SHIBUMI

"One of the year's best novels of international intrigue. It's hard to imagine a more nearly perfect spy story."

Milwaukee Journal

TREVANIAN

"Trevanian is in a class by himself. What he is beyond any doubt is a superior thriller spinner, an intricate plot-maker."

John Barkham Reviews

SHIBUMI

"A very unusual novel; action-packed from the very first pages, highly entertaining. Unique in its characters, it has great depth."

South Bend Tribune

SELECTED BY BOOK-OF-THE-MONTH CLUB

SHIBUMI

TREVANIAN

BALLANTINE BOOKS • NEW YORK

Library of Congress Catalog Card Number: 78-20950

ISBN 0-345-28585-9

This edition published by arrangement with
Crown Publishers, Inc.

Manufactured in the United States of America

First Ballantine Books Edition: June 1980
Sixth Printing: August 1980

*To the memories of the men
who here appear as: Kishikawa
                    Otake
                    de Lhandes
                    Le Cagot*

*All other characters and organizations
in this book lack any basis in reality—
although some of them do not realize that.*

Gameform of *Shibumi*

PART ONE

Fuseki

Washington

The screen flashed 9, 8, 7, 6, 5, 4, 3 . . . then the projector was switched off, and lights came up in recessed sconces along the walls of the private viewing room.

The projectionist's voice was thin and metallic over the intercom. "Ready when you are, Mr. Starr."

T. Darryl Starr, sole audience member, pressed the talk button of the communication console before him. "Hey, buddy? Tell me something. What are all those numbers in front of a movie for anyway?"

"It's called academy leader, sir," the projectionist answered. "I just spliced it onto the film as a sort of joke."

"Joke?"

"Yes, sir. I mean . . . considering the nature of the film . . . it's sort of funny to have a commercial leader, don't you think?"

"Why funny?"

"Well, I mean . . . what with all the complaints about violence in movies and all that."

T. Darryl Starr grunted and scrubbed his nose with the back of his fist, then he slipped down the pilot-style sunglasses he had pushed up into his cropped hair when the lights first went off.

Joke? It damn well better *not* be a joke, I shit thee not! If anything has gone wrong, my ass will be grass. And if the slightest little thing *is* wrong, you can bet your danglees that Mr. Diamond and his crew will spot it. Nit-picking bastards! Ever since they took control over Middle East operations of CIA, they seemed to get their cookies by pointing out every little boo-boo.

Starr bit off the end of his cigar, spat it onto the carpeted floor, pumped it in and out of his pursed lips, then lit it from a wooden match he struck with his thumbnail. As Most Senior Field Operative, he had access to Cuban cigars. After all, RHIP.

3

He scooted down and hooked his legs over the back of the seat before him, like he used to do when he watched movies at the Lone Star Theater as a boy. And if the boy in front objected, Starr would offer to kick his ass up amongst his shoulder blades. The other kid always backed off, because everybody in Flat Rock knew that T. Darryl Starr was some kind of fierce and could stomp a mud puddle in any kid's chest.

That was many years and knocks ago, but Starr was still some kind of fierce. That's what it took to become CIA's Most Senior Field Operative. That, and experience. And boo-coo smarts.

And patriotism, of course.

Starr checked his watch: two minutes to four. Mr. Diamond had called for a screening at four, and he would arrive at four—exactly. If Starr's watch did not read four straight up when Diamond walked into the theater, he would assume the watch was in need of repair.

He pressed his talk button again. "How does the film look?"

"Not bad, considering the conditions under which we shot it," the projectionist answered. "The light in Rome International is tricky . . . a mixture of natural light and fluorescent overheads. I had to use a combination of CC filters that brought my f-stop way down and made focus a real problem. And as for color quality—"

"I don't want to hear your piddly-assed problems!"

"Sorry, sir. I was just answering your question."

"Well, don't!"

"Sir?"

The door at the back of the private theater opened with a slap. Starr glanced at his watch; the sweep second hand was five seconds off four o'clock. Three men walked quickly down the aisle. In the lead was Mr. Diamond, a wiry man in his late forties whose movements were quick and adroit, and whose impeccably tailored clothes reflected his trim habits of mind. Following closely was Mr. Diamond's First Assistant, a tall, loosely jointed man with a vague academic air. Not a man to waste time, it was Diamond's practice to dictate memos, even while en route between meetings. The First Assistant carried a belt recorder at his hip,

4

the pinhead microphone of which was attached to his metal-rimmed glasses. He always walked close beside Mr. Diamond, or sat near him, his head bowed to pick up the flow of clipped monotonic directives.

Considering the heraldic stiffness of CIA mentality, it was inevitable that their version of wit would suggest a homosexual relationship between Diamond and his ever-hovering assistant. Most of the jokes had to do with what would happen to the assistant's nose, should Mr. Diamond ever stop suddenly.

The third man, trailing behind and somewhat confused by the brisk pace of action and thought surrounding him, was an Arab whose Western clothes were dark, expensive, and ill-fitting. The shabby look was not his tailor's fault; the Arab's body was not designed for clothes requiring posture and discipline.

Diamond slipped into an aisle seat across the auditorium from Starr; the First Assistant sat directly behind him, and the Palestinian, frustrated in his expectation that someone would tell him where to sit, finally shambled into a seat near the back.

Turning his head so the pinhead microphone could pick up the last of his rapid, atonic dictation, Diamond closed off the thoughts he had been pursuing. "Introduce the following topics to me within the next three hours: One—North Sea oil rig accident: the media suppression thereof. Two—This professor type who is investigating the ecological damage along the Alaska pipeline: the termination thereof by apparent accident."

Both these tasks were in their final phases, and Mr. Diamond was looking forward to getting in a little tennis over the weekend. Provided, of course, these CIA fools had not screwed up this Rome International action. It was a straightforward spoiling raid that should not have presented any difficulties, but in the six months since the Mother Company had assigned him to manage CIA activities involving the Middle East, he had learned that no action is so simple as to be beyond CIA's capacity for error.

Diamond understood why the Mother Company chose to maintain its low profile by working behind the cover of CIA and NSA, but that did not make his job any easier. Nor had he been particularly amused by the

5

Chairman's lighthearted suggestion that he think of the Mother Company's use of CIA operatives as Her contribution to the hiring of the mentally handicapped.

Diamond had not yet read Starr's action report, so he reached back for it now. The First Assistant anticipated him and had the report ready to press into his hand.

As he glanced over the first page, Diamond spoke without raising his voice. "Put the cigar out, Starr." Then he lifted his hand in a minimal gesture, and the wall lights began to dim down.

Darryl Starr pushed his sunglasses up into his hair as the theater went dark and the projector beam cut through slack threads of blue smoke. On the screen appeared a jerky pan over the interior of a large, busy airport.

"This here's Rome International," Starr drawled. "Time reference: thirteen thirty-four GMT. Flight 414 from Tel Aviv has just arrived. It's going to be a piece before the action starts. Those I-talian customs jokers ain't no speed balls."

"Starr?" said Diamond, wearily.

"Sir?"

"Why haven't you put that cigar out?"

"Well, to tell you God's own truth, sir, I never heard you ask me to."

"I didn't *ask* you."

Embarrassed at being ordered around in the presence of a foreigner, Starr unhooked his leg from the seat in front and ground out the almost fresh cigar on the carpet. To save face, he continued narrating as though nothing had happened. "I expect our A-rab friend here is going to be some impressed at how we handled this one. It went off slick as catshit on linoleum."

Wide shot: customs and immigration portal. A queue of passengers await the formalities with varying degrees of impatience. In the face of official incompetence and indifference, the only passengers who are smiling and friendly are those who anticipate trouble with their passports or luggage. An old man with a snow-white goatee leans over the counter, explaining something for the third time to the customs officer. Behind him in line are two young men in their twenties, deeply tanned, wearing khaki shorts and shirts open at the throat. As they

6

move forward, pushing their rucksacks along with their feet, camera zooms in to isolate them in mid-close-up.

"Those are our targets," Starr explained needlessly.

"Just so," the Arab said in a brittle falsetto. "I recognize one of them, one known within their organization as Avrim."

With a comically exaggerated bow of gallantry, the first young man offers to let a pretty red-headed girl precede them to the counter. She smiles thanks, but shakes her head. The Italian official in his too-small peaked cap takes the first young man's passport with a bored gesture and flicks it open, his eyes straying again and again to the girl's breasts, obviously unfettered beneath a denim shirt. He glances from the photograph to the young man's face and back again, frowning.

Starr explained. "The mark's passport picture was taken before he grew that silly-assed beard."

The immigration official shrugs and stamps the passport. The second young man is treated with the same combination of mistrust and incompetence. His passport is stamped twice, because the Italian officer was so engrossed in the red-headed girl's shirtfront that he forgot to use the ink pad the first time. The young men pick up their rucksacks, slinging them over their shoulders by one strap. Murmuring apologies and twisting sideways, they slip through a tangle of excited Italians, a large family pressing and standing on tiptoe to greet an arriving relative.

"Okay! Slow 'er down!" Starr ordered over the intercom. "Here's where it hits the fan."

The projector slowed to one-quarter speed.

From frame to flickering frame the young men move as though the air were gelatin. The leader turns back to smile at someone in the queue, the motion having the quality of a ballet in moon gravity. The second one looks out over the crowd. His nonchalant smile freezes. He opens his mouth and shouts silently, as the front of his khaki shirt bursts open and spouts blood. Before he can fall to his knees, a second bullet strikes his cheek and tears it off. The camera waves around dizzily before locating the other young man, who has dropped his rucksack and is running in nightmare slow motion toward the coin lockers. He pirouettes in the air as a slug takes him in the shoulder. He slams gracefully against the lockers and bounces back. His hip blossoms with gore, and he slips sideward to the polished granite floor. A third bullet blows off the back of his head.

The camera swishes over the terminal, seeking, losing, then finding again two men—out of focus—running toward the glass doors of the entrance. The focus is corrected, revealing them to be Orientals. One of them carries an automatic weapon. He suddenly arches his back, throws up his arms, and slides forward on his toes for a second before pitching onto his face. The gun clatters silently beside him. The second man has reached the glass doors, the smeared light of which haloes his dark outline. He ducks as a bullet shatters the glass beside his head; he veers and runs for an open elevator out of which a group of schoolchildren are oozing. A little girl slumps down, her hair billowing as though she were under water. A stray has caught her in the stomach. The next slug takes the Oriental between the shoulder blades and drives him gently into the wall beside the elevator. A grin of anguish on his face, he twists his arm up behind him, as though to pluck out the bullet. The next slug pierces his palm and enters his spine. He slides down the wall and falls with his head in the elevator car. The door closes, but reopens as the pressure pads meet the obstructing head. It closes again upon the head, then reopens. Closes. Opens.

Slow pan back over the terminal. High angle.

. . . A cluster of shocked and bewildered children around the fallen girl. One boy screams in silence . . .

. . . Two airport guards, their little Italian automatics drawn, run toward the fallen Orientals. One of them is still firing . . .

. . . The old man with the snow-white goatee sits stunned in a puddle of his own blood, his legs straight out before him, like a child playing in a sandbox. His expression is one of overwhelming disbelief. He was sure he had explained everything to the customs official . . .

. . . One of the young Israeli boys lies face down on his missing cheek, his rucksack improbably still over his shoulder . . .

. . . There is a largo minuet of stylized confusion

among the gaggle of Italians who were awaiting a relative. Three of them have fallen. Others are wailing, or kneeling, and one teenaged boy is turning around and around on his heel, seeking a direction in which to run for help—or safety . . .

. . . The red-headed girl stands stiff, her eyes round with horror as she stares at the fallen boy who just seconds ago offered to let her pass ahead . . .

. . . The camera comes to rest on the young man sprawled beside the coin lockers, the back of his head missing . . .

"That-a—that-a—that-a—that's all folks!" said Starr. The beam from the projector flickered out, and the wall lights dimmed up to full.

Starr turned in his seat to field questions from Mr. Diamond or the Arab. "Well?"

Diamond was still looking toward the white screen, three fingers pressed lightly against his lips, the action report on his lap. He let the fingers slip to beside his chin. "How many?" he asked quietly.

"Sir?"

"How many killed in the action?"

"I know what you mean, sir. Things got a little wetter than we expected. We'd arranged for the I-talian police to stay clear of the area, but they got their instructions all balled up—not that *that's* anything new. I even had some trouble myself. I had to use a Beretta so the slugs would match up for I-talian. And as a handgun, a Beretta isn't worth a fart in a hurricane, as my old daddy would have said. With an S&W, I could of dropped those Japs with two shots, and I wouldn't of hit that poor little girl that stepped out into my line of fire. Of course, in the first part of the action, our Nisei boys had been instructed to make it a little messy —make it look like a Black September number. But it was those panicked I-talian cops that started spattering slugs around like a cow pissing on a flat rock, as my old—"

"Starr?" Diamond's voice was heavy with disgust. "What was the question I asked you?"

"You asked how many were dead." Starr's tone was suddenly crisp, as he discarded the good ol' boy facade behind which he habitually took cover, to lull the target

9

with the assumption that it was dealing with a bucolic fool. "Nine dead in total." A sudden grin, and the down-home twang was back. "Let's see now. There was the two Jew targets, of course. Then our two Nisei agents I had to maximally demote. And that poor little girl that bumped into one of my slugs. And that old fella who collected a stray. And three of that family of locals that were loitering around when that second Jew ran past them. Loitering's dangerous. It ought to be against the law."

"Nine? Nine killed to get two?"

"Well, sir, you gotta remember that we were instructed to make this look like a Black September-type action. And those boys have this tendency to be some extravagant. It's their style to open eggs with sledge hammers—no offense intended to Mr. Haman here."

Diamond looked up from the report he was speed-reading. Haman? Then he remembered that the Arab observer seated behind him had been given Haman as a cover name by the imaginative CIA.

"I take no offense, Mr. Starr," said the Arab. "We are here to learn. That is why some of our own trainees are working with your men at the Riding Academy, under a Title Seventeen grant for cultural exchange. To tell truths, I am impressed that a man of your seniority took the time to deal with this matter personally."

Starr waved that aside with pleased modesty. "Think nothing of it. If you want a job done right, give it to a busy man."

"Is that something else your old daddy used to say?" Diamond asked, his eyes not leaving the report as they raced vertically down the center of the page, speed-reading.

"Matter of fact, it is, now you mention it."

"He was quite the folksy philosopher."

"I think of him more as a rotten son-of-a-bitch, sir. But he did have a way with words."

Diamond sighed nasally and returned his attention to the action report. During the months since the Mother Company had assigned him to control all CIA activities touching the interests of the oil-producing powers, he had learned that, despite their institutionalized ineptitude, men like Starr were not stupid. They were, in fact, surprisingly intelligent, in the mechanical, problem-solving sense of that word. None of the chitlin grammar, none of the scatalogical paucity of language ever appeared in Starr's written reports of wet-work assignments. Instead, one found concise, arid prose calculated to callus the imagination.

From going over his biographic printout, Diamond had learned that Starr was something of a hero figure among the younger CIA operatives—the last of the old breed from the precomputer era, from the days when Company operations had more to do with swapping shots across the Berlin Wall than with controlling the votes of congressmen by amassing evidence of their fiscal and sexual irregularities.

T. Darryl Starr was of the same stripe as his over-the-hill contemporary who left the Company to write inarticulate spy novels and dabble over his head in political crimes. When his gross ineptitude led to his being caught, he clung to truculent silence, while his cohorts sang mighty choruses of mea culpa and published at great profit. After serving a bit of soft time in federal prison, he sought to ennoble his panicked silence by falling back on The Unwritten Code, which declares, "Thou shalt not squeal—out of print." The world groaned as at an old joke, but Starr admired this bungling fool. They shared that blend of boy scout and mugger that characterizes old-timers in the CIA.

Diamond glanced up from the report. "According to this, Mr. . . . Haman, you went along on the spoiling raid as an observer."

"Yes. That is correct. As a trainee/observer."

"In that case, why did you want to see this confirmation film before reporting to your superiors?"

"Ah . . . yes. Well . . . in point of most absolute fact . . ."

"It wouldn't be possible for him to report his eyeball reactions, sir," Starr explained. "He was with us up on the mezzanine when it all started, but ten seconds later we couldn't find hide nor hair of him. A man we left behind to sweep up finally located him in the back stall of the public benjo."

The Arab laughed briefly and mirthlessly. "This is

true. The calls of nature are as inopportune as they are empirical."

The First Assistant frowned and blinked. Empirical? Did he mean imperative? Imperious?

"I see," Diamond said, and he returned to his scan-reading of the seventy-five-page report.

Uncomfortable with the silence, the Arab quickly filled in with: "I do not wish to be an inquisitor, Mr. Starr, but there is something I do not understand."

"Shoot, pal."

"Exactly why did we use Orientals to make the slap?"

"What? Oh! Well, you remember that we agreed to make it look as though your own men did the *hit*. But we don't have no A-rabs in the shop, and the boys we're training out to the Academy ain't up to this kind of number." Starr did not consider it tactful to add that, with their genetic disabilities, they probably never would be. "But your Black September boys have been members of the Japanese Red Army on their operations . . . and Japs we got."

The Arab frowned in confusion. "You are saying that the Japanese were your *own* men?"

"You got it. A couple of Nisei boys with the Agency in Hawaii. Good ol' boys too. It's a real pity we had to lose 'em, but their deaths put what you call your stamp of verisimilitude on your otherwise bald and unconvincing narrative. The slugs they dig out of them will be from a Beretta, and the local cops will get credit for pinching them off. They carried documents identifying them as Red Army members helping their A-rab brothers in what you call your unending struggle against the capitalist whatevers."

"Your *own* men?" the Arab repeated in awe.

"Don't sweat it. Their papers, their clothes, even the food that'll be found in their stomachs . . . it all makes them out to be from Japan. Matter of fact, they flew in from Tokyo just a couple of hours before the hit— or slap, as we sometimes call it."

The Arab's eyes shone with admiration. This was precisely the kind of organization his uncle—and president—had sent him to the United States to study, to the end of creating a similar one, and ending their dependence on their new-found allies. "But surely your

Japanese agents did not *know* they were going to be . . . what is your term for it?"

"Maximally demoted? No, they didn't know. There's a rule of thumb in the shop that actives shouldn't know more than they need to do the job. They were good men, but even so, if they'da known they were gonna do a Nathan Hale, they might'a lost some of their enthusiasm, if you catch my drift there."

Diamond continued to read, his vertical sweep of eye always well ahead of the mixing and analyzing operations of his mind, which sorted and reviewed the data in a way best described as intellectual peripheral vision. When some bit failed to fall into place, or rang false, he would pause and go back, scanning for the offending fragment.

He was on the last page when the internal alarms went off. He paused, turned back to the preceding page, and read carefully—this time horizontally. His jaw muscles rippled. He lifted his eyes and produced a characteristically understated exclamation: for a moment he did not breathe.

The First Assistant's eyes flickered. He knew the signs. There was trouble.

Diamond drew a long-suffering sigh as he handed the report back over his shoulder. Until he had evaluated the problem, he would not alert the Arab observer. His experience told him that it is unwise and wasteful to equip Arabs with unnecessary information. It is not a burden they carry gracefully.

"Well?" he asked, turning his head slightly. "Are you satisfied, Mr. Haman?"

For an instant the Arab failed to recognize his code name, then he started and giggled. "Oh, yes. Well, let us say that I am impressed by the evidence of the films."

"Does that mean impressed, but *not* satisfied?"

The Arab pulled in his neck, tilted his head, and lifted his palms, smiling in the oblique way of the rug merchant. "My good friends, it is not for me to be satisfied or unsatisfied. *Dis*satisfied? I am merely a messenger, a point of contact, what you might call . . . a . . ."

"Flunkey?" Diamond offered.

"Perhaps. I do not know that word. A short time ago,

our intelligence agents learned of a plot to assassinate the last two remaining heroes of the Munich Olympics Retaliation. My uncle—and president—expressed his desire to have this plot staunched . . . is that the word?"

"It's *a* word," Diamond admitted, his voice bored. He was out of patience with this fool, who was more a broad ethnic joke than a human being.

"As you recall, the staunching of this evil plot was a condition for continued amicable relations with the Mother Company in matters relating to oil supply. In its wisdom, the Mother Company decided to have CIA handle the matter—under your close personal supervisory, Mr. Diamond. I mean no offense to my brave friend, Mr. Starr, but it must be admitted that since certain bunglings of CIA-trained men led to the downfall of a most friendly and cooperative President, our confidence in that organization has not been without limits." The Arab tipped his head onto his shoulder and grinned apologetically at Starr, who examined his cuticles with deep interest.

The Arab continued. "Our intelligence organ was able to supply CIA with the names of the two Zionist gangsters assigned to this criminal attack, and with the approximate date of their departure from Tel Aviv. To this, Mr. Starr doubtless added his own sources of information; and he decided to avert the tragedy by technique of what you call a 'spoiling raid,' arranging that the criminals be executed before they committed their crime—a most economical judicial process. Now, you have shown me certain audiovisual medias proving that this raid was successful. I shall report this to my superiors. It is for them to be satisfied or nonsatisfied; not me."

Diamond, whose mind had been elsewhere through most of the Arab's singsong monologue, now rose. "That's it, then." Without further word, he strode up the aisle, followed immediately by his First Assistant.

Starr hooked his leg over the seat before him and drew out a cigar. "You want to see it again?" he asked the Arab over his shoulder.

"That would be pleasant."

Starr pressed the talk button of his console. "Hey, buddy? Let's have it again." He slipped his sunglasses up into his cropped hair as the lights dimmed down. "Here we go. A rerun. And on prime time." Pronounced: prahm tahm.

As he walked quickly down the white-walled corridor of the Center, Diamond's fury was manifest only in the sharp click of his leather heels over the tiles. He had trained himself to restrict his emotions to a very narrow band of expression, but the slight tension around his mouth and his half-defocused stare were sufficient to alert the First Assistant that anger was writhing within him.

They stepped into the elevator, and the First Assistant inserted a magnetic card into the slot that replaced the button for Floor 16. The car dropped rapidly from the main lobby to the subbasement suite coded as Floor 16. The first thing Diamond had done when he took over CIA activities on behalf of the Mother Company was to create a work area for himself in the bowels of the Center. No CIA personnel had access to Floor 16; the office suite was enclosed in lead sheeting with antibugging alarms designed to keep that organization in its traditional state of ignorance. As further security against governmental curiosity, Diamond's office was served by a direct computer link with the Mother Company through cables that were armored against the parallel-line/incidental capacitance method of eavesdropping by means of which NSA monitors telephone and telegraph communications in the United States.

In constant touch with the research and communications facilities of Mother Company, Diamond needed only a staff of two: his First Assistant, who was a gifted artist at computer search; and his secretary, Miss Swivven.

They stepped out into a large open work space, the walls and carpets all in matte white. In the center was a discussion area consisting of five lightly padded chairs around a table, with an etched glass top that served as a screen upon which television images generated by the computer complex could be projected. Of the five chairs, only one could swivel: Diamond's. The others were set rigidly into the floor and were designed to pro-

15

vide minimal comfort. The area was for quick, alert discussion—not for small-talk and social fencing.

Into the wall across from the discussion area was built a console that linked their computer with the Mother Company's master system: Fat Boy. The bank also contained television, telephoto and teletype connections back to Fat Boy for printout of verbal and visual data, together with local storage banks for short-term hold and cross-reference. The First Assistant's place was always before this console, upon which instrument he played with unique abstract artistry, and with great affection.

Raised slightly on a dais, Diamond's own desk was conspicuously modest, with its white plastic surface only fifty centimeters by sixty-five. It had no drawers or shelves, nowhere to lose or overlook material, no way to delay one matter by pushing it aside on the excuse of attending to something else. A priority system, ordered by a complicated set of strict criteria, brought each problem to his desk only when there was sufficient research available for decisions, which were made quickly, and matters disposed of. Diamond despised both physical and emotional clutter.

He crossed to his desk chair (constructed by an orthopedic specialist to reduce fatigue without providing narcotizing comfort) and sat with his back to the wide, floor-to-ceiling window beyond which could be seen a neat patch of park and the stele of the Washington Monument in the middle distance. He sat for a moment with his palms pressed together in a prayerlike attitude, forefingers lightly touching his lips. The First Assistant automatically took his place before the data console and awaited instructions.

Alerted by their entrance, Miss Swivven entered the work area from her anteoffice and sat in her chair beside and below Diamond's dais, her note pad ready. She was in her late twenties, lush of body, with thick honey-colored hair done up in an efficient bun. Her most salient feature was an extreme fairness of skin beneath which her veins traced faint bluish patterns.

Without raising his eyes, Diamond tilted his praying hands from his lips and directed the fingertips toward the First Assistant. "Those two Israeli boys. They belonged to some organization. Name?"

"The Munich Five, sir."

"Function?"

"To avenge the killing of Jewish athletes at the Munich Olympics. Specifically, to hunt down and kill the Palestinian terrorists involved. Not official. Nothing to do with the Israeli government."

"I see." Diamond turned his fingers toward Miss Swivven. "I'll dine here tonight. Something quick and light, but I'll need a protein shock. Make it brewer's yeast, liquid vitamins, egg yolks, and eight ounces of raw calf's liver. Do it up in a blender."

Miss Swivven nodded. It was going to be a long night.

Diamond turned in his desk chair and stared sightlessly out toward the Washington Monument. Walking across the lawn near the base was the same group of schoolchildren that passed every day at exactly this time. Without turning from the window, he said over his shoulder, "Give me a data pull on this Munich Five."

"What indices, sir?" the First Assistant asked.

"It's a small organization. And recent. Let's begin with history and membership."

"At what depth do I scan?"

"You work that out. It's what you do well."

The First Assistant turned in his chair and began instructing Fat Boy. His face was immobile, but his eyes behind the round glasses sparkled with delight. Fat Boy contained a medley of information from all the computers in the Western World, together with a certain amount of satellite-stolen data from Eastern Bloc powers. It was a blend of top-secret military information and telephone-billing records; of CIA blackmail material and drivers' permits from France, of names behind numbered Swiss bank accounts and mailing lists from direct advertising companies in Australia. It contained the most delicate information, and the most mundane. If you lived in the industrialized West, Fat Boy had you. He had your credit rating, your blood type, your political history, your sexual inclinations, your medical records, your school and university performance, random samplings of your personal telephone

17

conversations, a copy of every telegram you ever sent or received, all purchases made on credit, full military or prison records, all magazines subscribed to, all income tax records, driving licenses, fingerprints, birth certificates—all this, if you were a private citizen in whom the Mother Company had no special interest. If, however, the Mother Company or any of her input subsidiaries, like CIA, NSA, and their counterparts in the other democratic nations, took particular notice of you, then Fat Boy knew much, much more than this about you.

Programming facts into Fat Boy was the constant work of an army of mechanics and technicians, but getting useful information out of Him was a task for an artist, a person with training, touch, and inspiration. The problem lay in the fact that Fat Boy knew too much. If one scanned a given subject too shallowly, he might not discover what he wanted to know. If he scanned too deeply, he would be overwhelmed with an unreadable mass of minutia: results of former urine tests, boy scout merit badges won, predictions in high school annuals, preference in brand of toilet paper. The First Assistant's unique gift was his delicate touch in asking just the right questions of Fat Boy, and of demanding response at just the right depth of scan. Experience and instinct combined to send him after the right indices, the right permutations, the right rubrics, the right depths. He played the instrument of the computer masterfully, and he loved it. Working at his console was to him what sex was to other men—that is to say, what he assumed sex was to other men.

Diamond spoke over his shoulder to Miss Swivven. "When I'm ready, I'll want to talk to this Starr person, and to the Arab they call Mr. Haman. Have them kept on tap."

Under the First Assistant's manipulation, the console was warming and humming. The first responses were coming in; fragments were being stored in the local memory bank; the dialogue had begun. No two conversations with Fat Boy were alike; each took on its own patois, and the delights of the problem were beginning to stroke the First Assistant's considerable, if exclusively frontal, intellect.

It would be twenty minutes before a full picture was available. Diamond decided not to waste this time. He would take a little exercise and sun, tune up his body and clear his mind for the long haul to come. He gestured with a fingertip for Miss Swivven to follow him into the small exercise room off the principal work area.

As he stripped down to his abbreviated shorts, Miss Swivven put on a pair of round, dark eyecups, handed him a similar pair, and turned on the bank of sunlamps installed along the walls. Diamond began doing sit-ups on an inclined platform, his ankles held by a loop of velvet-covered rope, while Miss Swivven pressed against the wall, keeping her vulnerably pale skin as far away from the intense glare of ultraviolet as possible. Diamond did his sit-ups slowly, getting the most work out of the fewest repetitions. He was in excellent shape for a man of his age, but the stomach required constant attention. "Listen," he said, his voice tight with a withheld grunt as he rose and touched his right knee with his left elbow, "I'll have to bring some CIA clout in on this. Alert whoever is left at the top after that last round of cosmetic administrative shakeups."

The highest-ranking administrator below the political shills that came and went as sacrificial lambs to outraged public opinion was the Deputy International Liaison Duty Officer, who was typically referred to by his acronym. Miss Swivven informed her superior that he was still in the building.

"He'll do. Order him to keep himself on tap. Oh— and cancel my tennis date for this weekend."

Miss Swivven's eyebrows lifted above her dark eyecups. This must be something very serious indeed.

Diamond began to work with the weights. "I'll also want a Q-jump priority on Fat Boy for the rest of the afternoon, maybe longer."

"Yes, sir."

"Okay. What do you have on your pad?"

"High protein input in liquid form. Alert and freeze Mr. Starr and Mr. Haman. Alert and freeze the Deputy. Request Q-jump priority on Fat Boy."

"Good. Precede all that with a message to the Chairman." Diamond was breathing heavily with the effort of

19

exercise. "Message: Possible that Rome International spoiling raid was imperfect. Will seek, sort, and report alternatives."

When Miss Swivven returned seven minutes later, she was carrying a large glass of thick, foamy, purplish liquid, the color lent by the pulverized raw liver. Diamond was in the last phase of his exercise routine, working isometrically against a fixed steel pipe. He stopped and accepted his dinner, as she pressed close to the wall, avoiding the sunlamps as best she could, but knowing perfectly well that she had already had enough exposure to burn her delicate skin. Although there were many advantages of her job with the Mother Company —overtime, good retirement plan, medical benefits, company vacation resort in the Canadian Rockies, Christmas parties—Miss Swivven regretted two aspects of her career: this getting sunburnt every week or so, and the occasional impersonal use Mr. Diamond made of her to relieve his tensions. Still, she was philosophic. No job is perfect.

"Note pad cleared?" Diamond asked, shuddering slightly as he finished his drink.

"Yes, sir."

Disregarding her presence, Diamond stepped out of his shorts and into a glass-fronted shower stall, where he turned on a full spray of bracing cold water, over the noise of which he asked, "Did the Chairman respond to my message?"

"Yes, sir."

After a short silence, Diamond said, "Please feel free to tell me what the response was, Miss Swivven."

"Pardon me, sir?"

Diamond turned off the shower, stepped out, and began to dry off on the rough towels designed to heighten circulation.

"Do you want me to read the Chairman's message to you, sir?"

Diamond sighed deeply. If this twit had not been the only attractive one in the over-100 wpm pool . . . "That would be nice, Miss Swivven."

She referred to her note pad, squinting against the glare of the sunlamps. "Response: Chairman to Diamond, J.O.: 'Failure in this matter not acceptable.' "

Diamond nodded as he dried his crotch meditatively. It was as he had expected.

When he returned to the work area, he was crisp-minded and prepared for decision-making, having changed into his working clothes, a jumpsuit of pale yellow that was loose and comfortable, and set his rotisserie tan off to advantage.

The First Assistant was working at the console with narrow concentration and physical exhilaration, as he tickled a cogent printout of data on the Munich Five out of Fat Boy.

Diamond sat in his swivel chair above the milky etched glass tabletop. "Punch up the RP," he instructed. "Give me a roll-down rate of five hundred WPM." He could not absorb information faster than this because the data came from half a dozen international sources, and Fat Boy's mechanical translations into English were as stilted and unrefined of idiom as a Clint Eastwood film.

MUNICH FIVE, THE . . .
ORGANIZATION . . . UNOFFICIAL . . . SPLINTER . . . GOAL EQUALS TERMINATION OF BLACK SEPTEMBRISTS INVOLVED IN KILLING ISRAELI ATHLETES IN MUNICH OLYMPICS . . .
LEADER AND KEYMAN EQUALS STERN, ASA . . .
MEMBERS AND SATELLITES EQUAL LEVITSON, YOEL . . . YARIV, CHAIM . . . ZARMI, NEHEMIAH . . . STERN, HANNAH . . .

"Hold it," Diamond said. "Let's take a look at them one at a time. Just give me sketches."

STERN, ASA

BORN APRIL 13, 1909 . . . BROOKLYN, NEW YORK, USA . . . 1352 CLINTON AVENUE . . . APARTMENT 3B . . .

The First Assistant clenched his teeth. "Sorry, sir." He was probing just a shade too deeply. No one wanted to know the number of the apartment in which Asa Stern was born. Not yet, anyway. He shallowed the probe a micron.

21

STERN EMIGRATES TO PALESTINE PROTECTORATE . . .
1931 . . .
    PROFESSION AND/OR COVER . . . FARMER,
JOURNALIST, POET, HISTORIAN . . .
    INVOLVED IN STRUGGLE FOR INDEPENDENCE . . .
1945-1947 (details available) . . .
    IMPRISONED BY BRITISH OCCUPATION FORCES
(details available) . . .
    UPON RELEASE BECOMES CONTACT POINT FOR
STERN ORGANIZATION AND OUTSIDE SYMPATHETIC
GROUPS (details available) . . .
    RETIRES TO FARM . . . 1956 . . .
    REACTIVATES WITH MUNICH OLYMPICS AFFAIR (details
available) . . .
    CURRENT IRRITANT POTENTIAL TO MOTHER COMPANY
EQUALS COEFFICIENT .001 . . .
    REASON FOR LOW COEFFICIENT EQUALS:
        THISMAN NOW DEAD, sub CANCER, sub THROAT

"That's a surface scratch, sir," the First Assistant
said. "Shall I probe a little deeper? He's obviously the
pivot man."

"Obviously. But dead. No, just store the rest of his
stuff in the memory bank. I'll come back to him later.
Let's have a look at the other members of his group."

"It's rolling up on your screen now, sir."

LEVITSON, YOEL
    BORN DECEMBER 25, 1954 . . . NEGEV, ISRAEL . . .
    FATHER KILLED . . . COMBAT . . . 6-DAY WAR . . .
1967 . . .
    JOINS MUNICH FIVE . . . OCTOBER 1972 . . .
    KILLED . . . DECEMBER 25, 1976 . . . (IDENTITY
BETWEEN BIRTH AND DEATH DATES NOTED AND
CONSIDERED COINCIDENTAL)

"Hold that!" Diamond ordered. "Give me a little
depth on this boy's death."

"Yes, sir."

KILLED . . . DECEMBER 25, 1976 . . .
    VICTIM (PROBABLY PRIMARY TARGET) OF TERRORIST
BOMB . . .

22

SITE EQUALS CAFE IN JERUSALEM . . . BOMB ALSO
KILLED SIX ARAB BYSTANDERS. TWO CHILDREN
BLINDED . . .

"Okay, forget it. It's unimportant. Return to the light
scan."

CURRENT IRRITANT POTENTIAL TO MOTHER COMPANY
EQUALS COEFFICIENT .001 . . .
REASON FOR LOW COEFFICIENT EQUALS:
        THISMAN NOW DEAD, sub MULTIPLE FRACTURES,
sub COLLAPSED LUNGS . . .
****

YARIV, CHAIM
    BORN OCTOBER 11, 1952 . . . ELATH, ISRAEL . . .
    ORPHAN/KIBBUTZ BACKGROUND (details available) . . .
    JOINS MUNICH FIVE . . . SEPTEMBER 7, 1972 . . .
    CURRENT IRRITANT POTENTIAL TO MOTHER COMPANY
EQUALS COEFFICIENT .64 $\pm$ . . .
    REASON FOR MEZZO-COEFFICIENT EQUALS:
        THISMAN CAUSE-DEVOTED, BUT NOT
LEADERTYPE . . .
****

ZARMI, NEHEMIAH
    BORN JUNE 11, 1948 . . . ASHDOD, ISRAEL . . .
    KIBBUTZ/UNIVERSITY/ARMY BACKGROUND (details
available) . . .
    ACTIVE GUERRILLA, sub NONSPONSORED (details of
known/probable/possible actions available) . . .
    JOINS MUNICH FIVE . . . SEPTEMBER 7, 1972 . . .
    CURRENT IRRITANT POTENTIAL TO MOTHER COMPANY
EQUALS COEFFICIENT .96$\pm$
    REASON FOR HIGH COEFFICIENT EQUALS:
        THISMAN CAUSE-DEVOTED AND LEADERTYPE . . .

SEE THIS! SEE THIS! SEE THIS! SEE THIS! THISMAN MAY
BE TERMINATED ON SIGHT.
****

STERN, HANNAH
    BORN APRIL 1, 1952 . . . SKOKIE, ILLINOIS, USA . . .
    UNIVERSITY/SOCIOLOGY AND ROMANCE
LANGUAGES/ACTIVE CAMPUS RADICAL (NSA/CIA
DOSSIERS AVAILABLE) . . . SAYAGAINISAYAGAIN!
SAYAGAINISAYAGAIN!

Diamond looked up from the conference table screen. "What's the matter?"

"Something's in error, sir. Fat Boy is correcting himself."

"Well?"

"We'll know in a minute, sir. Fat Boy's cooking."

Miss Swivven entered from the machine room. "Sir? I have requested telephotos of the members of the Munich Five."

"Bring them as soon as they print out."

"Yes, sir."

The First Assistant lifted his hand for attention. "Here it comes. Fat Boy is correcting himself in terms of Starr's report on the spoiling raid in Rome. He just digested the information."

Diamond read the rear-projected roll-down.

NEGATE PRIOR, RE: YARIV, CHAIM sub CURRENT
IRRITANT POTENTIAL TO MOTHER COMPANY . . .
CORRECTED COEFFICIENT EQUALS .001 . . .
REASON FOR LOW COEFFICIENT EQUALS:
    THISPERSON TERMINATED . . .
NEGATE PRIOR, RE: ZARMI, NEHEMIAH sub CURRENT
IRRITANT POTENTIAL TO MOTHER COMPANY . . .
CORRECTED COEFFICIENT EQUALS .001 . . .
REASON FOR LOW COEFFICIENT EQUALS:
    THISPERSON TERMINATED . . .
****

Diamond leaned back and shook his head. "An eight-hour lag. That could hurt us someday."

"It's not Fat Boy's fault, sir. It's an effect of rising world population and our own information explosion. Sometimes I think we know *too* much about people!" The First Assistant chuckled at the very idea. "By the way, sir, did you notice the rephrase?"

"Which rephrase?"

"THISMAN is now expressed as THISPERSON. Fat Boy must have digested the Mother Company's becoming an equal opportunity employer." The First Assistant could not keep the pride from his voice.

"That's wonderful," Diamond said without energy.

Miss Swivven entered from the machine room and

placed five telephotos on Diamond's desk, then she took her position below his dais, her note pad at the ready.

Diamond shuffled through the photographs for that of the only member of the Munich Five not known to be dead: Hannah Stern. He scanned the face, nodded to himself, and sighed fatalistically. These CIA imbeciles!

The First Assistant turned from his console and adjusted his glasses nervously. "What's wrong, sir?"

His eyes half closed as he looked through the floor-to-ceiling window at the Washington Monument threatening to violate that same chubby cloud that always hung in the evening sky at this time, Diamond tapped his upper lip with his knuckle. "Did you read Starr's action report?"

"I scanned it, sir. Mostly checking for spelling."

"What was the ostensible destination of those Israeli youngsters?"

The First Assistant always felt uncomfortable with Mr. Diamond's rhetorical style of thinking aloud. He did not like answering questions without the aid of Fat Boy. "As I recall, their destination was London."

"Right. Presumably intending to intercept certain Palestinian terrorists at Heathrow Airport before they could hijack a plane to Montreal. All right. If the Munich Five team were going to London, why did they disembark at Rome? Flight 414 from Tel Aviv is a through flight to London with stops at Rome and Paris."

"Well, sir, there could be several—"

"And why were they going to England six days before their Black September targets were due to fly out to Montreal? Why sit in the open in London for all that time, when they could have stayed securely at home?"

"Well, perhaps they—"

"And why were they carrying tickets to Pau?"

"Pau, sir?"

"Starr's action report. Bottom of page thirty-two through middle of page thirty-four. Description of contents of victims' knapsacks and clothing. List prepared by Italian police. It includes two plane tickets for Pau."

The First Assistant did not mention that he had no idea where Pau was. He made a mental note to ask Fat Boy first chance he got. "What does all this mean, sir?"

"It means that once again CIA has lived up to the traditions of Bay of Pigs and Watergate. Once again, they have screwed up." Diamond's jaw tightened. "The mindless voters of this country are wrong to worry about the dangers of CIA's internal corruption. When they bring this nation to disaster, it won't be through their villainy; it will be because of their bungling." He returned to his pristine desk and picked up the telephoto of Hannah Stern. "Fat Boy interrupted himself with that correction while it was backgrounding this Hannah Stern. Start me up on that again. And give me a little more depth."

Evaluating both the data and the gaps, Diamond analyzed Miss Stern to be a fairly common sort found on the fringes of terrorist action. Young, intelligent mid-American, cause-oriented. He knew the type. She would have been a Liberal, back when that was still fashionable. She was the kind who sought "relevance" in everything; who expressed her lack of critical judgment as freedom from prejudice; who worried about Third World hunger, but shambled about a university campus with a huge protein-gobbling dog—symbol of her love for all living things.

She first came to Israel on a summer tour at a kibbutz, her purpose being to visit her uncle and—in her own words quoted in a NSA lift from a letter home—"to discover my Jewishness."

Diamond could not repress a sigh when he read that phrase. Miss Stern obviously suffered from the democratic delusion that all people are created interesting.

Fat Boy ascribed a low coefficient of irritant potential to Miss Stern, regarding her as a typical young American intellectual woman seeking a cause to justify her existence, until marriage, career, or artsy hobbies defused her. Her personality analysis turned up none of those psychotic warps that produce the urban guerrilla who finds sexual expression in violence. Nor was she flawed by that desperate hunger for notoriety that causes actors and entertainers who, unable to remain in the public eye by virtue of their talents, suddenly discover hitherto unnoticed social convictions.

No, there was nothing in Hannah Stern's printout that would nominate her for particular attention—save

26

for two facts: She was Asa Stern's niece. And she was the only surviving member of the Munich Five.

Diamond spoke to Miss Swivven. "Have Starr and that Arab . . . Mr. Haman . . . in the screening room in ten minutes."

"Yes, sir."

"And have the Deputy there too." He turned to the First Assistant. "You keep working on Fat Boy. I want a deep rescan of the leader, this Asa Stern. He's the one who will bleed through. Give me a list of his first-generation contacts: family, friends, accomplices, associates, acquaintances, affairs, and so on."

"Just a second, sir." The First Assistant introduced two questions into the computer, then one modifier. "Ah . . . sir? The first-generation list will have . . . ah . . . three hundred twenty-seven names, together with thumbnail sketches. And we'll cube as we move to second-generation lists—friends of friends, etc. That'll give us almost thirty-five million names. Obviously, sir, we have to have some kind of priority criterion."

The First Assistant was right; a critical decision; there are literally thousands of ways in which a list can be ordered.

Diamond thought back over the sketch on Asa Stern. His intuition was tickled by one line: Profession and/or cover . . . Farmer, Journalist, Poet, Historian. Not, then, a typical terrorist. Something worse—a romantic patriot.

"Order the list emotionally. Go for indices indicating love, friendship, trust—this sort of thing. Go from closest to most distant."

The First Assistant's eyes shone as he took a deep breath and lightly rubbed his fingers together. This was a fine challenge demanding console virtuosity. Love, friendship, trust—these imprecisions and shadows could not be located through approaches resembling the Schliemann Back-bit and Nonbit Theory. No computer, not even Fat Boy, can respond to such rubrics directly. Questions have to be phrased in terms of nonfrequency counts and non sequitur exchange relationships. In its simplest form, actions performed for no measurable reason, or contrary to linear logic, *might* indicate such underlying motives as love or friendship or trust. But

27

great care had to be exercised, because identical actions could derive from hate, insanity, or blackmail. Moreover, in the case of love, the nature of the action seldom helps to identify its motivational impulse. Particularly difficult is separating love from blackmail.

It was a delicious assignment, infinitely complicated. As he began to insert the first probes into Fat Boy, the First Assistant's shoulders twisted back and forth, as though he were guiding a pinball with body-english.

Miss Swivven returned to the work room. "They're waiting for you in the theater, sir."

"Good. Bring those telephotos along. What on earth is wrong with you, Miss Swivven?"

"Nothing, sir. My back itches, that's all."

"For Christ's sake."

Darryl Starr sensed trouble in the air when he and the Arab received curt orders to report to the viewing room at once. His fears were confirmed when he found his direct superior sitting gloomily in the auditorium. The Deputy International Liaison Duty Officer nodded a curt greeting to Starr and grunted once toward the Arab. He blamed the oil-rich Arabian sheikhdoms for many of his current problems, not the least of which was the interfering presence of Mr. Diamond in the bowels of the CIA, with his snide attitude toward every little operational peccadillo.

When first the oil-producing Arabs had run a petroleum boycott against the industrialized West to blackmail them into withdrawing their moral and legal commitments to Israel, the Deputy and other leaders of CIA proposed putting on line Contingency Plan NE385/8 (Operation Six Second War). In terms of this plan, CIA-sponsored troops of the Orthodox Islamic Maoist Falange would rescue the Arab states from the temptations of greed by occupying more than 80 percent of its oil facilities in an action calculated to require less than one minute of actual combat, although it was universally admitted that an additional three months would be required to round up such Arab and Egyptian troops as had fled in panic as far as Rhodesia and Scandinavia.

It was agreed that Operation Six Second War would be undertaken without burdening the President or Congress with those decision-making responsibilities so onerous in an election year. Phase One was instituted, and political leaders in both Black and Muslim Africa experienced an epidemic of assassinations, one or two at the hands of members of the victim's own family. Phase Two was in countdown, when suddenly everything froze up. Evidence concerning CIA operations was leaked to congressional investigating committees; lists of CIA agents were released to Leftist newspapers in France, Italy, and the Near East; internal CIA communications began to be jammed; massive tape erasures occurred in CIA memory banks, denying them the "biographic leverage" with which they normally controlled American elected officials.

Then one afternoon, Mr. Diamond and his modest staff walked into the Center carrying orders and directives that gave the Mother Company total control over all operations touching, either directly or tangentially, the oil-producing nations. Neither the Deputy nor his colleagues had ever heard of this "Mother Company," so a quick briefing was in order. They learned that the Mother Company was a consortium of major international petroleum, communications, and transportation corporations that effectively controlled the Western World's energy and information. After some consideration, the Mother Company had decided that she could not permit CIA to continue meddling in affairs that might harm or irritate those oil-producing friends in consort with whom she had been able to triple profits in two years.

No one at CIA seriously considered opposing Mr. Diamond and the Mother Company, which controlled the careers of most major governmental figures, not only through direct support, but also by the technique of using their public media subsidiaries to blacken and demoralize potential candidates, and to shape what the American masses took to be the Truth.

What chance had the scandal-ridden CIA to resist a force with enough power to build pipelines through tundra that had been demonstrated to be ecologically fragile? Who could stand against the organization that had reduced government research spending on solar, wind, tidal, and geothermal energy to a placating trick-

29

le, so as to avoid competition with their own atomic and fossil-fuel consortia? How could CIA effectively oppose a group with such overwhelming dominance that She was able, in conjunction with its Pentagon flunkies, to make the American public accept the storage of atomic wastes with lethal half-lives so long that failure and disaster were absolutely assured by the laws of anti-chance?

In Her takeover of CIA, the Mother Company had no interference from the executive branch of the government, as it was nearing election time, and all public business is arrested during this year of flesh-bartering. Nor did She really worry about the post-election pause of three years before the next democratic convulsion, for the American version of representative government assures that such qualities of intellect and ethics as might equip a man to lead a powerful nation responsibly are precisely the qualities that would prevent him from subjecting himself to the debasing performances of vote begging and delegate swapping. It is a truism of American politics that no man who can win an election deserves to.

There was one awkward moment for the Mother Company when a group of naïve young Senators decided to inquire into Arab millions in short-term paper that allowed them to manipulate American banks and hold the nation's economy hostage against the possibility—however remote—that the United States might attempt to fulfill its moral commitments to Israel. But these probes were cut short by Kuwait's threat to withdraw its money and crumble the banks, should the Senate pursue. With exceptional rhetorical adroitness, the committee reported that they could not say with certainty that the nation was vulnerable to blackmail, because they had not been permitted to continue their investigations.

This was the background to the Deputy's feelings of petulance over loss of control of his organization as he heard the doors of the auditorium bang open. He rose to his feet as Diamond entered at a brisk pace, followed by Miss Swivven who carried several rip-sheets from the Fat Boy printout and the stack of photographs of members of the Munich Five.

In minimal recognition of Diamond's arrival, Starr lifted most of the weight off his butt, then settled back with a grunt. The Arab's response to Miss Swivven's arrival was to jump to his feet, grin, and bow in jerky imitation of European suavity. Very nice looking woman, he told himself. Very lush. Skin like snow. And most gifted in what, in English, is referred to as the knockers.

"Is the projectionist in the booth?" Diamond asked, sitting apart from the others.

"Yes, sir," Starr drawled. "You fixin' to see the film again?"

"I want you fools to see it again."

The Deputy was not pleased to be grouped with a mere agent, and even less with an Arab, but he had learned to suffer in silence. It was his senior administrative skill.

"You never told us you wanted to see the film," Starr said. "I don't think the projectionist has rewound it yet."

"Have him run it backward. It doesn't matter."

Starr gave instructions through the intercom, and the wall lights dimmed.

"Starr?"

"Sir?"

"Put out the cigar."

. . . *the elevator door opens and closes on the dead Japanese gunman's head. The man returns to life and slides up the wall. The hole in his palm disappears, and he tugs the bullet out of his back. He runs backward through a gaggle of schoolchildren, one of whom floats up from the floor as a red stain on her dress is sucked back into her stomach. When he reaches the light-blurred main entrance, the Japanese ducks as fragments of broken glass rush together to form a window pane. The second gunman jumps up from the floor and catches a flying automatic weapon, and the two of them run backward, until a swish pan leaves them and discovers an Israeli boy on the tiled floor. A vacuum snaps the top of his skull back into place; the stream of gore recoils back into his hip. He leaps up and runs backward, snatching up his rucksack as he passes it. The camera waves around, then finds the second Israeli just*

31

*in time to see his cheek pop on. He rises from his knees,
and blood implodes into his chest as the khaki shirt
instantly mends itself. The two boys walk backward.
One turns and smiles. They saunter back through a
group of Italians pushing and standing tiptoe to greet
some arriving relative. They back down the lane to the
immigration counter, and the Italian official uses his
rubber stamp to suck the entrance permissions off their
passports. A red-headed girl shakes her head, then
smiles thanks . . .*

"Stop!" called Mr. Diamond, startling Miss Swivven,
who had never heard him raise his voice before.

The girl on the screen froze, a blow-back douser
dimming the image to prevent the frame from burning.

"See that girl, Starr?"

"Sure."

"Can you tell me anything about her?"

Starr was confused by this seemingly arbitrary demand. He knew he was in trouble of some sort, and he
fell back on his habit of taking cover behind his dumb,
good-ol'-boy facade.

"Well . . . let's see. She's got a fair set of boobs,
that's for sure. Taut little ass. A little skinny in the arms
and waist for my taste but, like my ol' daddy used to
say: the closer the bone, the sweeter the meat!" He
forced a husky laugh in which he was joined by the
Arab, who was anxious to prove he understood.

"Starr?" Diamond's voice was monotonic and dense.
"I want you to do something for me. For the next few
hours, I want you to try very hard to stop being an ass.
I don't want you to entertain me, and I don't want you
to supplement your answers with folksy asides. There
is nothing funny about what is going on here. True to
the traditions of the CIA, you have screwed up, Starr.
Do you understand that?"

There was silence as the Deputy considered objecting
to this defamation, but thought better of it.

"Starr? Do you understand that?"

A sigh, then quietly, "Yes, sir."

The Deputy cleared his throat and spoke in his most
authoritative voice. "If there's anything the Agency
can—"

"Starr? Do you recognize this girl?" Diamond asked.

Miss Swivven took the photograph from its folder and sidled down the aisle to Starr and the Arab.

Starr tilted the print to see it better in the dim light. "Yes, sir."

"Who is it?"

"It's the girl up there on the screen."

"That's right. Her name is Hannah Stern. Her uncle was Asa Stern, organizer of the Munich Five. She was the third member of the commando team."

"Third?" Starr asked. "But . . . we were told there were only two of them on the plane."

"Who told you that?"

"It was in the intelligence report we got from this fella here."

"That is correct, Mr. Diamond," the Arab put in. "Our intelligence men . . ."

But Diamond had closed his eyes and was shaking his head slowly. "Starr? Are you telling me that you based an operation on information provided by *Arab* sources?"

"Well, we . . . Yes, sir." Starr's voice was deflated. Put that way, it did seem a stupid thing to do. It was like having Italians do your political organization, or the British handle your industrial relations.

"It seems to me," the Deputy injected, "that if we have made an error based on faulty input from your Arab friends, they have to accept a goodly part of the responsibility."

"You're wrong," Diamond said. "But I suppose you're used to that. They don't have to accept anything. They own the oil."

The Arab representative smiled and nodded. "You reflect exactly the thinking of my president and uncle, who has often said that—"

"All right." Diamond rose. "The three of you remain on tap. In less than an hour, I'll call for you. I have background data coming in now. It's still possible that I may be able to make up for your bungling." He walked up the aisle, followed closely by Miss Swivven.

The Deputy cleared his throat to say something, then decided that the greater show of strength lay in silence. He fixed a long stare on Starr, glanced away from the Arab in dismissal, then left the theater.

33

"Well, buddy," Starr said as he pushed himself out of the theater seat, "we better get a bite to eat while the gettin's good. Looks like the shit has hit the fan."

The Arab chuckled and nodded, as he tried to envision an ardent supporter of sports fouled with camel dung.

For a time, the empty theater was dominated by the frozen image of Hannah Stern, smiling down from the screen. When the projectionist started to run the film out, it jammed. An amoeba of brown, bubbly scab spread rapidly over the young lady and consumed her.

Etchebar

Hannah Stern sat at a café table under the arcade surrounding the central place of Tardets. She stared numbly into the lees of her coffee, thick and granular. Sunlight was dazzling on the white buildings of the square; the shadows under the arcade were black and chill. From within the café behind her came the voices of four old Basque men playing *mousse,* to the accompaniment of a litany of *bai . . . passo . . . passo . . . alla Jainkoa! . . . passo . . . alla Jainkoa . . .* this last phrase passing through all conceivable permutations of stress and accent as the players bluffed, signaled, lied, and called upon God to witness this shit they had been dealt, or to punish this fool of a partner with whom God had punished them.

For the last seven hours, Hannah Stern had alternated between clawing through nightmare reality and floating upon escapist fantasy, between confusion and vertigo. She was stunned by emotional shock, spiritually evacuated. And now, teetering on the verge of nervous disintegration, she felt infinitely calm . . . even a little sleepy.

The real, the unreal; the important, the insignificant; the Now, the Then; the cool of her arcade, the rippling heat of the empty public square; these voices chanting in Europe's most ancient language . . . it was all indifferently tangled. It was all happening to someone else, someone for whom she felt great pity and sympathy, but whom she could not help. Someone past help.

After the massacre in Rome International, she had somehow got all the way from Italy to this café in a Basque market town. Dazed and mentally staggering, she had traveled fifteen hundred kilometers in nine hours. But now, with only another four or five kilometers to go, she had used up the last of her nervous energy. Her adrenaline well was empty, and it appeared that she was going to be defeated at the last moment by the caprice of a bumbling café owner.

First there had been terror and confusion at seeing her comrades shot down, neurasthenic incredulity during which she stood frozen as people rushed past her, knocking against her. More gunshots. Loud wailing from the family of Italians who had been awaiting a relative. Then panic clutched her; she walked blindly ahead, toward the main entrance of the terminal, toward the sunlight. She was breathing orally, shallow pants. Policemen rushed past her. She told herself to keep walking. Then she realized that the muscles in the small of her back were knotted painfully in anticipation of the bullet that never came. She passed an old man with a white goatee, sitting on the floor with his legs straight out before him, like a child at play. She could see no wound, but the pool of dark blood in which he sat was growing slowly wider. He did not seem to be in pain. He looked up at her interrogatively. She couldn't make herself stop. Their eyes locked together as she walked by. She muttered stupidly, "I'm sorry. I'm really sorry."

A fat woman in the group of waiting relatives was hysterical, wailing and choking. More attention was being paid to her than to the fallen members of the family. She was, after all, Mama.

Over the confusion, the running and shouting, a calm, singsong voice announced the first call for passengers on Air France flight 470 for Toulouse, Tarbes, and Pau. The recorded voice was ignorant of the chaos beneath its loudspeakers. When the announcement was repeated in French, the last fragment stuck to Hannah's consciousness. Gate Eleven, Gate Eleven.

The stewardess reminded Hannah to put up her seat back. "Yes. Yes. I'm sorry." A minute later, on her return down the aisle, the hostess reminded her to buckle her seat belt. "What? Oh, yes. I'm sorry."

The plane rose into thin cloud, then into crisp infinite blue. The drone of engines; the vibration of the fuselage. Hannah shivered with vulnerability and aloneness. There was a middle-aged man seated beside her, reading a magazine. From time to time his eyes slipped over the top of the page and glanced quickly at her suntanned legs below the khaki shorts. She could feel his eyes on her, and she buttoned one of the top two buttons of her shirt. The man smiled and cleared his throat. He was going to speak to her! The stupid son of a bitch was going to try to pick her up! My God!

And suddenly she was sick.

She made it to the toilet, where she knelt in the cramped space and vomited into the bowl. When she emerged, pale and fragile, the imprint of floor tile on her knees, the stewardess was solicitous but slightly superior, imagining that a short flight like this had made her airsick.

The plane banked on its approach to Pau, and Hannah looked out the window at the panorama of the Pyrenees, snow-tipped and sharp in the crystalline air, like a sea of whitecaps frozen in midstorm. Beautiful and awful.

Somewhere there, at the Basque end of the range, Nicholai Hel lived. If she could only get to Mr. Hel . . .

It was not until she was out of the terminal and standing in the chill sunlight of the Pyrenees that it occurred to her that she had no money. Avrim had carried all their money. She would have to hitchhike, and she didn't know the route. Well, she could ask the drivers. She knew that she would have no trouble getting rides. When you're pretty and young . . . and big-busted . . .

Her first ride took her into Pau, and the driver offered to find her a place to stay for the night. Instead, she talked him into taking her to the outskirts and directing her to Tardets. It must have been a hard car to shift, because his hand twice slipped off the lever and brushed her leg.

She got her next ride almost immediately. No, he wasn't going to Tardets. Only as far as Oléron. But he could find her a place to stay for the night . . .

One more car, one more suggestive driver, and Hannah reached the little village of Tardets, where she sought further directions at the café. The first barrier she met was the local accent, *langue d'oc* with heavy overlays of Soultine Basque in which *une petite cuillère* has eight syllables.

"What are you looking for?" the café owner asked, his eyes leaving her breasts only to stray to her legs.

"I'm trying to find the Château of Etchebar. The house of M. Nicholai Hel."

The proprietor frowned, squinted at the arches overhead, and scratched with one finger under the beret that Basque men take off only in bed, in coffin, or when adjudicating the game of *rebot*. No, he did not believe he had ever heard the name. Hel, you say? (He could pronounce the *h* because it is a Basque sound.) Perhaps his wife knew. He would ask. Would the Mademoiselle take something while she waited? She ordered coffee which came, thick, bitter, and often reheated, in a tin pot half the weight of which was tinker's solder, but which leaked nevertheless. The proprietor seemed to regret the leak, but to accept it with heavy fatalism. He hoped the coffee that dripped on her leg had not burned her. It was not hot enough to burn? Good. Good. He disappeared into the back of the café, ostensibly to inquire after M. Hel.

And that had been fifteen minutes ago.

Hannah's eyes dilated painfully as she looked out toward the bright square, deserted save for a litter of cars, mostly *Deu'ches* bearing '64 plates, parked at random angles, wherever their peasant drivers had managed to stop them.

With deafening roar of motor, grinding of gears, and outspewing of filthy exhaust, a German juggernaut lorry painfully navigated the corner with not ten centimeters to spare between vehicle and the *crepi* facades of the buildings. Sweating, cranking the wheel, and hiss-popping his air brakes, the German driver managed to introduce the monster into the ancient square, only to be met by the most formidable of barriers. Waddling side by side down the middle of the street, two Basque women with blank, coarse faces exchanged gossip out of the corners of their mouths. Middle-aged, dour, and vast, they plodded along on great barrel legs, indifferent to the frustration and fury of the truck driver, who crawled behind them muttering earnest imprecations and beating his fist against the steering wheel.

Hannah Stern had no way to appreciate this scene's iconographic representation of Franco-German relations in the Common Market, and at this moment the café owner reappeared, his triangular Basque face abeam with sudden comprehension.

"You are seeking M. Hel!" he told her.

"That's what I said."

"Ah, if I had known it was M. *Hel* you were seeking . . ." He shrugged from the waist, lifting his palms in a gesture implying that a little more clarity on her part would have saved them both a lot of trouble.

He then gave her directions to the Château d'Etchebar: first cross the *gave* from Tardets (the *r* rolled, both the *t* and the *s* pronounced), then pass through the village of Abense-de-Haut (five syllables, the *h* and *t* both pronounced) and on up through Lichans (no nasal, *s* pronounced), then take the right forking up into the hills of Etchebar; but not the left forking, which would carry you to Licq.

"Is it far?"

"No, not all that far. But you don't want to go to Licq, anyway."

"I mean to Etchebar! Is it far to Etchebar!" In her fatigue and nervous tension, the formidable task of getting simple information out of a Basque was becoming too much for Hannah.

"No, not far. Maybe two kilometers after Lichans."

"And how far is it to Lichans?"

He shrugged. "Oh, it could be two kilometers after Abense-de-Haut. You can't miss it. Unless you turn left at the forking. *Then* you'll miss it all right! You'll miss it because you'll be in Licq, don't you see."

The old *mousse* players had forsaken their game and were gathered behind the café owner, intrigued by all the confusion this foreign tourist was causing. They held a brief discussion in Basque, agreeing at last that if the girl took the left forking she would indeed end up in Licq. But then, Licq was not such a bad village. Was there not the famous story of the bridge at Licq built with the help of the Little People from the mountains who then . . .

"Listen!" Hannah pled. "Is there someone who could drive me to the Château of Etchebar?"

A quick conference was held between the café owner and the *mousse* players. There was some argument and

39

a considerable amount of clarification and restatement of positions. Then the proprietor delivered the consensus opinion.

"No."

It had been decided that this foreign girl wearing walking shorts and who had a rucksack was one of the young athletic tourists who were notorious for being friendly, but for tipping very little. Therefore, there was no one who would drive her to Etchebar, except for the oldest of the *mousse* players, who was willing to gamble on her generosity, but sadly he had no car. And anyway, he did not know how to drive.

With a sigh, Hannah took up her rucksack. But when the café owner reminded her of the cup of coffee, she remembered she had no French money. She explained this with expressions of lighthearted contrition, trying to laugh off the ludicrousness of the situation. But he steadfastly stared at the cup of unpaid-for coffee, and remained dolefully silent. The *mousse* players discussed this new turn of events with animation. What? The tourist took coffee without the money to pay for it? It was not impossible that this was a matter for the law.

Finally, the proprietor sighed a rippling sigh and looked up at her, tragedy in his moist eyes. Was she really telling him that she didn't have two francs for the coffee—forget the tip—just two francs for the coffee? There was a matter of principle involved here. After all, *he* paid for his coffee; *he* paid for the gas to heat the water; and every couple of years *he* paid the tinker to mend the pot. He was a man who paid his debts. Unlike some others he could mention.

Hannah was between anger and laughter. She could not believe that all these heavy theatrics were being produced for two francs. (She did not know that the price of a cup of coffee was, in fact, *one* franc.) She had never before met that especially French version of avarice in which money—the coin itself—is the center of all consideration, more important than goods, comfort, dignity. Indeed, more important than real wealth. She had no way to know that, although they bore Basque names, these village people had become thoroughly French under the corrosive cultural pressures of radio, television, and state-controlled education, in which modern history is creatively interpreted to confect that national analgesic, *la vérité à la Cinquième République*.

Dominated by the mentality of the *petit commercant,* these village Basques shared the Gallic view of gain in which the pleasure of earning a hundred francs is nothing beside the intense suffering caused by the loss of a centime.

Finally realizing that his dumb show of pain and disappointment was not going to extract the two francs from this young girl, the proprietor excused himself with sardonic politeness, telling her he would be right back.

When he returned twenty minutes later, after a tense conference with his wife in the back room, he asked, "You are a friend of M. Hel?"

"Yes," Hannah lied, not wanting to go into all that.

"I see. Well then, I shall assume that Mr. Hel will pay, should you fail to." He tore a sheet from the note pad provided by the Byrrh distributors and wrote something on it before folding it two times, sharpening the creases with his thumbnail. "Please give this to M. Hell," he said coldly.

His eyes no longer flicked to her breast and legs. Some things are more important than romance.

Hannah had been walking for more than an hour, over the Pont d'Abense and the glittering Gave de Saison, then slowly up into the Basque hills along a narrow tar road softened by the sun and confined by ancient stone walls over which lizards scurried at her approach. In the fields sheep grazed, lambs teetering beside the ewes, and russet *vaches de pyrénées* loitered in the shade of unkempt apple trees, watching her pass, their eyes infinitely gentle, infinitely stupid. Round hills lush with fern contained and comforted the narrow valley, and beyond the saddles of the hills rose the snow-tipped mountains, their jagged arêtes sharply traced on the taut blue sky. High above, a hawk balanced on the rim of an updraft, its wing feathers splayed like fingers constantly feeling the wind as it scanned the ground for prey.

The heat stewed a heady medley of aroma: the soprano of wild-flower, the mezzotones of cut grass and fresh sheep droppings, the insistent basso profundo of softened tar.

Insulated by fatigue from the sights and smells around her, Hannah plodded along, her head down and her concentration absorbed in watching the toes of her hiking boots. Her mind, recoiling from the sensory overload of the last ten hours, was finding haven in a tunnel-vision of the consciousness. She did not dare to think, to imagine, to remember; because looming out there, just beyond the edges of here-and-now, were visions that would damage her, if she let them in. Don't think. Just walk, and watch the toes of your boots. It is all about getting to the Château d'Etchebar. It is all about contacting Nicholai Hel. There is nothing before or beyond that.

She came to a forking in the road and stopped. To the right, the way rose steeply toward the hilltop village of Etchebar, and beyond the huddle of stone and *crepi* houses she could see the wide mansard facade of what must be the château peeking between tall pine trees and surrounded by a high stone wall.

She sighed deeply and trudged on, her fatigue blending with protective emotional neurasthenia. If she could just make the château . . . just get to Nicholai Hel . . .

Two peasant women in black dresses paused in their gossip over a low stone wall and watched the outlander girl with open curiosity and mistrust. Where was she going, this hussy showing her legs? Toward the château? Ah well, that explained it. All sorts of strange people go to the château ever since that foreigner bought it! Not that M. Hel was a bad man. Indeed, their husbands had told them he was much admired by the Basque freedom movement. But still . . . he was a newcomer. No use denying it. He had lived in the château only fourteen years, while everyone else in the village (ninety-three souls) could find his name on dozens of gravestones around the church, sometimes newly cut into pyrenean granite, sometimes barely legible on ancient stone scrubbed smooth by five centuries of rain and wind. Look! The hussy has not even bound her breasts! She wants men to look at her, that's what it is! She will have a nameless child if she is not careful! Who would marry her then? She will end up cutting vegetables and scrubbing floors in the household of her sister. And her sister's husband will pester her when he is drunk! And one day, when the sister is too far along with child to be able to do it, this one will succumb to the husband! Probably in the barn. It always happens so. And the sister will find out, and she will drive this one from the house! Where will she go then? She will become a whore in Bayonne, that's what!

A third woman joined the two. Who is that girl showing her legs? We know nothing about her—except that she is a whore from Bayonne. And not even Basque! Do you think she might be a Protestant? Oh no, I wouldn't go that far. Just a poor *putain* who has slept with the husband of her sister. It is what always happens, if you go about with your breasts unbound.

True, true.

As she passed, Hannah looked up and noticed the three women. *"Bonjour, mesdames,"* she said.

"Bonjour, mademoiselle," they chanted together, smiling in the open Basque way. "You are giving yourself a walk?" one asked.

"Yes, Madame."

"That's nice. You are lucky to have the leisure."

An elbow nudged, and was nudged back. It was daring and clever to come so close to saying it.

"You are looking for the château, Mademoiselle?"

"Yes, I am."

"Just keep going as you are, and you will find what you're looking for."

A nudge; another nudge. It was dangerous, but deliciously witty, to come so close to saying it.

Hannah stood before the heavy iron gates. There was no one in sight, and there did not seem to be any way of ringing or knocking. The château was set back a hundred meters, up a long curving allée of trees. Uncertain, she decided to try one of the smaller gates down the road, when a voice behind her asked in a singsong, "Mademoiselle?"

She returned to the gate where an old gardener in blue working apron was peering out from the other side of the barrier. "I am looking for M. Hel," she explained.

"Yes," the gardener said, with that inhaled *"oui"* that can mean almost anything, except yes. He told her to wait there, and he disappeared into the curving row of trees. A minute later she heard the hinges creak on one of the side gates, and he beckoned her with a rolling arm and a deep bow that almost cost him his balance. As she passed him, she realized that he was half-drunk. In fact, Pierre was never drunk. Also, he was never sober. The regular spacing of his daily twelve glasses of red protected him from either of those excesses.

Pierre pointed the way, but did not accompany her to the house; he returned to trimming the box hedges that formed a labyrinth. He never worked in haste, and he never avoided work, his day punctuated, refreshed, and blurred by his glass of red every half hour or so.

Hannah could hear the clip-clip-clip of his shears, the sound receding as she walked up the allée between tall blue-green cedars, the drooping branches of which wept and undulated, brushing the shadows with long kelplike sweeps. A susurrant wind hissed high in the trees like tide over sand, and the dense shade was chill. She shivered. She was dizzy after the long hot walk, having taken nothing but coffee all day long. Her emotions had been frozen by fear, then melted by despair. Frozen, then melted. Her hold on reality was slipping.

When she reached the foot of a double rank of marble steps ascending to the terraces, she stopped, uncertain which way to go.

"May I help you?" a woman's voice asked from above.

Hannah shaded her eyes and looked up toward the sunny terrace. "Hello. I am Hannah Stern."

"Well, come up, Hannah Stern." With the sunlight behind the woman, Hannah could not see her features, but from her dress and manner she seemed to be Oriental, although her voice, soft and modulated, belied the twittering stereotype of feminine Oriental speech. "We have one of those coincidences that are supposed to bring luck. My name is Hana—almost the same as yours. In Japanese, *hana* means flower. What does your Hannah mean? Perhaps, like so many Western names, it means nothing. How delightful of you to come just in time for tea."

They shook hands in the French fashion, and Hannah was struck by the calm beauty of this woman, whose eyes seemed to regard her with a mixture of kindness and humor, and whose manner made Hannah feel oddly protected and at ease. As they walked together across the broad flagstone terrace toward the house with its classic facade of four porte-fenêtres flanking the main entrance, the woman selected the best bloom from the flowers she had been cutting and offered it to Hannah with a gesture as natural as it was pleasant. "I must put these in water," she said. "Then we shall take our tea. You are a friend of Nicholai?"

"No, not really. My uncle was a friend of his."

"And you are looking him up in passing. How thoughtful of you." She opened the glass doors to a sunny reception room in the middle of which tea things were laid out on a low table before a marble fireplace with a brass screen. A door on the other side of the room clicked closed just as they entered. During the few days she was to spend at the Château d'Etchebar, all Hannah would ever see or hear of staff and servants would be doors that closed as she entered, or soft tiptoeing at the end of the hall, or the appearance of coffee or flowers on a bedside table. Meals were prepared in such a way that the mistress of the house could do the serving herself. It was an opportunity for her to show kindness and concern.

"Just leave your rucksack there in the corner, Hannah," the woman said. "And would you be so good as to pour, while I arrange these flowers?"

With sunlight flooding in through the French windows, walls of light blue, moldings of gold leaf, furniture blending Louis XV and oriental inlays, threads of gray vapor twisting up from the teapot through a shaft of sunlight, mirrors everywhere lightening, reflecting, doubling and tripling everything; this room was not in the same world as that in which young men are shot down in airports. As she poured from a silver teapot into Limoges with a vaguely Chinese feeling, Hannah was overwhelmed by reality vertigo. Too much had

45

happened in these last hours. She was afraid she was going to faint.

For no reason, she remembered feelings of dislocation like this when she was a child in school . . . it was summer, and she was bored, and there was the drone of study all around her. She had stared until objects became big/little. And she had asked herself, "Am I me? Am I here? Is this really me thinking these thoughts? Me? Me?"

And now, as she watched the graceful, economical movements of this slender Oriental woman stepping back to criticize the flower arrangement, then making a slight correction, Hannah tried desperately to find anchorage against the tide of confusion and fatigue that was tugging her away.

That's odd, she thought. Of all that had happened that day: the horrible things in the airport, the dreamlike flight to Pau, the babbling suggestive talk of the drivers she had gotten rides from, that fool of a café owner in Tardets, the long walk up the shimmering road to Etchebar . . . of all of it, the most profound image was her walk up the cedar-lined allée in sub-aqueous shadow . . . shivering in the dense shadow as the wind made sea sounds in the trees. It was another world. And odd.

Was it possible that she was sitting here, pouring tea into Limoges, probably looking quite the buffoon with her tight hiking shorts and clumsy, Vibram-cleated boots?

Was it just a few hours ago she had walked dazedly past the old man sitting on the floor of Rome International? "I'm sorry," she had muttered to him stupidly.

"I'm sorry," she said now, aloud. The beautiful woman had said something which had not penetrated the layers of thought and retreat.

The woman smiled as she sat beside her. "I was just saying it is a pity that Nicholai is not here. He's been up in the mountains for several days, crawling about in those caves of his. Appalling hobby. But I expect him back this evening or tomorrow morning. And that will give you a chance to bathe and perhaps sleep a little. That would be nice, wouldn't it."

The thought of a hot bath and cool sheets was almost swooningly seductive to Hannah.

The woman smiled and drew her chair closer to the marble tea table. "How do you take your tea?" Her eyes were calm and frank. In shape, they were Oriental, but their color was hazel, semé of gold flecks. Hannah could not have guessed her race. Surely her movements were Eastern, fine and controlled; but her skin tone was café au lait, and the body within its high-collared Chinese dress of green silk had a distinctly African development of breast and buttocks. Her mouth and nose, however, were Caucasian. And her voice was cultured, low and modulated, as was her laugh when she said, "Yes, I know. It is confusing."

"Pardon me?" Hannah said, embarrassed at having her thoughts read so transparently.

"I am what the kindly disposed call a 'cosmopolitan,' and others might term a mongrel. My mother was Japanese, and it would appear that my father was a mulatto American soldier. I never had the good fortune to meet him. Do you take milk?"

"What?"

"In your tea." Hana smiled. "Are you more comfortable in English?" she asked in that language.

"Yes, in fact I am," Hannah admitted also in English, but with an American tonality.

"I assumed as much from your accent. Good then. We shall speak in English. Nicholai seldom speaks English in the house, and I fear I am getting rusty." She had, in fact, a just-perceptible accent; not a mispronunciation, but a slightly mechanical overenunciation of her British English. It was possible that her French also bore traces of accent, but Hannah, with her alien ear, could not know that.

But something else did occur to her. "There are two cups set out. Were you expecting me, Mrs. Hel?"

"Do call me Hana. Oh, yes, I was expecting you. The man from the café in Tardets telephoned for permission to give you directions. And I received another call when you passed through Abense-de-Haut, and another when you reached Lichans." Hana laughed lightly. "Nicholai is very well protected here. You see, he has no great affection for surprises."

47

"Oh, that reminds me. I have a note for you." Hannah took from her pocket the folded note the café proprietor had given her.

Hana opened and glanced at it, then she laughed in her low, minor-key voice. "It is a bill. And very neatly itemized, too. Ah, these French. One franc for the telephone call. One franc for your coffee. And an additional one franc fifty—an estimate of the tip you would have left. My goodness, we have made a good bargain! We have the pleasure of your company for only three francs fifty." She laughed and set the bill aside. Then she reached across and placed her warm, dry hand upon Hannah's arm. "Young lady? I don't think you realize that you are crying."

"What?" Hannah put her hand to her cheek. It was wet with tears. My God, how long had she been crying? "I'm sorry. It's just . . . This morning my friends were . . . I *must* see Mr. Hel!"

"I know, dear. I know. Now finish your tea. There is something in it to make you rest. Then I will show you up to your room, where you can bathe and sleep. And you will be fresh and beautiful when you meet Nicholai. Just leave your rucksack here. One of the girls will see to it."

"I should explain—"

But Hana raised her hand. "You explain things to Nicholai when he comes. And he will tell me what he wants me to know."

Hannah was still sniffling and feeling like a child as she followed Hana up the wide marble staircase that dominated the entrance hall. But she could feel a delicious peace spreading within her. Whatever was in the tea was softening the crust of her memories and floating them off to a distance. "You're being very kind to me, Mrs. Hel," she said sincerely.

Hana laughed softly. "Do call me Hana. After all, I am not Nicholai's wife. I am his concubine."

Washington

The elevator door opened silently, and Diamond preceded Miss Swivven into the white workspace of the Sixteenth Floor.

" . . . and I'll want them available within ten minutes after call: Starr, the Deputy, and that Arab. Do you have that?"

"Yes, sir." Miss Swivven went immediately to her cubicle to make the necessary arrangements, while the First Assistant rose from his console.

"I have the scan of Asa Stern's first-generation contacts, sir. It's coming in now." He felt a justifiable pride. There were not ten men alive who had the skill to pull a list based upon amorphous emotional relationships out of Fat Boy.

"Give me a desk RP on it," Diamond ordered as he sat in his swivel chair at the head of the conference table.

"Coming up. Oops! Just a second, sir. The list is one-hundred-eighty percent inverted. It will only take a moment to flip it."

It was typical of the computer's systemic inability to distinguish between love and hate, affection and blackmail, friendship and parasitism, that any list organized in terms of such emotional rubrics stood a 50/50 chance of coming in inverted. The First Assistant had foreseen this danger and had seeded the raw list with the names of Maurice Herzog and Heinrich Himmler (both H's). When the printout showed Himmler to be greatly admired by Asa Stern, and Herzog to be detested, the First Assistant dared the assumption that Fat Boy had done a 180.

"It's not just a naked list, is it?" Diamond asked.

"No, sir. I've requested pinhole data. Just the most salient facts attached to each name, so we can make useful identification."

"You're a goddamned genius, Llewellyn."

The First Assistant nodded in absentminded agreement as he watched the list crawl up his screen in sans-serif IBM lettering.

STERN, DAVID
  RELATIONSHIP EQUALS SON . . . WHITE CARD . . .
STUDENT, AMATEUR ATHLETE . . . KILLED, 1972 sub
MUNICH OLYMPICS . . .
STERN, JUDITH
  RELATIONSHIP EQUALS WIFE . . . PINK CARD . . .
SCHOLAR, RESEARCHER . . .
  DEAD, 1956 sub NATURAL CAUSES . . .
ROTHMANN, MOISHE
  RELATIONSHIP EQUALS FRIEND . . . WHITE CARD . . .
PHILOSOPHER, POET . . . DEAD, 1958 sub NATURAL
CAUSES . . .
KAUFMANN, S.L.
  RELATIONSHIP EQUALS FRIEND . . . RED CARD . . .
POLITICAL ACTIVIST . . . RETIRED . . .
HEL, NICHOLAI ALEXANDROVITCH
  RELATIONSHIP EQUALS FRIEND . . .

"Stop!" Diamond ordered. "Freeze that!"

The First Assistant scanned the next fragments of information. "Oh, my goodness!"

Diamond leaned back in his chair and closed his eyes. When CIA screws up, they certainly do it in style! "Nicholai Hel," Diamond pronounced, his voice a monotone.

"Sir?" the First Assistant said softly, recalling the ancient practice of executing the messenger who brings bad news. "This Nicholai Hel is identified with a *mauve* card."

"I know . . . I know."

"Ah . . . I suppose you'll want a complete pull and printout on Hel, Nicholai Alexandrovitch?" the First Assistant asked, almost apologetically.

"Yes." Diamond rose and walked to the big window beyond which the illuminated Washington Monument stood out against the night sky, while double rows of automobile headlights crawled down the long avenue toward the Center—the same automobiles that were always at the same place at this time every evening. "You'll find the pull surprisingly thin."

"Thin, sir? On a mauve card?"

"On *this* mauve card, yes."

Within the color-coding system, mauve punch cards indicated the most elusive and dangerous of men, from the Mother Company's point of view: Those who operated without reference to nationalistic or ideological prejudices, free-lance agents and assassins who could not be controlled through pressure upon governments; those who killed for either side.

Originally, color-coding of punch cards was introduced into Fat Boy for the purpose of making immediately evident certain bold characteristics of a subject's life and work. But from the very first, Fat Boy's systemic inability to deal with abstractions and shadings reduced the value of the system. The problem lay in the fact that Fat Boy was permitted to color-code himself, in terms of certain input principles.

The first of these principles was that only such people as constituted real or potential threats to the Mother Company and the governments She controlled would be represented by color-coded cards, all others being identified by standard white cards. Another principle was that there be a symbolic relationship between the color of the card and the nature of the subject's affiliations. This worked well enough in its simplest forms: Leftist agitators and terrorists were represented by red cards; Rightist politicians and activists received blue cards; sympathizers of the Left had pink cards; abettors of ultra-conservatives had powder blue. (For a brief time, devoted Liberals were assigned yellow cards, in concurrence with British political symbolism, but when the potential for effective action by Liberals was assessed by Fat Boy, they were reassigned white cards indicating political impotence.)

The value of color-coding came under criticism when the system was applied to more intricate problems. For instance, active supporters of the Provisional IRA and of the various Ulster defense organizations were randomly assigned green or orange cards, because Fat Boy's review of the tactics, philosophy, and effec-

51

tiveness of the two groups made them indistinguishable from one another.

Another major problem arose from Fat Boy's mindless pursuit of logic in assigning colors. To differentiate between Chinese and European communist agents, the Chinese were assigned yellow cards; and the Europeans under their domination received a mixture of red and yellow, which produced for them orange cards, identical with those of the North Irish. Such random practices led to some troublesome errors, not the least of which was Fat Boy's longstanding assumption that Ian Paisley was an Albanian.

The most dramatic error concerned African nationalists and American Black Power actives. With a certain racial logic, these subjects were assigned black cards. For several months these men were able to operate without observation or interference from the Mother Company and her governmental subsidiaries, for the simple reason that black print on black cards is rather difficult to read.

With considerable regret, it was decided to end the color-code method, despite the millions of dollars of American taxpayers' money that had been devoted to the project.

But it is easier to introduce a system into Fat Boy than to cleanse it out, since His memory is eternal and His insistence on linear logic implacable. Therefore, color-coding remained in its vestigial form. Agents of the left were still identified with red and pink; while crypto-fascists, such as KKK members, were identified with blue, and American Legionnaires with powder blue. Logically enough, subjects who worked indifferently for both sides were identified with purple, but Fat Boy remembered His problem with Black Power actives, and so he gray'd the purple down to mauve.

Further, Fat Boy reserved the mauve card for men who dealt specifically in assassination.

The First Assistant looked up quizzically from his console. "Ah . . . I don't know what's wrong, sir. Fat Boy is running statement/correction/statement/correction patterns. On even the most basic information, his various input sources disagree. We have ages for this Nicholai Hel ranging from forty-seven to fifty-two. And look at this! Under nationality we have a choice among Russian, German, Chinese, Japanese, French, and Costa Rican. Costa Rican, sir?"

"Those last two have to do with his passports; he holds passports from France and Costa Rica. Right now he lives in France—or he did recently. The other nationalities have to do with his genetic background, his place of birth, and his major cultural inputs."

"So what is his real nationality?"

Mr. Diamond continued to look out the window, staring at nothing. "None."

"You seem to know something about this person, sir." The First Assistant's tone was interrogative but tentative. He was curious, but he knew better than to be inquisitive.

For several moments, Diamond did not answer. Then: "Yes. I know something about him." He turned away from the window and sat heavily at his desk. "Get on with the search. Turn up everything you can. Most of it will be contradictory, vague, or inaccurate, but we need to know everything we can discover."

"Then you feel that this Nicholai Hel is involved in this business?"

"With our luck? Probably."

"In what way, sir?"

"I don't know! Just get on with the search!"

"Yes, sir." The First Assistant scanned the next fragments of data. "Ah . . . sir? We have three possible birthplaces for him."

"Shanghai."

"You're sure of that, sir?"

"Yes!" Then, after a moment's pause, "Reasonably sure, that is."

Shanghai: 193?

As always at this season, cool evening breezes are drawn over the city from the sea, toward the warm land mass of China; and the draperies billow out from the glass doors to the veranda of the large house on Avenue Joffre in the French Concession.

General Kishikawa Takashi withdraws a stone from his lacquered *Gō ke* and holds it lightly between the tip of his middle finger and the nail of his index. Some minutes pass in silence, but his concentration is not on the game, which is in its 176th gesture and has begun to concrete toward the inevitable. The General's eyes rest on his opponent who, for his part, is completely absorbed in the patterns of black and white stones on the pale yellow board. Kishikawa-san has decided that the young boy must be sent away to Japan, and tonight he would have to be told. But not just now. It would spoil the flavor of the game; and that would be unkind because, for the first time, the young man is winning.

The sun has set behind the French Concession, over mainland China. Lanterns have been lighted in the old walled city, and the smell of thousands of cooking suppers fills the narrow, tangled streets. Along the Whangpoo and up Soochow Creek, the sampan homes of the floating city are alive with dim lights, as old women with trousers tied at the ankle arrange stones to level cooking fires on the canted decks, for the river is at low tide and the sampans have heeled over, their wooden bellies stuck in the yellow mud. People late for their suppers trot over Stealing Hen Bridge. A professional letter writer flourishes his brush carelessly, eager to finish his day's work, and knowing that his calligraphic insouciance will not be discovered by the illiterate young girl for whom he is composing a love letter on the model of one of his Sixteen Never-Fail Formulas. The Bund, that street of imposing commercial houses and hotels, gaudy statement of imperial might and confidence, is silent and dark; for the British taipans have fled; the *North China Daily News* no longer prints its gossip, its pious reprimands, its complaisant affirmations of the world situation. Even Sasson House, the most elegant facade on the Bund, built on profits from the opium trade, has been demoted to the mundane task of housing the Headquarters of the Occupation Forces. The greedy French, the swaggering British, the pompous Germans, the opportunistic Americans are all gone. Shanghai is under the control of the Japanese.

General Kishikawa reflects on the uncanny resemblance between this young man across the Gō board and his mother: almost as though Alexandra Ivanovna had produced her son parthenogenetically—a feat those who had experienced her overwhelming social presence would consider well within her capacity. The young man has the same angular line of jaw, the same broad forehead and high cheekbones, the fine nose that is spared the Slavic curse of causing interlocutors to feel they are staring into the barrels of a shotgun. But most intriguing to Kishikawa-san are comparisons between the boy's eyes and the mother's. Comparisons and contrasts. Physically, their eyes are identical: large, deepset, and of that startling bottle-green color unique to the Countess's family. But the polar differences in personality between mother and son are manifest in the articulation and intensity of gaze, in the dimming and crystallizing of those sinople eyes. While the mother's glance was bewitching, the son's is cool. Where the mother used her eyes to fascinate, the boy uses his to dismiss. What in her look was coquetry, in his is arrogance. The light that shone from her eyes is still and internal in his. Her eyes expressed humor; his express wit. She charmed; he disturbs.

Alexandra Ivanovna was an egotist; Nicholai is an egoist.

Although the General's Oriental frame of reference does not remark it, by Western criteria Nicholai looks very young for his fifteen years. Only the frigidity of his too-green eyes and a certain firm set of mouth keeps his face from being too delicate, too finely formed for a male. A vague discomfort over his physical beauty prompted Nicholai from an early age to engage in the most vigorous and combative of sports. He trained in classic, rather old-fashioned jiujitsu, and he played rugby with the international side against the sons of the British taipans with an effectiveness that bordered on brutality. Although Nicholai understood the stiff charade of fair play and sportsmanship with which the British protect themselves from real defeat, he preferred the responsibilities of victory to the comforts of losing with grace. But he did not really like team sports, preferring to win or lose by virtue of his own skill and toughness. And his emotional toughness was such that he almost always won, as a matter of will.

Alexandra Ivanovna almost always won too, not as a matter of will, but as a matter of right. When she appeared in Shanghai in the autumn of 1922 with an astonishing amount of baggage and no visible means of support, she relied upon her previous social position in St. Petersburg to grant her leadership in the growing community of displaced White Russians—so called by the ruling British, not because they came from Belorosskiya, but because they were obviously not "red." She immediately created about her an admiring court that included the most interesting men of the colony. To be interesting to Alexandra Ivanovna, one had to be rich, handsome, or witty; and it was the major annoyance of her life that she seldom found two of these qualities in one man, and never all three.

There were no other women near the core of her society; the Countess found women dull and, in her opinion, superfluous, as she could fully occupy the minds and attentions of a dozen men at one time, keeping a soirée atmosphere witty, brisk, and just naughty enough.

In retaliation, the unwanted ladies of the International Settlement declared that nothing in this world could tempt them to be seen in public with the Countess, and they fervently wished their husbands and fiancées shared their fine sense of propriety. By shrugs and hums and pursings of lips, these peripheral ladies made it known that they suspected a causal relationship between two social paradoxes: the first being that the Countess maintained a lavish household although she had arrived penniless; and the second being that she was constantly surrounded by the most desirable men of the international community, despite the fact that she lacked all those sterner virtues the ladies had been assured by their mothers were more important and durable than mere charm and beauty. These women would have been glad to include the Countess within that body of White Russian women who trickled into China from Manchuria, sold what pitiful goods and jewelry they had managed to escape with, and finally were driven to sustain themselves by vending the comfort of their laps. But these arid, righteous women were denied that facile dismissal by the knowledge that the Countess was one of those not uncommon anomalies of the Tzarist court, a Russian noblewoman without a drop of Slavic blood in her all-too-visible (and possibly available) body. Alexandra Ivanovna (whose father's given name had been Johann) was a Hapsburg with connections to a minor German royal family that had immigrated to England with nothing but their Protestantism to recommend them, and which had recently changed its name to one of less Hunnish sound as a gesture of patriotism. Still, the proper ladies of the settlement averred that even such deep quarterings were not proof of moral rectitude in those Flapper days; nor, despite the Countess's apparent assumption, an adequate substitute for it.

During the third season of her reign, Alexandra Ivanovna appeared to settle her attentions upon a vain young Prussian who possessed that pellucid, superficial intelligence untrammelled by sensitivity that is common to his race. Count Helmut von Keitel zum Hel became her companion of record—her pet and toy. Ten years younger than she, the Count possessed great physical beauty and athletic prowess. He was an expert horseman and a fencer of note. She thought of him as a decorative setting for her, and the only public statement she ever made concerning their relationship was to speak of him as "adequate breeding stock."

It was her practice to pass the heavy, humid months of summer in a villa in the uplands. One autumn she returned later than usual to Shanghai, and thenceforward there was a baby boy in the household. As a matter of form, young von Keitel zum Hel proposed marriage. She laughed lightly and told him that, while it had been her intention all along to create a child as a living argument against mongrel egalitarianism, she did not feel the slightest impulse to have *two* children about the house. He bowed with the rigid petulance that serves Prussians as a substitute for dignity, and made arrangements to return to Germany within the month.

Far from concealing the boy or the circumstances of his birth, she made him the ornament of her salon. When official requirements made it necessary that she name him, she called him Nicholai Hel, taking the last name from a little river bordering the Keitel estate. Alexandra Ivanovna's view of her own role in the production of the lad was manifest in the fact that his full name was Nicholai Alexandrovitch Hel.

A series of English nannies followed one another through the household, so English joined French, Russian, and German as the languages of the crib, with no particular preference shown, save for Alexandra Ivanovna's conviction that certain languages were best for expressing certain classes of thought. One spoke of love and other trivia in French; one discussed tragedy and disaster in Russian; one did business in German; and one addressed servants in English.

Because the children of the servants were his only companions, Chinese was also a cradle language for Nicholai, and he developed the habit of thinking in that language because his greatest childhood dread was that his mother could read his thoughts—and she had no Chinese.

Alexandra Ivanovna considered schools appropriate only for merchants' children, so Nicholai's education was confided to a succession of tutors, all decorative young men, all devoted to the mother. When it developed that Nicholai displayed an interest in, and a considerable capacity for, pure mathematics, his mother was not at all pleased. But when she was assured by the tutor of the moment that pure mathematics was a study without practical or commercial application, she decided it was appropriate to his breeding.

The more practical aspects of Nicholai's social education—and all of his fun—came from his practice of sneaking away from the house and wandering with street urchins through the narrow alleys and hidden courtyards of the seething, noisome, noisy city. Dressed in the universal loose-fitting blue, his close-cropped hair under a round cap, he would roam alone or with friends of the hour and return home to admonitions or punishments, both of which he accepted with great calm and an infuriating elsewhere gaze in his bottle-green eyes.

In the streets, Nicholai learned the melody of this city the Westerners had confected for themselves. He saw supercilious young British "griffins" being pulled about by cadaverous rickshaw "boys" cachectic with tuberculosis, sweating with effort and malnutrition, wearing gauze masks to avoid offending the European masters. He saw the compradores, fat and buttery middlemen who profited from the Europeans' exploitation of their own people, and who aped Western ways and ethics. After making profit and gorging on exotic foods, the greatest pleasure of these compradores was to arrange to deflower twelve- or thirteen-year-old girls who had been bought in Hangchow or Soochow and who were ready to enter the brothels licensed by the French. Their tactics of defloration were . . . irregular. The only revenge the girl might have was, if she had a gift for theatrics, the profitable ploy of being deflowered rather often. Nicholai learned that all of the beggars who threatened passers-by with contact with their rotting limbs, or stuck pins into babies to make them cry pitifully, or mobbed and frightened tourists with their demands for *kumshah*—all of them, from the old men who prayed for you or cursed you, to the half-starved children who offered to perform unnatural acts with one another for your entertainment, were under the control of His Heinous Majesty, the King of Beggars, who ran a peculiar combination of guild and protection racket. Anything lost in the city, anyone hiding in the city, any service wanted in the city, could be found through a modest contribution to His Majesty's treasury.

Down at the docks, Nicholai watched sweating stevedores dog-trot up and down the gangplanks of metal ships and wooden junks with strabismic eyes painted on their prows. In the evening, after they had already worked eleven hours, chanting their constant, narcotizing *hai-yo, hai-yo* the stevedores would begin to weaken, and sometimes one would stumble under his load. Then the Gurkhas would wade in with their blackjacks and iron bars, and the lazy would find new strength . . . or lasting rest.

Nicholai watched the police openly accept "squeeze money" from withered amahs who pimped for teenaged prostitutes. He learned to recognize the secret signs of the "Greens" and the "Reds," who constituted the world's largest secret societies, and whose protection and assassination rackets extended from beggars to politicians. Chiang Kai-shek himself was a "Green," sworn to obedience to the gang. And it was the "Greens" who murdered and mutilated young university students who attempted to organize the Chinese proletariat. Nicholai could tell a "Red" from a "Green" by the way he held his cigarette, by the way he spat.

During the days, Nicholai learned from tutors: Mathematics, Classical Literature, and Philosophy. In the evenings, he learned from the streets: Commerce, Politics, Enlightened Imperialism, and the Humanities.

And at night he would sit beside his mother as she entertained the cleverest of the men who controlled Shanghai and wrung it dry from their clubs and commercial houses of the Bund. What the majority of these men thought was shyness in Nicholai, and what the brightest of them thought was aloofness, was in fact cold hatred for merchants and the merchant mentality.

Time passed; Alexandra Ivanovna's carefully placed and expertly guided investments flourished, while the rhythms of her social life slowed. She became more comfortable of body, more languid, more lush; but her vivacity and beauty ripened, rather than waned, for she had inherited that family trait that had kept her mother and aunts looking vaguely thirtyish long after they passed the half-century mark. Former lovers became old friends, and life on Avenue Joffre mellowed.

Alexandra Ivanovna began to have little fainting spells, but she did not concern herself over them, beyond accepting the well-timed swoon as essential to the amorous arsenal of any lady of blood. When a doctor of her circle who had for years been eager to examine her ascribed the spells to a weak heart, she made a nominal accommodation to what she conceived to be a physical nuisance by reducing her at-homes to one a week, but beyond that she gave her body no quarter.

". . . and they tell me, young man, that I have a weak heart. It's an essentially romantic failing, and you must promise not to take advantage of it too frequently. You must also promise to seek out a responsible tailor. That suit, my boy!"

On the seventh of July, 1937, the *North China Daily News* reported that shots had been exchanged between Japanese and Chinese at the Marco Polo bridge near Peking. Down at number Three, the Bund, British taipans lounging about in the Shanghai Club agreed that this latest development in the pointless struggle between Orientals might get out of hand, if not dealt with briskly. They made it known to Generalissimo Chiang Kai-shek that they would prefer him to rush north and engage the Japanese along a front that would shield their commercial houses from the damned nuisance of war.

The Generalissimo decided, however, to await the Japanese at Shanghai in the hope that putting the International Settlement in jeopardy would attract foreign intervention on his behalf.

When that did not work, he began a systematic harassment of Japanese companies and civilians in the international community that culminated when, at six-thirty in the evening of August 9, Sub-Lieutenant Isao Oyama and his driver, first-class seaman Yozo Saito, who were driving to inspect Japanese cotton mills outside the city, were stopped by Chinese soldiers.

They were found beside Monument Road, riddled with bullets and sexually mutilated.

In response, Japanese warships moved up the Whangpoo. A thousand Japanese sailors were landed to protect their commercial colony at Chapei, across Soochow creek. They were faced by 10,000 elite Chinese soldiers dug in behind barricades.

The outcry of the comfortable British taipans was

reinforced by messages sent by European and American ambassadors to Nanking and Tokyo demanding that Shanghai be excluded from the zone of hostilities. The Japanese agreed to this request, provided that Chinese forces also withdraw from the demilitarized zone.

But on August 12, the Chinese cut all telephone lines to the Japanese Consulate and to Japanese commercial firms. The next day, Friday 13, the Chinese 88th Division arrived at North Station and blocked all roads leading out of the settlement. It was their intention to bottle up as large a buffer of civilians as possible between themselves and the vastly outnumbered Japanese.

On August 14, Chinese pilots in American-built Northrops flew over Shanghai. One high explosive bomb crashed through the roof of the Palace Hotel; another exploded in the street outside the Café Hotel. Seven hundred twenty-nine people dead; eight hundred sixty-one wounded. Thirty-one minutes later another Chinese plane bombed The Great World Amusement Park which had been converted into a refugee camp for women and children. One thousand twelve dead; one thousand seven wounded.

For the trapped Chinese there was no escape from Shanghai; the Generalissimo's troops had closed all the roads. For the foreign taipans, however, there was always escape. Sweating coolies grunted and chanted *hai-yo, hai-yo* as they struggled up gangplanks, carrying the loot of China under the supervision of white-suited young griffins with their checklists, and Gurkhas with their blackjacks. The British on the *Raj Putana,* Germans on the *Oldenburg,* Americans on the *President McKinley,* Dutchmen on the *Tasman* said good-bye to one another, the women daubing at eyes with tiny handkerchiefs, the men exchanging diatribes against the unreliable and ungrateful Orientals, as in the background ships' bands played a gallimaufry of national anthems.

That night, from behind its barricades of sandbags and trapped Chinese civilians, Chiang Kai-shek's artillery opened up on the Japanese ships at anchor in the river. The Japanese returned fire, destroying barricades of both kinds.

Through all of this, Alexandra Ivanovna refused to

leave her home on Avenue Joffre, now a deserted street, its shattered windows open to evening breezes and looters. As she was of no nationality, neither Soviet nor Chinese nor British, she was outside formal systems of protection. At any event, she had no intention at her age of leaving her home and carefully collected furnishings to reestablish herself God knows where. After all, she reasoned, the Japanese whom she knew were no duller than the rest, and they could hardly be less efficient administrators than the English had been.

The Chinese made their firmest stand of the war at Shanghai; it was three months before the outnumbered Japanese could drive them out. In their attempts to attract foreign intervention, the Chinese permitted a number of bombing "mistakes" to add to the toll in human lives and physical destruction caused by Japanese shelling.

And they maintained their barricades across the roads, keeping in place the protective buffer of tens of thousands of civilians . . . their own countrymen.

Throughout those terrible months, the resilient Chinese of Shanghai continued to go about their daily lives as best they could, despite the shelling from the Japanese and the bombings from American-made Chinese planes. Medicine, then food, then shelter, and finally water became scarce; but life went on in the teeming, frightened city; and the bands of boys clad in blue cotton with whom Nicholai roamed the streets found new, if grim, games involving the toppling ruins of buildings, desperate scrambles for make-shift air raid shelters, and playing in geysers from broken water mains.

Only once did Nicholai have a brush with death. He was with other street urchins in the district of the great department stores, the Wing On and The Sincere, when one of the common "mistakes" brought Chinese dive-bombers over densely packed Nanking Road. It was the lunch hour, and the crowds were thick when The Sincere received a direct hit, and one side of the Wing On was sheared away. Ornate ceilings caved in upon the faces of people staring up in horror. The occupants of a crowded elevator screamed in one voice as the cable was cut, and it plunged to the basement.

An old woman who had been facing an exploding window was stripped of flesh in front, while from behind she seemed untouched. The old, the lame, and children were crushed under foot by those who stampeded in panic. The boy who had been standing next to Nicholai grunted and sat down heavily in the middle of the street. He was dead; a chip of stone had gone through his chest. As the thunder of bombs and the war of collapsing masonry ebbed, there emerged through it the high-pitched scream from thousands of voices. A stunned shopper whimpered as she searched through shards of glass that had been a display counter. She was an exquisite young woman clothed in the Western "Shanghai" mode, an ankle-length dress of green silk slit to above the knee, and a stiff little collar standing around her curved, porcelain neck. Her extreme pallor might have come from the pale rice powders fashionable with the daughters of rich Chinese merchants, but it did not. She was searching for the ivory figurine she had been examining at the moment of the bombing, and for the hand in which she had been holding it.

Nicholai ran away.

A quarter of an hour later, he was sitting on a rubble heap in a quiet district where weeks of bombing had left blocks of empty and toppling shells. Dry sobs racked his body and seared his lungs, but he did not cry; no tears streaked the plaster dust that coated his face. In his mind, he repeated again and again: "Northrop bombers. American bombers."

When at last the Chinese soldiers were driven out, and their barricades broken, thousands of civilians fled the nightmare city of bombed-out buildings on the interior walls of which could be seen the checkerboard patterns of gutted apartments. In the rubble: a torn calendar with a date encircled, a charred photograph of a young woman, a suicide note and a lottery ticket in the same envelope.

By a cruel perversity of fate, the Bund, monument to foreign imperialism, was relatively unscathed. Its empty windows stared out over the desolation of the city the taipans had created, drained, then deserted.

Nicholai was among the small gaggle of blue-clad

Chinese children who lined the streets to watch the first parade of Japanese occupation troops. Army news photographers had passed out pieces of sticky candy and small *hinomaru* rising-sun flags, which the children were ordered to wave as the motion picture cameras recorded their bewildered enthusiasm. An officious young officer conducted the event, adding greatly to the confusion with his barked instructions in heavily accented Chinese. Uncertain of what to make of an urchin with blond hair and green eyes, he ordered Nicholai to the back of the crowd.

Nicholai had never seen soldiers like these, rough and efficient, but certainly no parade-ground models. They did not march with the robot synchronization of the German or the British; they passed in clean but rumpled ranks, marching jerkily behind serious young officers with moustaches and comically long swords.

Despite the fact that rather few dwellings were intact in the residential areas when the Japanese entered the city, Alexandra Ivanovna was surprised and annoyed when a staff car, little flags fluttering from its fenders, arrived in her driveway and a junior officer announced in a metallic French that General Kishikawa Takashi, governor of Shanghai, was to be billeted upon her. But her vivid instinct for self-preservation persuaded her that there might be some advantage to cultivating friendly relations with the General, particularly as so many of the good things of life were in short supply. Not for an instant did she doubt that this General would automatically enlist himself among her admirers.

She was mistaken. The General took time from a busy schedule to explain to her in a curiously accented but grammatically flawless French that he regretted any inconvenience the necessities of war might bring to her household. But he made it clear that she was a guest in his house, not he in hers. Always correct in his attitude toward her, the General was too occupied with his work to waste time on flirtations. At first Alexandra Ivanovna was puzzled, later annoyed, and finally intrigued by this man's polite indifference, a response she had never inspired from a heterosexual man. For his part, he found her interesting, but unnecessary. And he was not particularly impressed by the heritage that had made even the haughty women of Shanghai stand in reluctant awe. From the point of view of his thousand years of samurai breeding, her lineage appeared to be only a couple of centuries of Hunnish chieftainship.

Nevertheless, as a matter of politeness, he arranged weekly suppers, taken in the Western style, during the light conversation of which he learned a great deal about the Countess and her withdrawn, self-contained son; while they learned very little about the General. He was in his late fifties—young for a Japanese general—and a widower with one daughter living in Tokyo. Although an intensely patriotic man in the sense that he loved the physical things of his country—the lakes, mountains, misted valleys—he had never viewed his army career as the natural fulfillment of his personality. As a young man, he had dreamed of being a writer, although in his heart he had always known that the traditions of his family would ultimately conduct him into a military career. Pride in self and devotion to duty made him a hard-working and conscientious administrative officer but, although he had passed more than half his life in the army, his habits of mind caused him to think of the military as an avocation. His mind, not his heart; his time, not his passions, were given to his work.

In result of unstinting effort that often kept the General in his office on the Bund from early morning until midnight, the city began to recover. Public services were restored, the factories were repaired, and Chinese peasants began to trickle back into the city. Life and noise slowly returned to the streets, and occasionally one heard laughter. While not good by any civilized standards, living conditions for the Chinese worker were certainly superior to those he had experienced under the Europeans. There was work, clean water, basic sanitary services, rudimentary health facilities. The profession of begging was banned, but prostitution of course throve, and there were many acts of petty brutality, for Shanghai was an occupied city, and soldiers are men at their most beastly.

When General Kishikawa's health began to suffer from his self-imposed work load, he began a more salubrious routine that brought him to his home on Avenue Joffre in time for dinner each evening.

One evening after dinner, the General mentioned in passing that he was devoted to the game of Gō. Nicholai, who seldom spoke save in brief answer to direct questions, admitted that he also played the game. The General was amused and impressed by the fact that the boy said this in flawless Japanese. He laughed when Nicholai explained that he had been learning Japanese from textbooks and with the assistance of the General's own batman.

"You speak it well, for only six months' study," the General said.

"It is my fifth language, sir. All languages are mathematically similar. Each new one is easier to learn than the last. Then too"—the lad shrugged—"I have a gift for languages."

Kishikawa-san was pleased with the way Nicholai said this last, without braggadocio and without British coyness, as he might have said he was left-handed, or green-eyed. At the same time, the General had to smile to himself when he realized that the boy had obviously rehearsed his first sentence, for while that had been quite correct, his subsequent statements had revealed errors of idiom and pronunciation. The General kept his amusement to himself, recognizing that Nicholai was of an age to take himself very seriously and to be deeply stung by embarrassment.

"I shall help you with your Japanese, if you wish," Kishikawa-san said. "But first, let us see if you are an interesting opponent at Gō."

Nicholai was given a four-stone handicap, and they played a quick, time-limit game, as the General had a full day of work tomorrow. Soon they were absorbed, and Alexandra Ivanovna, who could never see much point in social events of which she was not the center, complained of feeling a bit faint and retired.

The General won, but not as easily as he should have. As he was a gifted amateur capable of giving professionals close combat with minimum handicaps, he was greatly impressed by Nicholai's peculiar style of play.

"How long have you been playing Gō?" he asked,

speaking in French to relieve Nicholai of the task of alien expression.

"Oh, four or five years, I suppose, sir."

The General frowned. "Five years? But . . . how old are you?"

"Thirteen, sir. I know I look younger than I am. It's a family trait."

Kishikawa-san nodded and smiled to himself as he thought of Alexandra Ivanovna who, when she had filled out her identity papers for the Occupation Authority, had taken advantage of this "family trait" by blatantly setting down a birth date that suggested she had been the mistress of a White Army general at the age of eleven and had given birth to Nicholai while still in her teens. The General's intelligence service had long ago apprised him of the facts concerning the Countess, but he allowed her this trivial gesture of coquetry, particularly considering what he knew of her unfortunate medical history.

"Still, even for a man of thirteen, you play a remarkable game, Nikko." During the course of the game, the General had manufactured this nickname that allowed him to avoid the troublesome "l." It remained forever his name for Nicholai. "I suppose you have not had any formal training?"

"No, sir. I have never had any instruction at all. I learned from reading books."

"Really? That is unheard of."

"Perhaps so, sir. But I am very intelligent."

For a moment, the General examined the lad's impassive face, its absinthe eyes frankly returning the officer's gaze. "Tell me, Nikko. Why did you choose to study Gō? It is almost exclusively a Japanese game. Certainly none of your friends played the game. They probably never even heard of it."

"That is precisely why I chose Gō, sir."

"I see." What a strange boy. At once both vulnerably honest and arrogant. "And has your reading given you to understand what qualities are necessary to be a fine player?"

Nicholai considered for a moment before answering. "Well, of course one must have concentration. Courage. Self-control. That goes without saying. But more im-

68

portant than these, one must have . . . I don't know how to say it. One must be both a mathematician and a poet. As though poetry were a science; or mathematics an art. One must have an affection for proportion to play Gō at all well. I am not expressing myself well, sir. I'm sorry."

"On the contrary. You are doing very well in your attempt to express the inexpressible. Of these qualities you have named, Nikko, where do you believe your own strengths lie?"

"In the mathematics, sir. In concentration and self-control."

"And your weaknesses?"

"In what I called poetry."

The General frowned and glanced away from the boy. It was strange that he should recognize this. At his age, he should not be able to stand outside himself and report with such detachment. One might expect Nikko to realize the need for certain Western qualities to play Gō well, qualities like concentration, self-control, courage. But to recognize the need for the receptive, sensitive qualities he called poetry was outside that linear logic that is the Western mind's strength . . . and limitation. But then—considering that Nicholai was born of the best blood of Europe but raised in the crucible of China—was he really Western? Certainly he was not Oriental either. He was of no racial culture. Or was it better to think of him as the sole member of a racial culture of his own?

"You and I share that weakness, sir." Nicholai's green eyes crinkled with humor. "We both have weaknesses in the area I called poetry."

The General looked up in surprise. "Ah?"

"Yes, sir. My play lacks much of this quality. Yours has too much of it. Three times during the game you relented in your attack. You chose to make the graceful play, rather than the conclusive one."

Kishikawa-san laughed softly. "How do you know I was not considering your age and relative inexperience?"

"That would have been condescending and unkind, and I don't believe you are those things." Nicholai's eyes smiled again. "I am sorry, sir, that there are no

69

honorifics in French. It must make my speech sound abrupt and insubordinate."

"Yes, it does a little. I was just thinking that, in fact."

"I am sorry, sir."

The General nodded. "I assume you have played Western chess?"

Nicholai shrugged. "A little. It doesn't interest me."

"How would you compare it with Gō?"

Nicholai thought for a second. "Ah . . . what Gō is to philosophers and warriors, chess is to accountants and merchants."

"Ah! The bigotry of youth. It would be more kind, Nikko, to say that Gō appeals to the philosopher in any man, and chess to the merchant in him."

But Nicholai did not recant. "Yes, sir, that would be more kind. But less true."

The General rose from his cushion, leaving Nicholai to replace the stones. "It is late, and I need my sleep. We'll play again soon, if you wish."

"Sir?" said Nicholai, as the General reached the door. "Yes?"

Nicholai kept his eyes down, shielding himself from the hurt of possible rejection. "Are we to be friends, sir?"

The General gave the question the consideration its serious tone requested. "That could be, Nikko. Let us wait and see."

It was that very night that Alexandra Ivanovna, deciding at last that General Kishikawa was not of the fabric of the men she had known in the past, came to tap at his bedroom door.

For the next year and half, they lived as a family. Alexandra Ivanovna became more subdued, more contented, perhaps a little plumper. What she lost in effervescence she gained in an attractive calm that caused Nicholai, for the first time in his life, to like her. Without haste, Nicholai and the General constructed a relationship that was as profound as it was undemonstrative. The one had never had a father; the other, a son. Kishikawa-san was of a temperament to enjoy guiding and shaping a clever, quick-minded young man, even

70

one who was occasionally too bold in his opinions, too confident of his attributes.

Alexandra Ivanovna found emotional shelter in the lee of the General's strong, gentle personality. He found spice and amusement in her flashes of temperament and wit. Between the General and the woman—politeness, generosity, gentleness, physical pleasure. Between the General and the boy—confidence, honesty, ease, affection, respect.

Then one evening after dinner, Alexandra Ivanovna joked as usual about the nuisance of her swooning fits and retired early to bed . . . where she died.

Now the sky is black to the east, purple over China. Out in the floating city the orange and yellow lanterns are winking out, as people make up beds on the canted decks of sampans heeled over in the mud. The air has cooled on the dark plains of inland China, and breezes are no longer drawn in from the sea. The curtains no longer billow inward as the General balances his stone on the nail of his index finger, his mind ranging far from the game before him.

It is two months since Alexandra Ivanovna died, and the General has received orders transferring him. He cannot take Nicholai with him, and he does not want to leave him in Shanghai where he has no friends and where his lack of formal citizenship denies him even the most rudimentary diplomatic protection. He has decided to send the boy to Japan.

The General examines the mother's refined face, expressed more economically, more angularly in the boy. Where will he find friends, this young man? Where will he find soil appropriate to his roots, this boy who speaks six languages and thinks in five, but who lacks the smallest fragment of useful training? Can there be a place in the world for him?

"Sir?"

"Yes? Oh . . . ah . . . Have you played, Nikko?"

"Some time ago, sir."

"Ah, yes, Excuse me. And do you mind telling me where you played?"

Nicholai pointed out his stone, and Kishikawa-san frowned because the unlikely placement had the taste

71

of a *tenuki*. He marshaled his fragmented attention and examined the board carefully, mentally reviewing the outcome of each placement available to him. When he looked up, Nicholai's bottle-green eyes were on him, smiling with relish. The game could be played on for several hours, and the outcome would be close. But it was inevitable that Nicholai would win. This was the first time.

The General regarded Nicholai appraisingly for some seconds, then he laughed. "You are a demon, Nikko!"

"That is true, sir," Nicholai admitted, enormously pleased with himself. "Your attention was wandering."

"And you took advantage of that?"

"Of course."

The General began to collect his stones and return them to the *Gō ke*. "Yes," he said to himself. "Of course." Then he laughed again. "What do you say to a cup of tea, Nikko?" Kishikawa-san's major vice was his habit of drinking strong, bitter tea at all hours of day and night. In the heraldry of their affectionate but reserved relationship, the offer of a cup of tea was the signal for a chat. While the General's batman prepared the tea, they walked out into the cool night air of the veranda, both wearing *yukatas*.

After a silence during which the General's eye wandered over the city, where the occasional light in the ancient walled town indicated that someone was celebrating, or studying, or dying, or selling herself, he asked Nicholai, seemingly apropos of nothing, "Do you ever think about the war?"

"No, sir. It has nothing to do with me."

The egoism of youth. The confident egoism of a young man brought up in the knowledge that he was the last and most rarefied of a line of selective breeding that had its sources long before tinkers became Henry Fords, before coinchangers became Rothschilds, before merchants became Medici.

"I am afraid, Nikko, that our little war is going to touch you after all." And with this entree, the General told the young man of the orders transferring him to combat, and of his plans to send Nicholai to Japan where he would live in the home of a famous player and teacher of Gō.

". . . my oldest and closest friend, Otake-san—whom you know by reputation as Otake of the Seventh *Dan*."

Nicholai did indeed recognize the name. He had read Otake-san's lucid commentaries on the middle game.

"I have arranged for you to live with Otake-san and his family, among the other disciples of his school. It is a very great honor, Nikko."

"I realize that, sir. And I am excited about learning from Otake-san. But won't he scorn wasting his instruction on an amateur?"

The General chuckled. "Scorn is not a style of mind that my old friend would employ. Ah! Our tea is ready."

The batman had taken away the *Gō ban* of *kaya,* and in its place was a low table set for tea. The General and Nicholai returned to their cushions. After the first cup, the General sat back slightly and spoke in a businesslike tone. "Your mother had very little money as it turns out. Her investments were scattered in small local companies, most of which collapsed upon the eve of our occupation. The men who owned the companies simply returned to Britain with the capital in their pockets. It appears that, for the Westerner, the great moral crisis of war obscures minor ethical considerations. There is this house . . . and very little more. I have arranged to sell the house for you. The proceeds will go for your maintenance and instruction in Japan."

"As you think best, sir."

"Good. Tell me, Nikko. Will you miss Shanghai?"

Nicholai considered for a second. "No."

"Will you feel lonely in Japan?"

Nicholai considered for a second. "Yes."

"I shall write to you."

"Often?"

"No, not often. Once a month. But you must write to me as often as you feel the need to. Perhaps you will be less lonely than you fear. There are other young people studying with Otake-san. And when you have doubts, ideas, questions, you will find Otake-san a valuable person to discuss them with. He will listen with interest, but will not burden you with advice." The General smiled. "Although I think you may find one of my friend's habits of speech a little disconcerting at times.

He speaks of everything in terms of Gō. All of life, for him, is a simplified paradigm of Gō."

"He sounds as though I shall like him, sir."

"I am sure you will. He is a man who has all my respect. He possesses a quality of . . . how to express it? . . . of *shibumi*."

"*Shibumi,* sir?" Nicholai knew the word, but only as it applied to gardens or architecture, where it connoted an understated beauty. "How are you using the term, sir?"

"Oh, vaguely. And incorrectly, I suspect. A blundering attempt to describe an ineffable quality. As you know, *shibumi* has to do with great refinement underlying commonplace appearances. It is a statement so correct that it does not have to be bold, so poignant it does not have to be pretty, so true it does not have to be real. *Shibumi* is understanding, rather than knowledge. Eloquent silence. In demeanor, it is modesty without pudency. In art, where the spirit of *shibumi* takes the form of *sabi,* it is elegant simplicity, articulate brevity. In philosophy, where *shibumi* emerges as *wabi,* it is spiritual tranquility that is not passive; it is being without the angst of becoming. And in the personality of a man, it is . . . how does one say it? Authority without domination? Something like that."

Nicholai's imagination was galvanized by the concept of *shibumi*. No other ideal had ever touched him so. "How does one achieve this *shibumi,* sir?"

"One does not achieve it, one . . . discovers it. And only a few men of infinite refinement ever do that. Men like my friend Otake-san."

"Meaning that one must learn a great deal to arrive at *shibumi?*"

"Meaning, rather, that one must pass through knowledge and arrive at simplicity."

From that moment, Nicholai's primary goal in life was to become a man of *shibumi;* a personality of overwhelming calm. It was a vocation open to him while, for reasons of breeding, education, and temperament, most vocations were closed. In pursuit of *shibumi* he could excel invisibly, without attracting the attention and vengeance of the tyrannical masses.

Kishikawa-san took from beneath the tea table a

small sandalwood box wrapped in plain cloth and put it into Nicholai's hands. "It is a farewell gift, Nikko. A trifle."

Nicholai bowed his head in acceptance and held the package with great tenderness; he did not express his gratitude in inadequate words. This was his first conscious act of *shibumi*.

Although they spoke late into their last night together about what *shibumi* meant and might mean, in the deepest essential they did not understand one another. To the General, *shibumi* was a kind of submission; to Nicholai, it was a kind of power.

Both were captives of their generations.

Nicholai sailed for Japan on a ship carrying wounded soldiers back for family leave, awards, hospitalization, a life under the burden of mutilation. The yellow mud of the Yangtze followed the ship for miles out to sea, and it was not until the water began to blend from khaki to slate blue that Nicholai unfolded the simple cloth that wrapped Kishikawa-san's farewell gift. Within a fragile sandalwood box, swathed in rich paper to prevent damage, were two *Gō ke* of black lacquer worked with silver in the Heidatsu process. On the lids of the bowls, lakeside tea houses wreathed in mist were implied, nestling against the shores of unstated lakes. Within one bowl were black Nichi stones from Kishiu. Within the other, white stones of Miyazaki clam shell . . . lustrous, curiously cool to the touch in any weather.

No one observing the delicate young man standing at the rail of the rusty freighter, his hooded green eyes watching the wallow and plunge of the sea as he contemplated the two gifts the General had given him—these *Gō ke,* and the lifelong goal of *shibumi*—would have surmised that he was destined to become the world's most highly paid assassin.

Washington

The First Assistant sat back from his control console and puffed out a long sigh as he pushed his glasses up and lightly rubbed the tender red spots on the bridge of his nose. "It's going to be difficult getting reliable information out of Fat Boy, sir. Each input source offers conflicting and contradictory data. You're sure he was born in Shanghai?"

"Reasonably, yes."

"Well, there's nothing on that. In a chronological sort, the first I come up with has him living in Japan."

"Very well. Start there, then!"

The First Assistant felt he had to defend himself from the irritation in Mr. Diamond's voice. "It's not as easy as you might think, sir. Here's an example of the kind of garble I'm getting. Under the rubric of 'languages spoken,' I get Russian, French, Chinese, German, English, Japanese, and Basque. *Basque?* That can't be right, can it?"

"It *is* right."

"Basque? Why would anyone learn to speak Basque?"

"I don't know. He studied it while he was in prison."

"Prison, sir?"

"You'll come to it later. He did three years in solitary confinement."

"You . . . you seem to be uniquely familiar with the data, sir."

"I've kept an eye on him for years."

The First Assistant considered asking why this Nicholai Hel had received such special attention, but he thought better of it. "All right, sir. Basque it is. Now how about this? Our first firm data come from immediately after the war, when it seems he worked for the Occupation Forces as a cryptographer and translator. Now, assuming he left Shanghai when we believe he did, we have six years unaccounted for. The only window Fat Boy gives me on that doesn't seem to make any sense. It suggests that he spent those six years studying some kind of game. A game called Gō—whatever that is."

"I believe that's correct."

"Can that be? Throughout the entire Second World War, he spent his time studying a board game?" The First Assistant shook his head. Neither he nor Fat Boy was comfortable with conclusions that did not proceed from solid linear logic. And it was not logical that a mauve-card international assassin would have passed five or six years (Christ! They didn't even know exactly how many!) learning to play some silly game!

Japan

For nearly five years Nicholai lived within the household of Otake-san; a student, and a member of the family. Otake of the Seventh *Dan* was a man of two contradictory personalities; in competition he was cunning, cold-minded, noted for his relentless exploitation of flaws in the opponent's play or mental toughness. But at home in his sprawling, rather disorganized household amid his sprawling extended family that included, besides his wife, father, and three children, never fewer than six apprenticed pupils, Otake-san was paternal, generous, even willing to play the clown for the amusement of his children and pupils. Money was never plentiful, but they lived in a small mountain village with few expensive distractions, so it was never a problem. When they had less, they lived on less; when they had more, they spent it freely.

None of Otake-san's children had more than average gifts in the art of Gō. And of his pupils, only Nicholai possessed that ineffable constellation of talents that makes the player of rank: a gift for conceiving abstract schematic possibilities; a sense of mathematical poetry in the light of which the infinite chaos of probability and permutation is crystallized under the pressure of intense concentration into geometric blossoms; the ruthless focus of force on the subtlest weakness of an opponent.

In time, Otake-san discovered an additional quality in Nicholai that made his play formidable: In the midst of play, Nicholai was able to rest in profound tranquility for a brief period, then return to his game fresh-minded.

It was Otake-san who first happened upon the fact that Nicholai was a mystic.

Like most mystics, Nicholai was unaware of his gift, and at first he could not believe that others did not have

78

similar experiences. He could not imagine life without mystic transport, and he did not so much pity those who lived without such moments as he regarded them as creatures of an entirely different order.

Nicholai's mysticism came to light later one afternoon when he was playing an exercise game with Otake-san, a very tight and classic game in which only vaguest nuances of development separated their play from textbook models. Partway through the third hour, Nicholai felt the gateway open to him for rest and oneness, and he allowed himself to expand into it. After a time, the feeling dissolved, and Nicholai sat, motionless and rested, wondering vaguely why the teacher was delaying in making an obvious placement. When he looked up, he was surprised to find Otake-san's eyes on his face and not on the *Gō ban*.

"What is wrong, Teacher? Have I made an error?"

Otake-san examined Nicholai's face closely. "No, Nikko. There was no particular brilliance in your last two plays, but also no fault. But . . . how can you play while you daydream?"

"Daydream? I was not daydreaming, Teacher."

"Were you not? Your eyes were defocused and your expression empty. In fact, you did not even look at the board while making your plays. You placed the stones while gazing out into the garden."

Nicholai smiled and nodded. Now he understood. "Oh, I see. In fact, I just returned from resting. So, of course, I didn't have to look at the board."

"Explain to me, please, why you did not have to look at the board, Nikko."

"I . . . ah . . . well, I was resting." Nicholai could see that Otake-san did not understand, and this confused him, assuming as he did that mystic experience was common.

Otake-san sat back and took another of the mint drops that he habitually sucked to relieve pains in his stomach resulting from years of tight control under the pressures of professional play. "Now tell me what you mean when you say that you were resting."

"I suppose 'resting' isn't the correct word for it, Teacher. I don't know what the word is. I have never heard anyone give a name to it. But you must know the sensation I mean. The departing without leaving. The . . . you know . . . the flowing into all things, and . . . ah . . . understanding all things." Nicholai was embarrassed. The experience was too simple and basic to explain. It was as though the Teacher had asked him to explain breathing, or the scent of flowers. Nicholai was sure that Otake-san knew exactly what he meant; after all, he had only to recall his own rest times. Why did he ask these questions?

Otake-san reached out and touched Nicholai's arm. "I know, Nikko, that this is difficult for you to explain. And I believe I understand a little of what you experience—not because I also have experienced it, but because I have read of it, for it has always attracted my curiosity. It is called mysticism."

Nicholai laughed. "Mysticism! But surely, Teacher—"

"Have you ever talked to anyone about this . . . how did you phrase it? . . . 'departing without leaving'?"

"Well . . . no. Why would anyone talk about it?"

"Not even our good friend Kishikawa-san?"

"No, Teacher. It never came up. I don't understand why you are asking me these questions. I am confused. And I am beginning to feel shame."

Otake-san pressed his arm. "No, no. Don't feel shame. Don't be frightened. You see, Nikko, what you experience . . . what you call 'resting' . . . is not very common. Few people experience these things, except in a light and partial way when they are very young. This experience is what saintly men strive to achieve through discipline and meditation, and foolish men seek through drugs. Throughout all ages and in all cultures, a certain fortunate few have been able to gain this state of calm and oneness with nature (I use these words to describe it because they are the words I have read) without years of rigid discipline. Evidently, it comes to them quite naturally, quite simply. Such people are called mystics. It is an unfortunate label because it carries connotations of religion and magic about it. In fact, all the words used to describe this experience are rather theatrical. What you call 'a rest,' others call ecstasy."

Nicholai grinned uncomfortably at this word. How could the most real thing in the world be called mysticism? How could the quietest emotion imaginable be called ecstasy?

"You smile at the word, Nikko. But surely the experience is pleasurable, is it not?"

"Pleasurable? I never thought of it that way. It is . . . necessary."

"Necessary?"

"Well, how would one live day in and day out without times of rest?"

Otake-san smiled. "Some of us are required to struggle along without such rest."

"Excuse me, Teacher. But I can't imagine a life like that. What would be the point of living a life like that?"

Otake-san nodded. He had found in his reading that mystics regularly reported an inability to understand people who lack the mystic gift. He felt a bit uneasy when he recalled that when mystics lose their gift—and most of them do at some time or other—they experience panic and deep depression. Some retreat into religion to rediscover the experience through the mechanics of meditation. Some even commit suicide, so pointless does life without mystic transport seem.

"Nikko? I have always been intensely curious about mysticism, so please permit me to ask you questions about this 'rest' of yours. In my readings, mystics who report their transports always use such gossamer terms, so many seeming contradictions, so many poetic paradoxes. It is as though they were attempting to describe something too complicated to be expressed in words."

"Or too simple, sir."

"Yes. Perhaps that is it. Too simple." Otake-san pressed his fist against his chest to relieve the pressure and took another mint drop. "Tell me. How long have you had these experiences?"

"Always."

"Since you were a baby?"

"Always."

"I see. And how long do these experiences last?"

"It doesn't matter, Teacher. There is not time there."

"It is timeless?"

"No. There is neither time nor timelessness."

Otake-san smiled and shook his head. "Am I to

have the gossamer terms and the poetic paradoxes from you as well?"

Nicholai realized that these bracketing oxymorons made that which was infinitely simple seem chaotic, but he didn't know how to express himself with the clumsy tools of words.

Otake-san came to his aid. "So you are saying that you have no sense of time during these experiences. You do not know how long they last?"

"I know exactly how long they last, sir. When I depart, I don't leave. I am where my body is, as well as everywhere else. I am not daydreaming. Sometimes the rest lasts a minute or two. Sometimes it lasts hours. It lasts for as long as it is needed."

"And do they come often, these . . . rests?"

"This varies. Twice or three times a day at most. But sometimes I go a month without a rest. When this happens, I miss them very much. I become frightened that they may never come back."

"Can you bring one of these rest periods on at will?"

"No. But I can block them. And I must be careful not to block them away, if I need one."

"How can you block them away?"

"By being angry. Or by hating."

"You can't have this experience if you hate?"

"How could I? The rest is the very opposite of hate."

"Is it love, then?"

"Love is what it might be, if it concerned people. But it doesn't concern people."

"What does it concern?"

"Everything. Me. Those two are the same. When I am resting, everything and I are . . . I don't know how to explain."

"You become one with everything?"

"Yes. No, not exactly. I don't *become* one with everything. I *return* to being one with everything. Do you know what I mean?"

"I am trying to. Please take this 'rest' you experienced a short time ago, while we were playing. Describe to me what happened."

Nicholai lifted his palms helplessly. "How can I do that?"

"Try. Begin with: we were playing, and you had just placed stone fifty-six . . . and . . . Go on."

"It was stone fifty-eight, Teacher."

"Well, fifty-eight then. And what happened?"

"Well . . . the flow of the play was just right, and it began to bring me to the meadow. It always begins with some kind of flowing motion . . . a stream or river, maybe the wind making waves in a field of ripe rice, the glitter of leaves moving in a breeze, clouds flowing by. And for me, if the structure of the Gō stones is flowing classically, that too can bring me to the meadow."

"The meadow?"

"Yes. That's the place I expand into. It's how I recognize that I am resting."

"Is it a real meadow?"

"Yes, of course."

"A meadow you visited at one time? A place in your memory?"

"It's not in my memory. I've never been there when I was diminished."

"Diminished?"

"You know . . . when I'm in my body and not resting."

"You consider normal life to be a diminished state, then?"

"I consider time spent at rest to be normal. Time like this . . . temporary, and . . . yes, diminished."

"Tell me about the meadow, Nikko."

"It is triangular. And it slopes uphill, away from me. The grass is tall. There are no animals. Nothing has ever walked on the grass or eaten it. There are flowers, a breeze . . . warm. Pale sky. I'm always glad to be the grass again."

"You *are* the grass?"

"We are one another. Like the breeze, and the yellow sunlight. We're all . . . mixed in together."

"I see. I see. Your description of the mystic experience resembles others I have read. And this meadow is what the writers call your 'gateway' or 'path.' Do you ever think of it in those terms?"

"No."

"So. What happens then?"

"Nothing. I am at rest. I am everywhere at once. And

everything is unimportant and delightful. And then . . . I begin to diminish. I separate from the sunlight and the meadow, and I contract again back into my body-self. And the rest is over." Nicholai smiled uncertainly. "I suppose I am not describing it very well, Teacher. It's not . . . the kind of thing one describes."

"No, you describe it very well, Nikko. You have evoked a memory in me that I had almost lost. Once or twice when I was a child . . . in summer, I think . . . I experienced brief transports such as you describe. I read once that most people have occasional mystic experiences when they are children, but soon outgrow them. And forget them. Will you tell me something else? How is it you are able to play Gō while you are transported . . . while you are in your meadow?"

"Well, I am here as well as there. I depart, but I don't leave. I am part of this room and that garden."

"And me, Nikko? Are you part of me too?"

Nicholai shook his head. "There are no animals in my rest place. I am the only thing that sees. I see for us all, for the sunlight, for the grass."

"I see. And how can you play your stones without looking at the board? How do you know where the lines cross? How do you know where I placed my last stone?"

Nicholai shrugged. It was too obvious to explain. "I am part of everything, Teacher. I share . . . no . . . I flow with everything. The *Gō ban,* the stones. The board and I are amongst one another. How could I not know the patterns of play?"

"You see from within the board then?"

"Within and without are the same thing. But 'see' isn't exactly right either. If one is everyplace, he doesn't have to 'see.' " Nicholai shook his head. "I can't explain."

Otake-san pressed Nikko's arm lightly, then withdrew his hand. "I won't question you further. I confess that I envy the mystic peace you find. I envy most of all your gift for finding it so naturally—without the concentration and exercise that even holy men must apply in search of it. But while I envy it, I also feel some fear on your behalf. If the mystic ecstasy has become —as I suspect it has—a natural and necessary part of your inner life, then what will become of you, should this gift fade, should these experiences be denied you?"

"I cannot imagine that happening, Teacher."

"I know. But my reading has revealed to me that these gifts can fade; the paths to inner peace can be lost. Something can happen that fills you with constant and unrelenting hate or fear, and then it would be gone."

The thought of losing the most natural and most important psychic activity of his life disturbed Nicholai. With a brief rush of panic, he realized that fear of losing it might be fear enough to cause him to lose it. He wanted to be away from this conversation, from these new and incredible doubts. His eyes lowered to the *Gō ban*, he considered his reaction to such a loss.

"What would you do, Nikko?" Otake-san repeated after a moment of silence.

Nicholai looked up from the board, his green eyes calm and expressionless. "If someone took my rest times from me, I would kill him."

This was said with a fatalistic calm that made Otake-san know it was not anger, only a simple truth. It was the quiet assurance of the statement that disturbed Otake-san most.

"But, Nikko. Let us say it was not a man who took this gift from you. Let us say it was a situation, an event, a condition of life. What would you do then?"

"I would seek to destroy it, whatever it was. I would punish it."

"Would that bring the path to rest back?"

"I don't know, Teacher. But it would be the least vengeance I could exact for so great a loss."

Otake-san sighed, part in regret for Nikko's particular vulnerability, part in sympathy for whoever might happen to be the agent of the loss of his gift. He had no doubt at all that the young man would do what he said. Nowhere is a man's personality so clearly revealed as in his Gō game, if his play be read by one with the experience and intelligence to interpret it. And Nicholai's play, brilliant and audacious as it was, bore the aesthetic blemishes of frigidity and almost inhuman concentration of purpose. From his reading of Nicholai's game, Otake-san knew that his star pupil might achieve greatness, might become the first non-Japanese to rise to the higher *dans;* but he knew also that the boy would never know peace or happiness in the smaller game of life. It was a blessed compensation that Nikko possessed the gift of retirement into mystic transport. But a gift with a poisoned core.

Otake-san sighed again and considered the pattern of stones. The game was about a third played out. "Do you mind, Nikko, if we do not finish? My nagging old stomach is bothering me. And the development is sufficiently classic that the seeds of the outcome have already taken root. I don't anticipate either of us making a serious error, do you?"

"No, sir." Nicholai was glad to leave the board, and to leave this small room where he had learned for the first time that his mystic retreats were vulnerable . . . that something could happen to deny him an essential part of his life. "At all events, Teacher, I think you would have won by seven or eight stones."

Otake-san glanced at the board again. "So many? I would have thought only five or six." He smiled at Nikko. It was their kind of joke.

In fact, Otake-san would have won by at least a dozen stones, and they both knew it.

The years passed, and the seasons turned easily in the Otake household where traditional roles, fealties, hard work, and study were balanced against play, devilment, and affection, this last no less sincere for being largely tacit.

Even in their small mountain village, where the dominant chords of life vibrated in sympathy with the cycle of the crops, the war was a constant tone in the background. Young men whom everybody knew left to join the army, some never to return. Austerity and harder work became their lot. There was great excitement when news came of the attack at Pearl Harbor on the eighth of December 1941; knowledgeable men agreed that the war would not last more than a year. Victory after victory was announced by enthusiastic voices over the radio as the army swept European imperialism from the Pacific.

But still, some farmers grumbled privately as almost impossible production quotas were placed on them, and they felt the pressures of decreasing consumer goods. Otake-san turned more to writing commentaries, as the number of Gō tournaments was restricted as a patriotic gesture in the general austerity. Occasionally the war touched the Otake household more directly. One winter evening, the middle son of the Otake family came home from school crushed and ashamed because he had been ridiculed by his classmates as a *yowamushi,* a weak worm, because he wore mittens on his sensitive hands during the bruising afternoon calisthenics when all the boys exercised on the snow-covered courtyard, stripped to the waist to demonstrate physical toughness and "samurai spirit."

And from time to time Nicholai overheard himself described as a foreigner, a *gaijin,* a "redhead," in tones of mistrust that reflected the xenophobia preached by jingoistic schoolteachers. But he did not really suffer from his status as an outsider. General Kishikawa had been careful that his identity papers designated his mother as a Russian (a neutral) and his father as a German (an ally). Too, Nicholai was protected by the great respect in which the village held Otake-san, the famed player of Gō who brought honor to their village by choosing to live there.

When Nicholai's game had improved sufficiently that he was allowed to play preliminary matches and accompany Otake-san as a disciple to the great championship games held in out-of-the-way resorts where the players could be "sealed in" away from the distractions of the world, he had opportunities to see at first hand the spirit with which Japan went to war. At railroad stations there were noisy send-offs for recruits, and large banners reading:
FELICITATIONS ON YOUR CALL TO COLORS and WE PRAY FOR YOUR LASTING MILITARY FORTUNE.

He heard of a boy from the neighboring village who, failing his physical examination, begged to be accepted in any role, rather than face the unspeakable *haji* of being unworthy to serve. His pleas were ignored, and he was sent home by train. He stood staring out the window, muttering again and again to himself, *"Haji desu, haji desu."* Two days later, his body was found along the tracks. He had chosen not to face the disgrace of returning to the relatives and friends who had sent him off with such joy and celebration.

For the people of Japan, as for the people of its enemies, this was a just war into which they had been forced. There was a certain desperate pride in the knowledge that tiny Japan, with almost no natural resources other than the spirit of the people, stood alone against the hordes of the Chinese, and the vast industrial might of America, Britain, Australia, and all the European nations but four. And every thinking person knew that, once Japan was weakened by the overwhelming odds against it, the crushing mass of the Soviet Union would descend upon them.

But at first there were only victories. When the village learned that Tokyo had been bombed by Doolittle, the news was received with bewilderment and outrage. Bewilderment, because they had been assured that Japan was invulnerable. Outrage, because although the effect of the bombing was slight, the American bombers had scattered their incendiaries randomly, destroying homes and schools and not touching—by ironic accident —a single factory or military establishment. When he heard of the American bombers, Nicholai remembered the Northrop planes that had bombed The Sincere department store in Shanghai. He could still see the doll-like Chinese girl in her green silk dress, a stiff little collar standing around her porcelain neck, her face pale beneath its rice powder as she searched for her hand.

Although the war tinted every aspect of life, it was not the dominant theme of Nicholai's formative years. Three things were more important to him: the regular improvement of his game; his rich and resuscitative returns to states of mystic calm whenever his psychic vigor flagged; and, during his seventeenth year, his first love.

Mariko was one of Otake-san's disciples, a shy and delicate girl only a year older than Nikko, who lacked the mental toughness to become a great player, but whose game was intricate and refined. She and Nicholai played many practice bouts together, drilling opening and middle games particularly. Her shyness and his aloofness suited one another comfortably, and frequently they would sit together in the little garden at evening, talking a little, sharing longish silences.

Occasionally they walked together into the village on some errand or other, and arms accidentally brushed, thrilling the conversation into an awkward silence. Eventually, with a boldness that belied the half hour of self-struggle that had preceded the gesture, Nicholai reached across the practice board and took her hand. Swallowing, and concentrating on the board with desperate attention, Mariko returned the pressure of his fingers without looking up at him, and for the rest of the morning they played a very ragged and disorganized game while they held hands, her palm moist with fear of discovery, his trembling with fatigue at the awkward position of his arm, but he could not lighten the strength of his grip, much less relinquish her hand, for fear that this might signal rejection.

They were both relieved to be freed by the call to the noon meal, but the tingle of sin and love was effervescent in their blood all that day. And the next day they exchanged a brushing kiss.

One spring night when Nicholai was almost eighteen, he dared to visit Mariko in her small sleeping room. In a household containing so many people and so little space, meeting at night was an adventure of stealthy movements, soft whispers, and breaths caught in the throat while hearts pounded against one another's chest at the slightest real or imagined sound.

Their lovemaking was bungling, tentative, infinitely gentle.

Although Nicholai exchanged letters with General Kishikawa monthly, only twice during the five years of his apprenticeship could the General free himself from administrative duties for brief leaves of absence in Japan.

The first of these lasted only one day, for the General spent most of his leave in Tokyo with his daughter, recently widowed when her naval officer husband went down with his ship during the victory of the Coral Sea, leaving her pregnant with her first child. After sharing in her bereavement and arranging for her welfare, the General stopped over in the village to visit the Otakes and to bring Nicholai a present of two boxes of books selected from confiscated libraries, and given with the injunction that the boy must not allow his gift of languages to atrophy. The books were in Russian, English, German, French and Chinese. These last were useless to Nicholai because, although he had picked up a fluid knowledge of rough-and-ready Chinese from the streets of Shanghai, he never learned to read the language. The General's own limitation to French was demonstrated by the fact that the boxes included four copies of *Les Miserables* in four different languages—and perhaps a fifth in Chinese, for all Nicholai knew.

That evening the General took dinner with Otake, both avoiding any talk about the war. When Otake-san praised the work and progress of Nicholai, the General assumed the role of Japanese father, making light of his ward's gifts and asserting that it was a great kindness on Otake's part to burden himself with so lazy and inept a pupil. But he could not mask the pride that shone in his eyes.

The General's visit coincided with *jusanya,* the Autumn Moon-Viewing Festival, and offerings of flowers and autumn grasses were placed on an altar in the garden where the moon's rays would fall on them. In normal times, there would have been fruit and food among the offerings, but with war shortages Otake-san tempered his traditionalism with common sense. He might, like his neighbors, have offered the food, then returned it to the family table the next day, but such a thing was unthinkable to him.

After dinner, Nicholai and the General sat in the garden, watching the rising moon disentangle itself from the branches of a tree.

"So, Nikko? Tell me. Have you attained the goal of *shibumi* as you once told me you would?" There was a teasing tone to his voice.

Nicholai glanced down. "I was rash, sir. I was young."

"Younger, yes. I assume you are finding flesh and youth considerable obstacles in your quest. Perhaps you will be able, in time, to acquire the laudable refinement of behavior and facade that might be called *shibusa*. Whether you will ever achieve the profound simplicity of spirit that is *shibumi* is moot. Seek it, to be sure. But be prepared to accept less with grace. Most of us have to."

"Thank you for your guidance, sir. But I would rather fail at becoming a man of *shibumi* than succeed at any other goal."

The General nodded and smiled to himself. "Yes, of course you would. I had forgotten certain facets of your personality. We have been apart too long." They shared the garden in silence for a time. "Tell me, Nikko, are you keeping your languages fresh?"

Nicholai had to confess that, when he had glanced at a few of the books the General had brought, he discovered that his German and English were rusting.

"You must not let that happen. Particularly your English. I shall not be in a position to help you much when this war is over, and you have nothing to rely upon but your gift for language."

"You speak as though the war will be lost, sir."

Kishikawa-san was silent for a long time, and Nicholai could read sadness and fatigue in his face, dim and pale in the moonlight. "All wars are lost ultimately. By both sides, Nikko. The day of battles between professional warriors is gone. Now we have wars between opposing industrial capacities, opposing populations. The Russians, with their sea of faceless people, will defeat the Germans. The Americans, with their anonymous factories, will defeat us. Ultimately."

"What will you do when this happens, sir?"

The General shook his head slowly. "That doesn't matter. Until the end, I shall do my duty. I shall continue to work sixteen hours a day on petty administrative problems. I shall continue to perform as a patriot."

Nicholai looked at him quizzically. He had never heard Kishikawa-san speak of patriotism.

The General smiled faintly. "Oh, yes, Nikko. I am a patriot after all. Not a patriot of politics, or ideology, or military bands, or the *hinomaru*. But a patriot all the same. A patriot of gardens like this, of moon festivals, of the subtleties of Gō, of the chants of women planting rice, of cherry blossoms in brief bloom—of things Japanese. The fact that I know we cannot win this war has nothing to do with the fact that I must continue to do my duty. Do you understand that, Nikko?"

"Only the words, sir."

The General chuckled softly. "Perhaps that is all there is. Go to your bed now, Nikko. Let me sit alone for a while. I shall leave before you arise in the morning, but it pleased me to have this little time with you."

Nicholai bowed his head and rose. Long after he had gone, the General was still sitting, regarding the moonlit garden calmly.

Much later, Nicholai learned that General Kishikawa had attempted to provide money for his ward's maintenance and training, but Otake-san had refused it, saying that if Nicholai were so unworthy a pupil as the General claimed, it would be unethical of him to accept payment for his training. The General smiled at his old friend and shook his head. He was trapped into accepting a kindness.

The tide of war turned against the Japanese, who had staked all their limited production capabilities on a short all-out struggle resulting in a favorable peace. Evidence of incipient defeat was everywhere: in the hysterical fanaticism of government morale broadcasts, in reports by refugees of devastating "carpet bombing" by American planes concentrating on residential areas, in ever-increasing shortages of the most basic consumer goods.

Even in their agricultural village, food was in short supply after farmers met their production quotas; and many times the Otake family subsisted on *zosui*, a gruel of chopped carrots and turnip tops boiled with rice, rendered palatable only by Otake-san's burlesque sense of humor. He would eat with many gestures and sounds of delight, rolling his eyes and patting his stomach in such a way as to make his children and students laugh and forget the bland, loamy taste of the food in their mouths. At first, refugees from the cities were cared for with compassion; but as time passed, these additional mouths to feed became a burden; the refugees were referred to by the mildly pejorative term *sokaijin;* and there was grumbling amongst the peasants about these urban drones who were rich or important enough to be able to escape the horrors of the city, but not capable of working to maintain themselves.

Otake-san had permitted himself one luxury, his small formal garden. Late in the war he dug it up and converted it to the planting of food. But, typical of him, he arranged the turnips and radishes and carrots in mixed beds so their growing tops were attractive to the eye. "They are more difficult to weed and care for, I confess. But if we forsake beauty in our desperate struggle to live, then the barbarian has already won."

Eventually, the official broadcasts were forced to admit the occasional loss of a battle or an island, because to fail to do so in the face of the contradictions of returning wounded soldiers would have cost them the last semblance of credibility. Each time such a defeat was announced (always with an explanation of tactical withdrawal, or reorganization of defense lines, or intentional shortening of supply lines) the broadcast was ended by the playing of the old, beloved song, "Umi Yukaba," the sweet autumnal strains of which became identified with this era of darkness and loss.

Otake-san now traveled to play in Gō tournaments very seldom, because transportation was given over to military and industrial needs. But the playing of the national game and reports of important contests in the newspapers were never given up entirely, because it was realized that this was one of the traditional refinements of culture for which they were fighting.

In the course of accompanying his teacher to these infrequent tournaments, Nicholai witnessed the effects of the war. Cities flattened; people homeless. But the bombers had not broken the spirit of the people. It is an ironic fiction that strategic (i.e., anti-civilian) bombing can break a nation's will to fight. In Germany, Britain, and Japan, the effect of strategic bombing was to give the people a common cause, to harden their will to resist in the crucible of shared difficulties.

Once, when their train was stopped for hours at a station because of damage to the railroad lines, Nicholai walked slowly back and forth on the platform. All along the facade of the station were rows of litters on which lay wounded soldiers on their way to hospitals.

Some were ashen with pain and rigid with the effort to contain it, but none cried out; there was not a single moan. Old people and children passed from stretcher to stretcher, tears of compassion in their eyes, bowing low to each wounded soldier and muttering, "Thank you. Thank you. *Gokuro sama. Gokuro sama.*"

One bent old woman approached Nicholai and stared into his Western face with its uncommon glass-green eyes. There was no hate in her expression, only a mixture of bewilderment and disappointment. She shook her head sadly and turned away.

Nicholai found a quiet end of the platform where he sat looking at a billowing cloud. He relaxed and concentrated on the slow churning within it, and in a few minutes he found escape into a brief mystic transport, in which state he was invulnerable to the scene about him, and to his racial guilt.

The General's second visit was late in the war. He arrived unannounced one spring afternoon and, after a private conversation with Otake-san, invited Nicholai to take a trip with him to view the cherry blossoms along the Kajikawa river near Niigata. Before turning inland over the mountains, their train brought them north through the industrialized strip between Yokohama and Tokyo, where it crawled haltingly over a roadbed weakened by bombing and overuse, past mile after mile of rubble and destruction caused by indiscriminate carpet bombing that had leveled homes and factories, schools and temples, shops, theaters, hospitals. Nothing stood higher than the chest of a man, save for the occasional jagged stump of a truncated smokestack.

The train was shunted around Tokyo, through sprawling suburbs. All around them was evidence of the great air raid of March 9 during which more than three hundred B-29's spread a blanket of incendiaries over residential Tokyo. Sixteen square miles of the city became an inferno, with temperatures in excess of 1800 degrees Fahrenheit melting roof tiles and buckling pavements. Walls of flame leapt from house to house, over canals and rivers, encircling throngs of panicked civilians who ran back and forth across ever-shrinking islands of safety, hopelessly seeking a break in the tightening ring of fire. Trees in the parks hissed and steamed as they approached their kindling points, then with a loud crack burst into flame from trunk to tip in one instant. Hordes waded out into the canals to avoid the terrible heat; but they were pushed farther out, over their heads, by screaming throngs pressing in from the shores. Drowning women lost their grip on babies held high until the last moment.

The vortex of flames sucked air in at its base, creating a firestorm of hurricane force that roared inward to feed the conflagration. So great were the blast-furnace winds that American planes circling overhead to take publicity photographs were buffeted thousands of feet upward.

Many of those who died that night were suffocated. The voracious fires literally snatched the breath from their lungs.

With no effective fighter cover left, the Japanese had no defense against the wave after wave of bombers that spread their jellied fire over the city. Firemen wept with frustration and shame as they dragged useless hoses toward the walls of flame. The burst and steaming water mains provided only limp trickles of water.

When dawn came, the city still smoldered, and in every pile of rubble little tongues of flame licked about in search of combustible morsels. The dead were everywhere. One hundred thirty thousand of them. The cooked bodies of children were stacked like cordwood in schoolyards. Elderly couples died in one another's arms, their bodies welded together in final embrace. The canals were littered with the dead, bobbing in the still-tepid water.

Silent groups of survivors moved from pile to pile of charred bodies in search of relatives. At the bottom of each pile were found a number of coins that had been heated to a white heat and had burned their way down through the dead. One fleshless young woman was discovered wearing a kimono that appeared unharmed by the flames, but when the fabric was touched, it crumbled into ashy dust.

In later years, Western conscience was to be shamed by what happened at Hamburg and Dresden, where the victims were Caucasians. But after the March 9 bombing of Tokyo, *Time* magazine described the event as "a dream come true," an experiment that proved that "properly kindled, Japanese cities will burn like autumn leaves."

And Hiroshima was still to come.

Throughout the journey, General Kishikawa sat stiff and silent, his breathing so shallow that one could see no movement beneath the rumpled civilian suit he wore. Even after the horror of residential Tokyo was behind them, and the train was rising into the incomparable beauty of mountains and high plateaus, Kishikawa-san did not speak. To relieve the silence, Nicholai asked politely about the General's daughter and baby grandson in Tokyo. Even as he spoke the last word, he realized what must have happened. Why else would the General have received leave during these last months of the war?

When he spoke, Kishikawa-san's eyes were kind, but wounded and void. "I looked for them, Nikko. But the district where they lived was ... it no longer exists. I have decided to say good-bye to them among the blossoms of Kajikawa, where once I brought my daughter when she was a little girl, and where I always planned to bring my ... grandson. Will you help me say good-bye to them, Nikko?"

Nicholai cleared his throat. "How can I do that, sir?"

"By walking among the cherry trees with me. By allowing me to speak to you when I can no longer support the silence. You are almost my son, and you ..." The General swallowed several times in succession and lowered his eyes.

Half an hour later, the General pressed his eye sockets with his fingers and sniffed. Then he looked across at Nicholai. "Well! Tell me about your life, Nikko. Is your game developing well? Is *shibumi* still a goal? How are the Otakes managing to get along?"

Nicholai attacked the silence with a torrent of trivia that shielded the General from the cold stillness in his heart.

For three days they stayed in an old-fashioned hotel in Niigata, and each morning they went to the banks of the Kajikawa and walked slowly between rows of cherry trees in full bloom. Viewed from a distance, the trees were clouds of vapor tinted pink. The path and road were covered with a layer of blossoms that were everywhere fluttering down, dying at their moment of greatest beauty. Kishikawa-san found solace in the insulating symbolism.

They talked seldom and in quiet tones as they walked. Their communication consisted of fragments of running thought concreted in single words or broken phrases, but perfectly understood. Sometimes they sat on the high embankments of the river and watched the water flow by until it seemed that the water was still, and they were flowing upstream. The General wore kimonos of browns and rusts, and Nicholai dressed in the dark-blue uniform of the student with its stiff collar and peaked cap covering his light hair. So much did they look like the typical father and son that passers-by were surprised to notice the striking color of the young man's eyes.

On their last day, they remained among the cherry trees later than usual, walking slowly along the broad avenue until evening. As light drained from the sky, an eerie gloaming seemed to rise from the ground, illuminating the trees from beneath and accenting the pink snowfall of petals. The General spoke quietly, as much to himself as to Nicholai. "We have been fortunate. We have enjoyed the three best days of the cherry blossoms. The day of promise, when they are not yet perfect. The perfect day of enchantment. And today they are already past their prime. So this is the day of memory. The saddest day of the three . . . but the richest. There is a kind of—solace? . . . no . . . perhaps comfort—in all that. And once again I am struck by what a tawdry magician's trick Time is after all. I am sixty-six years old, Nikko. Viewed from your coign of vantage—facing toward the future—sixty-six years is a great deal of time. It is all of the experience of your life more than three times over. But, viewed from my coign of vantage—facing toward the past—this sixty-six years was the fluttering down of a cherry petal. I feel that my life was a picture hastily sketched but never filled in . . . for lack of time. Time. Only yesterday— but more than fifty years ago—I walked along this river with my father. There were no embankments then; no cherry trees. It was only yesterday . . . but another century. Our victory over the Russian navy was still ten years in the future. Our fighting on the side of the allies in the Great War was still twenty and more years away. I can see my father's face. (And in my memory, I am always looking up at it.) I can remember how big and strong his hand felt to my small fingers. I can still feel in my chest . . . as though nerves themselves have independent memories . . . the melancholy tug I felt then over my inability to tell my father that I loved him. We did not have the habit of communicating in such bold and earthy terms. I can see each line in my father's stern but delicate profile. Fifty years. But all the insignificant, busy things—the terribly important, now forgotten things that cluttered the intervening time collapse and fall away from my memory. I used to think I felt sorry for my father because I could never tell him I loved him. It was for myself that I felt sorry. I needed the saying more than he needed the hearing."

The light from the earth was dimming, and the sky was growing purple, save to the west where the bellies of storm clouds were mauve and salmon.

"And I remember another yesterday when my daughter was a little girl. We walked along here. At this very moment, the nerves in my hand remember the feeling of her chubby fingers clinging to one of mine. These mature trees were newly planted saplings then—poor skinny things tied to supporting poles with strips of white cloth. Who would have thought such awkward, adolescent twigs could grow old and wise enough to console without presuming to advise? I wonder . . . I wonder if the Americans will have all these cut down because they do not bear obvious fruit. Probably. And probably with the best of intentions."

Nicholai was a little uneasy. Kishikawa-san had never opened himself in this way. Their relationship had always been characterized by understanding reticence.

"When last I visited, Nikko, I asked you to keep your gift of languages fresh. Have you done so?"

"Yes, sir. I have no chance to speak anything but Japanese, but I read all the books you brought, and sometimes I talk to myself in the various languages."

"Particularly in English, I hope."

Nicholai stared into the water. "Least often in English."

Kishikawa-san nodded to himself. "Because it is the language of the Americans?"

"Yes."

"Have you ever met an American?"

"No, sir."

"But you hate them all the same?"

"It is not difficult to hate barbarian mongrels. I don't have to know them as individuals to hate them as a race."

"Ah, but you see, Nikko, the Americans are not a race. That, in fact, is their central flaw. They are, as you say, mongrels."

Nicholai looked up in surprise. Was the General defending the Americans? Just three days ago they had ridden past Tokyo and seen the effects of the greatest firebombing of the war, one directed specifically against residential areas and civilians. Kishikawa-san's own daughter . . . his baby grandson . . .

"I have met Americans, Nikko. I served briefly with the military attaché in Washington. Did I ever tell you about that?"

"No, sir."

"Well, I was not a very successful diplomat. One must develop a certain obliquity of conscience, an elastic attitude toward the truth, to be effective in diplomacy. I lacked these gifts. But I came to know Americans and to appreciate their virtues and flaws. They are very skillful merchants, and they have a great respect for fiscal achievement. These may seem thin and tawdry virtues to you, but they are consonant with the patterns of the industrial world. You call the Americans barbarians, and you are right, of course. I know this better than you. I know they have tortured and sexually mutilated prisoners. I know they have set men afire with their flame-throwers to see how far they could run before they collapsed. Yes, barbarians. But Nikko, our own soldiers have done similar things, things ghastly and cruel beyond description. War and hatred and fear have made beasts of our own countrymen. And we are not barbarians; our morality should have been stiffened by a thousand years of civilization and culture. In a

99

way of speaking, the very barbarianism of the Americans is their excuse—no, such things cannot be excused. Their explanation. How can we condemn the brutality of the Americans, whose culture is a thin paste and patchwork thrown together in a handful of decades, when we ourselves are snarling beasts without compassion and humanity, despite our thousand years of pure breeding and tradition? America, after all, was populated by the lees and failures of Europe. Recognizing this, we must see them as innocent. As innocent as the adder, as innocent as the jackal. Dangerous and treacherous, but not sinful. You spoke of them as a despicable race. They are not a race. They are not even a culture. They are a cultural stew of the orts and leavings of the European feast. At best, they are a mannered technology. In place of ethics, they have rules. Size functions for them as quality functions for us. What for us is honor and dishonor, for them is winning and losing. Indeed, you must not think in terms of race; race is nothing, culture is everything. By race, you are Caucasian; but culturally you are not, and therefore you are not. Each culture has its strengths and weaknesses; they cannot be evaluated against one another. The only sure criticism that can be made is that a mixture of cultures always results in a blend of the worst of both. That which is evil in a man or a culture is the strong, vicious animal within. That which is good in a man or a culture is the fragile, artificial accretion of restraining civilization. And when cultures cross-breed, the dominant and base elements inevitably prevail. So, you see, when you accuse the Americans of being barbarians, you have really defended them against responsibility for their insensitivity and shallowness. It is only in pointing out their mongrelism that you touch their real flaw. And is flaw the right word? After all, in the world of the future, a world of merchants and mechanics, the base impulses of the mongrel are those that will dominate. The Westerner is the future, Nikko. A grim and impersonal future of technology and automation, it is true—but the future nevertheless. You will have to live in this future, my son. It will do you no good to dismiss the American with disgust. You must seek to understand him, if only to avoid being harmed by him."

100

Kishikawa-san had been speaking very softly, almost to himself, as they walked slowly along the wide path in the fading gloaming. The monologue had the quality of a lesson from loving teacher to wayward pupil; and Nicholai had listened with total attention, his head bowed. After a minute or two of silence, Kishikawa-san laughed lightly and clapped his hands together. "Enough of this! Advice helps only him who gives it, and that only insofar as it lightens the burdens of conscience. In the final event, you will do what fate and your breeding dictate, and my advice will affect your future as much as a cherry blossom falling into the river alters its course. There is really something else I wanted to talk to you about, and I have been avoiding it by technique of rambling on about cultures and civilizations and the future—subjects deep and vague enough to hide myself within."

They strolled on in silence as night came and with it an evening breeze that brought the petals down in a dense pink snow that brushed their cheeks and covered their hair and shoulders. At the end of the wide path they came to a bridge, and they paused on the rise to look down at the faintly phosphorescent foam where the river swirled around rocks. The General took a deep breath and let it out in a long stream through pursed lips as he steeled himself to tell Nicholai what was on his mind.

"This is our last chat, Nikko. I have been transferred to Manchukuo. We expect the Russians to attack as soon as we are so weak that they can participate in the war—and therefore in the peace—without risk. It is not likely that staff officers will survive being captured by the communists. Many intend to perform *seppuku*, rather than face the ignominy of surrender. I have decided to follow this course, not because I seek to avoid dishonor. My participation in this bestial war has dirtied me beyond the capacity of *seppuku* to cleanse—as it has every soldier, I fear. But, even if there is no sanctification in the act, there is at least . . . dignity. I have made this decision during these past three days, as we walked among the cherry trees. A week ago, I did not feel free to release myself from indignity, so long as my daughter and grandson were hostages held by fate. But

101

now . . . circumstances have released me. I regret leaving you to the storms of chance, Nikko, as you are a son to me. But . . ." Kishikawa-san sighed deeply. "But . . . I can think of no way to protect you from what is coming. A discredited, defeated old soldier would be no shield for you. You are neither Japanese nor European. I doubt if anyone can protect you. And, because I cannot help you by staying, I feel free to depart. Do I have your understanding, Nikko? And your permission to leave you?"

Nicholai stared into the rapids for some time before he found a way to express himself. "Your guidance, your affection will always be with me. In that way, you can never leave me."

His elbows on the railing, looking down at the ghost glow of the foam, the General slowly nodded his head.

The last few weeks in the Otake household were sad ones. Not because of the rumors of setbacks and defeats from all sides. Not because food shortages and bad weather combined to make hunger a constant companion. But because Otake of the Seventh *Dan* was dying.

For years, the tensions of top-level professional play had manifest themselves in almost continuous stomach cramps, which he kept at bay through his habit of taking mint drops; but the pain became ever more intense, and was finally diagnosed as stomach cancer.

When they learned that Otake-san was dying, Nicholai and Mariko discontinued their romantic liaison, without discussion and most naturally. That universal burden of illogical shame that marks the adolescent Japanese prevented them from engaging in so life-embracing an activity as lovemaking while their teacher and friend was dying.

In result of one of those ironies of life that continue to surprise us, although experience insists that irony is Fate's most common figure of speech, it was not until they ended their physical relationship that the household began to suspect them. While they had been engaged in their dangerous and exciting romance, fear of discovery had made them most circumspect in their public behavior toward one another. Once they were no longer guilty of shameful actions, they began to spend more time together, openly walking along the road or sitting in the garden; and it was only then that sly, if affectionate, rumors about them began to be signaled around the family through sidelong glances and lifted eyebrows.

Often, after practice games had been allowed to trail off inconclusively, they talked about what the future would hold, when the war was lost and their beloved teacher was gone. What would life be like when they were no longer members of the Otake household, when American soldiers occupied the nation? Was it true, as they had heard, that the Emperor would call upon them to die on the beaches in a last effort to repulse the invader? Would not such a death be preferable, after all, to life under the barbarians?

They were discussing such things when Nicholai was called by Otake-san's youngest son and told that the teacher would speak with him. Otake-san was waiting in his private six-mat study, the sliding doors of which gave onto the little garden with its decoratively arranged vegetables. This evening its green and brown tones were muted by an unhealthy mist that had descended from the mountains. The air in the room was humid and cool, and the sweet smell of rotting leaves was balanced by the delicious acrid aroma of burning wood. And there was also the faint tone of mint in the air, for Otake-san still took the mint drops that had failed to control the cancer that was draining away his life.

"It is good of you to receive me, Teacher," Nicholai said after several moments of silence. He did not like the formal sound of that, but he could find no balance between the affection and compassion he felt, and the native solemnity of the occasion. During the past three days, Otake-san had arranged long conversations with each of his children and students in turn; and Nicholai, his most promising apprentice, was the last.

Otake-san gestured to the mat beside him, where Nicholai knelt at right angles to the teacher in the polite position that permitted his own face to be read while it protected the privacy of the older man. Uncomfortable with the silence that endured several minutes, Nicholai felt impelled to fill with trivia. "Mist from the mountains is not common at this time of year, Teacher. Some say it is unhealthy. But it brings a new beauty to the garden and to . . ."

Otake-san lifted his hand and shook his head slightly. No time for this. "I shall speak in broad game plan, Nikko, recognizing that my generalizations will be tempered by small exigencies of localized play and conditions."

Nicholai nodded and remained silent. It was the teacher's practice to speak in terms of Gō whenever he dealt with anything of importance. As General Kishikawa had once said, for Otake-san life was a simplistic metaphor for Gō.

"Is this a lesson, Teacher?"

"Not exactly."

"A chastisement, then?"

"It may appear to you to be so. It is really a criticism. But not only of you. A criticism . . . an analysis . . . of what I perceive to be a volatile and dangerous mixture —you and your future life. Let us begin with the recognition that you are a brilliant player." Otake-san lifted his hand. "No. Do not bother with formulas of polite denial. I have seen brilliance of play equal to yours, but never in a man of your age, and not in any player now living. But there are other qualities than brilliance in the successful person, so I shall not burden you with unqualified compliments. There is something distressing in your play, Nikko. Something abstract and unkind. Your play is somehow inorganic . . . unliving. It has the beauty of a crystal, but lacks the beauty of a blossom."

Nicholai's ears were warming, but he gave no outward sign of embarrassment or anger. To chastise and correct is the right, the duty of a teacher.

"I am not saying that your play is mechanical and predictable, for it is seldom that. What prevents it from being so is your astonishing. . ."

Otake-san drew a sudden breath and held it, his eyes staring unseeing toward the garden. Nicholai kept his gaze down, not wishing to embarrass his teacher by observing his struggle with pain. Long seconds passed, and still Otake-san did not breathe. Then, with a little gasp, he unhitched his breath from the notch at which

104

he had held it and slowly let it out, testing for pain all along the exhalation. The crisis passed, and he took two long, thankful breaths through his open mouth. He blinked several times and . . .

". . . what prevents your play from being mechanical and predictable is your astonishing audacity, but even that flair is tainted with the unhuman. You play only against the situation on the board; you deny the importance—the existence even—of your opponent. Have you not yourself told me that when you are in one of your mystic transports, from which you garner rest and strength, you play without reference to your adversary? There is something devilish in this. Something cruelly superior. Arrogant, even. And at odds with your goal of *shibumi*. I do not bring this to your attention for your correction and improvement, Nikko. These qualities are in your bones and unchangeable. And I am not even sure I would have you change if you could; for these that are your flaws are also your strengths."

"Do we speak of Gō only, Teacher?"

"We speak in terms of Gō." Otake-san slipped his hands into his kimono and pressed the palm against his stomach while he took another mint drop. "For all your brilliance, dear student, you have vulnerabilities. There is your lack of experience, for instance. You waste concentration thinking your way through problems that a more experienced player reacts to by habit and memory. But this is not a significant weakness. You can gain experience, if you are careful to avoid empty redundancy. Do not fall into the error of the artisan who boasts of twenty years experience in his craft while in fact he has had only one year of experience—twenty times. And never resent the advantage of experience your elders have. Recall that they have paid for this experience in the coin of life and have emptied a purse that cannot be refilled." Otake-san smiled faintly. "Recall also that the old must make much of their experience. It is all they have left."

For a time, Otake-san's eyes were dull with inner focus as he gazed upon the drab garden, its features disintegrating in the mist. With an effort he pulled his mind from eternal things to continue his last lesson. "No, it is not your lack of experience that is your greatest flaw. It is your disdain. Your defeats will not come from those more brilliant than you. They will come from the patient, the plodding, the mediocre."

Nicholai frowned. This was consonant with what Kishikawa-san had told him as they walked along the cherry trees of the Kajikawa.

"Your scorn for mediocrity blinds you to its vast primitive power. You stand in the glare of your own brilliance, unable to see into the dim corners of the room, to dilate your eyes and see the potential dangers of the mass, the wad of humanity. Even as I tell you this, dear student, you cannot quite believe that lesser men, in whatever numbers, can really defeat you. But we are in the age of the mediocre man. He is dull, colorless, boring—but inevitably victorious. The amoeba outlives the tiger because it divides and continues in its immortal monotony. The masses are the final tyrants. See how, in the arts, *Kabuki* wanes and *Nō* withers while popular novels of violence and mindless action swamp the mind of the mass reader. And even in that timid genre, no author dares to produce a genuinely superior man as his hero, for in his rage of shame the mass man will send his *yojimbo,* the critic, to defend him. The roar of the plodders is inarticulate, but deafening. They have no brain, but they have a thousand arms to grasp and clutch at you, drag you down."

"Do we still speak of Gō, Teacher?"

"Yes. And of its shadow: life."

"What do you advise me to do then?"

"Avoid contact with them. Camouflage yourself with politeness. Appear dull and distant. Live apart and study *shibumi*. Above all, do not let him bait you into anger and aggression. Hide, Nikko."

"General Kishikawa told me almost the same thing."

"I do not doubt it. We discussed you at length his last night here. Neither of us could guess what the Westerner's attitude toward you will be, when he comes. And more than that, we fear your attitude toward him. You are a convert to our culture, and you have the fanaticism of the convert. It is a flaw in your character. And tragic flaws lead to . . ." Otake-san shrugged.

Nicholai nodded and lowered his eyes, waiting patiently for the teacher to dismiss him.

After a time of silence, Otake-san took another mint drop and said, "Shall I share a great secret with you, Nikko? All these years I have told people I take mint drops to ease my stomach. The fact is, I *like* them. But there is no dignity in an adult who munches candy in public."

"No *shibumi*, sir."

"Just so." Otake-san seemed to daydream for a moment. "Yes. Perhaps you are right. Perhaps the mountain mist is unhealthy. But it lends a melancholy beauty to the garden, and so we must be grateful to it."

After the cremation, Otake-san's plans for family and students were carried out. The family collected its belongings to go live with Otake's brother. The students were dispersed to their various homes. Nicholai, now over twenty, although he looked no more than fifteen, was given the money General Kishikawa had left for him and permitted to do what he chose, to go where he wanted. He experienced that thrilling social vertigo that accompanies total freedom in a context of pointlessness.

On the third day of August 1945, all the Otake household were gathered with their cases and packages on the train platform. There was neither the time nor the privacy for Nicholai to say to Mariko what he felt. But he managed to put special emphasis and gentleness into his promise to visit her as soon as possible, once he had established himself in Tokyo. He looked forward to his visit, because Mariko always spoke so glowingly of her family and friends in her home city, Hiroshima.

Washington

The First Assistant pushed back from his console and shook his head. "There's just not much to work with, sir. Fat Boy doesn't have anything firm on this Hel before he arrives in Tokyo." There was irritation in the First Assistant's tone; he was exasperated by people whose lives were so crepuscular or uneventful as to deny Fat Boy a chance to demonstrate his capacity for knowing and revealing.

"Hm-m," Mr. Diamond grunted absently, as he continued to sketch notes of his own. "Don't worry, the data will thicken up from this point on. Hel went to work for the Occupation Forces shortly after the war, and from then on he remained more or less within our scope of observation."

"Are you sure you really need this probe, sir? You seem to know all about him already."

"I can use the review. Look, something just occurred to me. All we have tying Nicholai Hel to the Munich Five and this Hannah Stern is a first-generation relationship between Hel and the uncle. Let's make sure we're not flying with the wild geese. Ask Fat Boy where Hel is living now." He pressed a buzzer at the side of his desk.

"Yes, sir," the First Assistant said, turning back to his console.

Miss Swivven entered the work area in response to Diamond's buzzer. "Sir?"

"Two things. First: get me all available photographs of Hel, Nicholai Alexandrovitch. Llewellyn will give you the mauve card ID code. Second: contact Mr. Able of the OPEC Interest Group and ask him to come here as soon as possible. When he arrives, bring him down here, together with the Deputy and those two idiots who screwed up. You'll have to escort them down; they don't have access to the Sixteenth Floor."

"Yes, sir." Upon leaving, Miss Swivven closed the door to the wirephoto room just a bit too firmly, and

Diamond looked up, wondering what on earth had gotten into her.

Fat Boy was responding to interrogation, His answer clattering up on the First Assistant's machine. "Ah . . . it seems this Nicholai Hel has several residences. There's an apartment in Paris, a place on the Dalmatian coast, a summer villa in Morocco, an apartment in New York, another in London—ah! Here we are. Last known residence equals a château in the bleeding village of Etchebar. This appears to be his principal residence, considering the amount of time he has spent there during the last fifteen years."

"And where is this Etchebar?"

"Ah . . . it's in the Basque Pyrenees, sir."

"Why is it called a 'bleeding' village?"

"I was wondering that myself, sir." The First Assistant queried the computer, and when the answer came he chuckled to himself. "Amazing! Poor Fat Boy had a little trouble translating from French to English. The word *bled* is evidently French for 'a small hamlet.' Fat Boy mistranslated it to 'bleeding.' Too much input from British sources just of late, I suspect."

Mr. Diamond glared across at the First Assistant's back. "Let's pretend that's interesting. So. Hannah Stern took a plane from Rome to the city of Pau. Ask Fat Boy what's the nearest airport to this Etchebar. If it's Pau, then we know we have trouble."

The question was passed on to the computer. The RP screen went blank, then flashed a list of airports arranged in order of their distance from Etchebar. The first on the list was Pau.

Diamond nodded fatalistically.

The First Assistant sighed and slipped his forefinger under his metal glasses, lightly rubbing the red dents. "So there it is. We have every reason to assume that Hannah Stern is now in contact with a mauve-card man. Only three mauve-card holders left alive in the world, and our girl has found one of them. Rotten luck!"

"That it is. Very well, now we know for sure that Nicholai Hel is in the middle of this business. Get back to your machine and root out all we know about him so we can fill Mr. Able in when he gets here. Begin with his arrival in Tokyo."

Japan

The Occupation was in full vigor; the evangelists of democracy were dictating their creed from the Dai Ichi Building across the moat from—but significantly out of sight of—the Imperial Palace. Japan was a physical, economic, and emotional shambles, but the Occupation put their idealistic crusade before mundane concerns for the well-being of the conquered people; a mind won was worth more than a life lost.

With millions of others, Nicholai Hel was flotsam on the chaos of the postwar struggle for survival. Rocketing inflation soon reduced his small store of money to a valueless wad of paper. He sought manual work with the crews of Japanese laborers clearing debris from the bombings; but the foremen mistrusted his motives and doubted his need, considering his race. Nor had he recourse to assistance from any of the occupying powers, as he was a citizen of none of their countries. He joined the flood of the homeless, the jobless, the hungry who wandered the city, sleeping in parks, under bridges, in railway stations. There was a surfeit of workers and a paucity of work, and only young women possessed services valuable to the gruff, overfed soldiers who were the new masters.

When his money ran out, he went two days without food, returning each night from his search for work to sleep in Shimbashi Station together with hundreds of others who were hungry and adrift. Finding places for themselves on or under the benches and in tight rows filling the open spaces, they dozed fitfully, or jolted up from nightmares, hag-ridden with hunger. Each morning the police cleared them out, so traffic could flow freely. And each morning there were eight or ten who did not respond to the prodding of the police. Hunger, sickness, old age, and loss of the will to live had come during the night to remove the burden of life.

Nicholai wandered the rainy streets with thousands of others, looking for any kind of work; looking, at last, for anything to steal. But there was no work, and nothing worth stealing. His high-collared student's uniform was muddy in patches and always damp, and his shoes leaked. He had ripped off the sole of one because it was loose, and the indignity of its flap-flap was unacceptable. He later wished he had bound it on with a rag.

The night of his second day without food, he returned late through the rain to Shimbashi Station. Crowded together under the vast metal vault, frail old men and desperate women with children, their meager belongings rolled up in scraps of cloth, arranged little spaces for themselves with a silent dignity that filled Nicholai with pride. Never before had he appreciated the beauty of the Japanese spirit. Jammed together, frightened, hungry, cold, they dealt with one another under these circumstances of emotional friction with the social lubrication of muttered forms of politeness. Once during the night, a man attempted to steal something from a young woman, and in a brief, almost silent scuffle in a dark corner of the vast waiting room, justice was dealt out quickly and terminally.

Nicholai had the good fortune to find a place under one of the benches where he would not be trod upon by people seeking to relieve themselves during the night. On the bench above him was a woman with two children, one a baby. She talked softly to them until they fell asleep after reminding her, without insistence, that they were hungry. She told them that grandfather was not really dead after all, and was coming to take them away soon. Later, she confected word pictures of her little village on the coast. After they fell asleep, she wept silently.

The old man on the floor beside Nicholai took great pains to set out his valuables on a folded bit of cloth close to his face before nestling down. They consisted of a cup, a photograph, and a letter that had been folded and refolded until the creases were thin and furry. It was a form letter of regret from the army. Before closing his eyes, the old man said good night to the young foreigner beside him, and Nicholai smiled and said good night.

Before a fitful sleep overtook him, Nicholai composed his mind and escaped from the acid gnaw of hunger into mystic transport. When he returned from his little meadow with its waving grasses and yellow sunlight, he was full although hungry, peaceful although desperate. But he knew that tomorrow he must find work or money, or soon he would die.

When the police rousted them shortly before dawn, the old man was dead. Nicholai wrapped the cup, photograph, and letter into his own bundle because it seemed a terrible thing to let all the old man had treasured be swept up and thrown away.

By noon Nicholai had drifted down to Hibiya Park in search of work or something to steal. Hunger was no longer a matter of unsatisfied appetite. It was a jagged cramp and a spreading weakness that made his legs heavy and his head light. As he drifted on the tide of desperate people, waves of unreality washed over him; people and things alternated between being indiscriminant forms and objects of surprising fascination. Sometimes he would find himself flowing within a stream of faceless people, allowing their energy and direction to be his, permitting his thoughts to spiral and short-circuit in a dreamy carousel without meaning. His hunger brought mystic transport close to the surface of his consciousness, and wisps of escape ended with sudden jolts of reality. He would find himself standing, staring at a wall or the face of a person, sensing that this was a remarkable event. No one had ever examined that particular brick with care and affection before. He was the very first! No one had ever looked at that man's ear in such sharp focus. That must mean something. Mustn't it?

The lightheaded hunger, the shattered spectrum of reality, the aimless drifting were all seductively pleasant, but something within him warned that this was dangerous. He must break out of it or he would die. Die? Die? Did that sound have any meaning?

A dense rivulet of humanity carried him out of the park through an entrance where two broad avenues intersected with a congestion of military vehicles, charcoal automobiles, clanging tramcars, and wobbling bicycles pulling two-wheeled carts loaded down with incredibly heavy and bulky cargoes. There had been a minor accident, and traffic was snarled for a block in every direction while a helpless Japanese traffic policeman in huge white gloves was trying to settle things between a Russian driving an American jeep and an Australian driving an American jeep.

Nicholai was pushed forward unwillingly by the curious crowd that seeped into the spaces around the congealed traffic, intensifying the confusion. The Russians spoke only Russian, the Australians only English, the policeman only Japanese; and all three were engaged in a vigorous discussion of blame and responsibility. Nicholai was pressed against the side of the Australian jeep, whose officer occupant was sitting, staring ahead with stoic discomfort, while his driver was shouting that he would gladly settle this thing man-to-man with the Russian driver, the Russian officer, both at once, or the whole fucking Red Army, if it came to that!

"Are you in a hurry, sir?"

"What?" The Australian officer was surprised to be addressed in English by this ragged lad in a tarnished Japanese student's uniform. It was a couple of seconds before he realized from the green eyes in the gaunt young face that the boy was not Oriental. "Of course I'm in a hurry! I have a meeting—" He snapped his wrist over and looked at his watch. "—twelve minutes ago!"

"I'll help you," Nicholai said. "For money."

"I beg your pardon?" The accent was comic-opera British raj, as is often the case with colonials who feel called upon to play it for more English than the English.

"Give me some money, and I'll help you."

The officer gave his watch another petulant glance. "Oh, very well. Get on with it."

The Australians did not understand what Nicholai said, first in Japanese to the policeman, then in Russian to the Red officer, but they made out the name "Mac-Arthur" several times. The effect of evoking the Emperor's emperor was immediate. Within five minutes a swath had been forced through the tangle of vehicles, and the Australian jeep was conducted onto the grass of the park, whence it was able to cross overland to a wide gravel path and make its way through astonished strollers, finally bouncing down over a curb into a side street that was beyond the jam of traffic, leaving behind a clotted chaos of vehicles sounding horns and bells angrily. Nicholai had jumped into the jeep beside the driver. Once they were free from their problem, the officer ordered the driver to pull over.

"Very well, now what do I owe you?"

Nicholai had no idea of the value of foreign money now. He clutched at a figure. "A hundred dollars."

"A hundred dollars? Are you mad?"

"Ten dollars," Nicholai amended quickly.

"Out for whatever you can get, is that it?" the officer sneered. But he tugged out his wallet. "Oh, God! I haven't any scrip at all. Driver?"

"Sorry, sir. Stony."

"Hm! Look. Tell you what. That's my building across the way." He indicated the San Shin Building, center of communications for Allied Occupation Forces. "Come along, and I'll have you taken care of."

Once within the San Shin Building, the officer turned Nicholai over to the office of Pay and Accounts with instructions to make out a voucher for ten dollars in scrip, then he left to make what remained of his appointment, but not before fixing Nicholai with a quick stare. "See here. You're not British, are you?" At that period, Nicholai's English had the accent of his British tutors, but the officer could not align the lad's public school accent with his clothes and physical appearance.

"No," Nicholai answered.

"Ah!" the officer said with obvious relief. "Thought not." And he strode off toward the elevators.

For half an hour, Nicholai sat on a wooden bench outside the office, awaiting his turn; while in the corridor around him people chatted in English, Russian, French, and Chinese. The San Shin Building was one of the few anodes on which the various occupying powers collected, and one could feel the reserve and mistrust underlying their superficial camaraderie. More than half the people working here were civilian civil servants, and Americans outnumbered the others by the same ratio as their soldiers outnumbered the others combined. It was the first time Nicholai heard the growled *r*'s and metallic vowels of American speech.

He was becoming ill and sleepy by the time an American secretary opened the door and called his name. Once in the anteroom, he was given a form to fill in while the young secretary returned to her typing, occasionally stealing glances at this improbable person in dirty clothes. But she was only casually curious; her real attention was on a date she had for that night with a major who was, the other girls all said, real nice and always brought you to a real fine restaurant and gave you a real good time before.

When he handed over his form, the secretary glanced at it, lifted her eyebrows and sniffed, but brought it in to the woman in charge of Pay and Accounts. In a few minutes, Nicholai was called into the inner office.

The woman in charge was in her forties, plumpish and pleasant. She introduced herself as Miss Goodbody. Nicholai did not smile.

Miss Goodbody gestured toward Nicholai's voucher form. "You really have to fill this out, you know."

"I can't. I mean, I can't fill in all the spaces."

"Can't?" Years of civil service recoiled at the thought. "What do you mean . . ." She glanced at the top line of the form. ". . . Nicholai?"

"I can't give you an address. I don't have one. And I don't have an identification card number. Or a—what was it?—sponsoring agency."

"Sponsoring agency, yes. The unit or organization for which you work, or for which your parents work."

"I don't have a sponsoring agency. Does it matter?"

"Well, we can't pay you without a voucher form filled out correctly. You understand that, don't you?"

"I'm hungry."

For a moment, Miss Goodbody was nonplussed. She leaned forward. "Are your parents with the Occupation Forces, Nicholai?" She had come to the assumption that he was an army brat who had run away from home.

"No."

"Are you here alone?" she asked with disbelief.

"Yes."

"Well . . ." She frowned and made a little shrug of futility. "Nicholai, how old are you?"

"I'm twenty-one years old."

"Oh, my. Excuse me. I assumed—I mean, you look no more than fourteen or fifteen. Oh, well, that's a different matter. Now, let's see. What shall we do?" There was a strong maternal urge in Miss Goodbody, the sublimation of a life of untested sexuality. She was oddly attracted to this young man who had the appearance of a motherless child, but the age of a potential mate. Miss Goodbody identified this mélange of contradictory feelings as Christian concern for a fellow being.

"Couldn't you just give me my ten dollars? Maybe five dollars?"

"Things don't work like that, Nicholai. Even assuming we find a way to fill out this form, it will be ten days before it clears AP&R."

Nicholai felt hope drain away. He lacked the experience to know that the gossamer barriers of organizational dysfunction were as impenetrable as the pavements he trod all day. "I can't have any money then?" he asked atonally.

Miss Goodbody half-shrugged and rose. "I'm sorry, but . . . Listen. It's after my lunch hour. Come with me to the employees' cafeteria. We'll have a bite to eat, and we'll see if we can work something out." She smiled at Nicholai and laid her hand on his shoulder. "Is that all right?"

Nicholai nodded.

The next three months before Miss Goodbody was transferred back to the United States remained forever thrilling and shimmering in her memory. Nicholai was the closest thing to a child she would ever have, and he was her only prolonged affair. She never dared to talk out, or even to analyze for herself, the complex of feelings that tingled through her mind and body during those months. Certainly she enjoyed being needed by someone, enjoyed the security of dependency. Also, she was a genuinely good person who liked giving help to someone who needed it. And in their sexual relations there was a tang of delicious shame, the spice of being at one time mother and lover, a heady brew of affection and sin.

116

Nicholai never did get his ten dollars; the task of sending through a voucher without an identification card number proved too much even for Miss Goodbody's twenty-odd years of bureaucratic experience. But she did manage to introduce him to the director of translation services, and within a week he was working eight hours a day, translating documents, or sitting in interminable conferences, repeating in two or three languages such overworded and cautious statements as a given representative dared to make in public. He learned that, in diplomacy, the principal function of communication is to mask meaning.

His relations with Miss Goodbody were friendly and polite. As soon as possible he repaid, over her protests, her outlay for clothes and toilet articles, and he insisted on assuming his share of their living expenses. He did not like her enough to be willing to owe her anything. This is not to say he disliked her—she was not the kind one could dislike; she did not arouse feelings of that intensity. At times her mindless babble was annoying; and her hovering attention could be burdensome; but she tried so hard, if clumsily, to be considerate, and she was so dewily grateful for her sexual experiences that he tolerated her with some real affection, affection of the kind one has for a maladroit pet.

Nicholai suffered only one significant problem in living with Miss Goodbody. Because of the high concentration of animal fat in their diets, Westerners have a faintly unpleasant smell that offends the Japanese olfactory sense and dampens ardor notably. Before he became acclimated to this, Nicholai had some difficulty giving himself over to physical transports, and it took him rather a long time to achieve climax. To be sure, Miss Goodbody benefited experientially from her unconscious taint; but as she had minimal grounds for comparison, she assumed that Nicholai's sexual endurance was common. Emboldened by her experience with him, after she returned to the United States she launched into several short-lived affairs, but they were all relative disappointments. She ended with becoming the "grand old woman" of the Feminist Movement.

It was not totally without relief that Nicholai saw

Miss Goodbody off on her homeward-bound ship and returned to move out of her government-allotted quarters to a house he had rented in the Asakusa district of northwest Tokyo where, in this rather old-fashioned quarter, he could live with invisible elegance—nearly *shibumi*—and deal with Westerners only during the forty hours a week that produced his living, a luxurious level of living by Japanese standards because of his relatively high pay and, even more important, his access to goods at American post exchanges and commissaries. For Nicholai was now in possession of that most important of human endowments: identification papers. These had been obtained by means of a little winking collusion between Miss Goodbody and friends in the civil service. Nicholai had one ID card that identified him as an American civilian employee, and another that identified him as Russian. On the unlikely event that he might be questioned by American military police, he could produce his Russian identity; and for all other curious nationals, his American papers. Relations between the Russians and Americans were founded in mistrust and mutual fear, and they avoided interfering with one another's nationals over petty events, much as a man crossing the street to rob a bank might avoid jaywalking.

During the next year, Nicholai's life and work expanded. So far as work went, he was sometimes called upon to serve in the cryptography section of Sphinx/FE, before that intelligence organization was consumed by the insatiable new bureaucratic infragovernment of the CIA. Upon one occasion it was not possible to translate the decoded message into English because the Russian into which it had been reduced was almost gibberish. Nicholai asked to see the original cryptograph. Combining his childhood penchant for pure mathematics, his ability to conceive in abstract permutations as developed and displayed in his Gō training, and his native facility in six languages, he was able to locate the errors in decoding fairly easily. He discovered that the original message had been wrongly encoded by someone who wrote a stilted Russian that was organized, quaintly enough, in the Chinese word order, producing by chance a message that baffled the complicated

118

decoding machines of Sphinx/FE. Nicholai had known Chinese who spoke their imperfectly learned Russian in this stilted way, so once he stumbled on the key, the content of the communication fell into place easily. But the clerk/accountant mentalities of the Cryptology Section were impressed, and Nicholai was heralded a "boy wonder"—for most of them assumed he was still a boy. One thoroughly "hep" young code clerk fanned his fingers at Nicholai, calling him a real "quiz kid" and describing the decoding job as "reet, neat, and complete!"

So Nicholai was transferred to Sphinx/FE on a permanent basis, given a raise in rank and salary, and allowed to pass his days in a small secluded office, amusing himself with the game of untangling and translating messages in which he had not the slightest interest.

In time, and somewhat to his surprise, Nicholai arrived at a kind of emotional truce with the Americans among whom he worked. This is not to say that he came to like them, or to trust them; but he came to realize that they were not the amoral, depraved people their political and military behavior suggested they were. True, they were culturally immature, brash and clumsy, materialistic and historically myopic, loud, bold, and endlessly tiresome in social encounters; but at bottom they were good-hearted and hospitable; willing to share—indeed insistent upon sharing—their wealth and ideology with all the world.

Above all, he came to recognize that all Americans were merchants, that the core of the American Genius, of the Yankee Spirit, was buying and selling. They vended their democratic ideology like hucksters, supported by the great protection racket of armaments deals and economic pressures. Their wars were monumental exercises in production and supply. Their government was a series of social contracts. Their education was sold as so much per unit hour. Their marriages were emotional deals, the contracts easily broken if one party failed in his debt-servicing. Honor for them consisted in fair trading. And they were not, as they thought, a classless society; they were a one-class society—the mercantile. Their elite were the rich; their workers and farmers were best viewed as flawed and failed scramblers up the middle-class monetary ladder. The peasants and proletariat of America had values identical to those of the insurance salesmen and business executives, the only difference being that these values were expressed in more modest fiscal terms: the motor boat rather than the yacht; the bowling league rather than the country club; Atlantic City rather than Monaco.

Training and inclination had combined to make Nicholai respect and feel affection for all members of the real classes: farmers, artisans, artists, warriors, scholars, priests. But he could feel nothing but disdain for the artificial class of the merchant, who sucks up his living through buying and selling things he does not create, who collects power and wealth out of proportion to his discrimination, and who is responsible for all that is kitsch, for all that is change without progress, for all that is consumption without use.

Following the advice of his mentors to maintain a diffident facade of distant *shibumi,* Nicholai was careful to mask his attitudes from his fellow workers. He avoided their envy by occasionally asking advice on some simple decoding problem, or phrasing his questions so as to guide them to the correct answers. For their parts, they treated him as a kind of freak, an intellectual phenomenon, a boy wonder who had dropped from another planet. To this degree, they were numbly aware of the genetic and cultural gulf separating him from them, but as they saw it, it was they who were within, and he who was without.

And that suited him perfectly, for his real life was centered on his house, built around a courtyard, off a narrow side street in the Asakusa district. Americanization was slow to penetrate this old-fashioned quarter in the northwest section of the city. To be sure, there were little shops engaged in producing imitations of Zippo lighters and cigarette cases bearing the image of the one-dollar bill, and from some bars came the music of Japanese orchestras imitating the "big band" sound, and peppy girl singers squeaking their way through "Don't Sit Under the Apple Tree With Anyone Else But Me," and one saw the occasional young man dressed like a movie gangster in the thought that he looked modern and American, and there were radio advertisements in English promising that Akadama wine would make you bery-bery happy. But the veneer was thin, and still in late May the district celebrated the Festival of Sanja Matsuri, the streets blocked by sweating young men staggering under the weight of black-lacquered, lavishly gilted palanquins, their eyes shining with saki-reinforced trance as they reeled under the weight of their burdens and chanted *washoi, washoi, washoi,* under the direction of magnificently tattooed men wearing only *fundoshi* breech-cloths that revealed the complicated "suits of ink" covering their shoulders, backs, arms, and thighs.

Nicholai was returning home through the rain, somewhat fogged with saki after participating in the Festival, when he met Mr. Watanabe, a retired printmaker who was selling matches on the street because his pride would not allow him to beg, although he was seventy-two and all his family was gone. Nicholai declared himself to be in desperate need of matches and offered to buy the entire stock. Mr. Watanabe was delighted to be of service, as the sale would forestall hunger for another day. But when he discovered that the rain had made the matches useless, his sense of honor would not allow him to sell them, despite the fact that Nicholai declared he was particularly seeking soggy matches for an experiment he had in mind.

The next morning, Nicholai woke up with a heavy saki hangover behind his eyes, and no very clear recollection of his conversation with Mr. Watanabe as they had taken a supper of *soba* eaten standing beside the booth, hunched over to keep the rain out of the noodle soup; but he soon learned that he had a permanent house guest. Within a week, Mr. Watanabe came to feel that he was essential to Nicholai and the daily routine of the Asakusa house, and that it would be unkind of him to abandon the friendless young man.

It was a month later that the Tanaka sisters became part of the household. Nicholai was taking a lunchtime stroll in Hibiya Park when he encountered the sisters, robust country girls of eighteen and twenty-one who had fled the starvation that followed floods in the north, and who were reduced to offering themselves to passers-by. Nicholai was their first prospective client, and they approached him so awkwardly and shyly that his compassion was mixed with laughter, for more experienced hookers had equipped them with a scant vocabulary of English consisting solely of the most graphic and vulgar names for items of anatomy and sexual variants. Once installed in the Asakusa house, they reverted to their hard-working, merry, giggling peasant selves, and were the constant concern—and objects of harried affection—for Mr. Watanabe, who had very strict views of proper behavior for young girls. In the natural course of things, the Tanaka sisters came to share Nicholai's bed, where their natural rural vigor was expressed in playful explorations of uncommon and often ballistically improbable combinations. They satisfied the young man's need for sexual expression, unencumbered by emotional involvement beyond affection and gentleness.

Nicholai was never sure just how Mrs. Shimura, the last addition to the family, first entered the household. She simply was there when he returned one evening, and she stayed on. Mrs. Shimura was in her mid-sixties, dour, crabby, constantly grumbling, infinitely kind, and a wonderful cook. There was a brief struggle for territorial domination between Mr. Watanabe and Mrs. Shimura, which was fought out on the grounds of daily marketing, for Mr. Watanabe was in charge of household funds, while Mrs. Shimura was responsible for their daily menus. They came finally to doing the food shopping together, she in charge of quality, he in charge of price; and hard was the lot of the poor greengrocer caught in the crossfire of their bickering.

Nicholai never thought of his guests as a staff of servants because they never thought of themselves in that way. Indeed, it was Nicholai who seemed to lack any precise role with concomitant rights, save that he procured the money on which they all lived.

During these months of freedom and new experience, Nicholai's mind and sensations were exercised in many directions. He maintained body tone through the study and practice of an occult branch of martial arts that accented the use of common household articles as lethal weapons. He was attracted by the mathematical clarity

122

and calculating precision of this rarefied system of combat, the name of which was, by tradition, never spoken aloud, but was formed by a superimposition of the symbols *hoda* (naked) and *korosu* (kill). Throughout his future life, although he was seldom armed, he was never unarmed; for in his hands a comb, a matchbox, a rolled magazine, a coin, even a folded piece of writing paper could be put to deadly use.

For his mind, there was the fascination and intellectual cushion of Gō. He no longer played, because for him the game was intimately tied to his life with Otakesan, to rich and gentle things now gone; and it was safer to close the gates of regret. But he still read commentaries of games and worked out problems for himself on the board. The work at the San Shin Building was mechanical and had no more intellectual challenge than solving crossword puzzles; so, to sop up some of his mental energy, Nicholai began work on a book called *Blossoms and Thorns on the Path Toward Gō,* which was eventually published privately under a pseudonym and enjoyed a certain popularity among the most advanced aficionados of the game. The book was an elaborate joke in the form of a report and commentary on a fictional master's game played at the turn of the century. While the play of the "masters" seemed classic and even brilliant to the average player, there were little blunders and irrelevant placements that brought frowns to the more experienced of the readers. The delight of the book lay in the commentary by a well-informed fool who found a way to make each of the blunders seem a touch of audacious brilliance, and who stretched the limits of imagination by attaching to the moves metaphors for life, beauty, and art, all stated with great refinement and demonstrations of scholarship, but all empty of significance. The book was, in fact, a subtle and eloquent parody of the intellectual parasitism of the critic, and much of the delight lay in the knowledge that both the errors of play and the articulate nonsense of the commentary were so arcane that most readers would nod along in grave agreement.

The first of every month, Nicholai wrote to Otakesan's widow and received in reply fragments of family news concerning ex-pupils and the Otake children. It was by this means that Mariko's death in Hiroshima was confirmed.

When he had learned of the atomic bombing, he had feared that Mariko might be among the victims. He wrote several times to the address she had given him. The first letters simply disappeared into the vortex of disorder left by the bombing, but the last one was returned with the note that this address no longer existed. For a time he played avoidance games in his mind, imagining that Mariko might have been visiting a relative when the bomb was dropped, or she might have been fetching something from a deep cellar, or she might . . . he constructed dozens of improbable narratives accounting for her survival. But she had promised to write him through Mrs. Otake, and no letter ever came.

He was emotionally prepared to receive the final news when it came from Otake-san's widow. Still, for a time, he was diminished and voided, and he felt acid hate for the Americans among whom he worked. But he struggled to cleanse himself of this hate, because such black thoughts blocked the path to mystic transport wherein lay his salvation from the draining effects of depression and sadness. So, for all of one day, he wandered alone and sightless through the streets of his district, remembering Mariko, turning images of her over with the fingers of his mind, recalling the delight and fear and shame of their sexual unions, smiling to himself over private jokes and nonsense. Then, late in the evening, he said good-bye to her and set her aside with gentle affection. There remained autumnal emptiness, but no searing pain and hate, so he was able to cross into his triangular meadow and become one with the sunlight and the waving grass, and he found strength and rest there.

He had also come to peace with the loss of General Kishikawa. After their last long chat among the snowing cherry trees of the Kajikawa, Nicholai received no further word. He knew that the General had been transferred to Manchuria; he learned that the Russians had attacked across the border during the last days of the war when the action involved no military risk and great political gain; and he knew from talking to survivors

124

that some ranking officers had escaped into *seppuku*, and none of those captured by the communists survived the rigors of the "reeducation" camps.

Nicholai consoled himself with the thought that Kishikawa-san had at least escaped the indignity of facing the brutal machinery of the Japanese War Crimes Commission, where justice was perverted by deeply imbedded racism of the kind that had sent Japanese-Americans into concentration camps, while German- and Italian-Americans (formidable voting blocs) were free to profit from the defense industry; this despite the fact that Nisei soldiers in the American army proved their patriotism by being the most decorated and casualty-ridden of all units, although insulted by restriction to the European theater for fear of their loyalty if faced by Japanese troops. The Japanese War Crimes Trials were infected by the same racist assumptions of subhumanity as had condoned the dropping of a uranium bomb on a defeated nation already suing for peace, and the subsequent dropping of a larger plutonium bomb for reasons of scientific curiosity.

What troubled Nicholai most was that the mass of the Japanese condoned the punishment of their military leaders, not for the Japanese reason that many of them had placed their personal glorification and power lust before the interests of their nation and people, but for the Western reason that these men had somehow sinned against retroactive rules of human behavior based on a foreign notion of morality. Many Japanese seemed not to realize that the propaganda of the victor becomes the history of the vanquished.

Young and emotionally alone, surviving precariously in the shadow of the Occupying Forces, whose values and methods he did not care to learn, Nicholai needed an outlet for his energies and frustrations. He found one during his second year in Tokyo, a sport that would take him out of the crowded, sordid city to the unoccupied, un-American mountains: caving.

It was his practice to take lunch with the young Japanese who worked in the San Shin motor pool, because he felt more comfortable with them than with the wisecracking, metal-voiced Americans of the Crypto Center. Since knowing some English was a prerequisite for even the most menial job, most of the men in the motor pool had attended the university, and some of those who washed jeeps and chauffeured officers were graduate mechanical engineers unable to sustain themselves in a jobless, ruined economy.

At first the young Japanese were stiff and uncomfortable in Nicholai's company, but it was not long before, in the open and free way of youth, they accepted him as a green-eyed Japanese who had had the misfortune to misplace his epicanthic fold. He was admitted to their circle and even joined in their hoarse, bawdy laughter concerning the sexual misadventures of the American officers they chauffeured. All these jokes had the same central figure of ridicule: the stereotypic American who was constantly and blindly randy, but tactically incompetent.

The subject of caving came up during one of these lunch breaks when they were all squatting under the corrugated metal roof of a rain shelter, eating from metal boxes the rice and fish that were the rations for Japanese workers. Three of the ex-university men were caving enthusiasts, or had been, before the last desperate year of the war and the chaos of the Occupation. They talked about the fun and difficulty of their expeditions into the mountains and lamented their lack of money and basic supplies to return. By this time, Nicholai had been long in the city, and its noise and congestion were eroding his village-life sensibilities. He drew the young men out on the subject of exploring caves and asked what supplies and equipment were needed. It turned out that their requirements were minimal, although inaccessible on the pittance they were paid by the Occupation Forces. Nicholai suggested that he collect whatever was needed, if they would take him along and introduce him to the sport. The offer was snatched up eagerly, and two weeks later four of them passed a weekend in the mountains, cave-bashing by day and spending their nights at cheap mountain inns where they drank too much saki and talked late into the night in the way of bright young men the world over, the conversation drifting from the Nature of Art, to bawdy double entendre, to plans for the future, to strained

126

puns, to improvised haiku, to horseplay, to politics, to sex, to memories, to silence.

After his first hour underground, Nicholai knew this was the sport for him. His body, lithe and wiry, seemed designed for slithering through tight spots. The rapid and narrow calculations of method and risk were consonant with the mental training Gō had given him. And the fascination of danger was seductive to him. He could never have climbed mountains, because the public bravado of it offended his sense of *shibumi* and dignified reserve. But the moments of risk and daring in the caves were personal, silent, and unobserved; and they had the special spice of involving primitive animal fears. In vertical work down a shaft, there was the thrill and fear of falling, native to all animals and honed keener by the knowledge that the fall would be into a black void below, rather than into the decorative landscape beneath the mountain climber. In the caves, there was the constant presence of cold and damp, primordial fears for man, and real ones for the caver, as most grave accidents and deaths result from hypothermia. There was also the animal dread of the dark, of endless blackness and the ever-present thought of getting lost in mazes of slits and belly crawls so tight that retreat was impossible because of the jointing of the human body. Flash flooding could fill the narrow caves with water with only minutes of warning, or none. And there was the constant mental pressure of knowing that just above him, often scraping against his back as he wriggled through a tight cave, were thousands of tons of rock that must inevitably one day obey gravity and fill in the passage.

It was the perfect sport for Nicholai.

He found the subjective dangers particularly attractive and exhilarating. He enjoyed pitting mental control and physical skill against the deepest and most primitive dreads of the animal within him, the dark, fear of falling, fear of drowning, the cold, solitude, the risk of being lost down there forever, the constant mental erosion of those tons of rock above. The senior ally of the caver is logic and lucid planning. The senior foes are imagination and the hounds of panic. It is easy for the caver to be a coward and difficult to be brave, for he works alone, unseen, uncriticized, unpraised. Nicholai enjoyed the foes he met and the private arena in which he met them. He delighted in the idea that most of the foes were within himself, and the victories unobserved.

Too, there were the unique delights of emerging. Dull, quotidian things took on color and value after hours inside the earth, particularly if there had been danger and physical victory. The sweet air was drunk in with greedy breaths. A cup of bitter tea was something to warm stiff hands, something to delight the eye with its rich color, something to smell gorgeously, a rush of heat down the throat, a banquet of subtly varying flavors. The sky was significantly blue, the grass importantly green. It was good to be slapped on the back by a comrade, touched by a human hand. It was good to hear voices and make sounds that revealed feelings, that shared ideas, that amused friends. Everything was novel and there to be tasted.

For Nicholai, the first hour after emerging from a cave had almost the quality of the life he knew during mystic transport. For that brief hour before objects and experiences retreated again into the commonplace he was almost united with the yellow sunlight and the fragrant grasses.

The four young men went into the mountains every free weekend, and although their amateur class and jury-rigged equipment limited them to bashing about in cave networks that were modest by international caving standards, it was always a thorough test of their will, endurance, and skill, followed by nights of fellowship, talk, saki, and bad jokes richly appreciated. Although in later life Nicholai was to gain a wide reputation for his participation in significant underground expeditions, these apprentice outings were never surpassed for pure fun and adventure.

By the time he was twenty-three, Nicholai had a lifestyle that satisfied most of his needs and compensated for most of his losses, save that of General Kishikawa. To replace the household of Otake-san, he had filled his home in Asakusa with people who took roughly the territorial roles of family members. He had lost his boyhood, and largely boyish, love; but he satisfied his body needs with the irrepressible and inventive Tanaka sisters. His once consuming involvement with the mental disciplines and delights of Gō had been replaced by the emotional and physical ones of caving. In a peculiar and not altogether healthy way, his training in Naked/ Kill combat gave vent to the most corrosive aspects of his hatred for those who had destroyed his nation and youth; for during his practice periods he fantasized round-eyed opponents, and felt better for it.

Most of what he had lost was personal and organic, most of his substitutes were mechanical and external; but the gap in quality was bridged in large part by his occasional retreats into the soul-rest of mystic experience.

The most onerous part of his life was the forty hours a week he passed in the basement of the San Shin Building in remunerative drudgery. Breeding and training had given him the inner resources to satisfy his needs without the energy sponge of gainful employment so vital to the men of the egalitarian WAD who have difficulty filling their time and justifying their existence without work. Pleasure, study, and comfort were adequate to him; he did not need the crutch of recognition, the reassurance of power, the narcotic of fun. Unfortunately, circumstance had made it necessary to earn a living, and yet more ironic, to earn it amongst the Americans. (Although Nicholai's co-workers were a mixture of Americans, Britons, and Australians, American methods, values, and objectives were dominant, so he soon came to think of Britons as incompetent Americans and Australians as Americans-in-training.)

English was the language of the Crypto Center, but Nicholai's sense of euphony recoiled at the swallowed mushiness or effete whine of upper class British speech, and the metallic clatter and bow-string twang of American, so he developed an accent of his own, one that took a middle course between the American and the British noises. The effect of this artifice was to cause his Anglophonic associates, throughout his life, to assume he was a native English speaker, but from "somewhere else."

Occasionally, his co-workers would seek to include Nicholai in their plans for parties or outings, never dreaming that what they intended as benevolent condescension toward the foreigner was regarded by Nicholai as presumptuous egalitarianism.

It was not their irritating assumption of equality that annoyed Nicholai so much as their cultural confusions. The Americans seemed to confuse standard of living with quality of life, equal opportunity with institutionalized mediocrity, bravery with courage, machismo with manhood, liberty with freedom, wordiness with articulation, fun with pleasure—in short, all of the misconceptions common to those who assume that justice implies equality for all, rather than equality for equals.

In his most benevolent moods, he thought of Americans as children—energetic, curious, naïve, goodhearted, badly brought up children—in which respect he could detect very little difference between Americans and Russians. Both were hale, vigorous, physical peoples, both excelling in things material, both baffled by beauty, both swaggeringly confident that theirs was the ultimate ideology, both infantile and contentious, and both terribly dangerous. Dangerous because their toys were cosmic weapons that threatened the existence of civilization. The danger lay less in their malice than in their blundering. It was ironic to realize that the destruction of the world would not be the work of Machiavelli, but of Sancho Panza.

He never felt comfortable, having his source of survival dependent on these people, but there was no alternative, and he lived with his discomfort by ignoring it. It was not until the damp and blustery March of his second year that he was forced to learn that, when one dines with wolves, it is moot if one is guest or entrée.

Despite the melancholy weather, the eternal resilience of the Japanese spirit was expressed by the light, optimistic song "Ringo no Uta," which was sweeping the nation and could be heard sung at half voice or hummed under the breath by thousands of people rebuilding from the physical and emotional rubble of the war. The cruel winters of famine were past; the springs of flood and poor harvest were behind; and there was a feeling abroad that the world was on the mend. Even beneath

130

the damp winds of March, trees had begun to collect the faint greenish haze of early spring, the ghost of plenty.

When he arrived at his office that morning, his mood was so benevolent that he even found comic charm in the precious military obscurantism of the sign on his door: SCAP/COMCEN/SPHINX-FE (N-CODE/D-CODE).

His mind ranging elsewhere, he set himself to cleaning up a machine breakout of intercepted messages from the Soviet Occupation Forces of Manchuria, routine communications framed in low-grade code. As he had no interest in the military and political games of the Russians and Americans, he normally worked messages without attending to their content, much as a good stenographer types without reading. It was for this reason that he had already begun on another problem when the import of what he had just read blossomed in his mind. He pulled the sheet from his out box and read it again.

General Kishikawa Takashi was being flown to Tokyo by the Russians to face trial as a Class A War Criminal.

Washington

Conducted by Miss Swivven, the four men entered the elevator and stood in silence as she slipped her magnetically coded card into the slot marked "Floor 16." The Arab trainee-in-terror whose code name was Mr. Haman lost his balance when, contrary to expectation, the elevator dropped rapidly into the bowels of the building. He bumped into Miss Swivven, who made a slight squeak as his shoulder brushed hers.

"I am so sorry, Madame. I had the assumption that the direction from the first floor to the sixteenth was upward. It should be so, mathematically speaking, but—"

A frown from his OPEC superior stemmed the falsetto babble, so he turned his attention to the taut nape of Miss Swivven's neck.

The OPEC troubleshooter (codetermed Mr. Able, because he was top man in an able-baker-charlie-dog sequence) was embarrassed by his fellow Arab's twittering voice and blundering ways. A third-generation Oxford man whose family had long enjoyed the cultural advantages of participating with the British in the exploitation of their people, Mr. Able scorned this parvenu son of a goatherd who had probably struck oil while overzealously driving a tent peg.

He was further annoyed at being called away from an intimate social affair to deal with some unexplained problem resulting, no doubt, from the incompetence of his compatriot and these CIA ruffians. Indeed, had the summons not borne the authority of the Chairman of the Mother Company, he would have ignored it, for at the moment of interruption he had been enjoying a most charming and titillating chat with a lovely young man whose father was an American senator.

Reacting to the OPEC man's frigid disdain, the Deputy stood well back in the elevator, attempting to

132

appear occupied with more important worries than this little matter.

Darryl Starr, for his part, sought to maintain an image of cool indifference by jingling the coins in his pocket while he whistled between his teeth.

With palpable G-press, the elevator stopped, and Miss Swivven inserted a second magnetic card into the slot to open the doors. The goatherd took this opportunity to pat her ass. She flinched and drew away.

Ah, he thought. A woman of modesty. Probably a virgin. So much the better. Virginity is important to Arabs, who dread comparison, and with good reason.

Darryl Starr quite openly, and the Deputy more guardedly, examined their surroundings, for neither had ever before been admitted to the "Sixteenth Floor" of their building. But Mr. Able shook hands with Diamond curtly and demanded, "What is this all about? I am not pleased to be called here summarily, particularly on an evening when I had something else in hand."

"You'll be even less pleased when I explain," Diamond said. He turned to Starr. "Sit down. I want you to learn the magnitude of your screw-up in Rome."

Starr shrugged with pretended indifference and slid into a white plastic molded chair at the conference table with its etched glass surface for rear projection of computer data. The goatherd was lost in admiring the view beyond the picture window.

"Mr. Haman?" Diamond said.

The Arab's nose touched the glass as he watched with delight the patterns of headlights making slow progress past the Washington Monument—the same cars that always crawled down that avenue at precisely this time of night.

"Mr. Haman?" Diamond repeated.

"What? Oh, yes! I always forget this code name I have been assigned. How humorous of me!"

"Sit," Diamond said dully.

"Pardon me?"

"Sit!"

Grinning awkwardly, the Arab joined Starr at the table as Diamond gestured the OPEC representative to the head of the table, and he himself occupied his orthopedically designed swivel chair on its raised dais.

133

the needed oil happened to be under their rock and sand, to convert that oil and concomitant political power into more enduring sources of wealth before the earth was drained of the noxious ooze, to which end they were energetically purchasing land all over the world, buying out companies, infiltrating banking systems, and exercising financial control over political figures throughout the industrialized West. They had certain advantages in effecting these designs. First, they could maneuver quickly because they were not burdened by the viscous political systems of democracy. Second, the politicians of the West are corrupt and available. Third, the mass of Westerners are greedy, lazy, and lacking any sense of history, having been conditioned by the atomic era to live on the rim of doomsday, and therefore only concerned with ease and prosperity in their own lifetimes.

The cluster of energy corporations that constitute the Mother Company could have broken the blackmail stranglehold of the Arab nations at any time. Raw oil is worthless until it is converted into a profitable pollutant, and they alone controlled the hoarding and distribution facilities. But the Mother Company's long-range objective was to use the bludgeon of contrived oil shortages to bring into their control all sources of energy: coal, atomic, solar, geothermic. As one aspect of their symbiotic affair, OPEC served the Mother Company by creating shortages when She wanted to build pipelines over fragile tundra, or block major governmental investment in research into solar and wind energy, or create natural gas shortfalls when pressing for removal of price controls. In return, the Mother Company serviced the OPEC nations in many ways, not the least of which was applying political pressure during the oil embargo to prevent the Western nations from taking the obvious step of occupying the land and liberating the oil for the common good. Doing this required more rhetorical suppleness than the Arabs realized, because the Mother Company was, at the same time, mounting vast propaganda programs to make the masses believe She was working to make America independent from foreign oil imports, using major stockholders who were also beloved figures from the entertainment world to gain popular support for their exploration of fossil fuel, their endangering of mankind with atomic wastes, their contaminating of the seas with off-shore drilling and reckless mishandling of oil freighters.

Both the Mother Company and the OPEC powers were passing through a delicate period of transition; the one attempting to convert Her oil monopoly into a hegemony over all other energy sources, so Her power and profit would not wane with the depletion of the world's oil supply; the other striving to transform its oil wealth into industrial and territorial possessions throughout the Western world. And it was to ease their way through this difficult and vulnerable period that they granted unlimited authority to Mr. Diamond and Mr. Able to deal with the three most dangerous obstacles to their success: the vicious efforts of the PLO to use their nuisance value to gain a share of the Arab spoils; the mindless and bungling interference of the CIA and its sensory organ the NSA; and Israel's tenacious and selfish insistence upon survival.

In bold, it was Mr. Diamond's role to control the CIA and, through the international power of the Mother Company, the actions of the Western states; while Mr. Able was assigned the task of keeping the individual Arab states in line. This last was particularly difficult as those powers are an uneasy blend of medieval dictatorships and chaotic military socialisms.

Keeping the PLO in line was their major problem. Both OPEC and the Mother Company agreed that the Palestinians were a pest out of all proportion to their significance, but the vagaries of history had made them and their petty cause a rallying point for the divergent Arab nations. Everyone would gladly have been rid of their stupidity and viciousness, but unfortunately these diseases, although communicable, are not fatal. Still, Mr. Able did what he could to keep them defused and impotent, and had recently drained much of the potency from them by creating the Lebanon disaster.

But he had not been able to prevent Palestinian terrorists from making the Munich Olympics blunder, which wasted years of anti-Jewish propaganda that had been thriving on the basis of latent anti-semitism throughout the West. Mr. Able had done what he could; he had alerted Mr. Diamond of the event beforehand. And Diamond sent the information on to the West German government, assuming they would handle the matter. Instead, they lay back and let it happen, not that protection of Jews has ever been a dominant theme in the German conscience.

Although there was a long history of cooperation between Diamond and Able, and a certain mutual admiration, there was no friendship. Diamond was uncomfortable with Mr. Able's sexual ambiguity. Beyond that, he detested the Arab's cultural advantages and social ease, for Diamond had been raised on the streets of New York's West Side, and like many risen plebes was driven by that reverse snobbism that assumes breeding to be a personality flaw.

For his part, Mr. Able viewed Diamond with disdain he never bothered to disguise. He saw his own role as a patriotic and noble one, laboring to create a power base for his people when their oil was gone. But Diamond was a whore, willing to submerge the interests of his own people in return for wealth and an opportunity to play at the game of power. He dismissed Diamond as a prototypic American, one whose view of honor and dignity was circumscribed by lust for gain. He thought of Americans as a decadent people whose idea of refinement is fluffy toilet paper. Affluent children who race about their highways, playing with their CB radios, pretending to be World War II pilots. Where is the fiber in a people whose best-selling poet is Rod McKuen, the Howard Cosell of verse?

Mr. Able's mind was running to thoughts like these, as he sat at the head of the conference table, his face impassive, a slight smile of polite distance on his lips. He never permitted his disgust to show, knowing that his people must continue to cooperate with the Americans—until they had finished the task of buying their nation out from under them.

Mr. Diamond was sitting back in his chair, examining the ceiling while he thought of a way to introduce this problem so that it would not seem to be entirely his fault. "All right," he said, "a little background. After the Munich Olympics screw-up, we had your commitment that you would control the PLO and avoid that kind of bad press in the future."

Mr. Able sighed. Well, at least Diamond had not begun his story with the escape of the Israelites across the Red Sea.

"As a sop to them," Diamond continued, "we arranged that whatshisname would be permitted to appear on the UN floor and unleash his slobbering fulminations against the Jews. But despite your assurances, we recently discovered that a cell of Black Septembrists—including two who had participated in the Munich raid—had your permission to run a stupid skyjacking out of Heathrow."

Mr. Able shrugged. "Circumstances alter intentions. I do not owe you an explanation for everything we do. Suffice it to say that this last exercise in blood lust was their price for biding their time until American pressure saps Israel's ability to defend itself."

"And we went along with you on that. As passive assistance, I ordered CIA to avoid any counteraction against the Septembrists. These orders were probably redundant, as the traditions of incompetence within the organization would have effectively neutralized them anyway."

The Deputy cleared his throat to object, but Diamond hushed him with a lift of the hand and continued. "We went a step beyond passive assistance. When we learned that a small, informal group of Israelis was on the track of those responsible for the Munich massacre, we decided to interdict them with a spoiling raid. The leader of this group was one Asa Stern, an ex-political whose son was among the athletes killed in Munich. Because we knew that Stern was suffering from terminal cancer—he died two weeks ago—and his little group consisted only of a handful of idealistic young amateurs, we assumed the combined forces of your Arab intelligence organization and our CIA would be adequate to blow them away."

"And it was not?"

"And it was not. These two men at the table were responsible for the operation, although the Arab was really no more than an agent-in-training. In a very wet and public action they managed to terminate two of the three members of Stern's group . . . along with seven bystanders. But one member, a girl named Hannah Stern, niece of the late leader, slipped through them."

Mr. Able sighed and closed his eyes. Did nothing ever work correctly in this country with its cumbersome form of government? When would they discover that the world is in a post-democratic era? "You say that *one* young woman escaped this spoiling raid? Surely this is not very serious. I cannot believe that one woman is going to London alone and manage singlehandedly to kill six highly trained and experienced Palestinian terrorists who have not only the protection of your organization and mine but, through your good offices, that of British MI-5 and MI-6! It is ridiculous."

"It would be ridiculous. But Miss Stern is not going to London. We are quite sure she went to France. We are also sure that she is now, or soon will be, in contact with one Nicholai Hel—a mauve-card man who is perfectly capable of penetrating your people and mine and all the British, of terminating the Black Septembrists, and of being back in France in time for a luncheon engagement."

Mr. Able looked at Diamond quizzically. "Is that admiration I detect in your voice?"

"No! I would not call it admiration. But Hel is a man we must not ignore. I am going to fill you in on his background so you can appreciate the special lengths to which we may have to go to remedy this screw-up." Diamond turned to the First Assistant, who sat unobtrusively at his console. "Roll up the printout on Hel."

As Fat Boy's lean, prosaic data appeared, rear-projected on the tabletop before them, Diamond quickly sketched out biographic details leading to Nicholai Hel's learning that General Kishikawa was a prisoner of the Russians and scheduled for trial before the War Crimes Commission.

Japan

Nicholai requested and received a leave of absence, to free his time and energy for the task of locating the General. The next week was nightmarish, a desperate struggle in slow motion against the spongy but impenetrable barricades of red tape, autonomic secrecy, international mistrust, bureaucratic inertia, and individual indifference. His efforts through the Japanese civil government were fruitless. Its systems were static and mired because grafted upon the Japanese propensity toward overorganization and shared authority designed to lessen the burden of individual responsibility for error were elements of alien democracy that brought with them the busy inaction characteristic of that wasteful form of government.

Nicholai then turned to the military governments and, through perseverance, managed to piece together a partial mosaic of events leading to the General's arrest. But in doing so, he had to make himself dangerously visible, although he realized that for one living on forged identity papers and lacking the protection of formal nationality, it was perilous to irritate bureaucrats who thrive on the dysfunctional status quo.

The results of this week of probing and pestering were meager. Nicholai learned that Kishikawa-san had been delivered to the War Crimes Commission by the Soviets, who would be in charge of prosecuting his case, and that he was currently being held in Sugamo Prison. He discovered that an American legal officer was responsible for the defense, but it was not until he had deluged that man with letters and telephone calls that he was granted an interview, and the best he could get was a half hour squeezed into the early morning.

Nicholai rose before dawn and took a crowded tram to the Yotsuya district. A damp, slate-gray morning was smudging the eastern sky as he walked across the Akebonobashi, Bridge of Dawn, beyond which crouched the forbidding bulk of the Ichigaya Barracks which had become symbolic of the inhuman machinery of Western justice.

For three-quarters of an hour, he sat on a wooden bench outside the counsel's office in the basement. Eventually a short-tempered overworked secretary showed him into Captain Thomas's cluttered work room. The Captain waved him to a chair without looking up from a deposition he was scanning. Only after finishing it and scribbling a marginal note did Captain Thomas raise his eyes.

"Yes?" There was more fatigue than curtness in his tone. He was personally responsible for the defense of six accused war criminals, and he had to work with limited personnel and resources, compared to the vast machinery of research and organization at the disposal of the prosecution in their offices above. Unfortunately for his peace of mind, Captain Thomas was idealistic about the fairness of Anglo-Saxon law, and he drove himself so hard that weariness, frustration, and bitter fatalism tainted his every word and gesture. He wanted nothing more than to see all this mess over and return to civilian life and to his small-town legal practice in Vermont.

Nicholai explained that he was seeking information about General Kishikawa.

"Why?"

"He is a friend."

"A friend?" The Captain was dubious.

"Yes, sir. He . . . he helped me when I was in Shanghai."

Captain Thomas tugged the Kishikawa brief from under a stack of similar folders. "But you were just a child then."

"I am twenty-three, sir."

The Captain's eyebrows went up. Like everyone else, he was fooled by Nicholai's genetic disposition toward youthful appearance. "I'm sorry. I assumed you were much younger. What do you mean when you say that Kishikawa helped you?"

"He cared for me when my mother died."

141

"I see. You're British, are you?"

"No."

"Irish?" Again the accent that was always identified as being from "someplace else."

"No, Captain. I work for SCAP as a translator." It was best to sidestep the irrelevant tangle of his nationality—or rather, his lack thereof.

"And you're offering yourself as a character witness, is that it?"

"I want to help in any way I can."

Captain Thomas nodded and fumbled about for a cigarette. "To be perfectly frank, I don't believe you can help all that much. We're understaffed here, and overworked. I've had to decide to concentrate my energy on cases where there is some chance of success. And I wouldn't put Kishikawa's in that category. That probably sounds cold-blooded to you, but I might as well be honest."

"But . . . I can't believe General Kishikawa was guilty of anything! What is he being accused of?"

"He's in the Class A grab bag: crimes against humanity—whatever the hell that means."

"But who's testifying against him? What do they say he did?"

"I don't know. The Russians are handling the prosecution, and they're not permitting me to examine their documents and sources until the day before the trial. I assume the charges will center around his actions as military governor of Shanghai. Their propaganda people have several times used the label: 'The Tiger of Shanghai.'"

"'The Tiger of'—! That is insane! He was an administrator. He got the water supply working again—the hospitals. How can they . . . ?"

"During his governorship, four men were sentenced and executed. Did you know that?"

"No, but—"

"For all I know, those four men might have been murderers or looters or rapists. I *do* know that the average number of executions for capital crimes during the ten years of British control was fourteen point six. You would think that comparison would be in your general's favor. But the men executed under him are

142

being described as 'heroes of the people.' And you can't go around executing heroes of the people and get away with it. Particularly if you are known as 'The Tiger of Shanghai.' "

"He was never called that!"

"That's what they're calling him now." Captain Thomas sat back and pressed his forefingers into his sunken eye sockets. Then he tugged at his sandy hair in an effort to revive himself. "And you can bet your Aunt Tilly's twat that that title will be used a hundred times during the trial. I'm sorry if I sound defeatist, but I happen to know that winning this one is very important to the Soviets. They're making a big propaganda number out of it. As you probably know, they've picked up a lot of flack for failing to repatriate their war prisoners. They've been keeping them in 'reeducation camps' in Siberia until they can be returned fully indoctrinated. And they have not delivered a single war criminal, other than Kishikawa. So this is a set piece for them, a chance to let the people of the world know they're doing their job, vigorously purging Japanese Capitalist Imperialists, making the world safe for socialism. Now, you seem to think this Kishikawa is innocent. Okay, maybe so. But I assure you that he qualifies as a war criminal. You see, the primary qualification for that honor is to be on the losing side—and that he was." Captain Thomas lighted one cigarette from another and stubbed out the punk in an overflowing ashtray. He puffed out a breath in a mirthless chuckle. "Can you imagine what would have happened to FDR or General Patton if the other side had won? Assuming they had been so self-righteous as to set up war-crimes trials. Shit, the only people who would have escaped being labeled 'warmongers' would have been those isolationist hicks who kept us out of the League of Nations. And chances are they would have been set up as puppet rulers, just as we have set up their opposite numbers in the Diet. That's the way it is, son. Now, I've got to get back to work. I go to trial tomorrow representing an old man who's dying of cancer and who claims he never did anything but obey the commands of his Emperor. But he'll probably be called the 'Leopard of Luzon' or the 'Puma of Pago-Pago.' And you know what, kid? For all I know, he might really have been the Leopard of Luzon. It won't matter much one way or the other."

"Can I at least see him? Visit him?"

Captain Thomas's head was down; he was already scanning the folder on the forthcoming trial. "What?"

"I want to visit General Kishikawa. May I?"

"I can't do anything about that. He's a Russian prisoner. You'll have to get permission from them."

"Well, how do *you* get to see him?"

"I haven't yet."

"You haven't even talked to him?"

Captain Thomas looked up blearily. "I've got six weeks before he goes to trial. The Leopard of Luzon goes up tomorrow. Go see the Russians. Maybe they can help you."

"Whom do I see?"

"Shit, boy, I don't know!"

Nicholai rose. "I see. Thank you."

He had reached the door when Captain Thomas said, "I'm sorry, son. Really."

Nicholai nodded and left.

In months to come, Nicholai was to reflect on the differences between Captain Thomas and his Russian opposite number, Colonel Gorbatov. They were symbolic variances in the superpowers' ways of thinking and dealing with men and problems. The American had been genuinely concerned, compassionate, harried, ill-organized . . . ultimately useless. The Russian was mistrustful, indifferent, well prepared and informed, and ultimately of some value to Nicholai, who sat in a large, overstuffed chair as the Colonel stirred his glass of tea thoughtfully until two large lumps of sugar disintegrated and swirled at the bottom, but never completely dissolved.

"You are sure you will not take tea?" the Colonel asked.

"Thank you, no." Nicholai preferred to avoid wasting time on social niceties.

"For myself, I am addicted to tea. When I die, the fellow who does my autopsy will find my insides tanned like boot leather." Gorbatov smiled automatically at the old joke, then set down the glass in its metal holder.

He unthreaded his round metal-rimmed glasses from his ears and cleaned them, or rather distributed the smudge evenly, using his thumb and finger. As he did so, he settled his hooded eyes on the young man sitting across from him. Gorbatov was farsighted and could see Nicholai's boyish face and startling green eyes better with his glasses off. "So you are a friend of General Kishikawa? A friend concerned with his welfare. Is that it?"

"Yes, Colonel. And I want to help him, if I can."

"That's understandable. After all, what are friends for?"

"At very least, I would like permission to visit him in prison."

"Yes, of course you would. That's understandable." The Colonel replaced his glasses and sipped his tea. "You speak Russian very well, Mr. Hel. With quite a refined accent. You have been trained very carefully."

"It's not a matter of being trained. My mother was Russian."

"Yes, of course."

"I never learned Russian formally. It was a cradle language."

"I see. I see." It was Gorbatov's style to place the burden of communication on the other person, to draw him out by contributing little beyond constant indications that he was unconvinced. Nicholai allowed the transparent tactic to work because he was tired of fencing, frustrated with short leads and blind alleys, and eager to learn about Kishikawa-san. He offered more information than necessary, but even as he spoke, he realized that his story did not have the sound of truth. That realization made him explain even more carefully, and the meticulous explanations made it sound more and more as though he were lying.

"In my home, Colonel, Russian, French, German, and Chinese were all cradle languages."

"It must have been uncomfortable, sleeping in so crowded a cradle."

Nicholai tried to laugh, but the sound was thin and unconvincing.

"But of course," Gorbatov went on, "you speak

English as well?" The question was posed in English with a slight British accent.

"Yes," Nicholai answered in Russian. "And Japanese. But these were learned languages."

"Meaning: not cradle?"

"Meaning just that." Nicholai instantly regretted the brittle sound his voice had assumed.

"I see." The Colonel leaned back in his desk chair and regarded Nicholai with a squint of humor in his Mongol-shaped eyes. "Yes," he said at last, "very well trained. And disarmingly young. But for all your cradle and post-cradle languages, Mr. Hel, you are an American, are you not?"

"I *work* for the Americans. As a translator."

"But you showed an American identification card to the men downstairs."

"I was issued the card because of my work."

"Oh, of course. I see. But as I recall, my question was not *whom* you worked for—we already knew that—but what your nationality is. You are an American, are you not?"

"No, Colonel, I am not."

"What then?"

"Well . . . I suppose I am more Japanese than anything."

"Oh? You will excuse me if I mention that you do not look particularly Japanese?"

"My mother was Russian, as I told you. My father was German."

"Ah! That clarifies everything. A typical Japanese ancestry."

"I cannot see what difference it makes what my nationality is!"

"It's not important that you be able to see it. Please answer my question."

The sudden frigidity of tone caused Nicholai to calm his growing anger and frustration. He drew a long breath. "I was born in Shanghai. I came here during the war—under the protection of General Kishikawa—a family friend."

"Then of what nation are you a citizen?"

"None."

"How awkward that must be for you."

146

"It is, yes. It made it very difficult to find work to support myself."

"Oh, I am sure it did, Mr. Hel. And in your difficulties, I understand how you might be willing to do almost anything to secure employment and money."

"Colonel Gorbatov, I am not an agent of the Americans. I am in their employ, but I am not their agent."

"You make distinctions in shading which, I confess, are lost upon me."

"But why would the Americans want to interview General Kishikawa? What reason would they have to go through an elaborate charade just to contact an officer with a largely administrative career?"

"Precisely what I hoped you would clarify for me, Mr. Hel." The Colonel smiled.

Nicholai rose. "It is evident to me, Colonel, that you are enjoying our conversation more than I. I must not squander your valuable time. Surely there are flies waiting to have their wings pulled off."

Gorbatov laughed aloud. "I haven't heard that tone for years! Not only the cultivated sound of court Russian, but even the snide disdain! That's wonderful! Sit down, young man. Sit down. And tell me why you must see General Kishikawa."

Nicholai dropped into the overstuffed chair, voided, weary. "It is more simple than you are willing to believe. Kishikawa-san is a friend. Almost a father. Now he is alone, without family, and in prison. I must help him, if I can. At very least, I must see him . . . talk to him."

"A simple gesture of filial piety. Perfectly understandable. Are you sure you won't have a glass of tea?"

"Quite sure, thank you."

As he refilled his glass, the Colonel opened a manila folder and glanced at the contents. Nicholai assumed that the preparation of this file was the cause of his three-hour wait in the outer offices of the headquarters of Soviet Occupation Forces. "I see that you also carry papers identifying you as a citizen of the USSR. Surely that is sufficiently uncommon as to merit an explanation?"

"Your sources of information within SCAP are good."

The Colonel shrugged. "They are adequate."

"I had a friend—a woman—who helped me get employment with the Americans. It was she who got my American identification card for me—"

"Excuse me, Mr. Hel. I seem to be expressing myself poorly this afternoon. I did not ask you about your American papers. It was your Russian identity card that interested me. Will you forgive my vagueness?"

"I was trying to explain that."

"Oh, do excuse me."

"I was going to tell you that this woman realized I might get into some trouble if the Americans discovered I was not a citizen. To avoid this, she also had papers made up indicating a Russian nationality, so I could show them to curious American MP's and avoid questioning."

"And how often have you been driven to this baroque expedient?"

"Never."

"Hardly a frequency that justifies the effort. And why Russian? Why was not some other nationality selected from that crowded cradle of yours?"

"As you have pointed out, I do not look convincingly Oriental. And the attitude of the Americans toward German nationals is hardly friendly."

"While their attitude toward Russians, on the other hand, is fraternal and compassionate? Is that it?"

"Of course not. But they mistrust and fear you, and for that reason, they do not treat Soviet citizens highhandedly."

"This woman friend of yours was very astute. Tell me why she went to such efforts on your behalf. Why did she take such risks?"

Nicholai did not answer, which was sufficient answer.

"Ah, I see," Colonel Gorbatov said. "Of course. Then too, Miss Goodbody was a woman no longer burdened with her first youth."

Nicholai flushed with anger. "You know all about this!"

Gorbatov tugged off his glasses and redistributed the sneer. "I know certain things. About Miss Goodbody, for instance. And about your household in the Asakusa district. My, my, my. *Two* young ladies to share your bed? Profligate youth! And I know that your mother was the Countess Alexandra Ivanovna. Yes, I know certain things about you."

"And you have believed me all the while, haven't you."

Gorbatov shrugged. "It would be more accurate to say that I have believed the details with which your story is garnished. I know that you visited Captain Thomas of the War Crimes Tribunal Staff last . . ." He glanced at the folder. ". . . last Tuesday morning at seven-thirty. I presume he told you there was nothing he could do for you in the matter of General Kishikawa who, apart from being a major war criminal guilty of sins against humanity, is also the only high-ranking officer of the Japanese Imperial Army to survive the rigors of reeducation camp, and is therefore a figure of value to us from the point of view of prestige and propaganda." The Colonel threaded his glasses from ear to ear. "I am afraid there is nothing you can do for the General, young man. And if you pursue this, you will expose yourself to investigation by American Intelligence—a title more indicative of what they seek than of what they possess. And if there was nothing my ally and brother-in-arms, Captain Thomas, could do for you, then certainly there is nothing I can do. He, after all, represents the defense. I represent the prosecution. You are quite sure you will not take a glass of tea?"

Nicholai grasped for whatever he could get. "Captain Thomas told me I would need your permission to visit the General."

"That is true."

"Well?"

The Colonel turned in his desk chair toward the window and tapped his front teeth with his forefinger as he looked out on the blustery day. "Are you sure he would want a visit from you, Mr. Hel? I have talked to the General. He is a man of pride. It might not be pleasant for him to appear before you in his present state. He has twice attempted to commit suicide, and now he is watched over very strictly. His present condition is degrading."

"I must try to see him. I owe him . . . very much."

The Colonel nodded without looking back from the window. He seemed lost in thoughts of his own.

"Well?" Nicholai asked after a time.

Gorbatov did not answer.

"May I visit the General?"

His voice distant and atonic, the Colonel said, "Yes, of course." He turned to Nicholai and smiled. "I shall arrange it immediately."

Although so crowded into the swaying elevated car of the Yamate loop line that he could feel the warmth of pressing bodies seep through the damp of their clothing and his, Nicholai was isolated within his confusion and doubts. Through gaps between people, he watched the city passing beneath, dreary in the chill wet day, sucked empty of color by the leaden skies.

There had been subtle threat in Colonel Gorbatov's atonic permission to visit Kishikawa-san, and all morning Nicholai had felt diminished and impotent against the foreboding he felt. Perhaps Gorbatov had been right when he suggested that this visit might not, after all, be an act of kindness. But how could he allow the General to face his forthcoming trial and disgrace alone? It would be an act of indifference for which he could never forgive himself. Was it for his own peace of mind, then, that he was going to Sugamo Prison? Were his motives at base selfish?

At the Komagome Station, one stop before Sugamo Prison, Nicholai had a sudden impulse to get off the train—to return home, or at least wander about for a while and consider what he was doing. But this survival warning came too late. Before he could push his way to the doors, they clattered shut, and the tram jerked away. He was certain he should have gotten off. He was equally certain that now he would go through with it.

Colonel Gorbatov had been generous; he had arranged that Nicholai would have an hour with Kishikawa-san. But now as Nicholai sat in the chilly visiting room, staring at the flaking green paint on the walls, he wondered if there would be anything to say that could fill a whole hour. A Japanese guard and an American MP stood by the door, ignoring one another, the Japanese staring at the floor before him, while the American devoted his attention to the task of snatching

150

hairs from his nostrils. Nicholai had been searched with embarrassing thoroughness in an anteroom before being admitted to the visiting area. The rice cakes he had brought along wrapped in paper had been taken from him by the American MP, who took Nicholai for an American on the strength of his identification card and explained, "Sorry, pal. But you can't bring chow with you. This—ah—whatshisname, the gook general —he's tried to bump himself off. We can't run the risk of poison or whatever. You dig?"

Nicholai said that he dug. And he joked with the MP, realizing that he must put himself on the good side of the authorities, if he was to help Kishikawa-san in any way. "Yeah, I know what you mean, sergeant. I sometimes wonder how any Japanese officers survived the war, what with their inclination toward suicide."

"Right. And if anything happened to this guy, my ass would be in a sling. Hey. What in hell's this?" The sergeant held up a small magnetic Gō board Nicholai had thought to bring along at the last minute, in case there was nothing to say and the embarrassment should hang too heavily.

Nicholai shrugged. "Oh, a game. Sort of a Japanese chess."

"Oh yeah?"

The Japanese guard, who stood about awkwardly in the knowledge of his redundancy in this situation, was glad to be able to tell his American opposite number in broken English that it was indeed a Japanese game.

"Well, I don't know, pal. I don't know if you can bring this in with you."

Nicholai shrugged again. "It's up to you, sergeant. I thought it might be something to pass the time if the General didn't feel like talking."

"Oh? You talk gook?"

Nicholai had often wondered how that word, a corruption of the Korean name for its people, had become the standard term of derogation in the American military vocabulary for all Orientals.

"Yes, I speak Japanese." Nicholai recognized the need for duplicity where sensibility meets stony ignorance. "You probably noticed from my ID card that I work for Sphinx?" He looked steadily at the sergeant and

151

tipped his head slightly toward the Japanese guard, indicating that he didn't want to go into this too deeply with alien ears around.

The MP frowned in his effort to think, then he nodded conspiratorily. "I see. Yeah, I sort of wondered how come an American was visiting this guy."

"A job's a job."

"Right. Well, I guess it's okay. What harm can a game do?" He returned the miniature Gō board and conducted Nicholai to the visiting room.

Five minutes later the door opened, and General Kishikawa entered, followed by two more guards, another Japanese, and a thick-set Russian with the immobile, meaty face of the Slavic peasant. Nicholai rose in greeting, as the two new protectors took up their positions against the wall.

As Kishikawa-san approached, Nicholai automatically made a slight head bow of filial obeisance. The gesture was not lost upon the Japanese guards, who exchanged brief glances, but remained silent.

The General shuffled forward and took the chair opposite Nicholai, across the rough wooden table. When at last he lifted his eyes, the young man was struck by the General's appearance. He had expected an alteration in Kishikawa-san's features, an erosion of his gentle virile manner, but not this much.

The man sitting opposite him was old, frail, diminished. There was an oddly priestly look to his transparent skin and slow, uncertain movements. When finally he spoke, his voice was soft and monotonic, as if communication was a pointless burden.

"Why have you come, Nikko?"

"To be with you, sir."

"I see."

There followed a silence during which Nicholai could think of nothing to say, and the General had nothing to say. Finally, with a long, fluttering sigh, Kishikawa-san assumed the responsibility for the conversation because he did not want Nicholai to feel uncomfortable with the silence. "You look well, Nikko. Are you?"

"Yes, sir."

"Good. Good. You grow more like your mother each day. I can see her eyes in yours." He smiled faintly.

152

"Someone should have advised your family that this particular color of green was meant for jade or ancient glass, not for human eyes. It is disconcerting."

Nicholai forced a smile. "I shall speak to an ophthalmologist, sir, to see if there is a remedy for our blunder."

"Yes. Do that."

"I shall."

"Do." The General gazed away and seemed for a second to forget Nicholai's presence. Then: "So? How are you getting on?"

"Well enough. I work for the Americans. A translator."

"So? And do they accept you?"

"They ignore me, which is just as well."

"Better, really."

There was another brief silence, which Nicholai was going to break with small talk when Kishikawa-san raised his hand.

"Of course you have questions. I will tell you things quickly and simply, then we shall discuss them no further."

Nicholai bowed his head in compliance.

"I was in Manchuria, as you know. I became sick—pneumonia. I was in fever and coma when the Russians attacked the hospital unit where I was. When I became myself again, I was in a reeducation camp, under constant surveillance and unable to use the portal through which so many of my brother officers had escaped the indignity of surrender and the humiliations of . . . reeducation. Only a few other officers were captured. They were taken away somewhere and not heard of again. Our captors assumed that officers were either incapable or unworthy of . . . reeducation. I assumed this would be my fate also, and I awaited it with such calm as I could manage. But no. Evidently, the Russians thought that one thoroughly reeducated officer of general rank would be a useful thing to introduce into Japan, to aid them with their plans for the future of our country. Many . . . many . . . many methods of reeducation were employed. The physical ones were easiest to bear—hunger, sleeplessness, beatings. But I am a stubborn old man, and I do not reeducate easily. As I had no family left alive in Japan, as hostages, they were denied the emotional whip with which they had reeducated others. A long time passed. A year and a half, I think. It is difficult to tell the seasons when you never see the light of day, and when endurance is measured in five more minutes . . . five more minutes . . . I can stand this for five more minutes." The General was lost for a time in memories of specific torments. Then, with a faint start, he returned to his story. "Sometimes they lost patience with me and made the error of giving me periods of rest in unconsciousness. A long time passed in this way. Months measured in minutes. Then suddenly they stopped all efforts toward my reeducation. I assumed, of course, that I would be killed. But they had something more degrading in mind for me. I was cleaned and deloused. A plane trip. A long ride on a railroad. Another plane trip. And I was here. For a month, I was kept here with no idea of their intentions. Then, two weeks ago, a Colonel Gorbatov visited me. He was quite frank with me. Each occupying nation has offered up its share of war criminals. The Soviets have had none to offer, no direct participation in the machinery of international justice. Before me, that is."

"But, sir—"

Kishikawa-san lifted his hand for silence. "I decided I would not face this final humiliation. But I had no way to release myself. I have no belt. My clothes, as you see, are of stout canvas that I have not the strength to tear. I eat with a wooden spoon and bowl. I am permitted to shave only with an electric razor, and only under close surveillance." The General smiled a gray smile. "The Soviets prize me, it would appear. They are concerned not to lose me. Ten days ago, I stopped eating. It was easier than you might imagine. They threatened me, but when a man decides to live no longer, he removes the power of others to make potent threats. So . . . they held me down on a table and forced a rubber tube down my throat. And they fed me liquids. It was ghastly . . . humiliating . . . eating and vomiting all at once. It was without dignity. So I promised to start eating again. And here I am."

Throughout this minimal explanation, Kishikawa-san had riveted his eyes on the rough surface of the table, intense and defocused.

154

Nicholai's eyes stung with brimming tears. He stared ahead, not daring to blink and send tears down his cheeks that would embarrass his father—his friend, that is.

Kishikawa-san drew a long breath and looked up. "No, no. There's no point in that, Nikko. The guards are looking on. Don't give them this satisfaction." He reached across and patted Nicholai's cheek with a firmness that was almost an admonitory slap.

At this point, the American sergeant straightened up, ready to protect his Sphinx compatriot from this gook general.

But Nicholai scrubbed his face with his hands, as though in fatigue, and with this gesture he rid himself of the tears.

"So!" Kishikawa-san said with new energy. "It is nearly time for the blossoms of Kajikawa. Do you intend to visit them?"

Nicholai swallowed. "Yes."

"That's good. The Occupation Forces have not chopped them down, then?"

"Not physically."

The General nodded. "And have you friends in your life, Nikko?"

"I . . . I have people living with me."

"As I recall from a letter from our friend Otake shortly before his death, there was a girl in his household, a student—I am sorry, but I don't remember her name. Evidently you were not totally indifferent to her charms. Do you still see her?"

Nicholai considered before answering. "No, sir, I don't."

"Not a quarrel, I hope."

"No. Not a quarrel."

"Ah, well, at your age affections ebb and flow. When you get older, you will discover that you cling to some with desperation." The effort to make Nicholai comfortable with social talk seemed to exhaust Kishikawa-san. There was really nothing he wanted to say, and after his experiences of the past two years, nothing he wanted to know. He bowed his head and stared at the table, slipping into the tight cycle of abbreviated thoughts and selected memories from his childhood with which he had learned to narcotize his imagination.

At first, Nicholai found comfort in the silence too. Then he realized that they were not together in it, but alone and apart. He drew the miniature Gō board and packet of metal stones from his pocket and set it on the table.

"They have given us an hour together, sir."

Kishikawa-san tugged his mind to the present. "What? Ah, yes. Oh, a game. Good, yes. It is something we can do together painlessly. But I have not played for a long time, and I shall not be an interesting opponent for you, Nikko."

"I haven't played since the death of Otake-san myself, sir."

"Oh? Is that so?"

"Yes. I am afraid I have made a waste of the years of training."

"No. It is one of the things one cannot waste. You have learned to concentrate deeply, to think subtly, to have affection for abstractions, to live at a distance from quotidian things. Not a waste. Yes, let's play."

Automatically returning to their first days together, and forgetting that Nicholai was now a far superior player, General Kishikawa offered a two stone advantage, which Nicholai of course accepted. For a time they played a vague and undistinguished game, concentrating only deeply enough to absorb mental energy that would otherwise have tormented them with memories, and with anticipations of things to come. Eventually the General looked up and sighed with a smile. "This is no good. I have played poorly and driven all *aji* out of the game."

"So have I."

Kishikawa-san nodded. "Yes. So have you."

"We'll play again, if you wish, sir. During my next visit. Perhaps we'll play better."

"Oh? Have you permission to visit me again?"

"Yes. Colonel Gorbatov has arranged that I may come tomorrow. After that . . . I'll apply to him again and see."

The General shook his head. "He is a very shrewd man, this Gorbatov."

156

"In what way, sir?"

"He has managed to remove my 'stone of refuge' from the board."

"Sir?"

"Why do you think he let you come here, Nikko? Compassion? You see, once they had removed from me all means of escape into an honorable death, I decided that I would face the trial in silence, in a silence as dignified as possible. I would not, as others have done, struggle to save myself by implicating friends and superiors. I would refuse to speak at all, and accept their sentence. This did not please Colonel Gorbatov and his compatriots. They would be cheated out of the propaganda value of their only war criminal. But there was nothing they could do. I was beyond the sanctions of punishment and the attractions of leniency. And they lacked the emotional hostages of my family, because, so far as they knew, my family had died in the carpet bombing of Tokyo. Then . . . then fate offered them you."

"Me, sir?"

"Gorbatov was perceptive enough to realize that you would not expose your delicate position with the Occupation Forces by making efforts to visit me unless you honored and loved me. And he reasoned—not inaccurately—that I reciprocate these feelings. So now he has his emotional hostage. He allowed you to come here to show me that he had you. And he does have you, Nikko. You are uniquely vulnerable. You have no nationality, no consulate to protect you, no friends who care about you, and you live on forged identity papers. He told me all of this. I am afraid he has 'confined the cranes to their nest,' my son."

The impact of what Kishikawa-san was saying grew in Nicholai. All the time and effort he had spent trying to contact the General, all this desperate combat against institutional indifference, had had the final effect of stripping the General of his armor of silence. He was not a consolation to Kishikawa-san; he was a weapon against him. Nicholai felt a medley of anger, shame, outrage, self-pity, and sorrow for Kishikawa-san.

The General's eyes crinkled into a listless smile. "This

is not your fault, Nikko. Nor is it mine. It is fate only. Bad luck. We will not talk about it again. We will play when you come back, and I promise to offer you a better game."

The General rose and walked to the door, where he waited to be escorted out by the Japanese and Russian guards, who left him standing there until Nicholai nodded to the American MP, who in turn nodded to his opposite numbers.

For a time, Nicholai sat numbly, picking the metal stones off the magnetic board with his fingernail.

The American sergeant approached and asked in a low, conspiratorial voice, "Well? You find out what you were looking to?"

"No," Nicholai said absently. Then more firmly: "No, but we'll talk again."

"You going to soften him up with that silly-assed gook game again?"

Nicholai stared at the sergeant, his green eyes arctic.

Uncomfortable under the gaze, the MP explained, "I mean . . . well, it's only a sort of chess or checkers or something, isn't it?"

Intending to scour this prole with his disdain for things Western, Nicholai said, "Gō is to Western chess what philosophy is to double-entry accounting."

But obtuseness is its own protection against both improvement and punishment. The sergeant's response was frank and naïve: "No shit?"

A needle-fine rain stung Nicholai's cheek as he stared across from the Bridge of Dawn to the gray bulk of the Ichigaya Barracks, blurred but not softened by the mist, its rows of windows smeared with wan yellow light, indicating that the Japanese War Crimes Trials were in progress.

He leaned against the parapet, his eyes defocused, rain running from his hair, down his face and neck. His first thought after leaving Sugamo Prison had been to appeal to Captain Thomas for help against the Russians, against this emotional blackmail of Colonel Gorbatov. But even as he formed the idea, he realized the pointlessness of appealing to the Americans, whose basic attitudes and objectives regarding the disposition of Japanese leaders were identical with the Soviets'.

After descending from the tramcar and wandering without destination in the rain, he had stopped at the rise of the bridge to look down for a few seconds and collect his thoughts. That was half an hour ago, and still he was stunned to inaction by a combination of churning fury and draining helplessness.

Although his fury had its roots in love of a friend and filial obligation, it was not without base self-pity. It was anguishing that *he* should be the means by which Gorbatov would deny Kishikawa-san the dignity of silence. The ironic unfairness of it was overwhelming. Nicholai was still young, and still assumed that equity was the basic impulse of Fate; that karma was a system, rather than a device.

As he stood on the bridge in the rain, his thoughts descending into bittersweet self-pity, it was natural that he should entertain the idea of suicide. The thought of denying Gorbatov his principal weapon was comforting, until he realized that the gesture would be empty. Surely, Kishikawa-san would not be informed of his death; he would be told that Nicholai had been taken into custody as hostage against the General's cooperation. And probably, after Kishikawa had disgraced himself with confessions that implicated associates, they would deliver the final punishment: they would tell him that Nicholai had been dead all the time, and that he had shamed himself and involved innocent friends in vain.

The wind gusted and drilled the needle rain into his cheek. Nicholai swayed and gripped the edge of the parapet as he felt waves of helplessness drain him. Then, with an involuntary shudder, he remembered a terrible thought that had strayed into his mind during his conversation with the General. Kishikawa had spoken of his attempt to starve himself to death, and of the disgusting humiliation of being force-fed through a tube shoved down his gagging throat. At that moment, the thought flashed through Nicholai's mind that, had he been with the General during this humiliation, he would have reached out and given him escape into death. The plastic identity card in Nicholai's pocket would have been weapon enough, used in the styles of Naked/Kill. The thing would have been over in an instant.*

The image of releasing Kishikawa-san from the trap of life had scarcely sketched itself in Nicholai's mind before he rejected it as too ghastly to consider. But now, in the rain, within sight of that machine for racial vengeance, the War Crimes Trials, the idea returned again, and this time it lingered. It was particularly bitter that fate was demanding that he kill the only person close to him. But honorable death was the only gift he could offer. And he recalled the ancient adage: Who must do the harsh things? He who can.

The act would, of course, be Nicholai's last. He would attract to himself all their fury and disappointment, and they would punish him. Obviously, suicide would be easier for Nicholai than releasing the General with his own hands. But it would be pointless . . . and selfish.

As he walked in the rain toward the underground station, Nicholai felt a chill in the pit of his stomach, but he was calm. Finally he had a path.

There was no sleep that night, nor could Nicholai abide the company of the vigorous, life-embracing Tanaka sisters, whose peasant energy seemed part of some alien world of light and hope, and for that reason both banal and irritating.

Alone in the dark of a room that gave out onto the small garden, the panels slid back so he could hear the

---

* In the course of this book, Nicholai Hel will avail himself of the tactics of Naked/Kill, but these will never be described in detail. In an early book, the author portrayed a dangerous ascent of a mountain. In the process of converting this novel into a vapid film, a fine young climber was killed. In a later book, the author detailed a method for stealing paintings from any well-guarded museum. Shortly after the Italian version of this book appeared, three paintings were stolen in Milan by the exact method described, and two of these were irreparably mutilated.

Simple social responsibility now dictates that he avoid exact descriptions of tactics and events which, although they might be of interest to a handful of readers, might contribute to the harm done to (and by) the uninitiated.

In a similar vein, the author shall keep certain advanced sexual techniques in partial shadow, as they might be dangerous, and would certainly be painful, to the neophyte.

rain pattering on broad-leafed plants and hissing softly in the gravel, protected from the cold by a padded kimono, he knelt beside a charcoal brazier that had long ago gone out and was barely warm to the touch. Twice he sought retreat into mystic transport, but his mind was too charged with fear and hate to allow him to cross over the lower path. Although he could not know it at this time, Nicholai would not again be able to find his way to the small mountain meadow where he enriched himself by being one with the grass and yellow sunlight. Events were to leave him with an impenetrable barrier of hate that would block him from ecstasy.

In the early morning, Mr. Watanabe found Nicholai still kneeling in the garden room, unaware that the rain had stopped and had been succeeded by a raw cold. Mr. Watanabe closed the panels fussily and lighted the brazier, all the while muttering about negligent young people who would ultimately have to pay the price in poor health for their foolishness.

"I should like to have a talk with you and Mrs. Shimura," Nicholai said in a quiet tone that staunched the flow of Mr. Watanabe's avuncular grumpiness.

An hour later, having had a light breakfast, the three of them knelt around a low table on which were the rolled-up deed to the house and a rather informally worded paper Nicholai had drawn up giving his possessions and furnishings to the two of them equally. He informed them that he would leave later that afternoon, probably never to return. There would be difficulty; there would be strangers asking questions and making life complicated for a few days; but after that it was not likely that the foreigners would concern themselves with the little household. Nicholai did not have much money, as he spent most of what he earned as it came in. What little he had was wrapped in cloth on the table. If Mr. Watanabe and Mrs. Shimura could not earn enough to support the house, he gave them permission to sell it and use the income as they would. It was Mrs. Shimura who insisted that they set aside a portion as dowry for the Tanaka sisters.

When this was settled, they took tea together and talked of business details. Nicholai had hoped to avoid the burden of silence, but soon their modest affairs were exhausted, and there was nothing more to say.

A cultural blemish of the Japanese is their discomfort with genuine expression of emotions. Some tend to mask feelings with stoic silence or behind the barricade of polite good form. Others hide in emotional hyperbole, in extravagances of gratitude or sorrow.

It was Mrs. Shimura who anchored herself in silence, while Mr. Watanabe wept uncontrollably.

With the same excessive consideration of security as yesterday, the four guards stood along the wall on the door side of the small visitors' room. The two Japanese looked tense and uncomfortable; the American MP yawned in boredom; and the stocky Russian seemed to daydream, which certainly he was not doing. Early in his conversation with Kishikawa-san, Nicholai had tested the guards, speaking first in Japanese. It was clear that the American did not understand, but he was less sure of the Russian, so he made up a nonsense statement and read a slight frown on the broad brow. When Nicholai shifted to French, losing the Japanese guards, but not the Russian, he was sure this man was no common soldier, despite his appearance of Slavic intellectual viscosity. It was necessary, therefore, to find another code in which to speak, and he chose the cryptography of Gō, reminding the General, as he took out the small magnetic board, that Otake-san had always used the idioticon of his beloved game when discussing important things.

"Do you want to continue the game, sir?" Nicholai asked. "The fragrance has gone bad: *Aji ga warui.*"

Kishikawa-san looked up in mild confusion. They were only four or five plays into the game; this was a most peculiar thing to say.

Three plays passed in silence before the General began to glimpse what Nicholai might have meant. He tested this out by saying, "It seems to me that the game is in *korigatachi,* that I am frozen into position without freedom of development."

"Not quite, sir. I see the possibility of a *sabaki,* but of course you would join the *hama.*"

"Isn't that dangerous for you? Isn't it in fact a *ko* situation?"

162

"More a *uttegae*, in truth. And I see nothing else for your honor—and mine."

"No, Nikko. You are too kind. I cannot accept the gesture. For you such a play would be a most dangerous aggression, a suicidal *de*."

"I am not asking your permission. I could not put you in that impossible position. Having decided how I shall play it, I am explaining the configuration to you. They believe they have *tsuru no sugomori*. In fact they face a *seki*. They intended to drive you to the wall with a *shicho*, but I have the privilege of being your *shicho atari*."

Out of the corner of his eye, Nicholai saw one of the Japanese guards frown. Obviously he played a bit, and he realized this conversation was nonsense.

Nicholai reached across the rough wooden table and placed his hand on the General's arm. "Foster-father, the game will end in two minutes. Permit me to guide you."

Tears of gratitude stood in Kishikawa-san's eyes. He seemed more frail than before, both very old and rather childlike. "But I cannot permit . . ."

"I act without permission, sir. I have decided to perform a loving disobedience. I do not even seek your forgiveness."

After a moment of consideration, Kishikawa-san nodded. A slight smile squeezed the tears from his eyes and sent one down each side of his nose. "Guide me, then."

"Turn your head and look out the window, sir. It is all overcast and damp, but soon the season of the cherry will be with us."

Kishikawa-san turned his head and looked calmly out into the rectangle of moist gray sky. Nicholai took a lead pencil from his pocket and held it lightly between his fingers. As he spoke, he concentrated on the General's temple where a slight pulse throbbed under the transparent skin.

"Do you recall when we walked beneath the blossoms of Kajikawa, sir? Think of that. Remember walking there years before with your daughter, her hand small in yours. Remember walking with your father

163

along the same bank, your hand small in his. Concentrate on these things."

Kishikawa-san lowered his eyes and reposed his mind, as Nicholai continued speaking quietly, the lulling drone of his voice more important than the content. After a few moments, the General looked at Nicholai, the hint of a smile creasing the corners of his eyes. He nodded. Then he turned again to the gray, dripping scene beyond the window.

As Nicholai continued to talk softly, the American MP was engrossed in dislodging a bit of something from between his teeth with his fingernail; but Nicholai could feel tension in the attitude of the brighter of the Japanese guards, who was bewildered and uncomfortable with the tone of this conversation. Suddenly, with a shout, the Russian "guard" leapt forward.

He was too late.

For six hours Nicholai sat in the windowless interrogation room after surrendering himself without struggle or explanation to the stunned, confused, and therefore violent guards. In his first fury the American MP sergeant had hit him twice with his truncheon, once on the point of the shoulder, once across the face, splitting his eyebrow against the sharp bone behind it. There was little pain, but the eyebrow bled profusely, and Nicholai suffered from the messy indignity of it.

Frightened by anticipation of repercussions for allowing their prisoner to be killed under their eyes, the guards screamed threats at Nicholai as they raised the alarm and summoned the prison doctor. When he arrived, there was nothing the fussy, uncertain Japanese doctor could do for the General, who had been nerve-dead seconds after Nicholai's strike, and body-dead within a minute. Shaking his head and sucking breaths between his teeth, as though admonishing a mischievous child, the doctor attended to Nicholai's split eyebrow, relieved to have something to do within the scope of his competence.

While two fresh Japanese guards watched over Nicholai, the others reported to their superiors, giving versions of the event that showed them to be blameless, while their opposite numbers were revealed to be something between incompetent and perfidious.

When the MP sergeant returned, he was accompanied by three others of his nationality; no Russians, no Japanese. Dealing with Nicholai was to be an American show.

In grim silence, Nicholai was searched and stripped, dressed in the same coarse "suicide-proof" uniform the General had worn, and brought down the hall to be left, barefoot and with his wrists handcuffed behind his back, in the stark interrogation room, where he sat in silence on a metal chair bolted to the floor.

To subdue his imagination, Nicholai focused his mind on the middle stages of a famous contest between Gō masters of the major schools, a game he had memorized as a part of his training under Otake-san. He reviewed the placements, switching by turns from one point of view to the other, examining the implications of each. The considerable effort of memory and concentration was sufficient to close out the alien and chaotic world around him.

There were voices beyond the door, then the sound of keys and bolts, and three men entered. One was the MP sergeant who had been industriously picking his teeth when Kishikawa-san died. The second was a burly man in civilian dress whose porcine eyes had that nervous look of superficial intelligence thinned by materialistic insensitivity one sees in politicians, film producers, and automobile salesmen. The third, the leaves of a major on his shoulders, was a taut, intense man with large bloodless lips and drooping lower eyelids. It was this third who occupied the chair opposite Nicholai, while the burly civilian stood behind Nicholai's chair, and the sergeant stationed himself near the door.

"I am Major Diamond." The officer smiled, but there was a flat tone to his accent, that metallic mandibular sound that blends the energies of the garment district with overlays of acquired refinement—the kind of voice one associates with female newscasters in the United States.

At the moment of their arrival, Nicholai had been puzzling over a move in the recalled master game that had the fragrance of a *tenuki,* but which was in fact a subtle reaction to the opponent's preceding play. Before looking up, he concentrated on the board, freezing its patterns in his memory so he could return to it later. Only then did he lift his expressionless bottle-green eyes to the Major's face.

"What did you say?"

"I am Major Diamond, CID."

"Oh?" Nicholai's indifference was not feigned.

The Major opened his attaché case and drew out three typed sheets stapled together. "If you will just sign this confession, we can get on with it."

Nicholai glanced at the paper. "I don't think I want to sign anything."

Diamond's lips tightened with irritation. "You're denying murdering General Kishikawa?"

"I am not denying anything. I helped my friend to his escape from . . ." Nicholai broke off. What was the point of explaining to this man something his mercantile culture could not possibly comprehend? "Major, I don't see any value in continuing this conversation."

Major Diamond glanced toward the burly civilian behind Nicholai, who leaned over and said, "Listen. You might as well sign the confession. We know all about your activities on behalf of the Reds!"

Nicholai did not bother to look toward the man.

"You're not going to tell us you haven't been in contact with a certain Colonel Gorbatov?" the civilian persisted.

Nicholai took a long breath and did not answer. It was too complicated to explain; and it didn't matter if they understood or not.

The civilian gripped Nicholai's shoulder. "You're in maximum trouble, boy! Now, you'd better sign this paper, or—"

Major Diamond frowned and shook his head curtly, and the civilian released his grip. The Major put his hands on his knees and leaned forward, looking into Nicholai's eyes with worried compassion. "Let me try to explain all this to you. You're confused right now, and that's perfectly understandable. We know the Russians are behind this murder of General Kishikawa. I'll admit to you that we don't know why. That's one of the things we want you to help us with. Let me be open

166

and frank with you. We know you've been working for the Russians for some time. We know you infiltrated a most sensitive area in Sphinx/FE with forged papers. A Russian identity card was found on you, together with an American one. We also know that your mother was a communist and your father a Nazi; that you were in Japan during the war; and that your contacts included militarist elements of the Japanese government. One of these contacts was with this Kishikawa." Major Diamond shook his head and sat back. "So you see, we know rather a lot about you. And I'm afraid it's all pretty damning. That's what my associate means when he says that you're in great trouble. It's possible that I may be able to help you . . . if you are willing to cooperate with us. What do you say?"

Nicholai was overwhelmed by the irrelevance of all this. Kishikawa-san was dead; he had done what a son must do; he was ready to face punishment; the rest didn't matter.

"Are you denying what I have said?" the Major asked.

"You have a handful of facts, Major, and from them you have made ridiculous conclusions."

Diamond's lips tightened. "Our information came from Colonel Gorbatov himself."

"I see." So Gorbatov was going to punish him for snatching away his propaganda prey by giving the Americans certain half-truths and allowing them to do his dirty work. How Slavic in its duplicity, in its involute obliquity.

"Of course," Diamond continued, "we don't take everything the Russians tell us at face value. That's why we want to give you a chance to tell us your side of the story."

"There is no story."

The civilian touched his shoulder again. "You deny that you knew General Kishikawa during the war?"

"No."

"You deny that he was a part of the Japanese military/industrial machine?"

"He was a soldier." The more accurate response would have been that he was a warrior, but that distinction would have meant nothing to these Americans with their mercantile mentalities.

"Do you deny being close to him?" the civilian pursued.

"No."

Major Diamond took up the questioning, his tone and expression indicating that he was honestly uncertain and sought to understand. "Your papers *were* forged, weren't they, Nicholai?"

"Yes."

"Who helped you obtain forged papers?"

Nicholai was silent.

The Major nodded and smiled. "I understand. You don't want to implicate a friend. I understand that. Your mother was Russian, wasn't she?"

"Her nationality was Russian. There was no Slavic blood in her."

The civilian cut in. "So you admit that your mother was a communist?"

Nicholai found a bitter humor in the thought of Alexandra Ivanovna being a communist. "Major, to the degree my mother took any interest in politics—a very modest degree indeed—she was to the political right of Attila." He repeated "Attila" again, mispronouncing it with an accent on the second syllable, so the Americans would understand.

"Sure," the civilian said. "And I suppose you're going to deny that your father was a Nazi?"

"He might have been. From what I understand, he was stupid enough. I never met him."

Diamond nodded. "So what you're really saying, Nicholai, is that the bulk of our accusations are true."

Nicholai sighed and shook his head. He had worked with the American military mentality for two years, but he could not pretend to understand its rigid penchant for forcing facts to fit convenient preconceptions. "If I understand you, Major—and frankly I don't much care if I do—you are accusing me of being both a communist and a Nazi, of being both a close friend of General Kishikawa's and his hired assassin, of being both a Japanese militarist and a Soviet spy. And you seem to believe that the Russians would arrange the killing of a man they intended to subject to the indignities of a

War Crimes Trial to the end of garnering their bit of the propaganda glory. None of this offends your sense of rational probability?"

"We don't pretend to understand every twist and turn of it," Major Diamond admitted.

"Don't you really? What becoming humility."

The civilian's grip tightened painfully on his shoulder. "We don't need wise-assed talk from you! You're in heavy trouble! This country is under military occupation, and you're not a citizen of anywhere, boy! We can do anything we want with you, with no interference from consulates and embassies!"

The Major shook his head, and the civilian released his grip and stepped back. "I don't think that tone is going to do us any good. It's obvious that Nicholai isn't easily frightened." He smiled half shyly, then said, "But still, what my associate says is true. You have committed a capital crime, the penalty for which is death. But there are ways in which you can help us in our fight against international communism. A little cooperation from you, and something might be arranged to your advantage."

Nicholai recognized the haggling tone of the marketplace. Like all Americans, this Major was a merchant at heart; everything had a price, and the good man was he who bargained well.

"Are you listening to me?" Diamond asked.

"I can hear you," Nicholai modified.

"And? Will you cooperate?"

"Meaning sign your confession?"

"That and more. The confession implicates the Russians in the assassination. We'll also want to know about the people who helped you infiltrate Sphinx/FE. And about the Russian intelligence community here, and their contacts with unpurged Japanese militarists."

"Major. The Russians had nothing to do with my actions. Believe me that I don't care one way or the other about their politics, just as I don't care about yours. You and the Russians are only two slightly different forms of the same thing: the tyranny of the mediocre. I have no reason to protect the Russians."

"Then you will sign the confession?"

"No."

169

"But you just said—"

"I said that I would not protect or assist the Russians. I also have no intention of assisting your people. If it is your intention to execute me—with or without the mockery of a military trial—then please get to it."

"Nicholai, we *will* get your signature on that confession. Please believe me."

Nicholai's green eyes settled calmly on the Major's. "I am no longer a part of this conversation." He lowered his eyes and returned his concentration to the patterns of stones in the Gō game he had temporarily frozen in his memory. He began again considering the alternative responses to that clever seeming *tenuki*.

There was an exchange of nods between the Major and the burly civilian, and the latter took a black leather case from his pocket. Nicholai did not break his concentration as the MP sergeant pushed up his sleeve and the civilian cleared the syringe of air by squirting an arcing jet into the air.

When, much later, he tried to remember the events of the subsequent seventy-two hours, Nicholai could only recall shattered tesserae of experience, the binding grout of chronological sequence dissolved by the drugs they pumped into him. The only useful analogy he could devise for the experience was that of a motion picture in which he was both actor and audience member—a film with both slow and fast motion, with freeze frames and superimpositions, with the sound track from one sequence playing over the images of another, with single-frame subliminal flashes that were more felt than perceived, with long stretches of underexposed, out-of-focus pictures, and dialogue played under speed, mushy and basso.

At this period, the American intelligence community had just begun experimenting with the use of drugs in interrogation, and they often made errors, some mind-destroying. The burly civilian "doctor" tried many chemicals and combinations on Nicholai, sometimes accidentally losing his victim to hysteria or to comatose indifference, sometimes creating mutually cancelling effects that left Nicholai perfectly calm and lucid, but so displaced in reality that while he responded willingly to interrogation, his answers were in no way related to the questions.

Throughout the three days, during those moments when Nicholai drifted into contact with himself, he experienced intense panic. They were attacking, probably damaging, his mind; and Nicholai's genetic superiority was as much intellectual as sensual. He dreaded that they might crush his mind, and hundreds of years of selective breeding would be reduced to their level of humanoid rubble.

Often he was outside himself, and Nicholai the audience member felt pity for Nicholai the actor, but could do nothing to help him. During those brief periods when he could reason, he tried to flow with the nightmare distortions, to accept and cooperate with the insanity of his perceptions. He knew intuitively that if he struggled against the pulsing warps of unreality, something inside might snap with the effort, and he would never find his way back again.

Three times during the seventy-two hours, his interrogators' patience broke, and they allowed the MP sergeant to pursue the questioning in more conventional third-degree ways. He did this with the aid of a nine-inch tube of canvas filled with iron filings. The impact of this weapon was terrible. It seldom broke the surface of the skin, but it crushed bone and tissue beneath.

A civilized man who could not really condone this sort of thing, Major Diamond left the interrogation during each of the beatings, unwilling to witness the torture he had ordered. The "doctor" remained, curious to see the effects of pain inflicted under heavily drugged conditions.

The three periods of physical torture registered differently upon Nicholai's perception. Of the first, he remembered nothing. Had it not been for his right eye swollen closed and a loose tooth oozing the saline taste of blood, the thing might never have happened. The second beating was excruciatingly painful. The combined and residual effects of the drugs at this moment were such that he was intensely aware of sensation. His skin was so sensitive that the brush of his clothes against it was painful, and the air he breathed stung his nostrils. In this hypertactile condition, the torture was indescribable. He yearned for unconsciousness, but the sergeant's talents were such that he could deny blissful emptiness forever.

The third session was not painful at all, but it was by far the most frightening. With perfect, but insane, lucidity, Nicholai both received and observed the punishment. Again, he was both audience and actor, and he watched it happen with only mild interest. He felt nothing; the drugs had short-circuited his nerves. The terror lay in the fact that he could *hear* the beating as though the sound were amplified by powerful microphones within his flesh. He heard the liquid crunch of tissue; he heard the crisp splitting of skin; he heard the granular grating of fragmented bone; he heard the lush pulsing of his blood. In the mirror of the mirror of his consciousness, he was calmly terrified. He realized that to be able to hear all this while feeling nothing was insane, and to experience anesthetized indifference to the event was beyond the verge of madness.

At one moment, his mind swam to the surface of reality and he spoke to the Major, telling that he was the son of General Kishikawa and that they would be making a terminal error not to kill him, because if he lived, there was no escaping him. He spoke mushily; his tongue was thick with the drugs and his lips were split with the beating; but his tormentors would not have understood him anyway. He had unknowingly spoken in French.

Several times during the three days of interrogation the handcuffs that bound his wrists behind him were removed. The "doctor" noticed that his fingers were white and cold with lack of circulation, so the cuffs were taken off for a few minutes while his wrists were massaged, then they were replaced. Throughout the rest of his life, Nicholai carried shiny tan bracelets of scar from the handcuffs.

During the seventy-third hour, neither knowing what he was doing nor caring, Nicholai signed the confession implicating the Russians. So lost to reality was he that he signed it in Japanese script and in the middle of the typewritten page, though they had tried to direct his trembling hand to the bottom. So useless was this confession that the Americans were finally reduced to forging his signature, which of course they might have done at the outset.

The final fate of this "confession" is worth noting as a metaphor of intelligence-community bungling. Some months later, when American Sphinx people thought an opportune time had come to make a threatening shot across the bow of their Russian counterparts, the document was brought to Colonel Gorbatov by Major Diamond, who sat in silence on the other side of the Colonel's desk and awaited his reaction to this damning proof of active espionage.

The Colonel glanced over the pages with operatic indifference, then he unhooked his round metal-rimmed glasses from each ear and polished them between thumb and finger with excruciating care before threading the temples on again. With the bottom of his spoon, he crushed the undissolved lump of sugar in his teacup, drank off the tea in one long sip, then replaced the cup exactly in the center of the saucer.

"So?" he said lazily.

And that was all there was to that. The threatening gesture had been made and ignored, and it had not the slightest effect on the covert operation of the two powers in Japan.

For Nicholai the last hours of the interrogation dissolved into confusing but not unpleasant dreams. His nervous system was so shattered by the various drugs that it functioned only minimally, and his mind had recoiled into itself. He dozed from level of unreality to level of unreality, and soon he found himself walking along the banks of the Kajikawa beneath a snowfall of blossoms. Beside him, but far enough away so that General Kishikawa might have walked between them, had he been there, was a young girl. Though he had never met her, he knew she was the General's daughter. The girl was talking to him about how she would marry one day and have a son. And quite conversationally, the girl mentioned that both she and the son would die, incinerated in the firebombing of Tokyo. Once she had mentioned this, it was logical that she should become Mariko, who had died at Hiroshima. Nicholai was delighted to see her again, and so they played a practice game of Gō, she using black cherry petals for stones, he using white. Nicholai then became one of the stones, and from his microscopic position on the board, he looked around at the enemy stone forming thicker and thicker walls of containment. He tried to form defensive "eyes," but all of them turned out to be false, so he fled, rushing along the yellow surface of the board, the black lines blurring past him as he gathered momentum, until he shot off the edge of the board into thick darkness that dissolved into his cell . . .

. . . Where he opened his eyes.

It was freshly painted gray, and there were no windows. The overhead light was so painfully bright that he squinted to keep his vision from smearing.

Nicholai lived in solitary confinement in that cell for three years.

The transition from the nightmare of interrogation to the years of solitary existence under the burden of "silent treatment" was not abrupt. Daily at first, then less often, Nicholai was visited by the same fussy, distracted Japanese prison doctor who had confirmed the General's death. The treatments consisted only of prophylactic dressings with no cosmetic efforts to close cuts or remove crushed bone and cartilage. Throughout each session the doctor repeatedly shook his head and sucked his teeth and muttered to himself, as though he disapproved of him for participating in this senseless violence.

The Japanese guards had been ordered to deal with the prisoner in absolute silence, but during the first days it was necessary that they instruct him in the rudiments of routine and behavior. When they spoke to him they used the brusque verb forms and a harsh staccato tone that implied no personal antipathy, only recognition of the social gulf between prisoner and master. Once routine was established, they stopped speaking to him, and for the greater part of three years he heard no other human voice than his own, save for one half hour each three months when he was visited by a minor prison official who was responsible for the social and psychological welfare of the inmates.

Almost a month passed before the last effects of the drugs leached from his mind and nerves, and only then could he dare to relax his guard against those unexpected plunges into waking nightmares of space/time distortion that would grip him suddenly and rush him toward madness, leaving him panting and sweating in the corner of his cell, drained of energy and frightened lest the damage to his mind be permanent.

There were no inquiries into the disappearance of Hel, Nicholai Alexandrovitch (TA/737804). There were no efforts to free him, or to hasten his trial. He was a citizen of no nation; he had no papers; no consulate official came forward to defend his civil rights.

The only faint ripple on the surface of routine caused by Nicholai Hel's disappearance was a brief visit to the San Shin Building some weeks later by Mrs. Shimura and Mr. Watanabe, who had spent nights of whispered conversation, screwing up their courage to make this hopeless gesture on behalf of their benefactor. Fobbed off on a minor official, they made their inquiries in hushed, rapid words and with every manifestation of diffident humility. Mrs. Shimura did all of the talking, Mr. Watanabe only bowing and keeping his eyes down in the face of the incalculable power of the Occupation Forces and their inscrutable ways. They knew that by coming to the den of the Americans they were exposing themselves to the danger of losing their home and the little security Nicholai had provided, but their sense of honor and fairness dictated that they run this risk.

The only effect of this tentative and frightened inquiry was a visit to the Asakusa house by a team of military police searching for evidence of Nicholai's wrongdoing. In the course of this search, the officer in charge appropriated as material to the investigation Nicholai's small collection of prints by Kiyonobu and Sharaku, which he had purchased when he could afford them, feeling distressed that the owners were forced by the economic and moral anarchy of the Occupation to relinquish these national treasures, and eager to do what little he could to keep them out of the hands of the barbarians.

As it turned out, these prints had a minor influence on the downward path of egalitarian American art. They were sent home by the confiscating officer, whose twilight child promptly filled in the open spaces with Crayola, so ingeniously managing to stay within the lines that the doting mother was convinced anew of her boy's creative potential and directed its education toward art. This gifted youngster eventually became a leader in the Pop Art movement because of the mechanical precision of his reproductions of tinned foods.

Throughout the three years of confinement, Nicholai was technically awaiting trial for espionage and murder, but no legal proceedings were ever instigated; he was never tried or sentenced, and for this reason he lacked access to even the spartan privileges enjoyed by the ordinary prisoner. The Japanese administrators of Sugamo Prison were under the thrall of the Occupation, and they held Nicholai in close confinement because they were ordered to, despite the fact that he was an embarrassing exception to their rigid organizational pattern. He was the only inmate who was not a Japanese citizen, the only one who had never been sentenced, and the only one being held in solitary confinement with no record of misbehavior in prison. He would have been a troublesome administrative anomaly, had not those in charge treated him as institutional people treat all manifestations of disturbing individuality: they ignored him.

Once he was no longer tormented by unexpected returns of drug panic, Nicholai began to accommodate himself to the routines and chronological articulations of solitary life. His cell was a windowless six-foot cube of gray cement with one overhead light recessed into the ceiling and covered by thick shatterproof glass. The light was on twenty-four hours a day. At first Nicholai hated the constant glare that denied him retreat into the privacy of darkness and made sleeping fitful and thin. But when, three times in the course of his confinement, the light burned out and he had to live in total dark until the guard noticed it, he realized that he had become so accustomed to constant light that he was frightened by the weight of absolute dark closing in around him. These three visits by a trustee prisoner to replace the light bulb under the close surveillance of a guard were the only events outside the established and predictable routine of Nicholai's life, save for one brief power failure that occurred in the middle of the night during his second year. The sudden darkness woke

176

Nicholai from his sleep, and he sat on the edge of his metal bunk, staring into the black, until the light came back on, and he could return to sleep.

Other than the light, only three features characterized the freshly painted gray cube in which Nicholai lived: the bed, the door, the toilet. The bed was a narrow tray of steel secured to the wall, its two front legs sunken into the cement of the floor. For reasons of hygiene, the bunk was off the floor in the Western style, but only by eight inches. For reasons of security, and to deny materials that might be used to commit suicide, the bed had neither boards nor wire mesh, only the flat shelf of metal on which there were two quilted pads for warmth and comfort. This bed was opposite the door, which was the most intricate feature of the cell. It was of heavy steel and opened out on silent, well-greased hinges, and it fit into its sill so exactly that the air in the cell was compressed when the door was closed and the prisoner felt some temporary discomfort in his eardrums. Let into the door was an observation window of thick wire-reinforced glass through which guards routinely monitored the actions of the prisoner. At the base of the door was a riveted steel panel that hinged from the bottom for passing in food. The third feature of the cell was a tiled depression that was the squat toilet. With Japanese nicety of concern for dignity, this was in the corner on the same wall as the door, so the inmate could attend to his physical needs out of range of observation. Directly above this convenience was a ventilation pipe three inches in diameter set flush into the cement ceiling.

Within the strict context of solitary confinement, Nicholai's life was crowded with events that punctuated and measured his time. Twice a day, morning and evening, he received food through the hinged inner door, and in the mornings there was also a pail of water and a small bar of gritty soap that made a thin, greasy lather. Every day, he bathed from head to foot, splashing up water with cupped hands to rinse himself, drying himself off with his rough padded shirt, then using what was left of the water to rinse down the toilet.

His diet was minimal but healthy: unpolished rice, a stew of vegetables and fish, and thin tepid tea. The vegetables varied slightly with the seasons and were always crisp enough not to have had the value cooked out of them. His food was served on a compartmented metal tray with one set of throwaway wooden chopsticks joined at the base. When the small door opened, the trustee always waited until the prisoner had passed out his soiled tray together with the used chopsticks and paper wrapper (even this had to be accounted for) before he would pass in the new meal.

Twice a week, at midday, the cell door was opened, and a guard beckoned him out. Since the guards were prohibited from speaking to him, all communications were carried out in uneconomical and sometimes comic mime. He followed the guard to the end of the corridor, where a steel door was opened (it always groaned on its hinges), and he was permitted to step out into the exercise area, a narrow alley between two featureless buildings, both ends of which were blocked off by high brick walls, where he could walk alone for twenty minutes with a rectangle of open sky above him and fresh air to breathe. He knew that he was under the constant surveillance of guards in the tower at the end of the lane, but their glass windows always reflected the sky, and he could not see them, so the illusion of being alone and almost free was maintained. Except for two times when he was sick with fever, he never declined to take his twenty minutes in the open air, even during rain or snow; and after the first month, he always used this time to run as hard as he could, up and down the short alley, stretching his muscles and burning off as much as he could of the energy that seethed within him.

By the end of the first month, when the lingering effects of the drugs had worn off, Nicholai made a decision for survival, part of the impulse for which came from bone-deep stubbornness and part from sustaining thoughts of vengeance. He always ate every morsel of food, and twice a day, after each meal, he exercised vigorously in his cell, developing routines that kept every muscle in his wiry body taut and quick. After each exercise period, he would sit in lotus in the corner of his cell and concentrate on the pulse of blood in his temples until he achieved the peace of middle-density meditation which, although it was a pallid substitute for

178

the lost soul-rest of mystic transportation, was sufficient to keep his mind calm and dry, unspoiled by despair and self-pity. He trained himself never to think of the future, but to assume there would be one, because the alternative would lead to destructive despair.

After several weeks, he decided to keep mental track of the days as a gesture of confidence that someday he would get out and rejoin his life. He arbitrarily decided to call the next day Monday and to assume it was the first day of April. He was wrong by eight days, but he did not discover this for three years.

His solitary life was busy. Two meals, one bath, two exercise periods, and two terms of meditation each day. Twice a week, the pleasure of running up and down the narrow exercise lane. And there were two other bold demarcations of time. Once a month, he was visited by a barber/trustee who shaved him and went over his head with hand-operated clippers that left a half-inch of stubbly hair. This old prisoner obeyed the injunction against speaking, but he winked and grinned constantly to express brotherhood. Also once a month, always two days after the visit of the barber, he would return from his exercise run to find his bedding changed, and the walls and floor of his cell dripping with water laced with disinfectant, the stench of which lasted three and sometimes four days.

One morning, after he had passed six months in silence in that cell, he was startled out of his meditation by the sound of the door being unlocked. His first reaction was to be annoyed, and a little fearful, at this rupture in reliable routine. Later he learned that this visit was not a break in routine, but only the final element in the cycles that measured his life out. Once every six months he was to be visited by an elderly, overworked civil servant whose duty it was to attend to the social and psychological needs of the inmates of this enlightened prison. The old man introduced himself as Mr. Hirata and told Nicholai that they had permission to speak. He sat on the edge of Nicholai's low bed-shelf, placed his overstuffed briefcase beside him, opened it, fumbled within for a fresh questionnaire, and inserted it into the spring clamp of the clipboard on his lap. In an atonic, bored voice, he asked questions about Nicholai's health and well-being, and with every nod of Nicholai's head, he made a check mark beside the appropriate question.

After scanning with the tip of his pen to make sure he had checked off all the required questions, Mr. Hirata looked up with moist, fatigued eyes and asked if Mr. Hel (Heru) had any formal requests or complaints to make.

Nicholai automatically shook his head . . . then he changed his mind. "Yes," he tried to say. But his throat was thick and only a creaking sound came out. It occurred to him suddenly that he had fallen out of the habit of speaking. He cleared his throat and tried again. "Yes, sir. I would like books, paper, brushes, ink."

Mr. Hirata's thick, hooked eyebrows arched, and he cast his eyes to the side as he sucked in a great breath between his teeth. Clearly, the request was extravagant. It would be very difficult. It would make trouble. But he dutifully registered the request in the space provided for that purpose.

Nicholai was surprised to realize how desperately he wanted the books and paper, although he knew that he was making the error of hoping for something and risking disappointment, thus damaging the fine balance of his twilight existence in which desire had been submerged and hope diminished to the size of expectation. He plunged ahead recklessly. "It is my only chance, sir."

"So? Only chance?"

"Yes, sir. I have nothing . . ." Nicholai growled and cleared his throat again. Speaking was so difficult! "I have nothing to occupy my mind. And I believe I am going mad."

"So?"

"I have found myself thinking often of suicide."

"Ah." Mr. Hirata frowned deeply and sucked in his breath. Why must there always be problems such as these? Problems for which there are no clear instructions in the manual of regulations? "I shall report your request, Mr. Heru."

From the tone, Nicholai knew that the report would be made without energy, and his request would fall into the bureaucratic abyss. He had noticed that Mr. Hirata's glance fell often upon his battered face, where the scars and swellings of the beatings he had taken were still purplish, and each time the glance had flicked away with discomfort and embarrassment.

Nicholai touched his fingers to his broken eyebrow. "It was not your guards, sir. Most of these wounds came from my interrogation at the hands of the Americans."

"*Most* of them? And the rest?"

Nicholai looked down at the floor and cleared his throat. His voice was raspy and weak, and he needed to be glib and persuasive just now. He promised himself that he would not let his voice fall into disuse again through lack of exercise. "Yes, most. The rest . . . I must confess that I have done some harm to myself. In despair I have run my head against the wall. It was a stupid and shameful thing to do, but with nothing to occupy my mind . . ." He allowed his voice to trail off, and he kept his eyes on the floor.

Mr. Hirata was disturbed as he considered the ramifications of madness and suicide on his career, particularly now when he was only a few years from retirement. He promised he would do what he could, and he left the cell troubled by that most harrowing of torments for civil servants: the need to make an independent decision.

Two days later, upon returning from his twenty minutes of fresh air, Nicholai found a paper-wrapped package at the foot of his iron bed. It contained three old books that smelled of mildew, a fifty-sheet pad of paper, a bottle of Western-style ink, and a cheap but brand-new fountain pen.

When he examined the books, Nicholai was crestfallen. They were useless. Mr. Hirata had gone to a secondhand bookstore and had purchased (out of his own money, to avoid the administrative complexity of a formal requisition for articles that might turn out to be prohibited) the three cheapest books he could find. Having no language but Japanese, and knowing from Hel's record that he read French, Mr. Hirata bought what he assumed were French books from a stack that had once been part of the library of a missionary priest, confiscated by the government during the war. The priest had been Basque, and so were the books. All printed before 1920, one was a description of Basque life written for children and including stiff, touched-up photographs and etchings of rural scenes. Although the book was in French, it had no apparent value to Nicholai. The second book was a slim volume of Basque *dictons,* parables, and folktales written in Basque on the left-hand page, and in French on the right. The third was a French/Basque dictionary compiled in 1898 by a priest from Haute Soule, who attempted, in a turgid and lengthy introduction, to identify scholarship in the Basque language with the virtues of piety and humility.

Nicholai tossed the books aside and squatted in the corner of the cell he reserved for meditation. Having made the error of hoping for something, he paid the penalty of disappointment. He found himself weeping bitterly, and soon chest-racking sobs were escaping from him involuntarily. He moved over to the toilet corner, so that the guards might not see him break down like this. He was surprised and frightened to discover how close to the surface was this terrible despair, despite the fact that he had trained himself to live by taut routine and avoid all thoughts of the past and the future. Worn out at last and empty of tears, he brought himself to middle-density meditation, and when he was calmed, he faced his problem.

Question: Why had he hoped for the books so desperately that he made himself vulnerable to the pains of disappointment? Answer: Without admitting it to himself, he had realized that his intellect, honed through Gō training, had something of the properties of a series-wound motor which, if it bore no load, would run ever faster and faster until it burned itself out. This is why he had diminished his life through rigid routine, and why he passed more time than was necessary in the pleasant vacuum of meditation. He had no one to speak to, and he even avoided thought. To be sure, impressions passed unsummoned through his mind, but they were, for the greater part, surd images lacking the linear logic of worded thought. He had not been conscious of avoiding the use of his mind for fear it would run toward panic and despair in this solitary and silent cell, but that was why he had leapt at the chance to have books and paper, why he had yearned terribly for the company and mental occupation of the books.

And *these* were the books? A children's travelogue; a thin volume of folk wisdom; and a dictionary compiled by a preciously pious priest!

And most of it in Basque, a language Nicholai had barely heard of, the most ancient language of Europe and no more related to any other language in the world than the Basque people, with their peculiar blood-type distribution and cranial formation, are unrelated to any other race.

Nicholai squatted in silence and confronted his problem. There was only one answer: he must somehow use these books. With them, he would teach himself Basque. After all, he had much more than the Rosetta stone here; he had page-by-page translation, and a dictionary. His mind was trained to the abstract crystalline geometry of Gō. He had worked in cryptography. He would construct a Basque grammar. And he would keep his other languages alive too. He would translate the Basque folktales into Russian, English, Japanese, German. In his mind, he could translate them also into his ragged street Chinese, but he could go no further, for he had never learned to write the language.

He stripped the bedding off and made a desk of the iron shelf beside which he knelt as he arranged his books and pen and paper. At first he attempted to hold rein on his excitement, lest they decide to take his treasures back, plunging him into what Saint-Exupéry had called the torture of hope. Indeed, his next exercise period in the narrow lane was a torment, and he returned having steeled himself to find that they had confiscated his books. But when they were still there, he abandoned himself to the joys of mental work.

After his discovery that he had all but lost the use of his voice, he initiated the practice of talking to himself for several hours each day, inventing social situations or recounting aloud the political or intellectual histories of each of the nations whose language he spoke. At first, he was self-conscious about talking to himself, not wanting the guards to think his mind was going. But soon thinking aloud became a habit, and he would mutter to himself throughout the day. From his years in prison came Hel's lifelong characteristic of speaking in a voice so soft it was nearly a whisper and was rendered understandable only by his great precision of pronunciation.

In later years, this precise, half-whispered voice was to have a daunting and chilling effect on the people with whom his bizarre profession brought him in contact. And for those who made the fatal error of acting treacherously against him, the stuff of nightmare was hearing his soft, exact voice speak to them out of the shadows.

The first *dicton* in the book of adages was *"Zahar hitzak, zuhur hitzak,"* which was translated as "Old sayings are wise sayings." His inadequate dictionary provided him only with the word *zahar* meaning old. And the first notes of his amateur little grammar were:

Zuhur = wise.
Basque plural either "ak" or "zak."
Radical for "adages/sayings" is either "hit" or "hitz."
Note: verb "to say/to speak" probably built on this radical.
Note: is possible that parallel structures do not require verb of simple being.

And from this meager beginning Nicholai constructed a grammar of the Basque language word by word, concept by concept, structure by structure. From the first, he forced himself to pronounce the language he was learning, to keep it alive and vital in his mind. Without guidance, he made several errors that were to haunt his spoken Basque forever, much to the amusement of his Basque friends. For instance, he decided that the *h* would be mute, as in French. Also, he had to choose how he would pronounce the Basque *x* from a range of possibilities. It might have been a *z,* or a *sh,* or a *tch,* or a guttural Germanic *ch.* He arbitrarily chose the latter. Wrongly, to his subsequent embarrassment.

His life was now full, even crowded, with events he had to leave before he tired of them. His day began with breakfast and a bath of cold water. After burning off excess physical energy with isometric exercise, he would allow himself a half hour of middle-density meditation. Then the study of Basque occupied him until supper, after which he exercised again until his body was worn and tired. Then another half hour of meditation. Then sleep.

His biweekly runs in the narrow exercise lane were taken out of time for Basque study. And each day, as he ate or exercised, he talked to himself in one of his languages to keep them fresh and available. As he had seven languages, he assigned one day of the week to each, and his personal weekly calendar read: Monday, вторник, lai-bai-sam, jeudi, Freitag, Larunbat, and Nitiyoo-bi.

The most significant event of Nicholai Hel's years in solitary imprisonment was the flowering of his proximity sense. This happened quite without his will and, in its incipient stages, without his conscious recognition. It is assumed by those who study paraperceptual phenomena that the proximity sense was, early in the development of man, as vigorous and common as the five other perceptual tools, but it withered through disuse as man developed away from his prey/hunter existence. Too, the extraphysical nature of this "sixth sense" derived from central cortex energies that are in diametric contradiction to rational reasoning, which style of understanding and arranging experience was ultimately to characterize the man animal. To be sure, certain primitive cultures still maintain rudimentary proximity skills, and even thoroughly acculturated people occasionally receive impulses from the vestigial remnants of their proximity system and find themselves tingling with the awareness that somebody is staring at them from behind, or somebody is thinking of them, or they experience vague, generalized senses of well-being or doom; but these are passing and gossamer sensations that are shrugged away because they are not and cannot be understood within the framework of pedestrian logical comprehension, and because acceptance of them would undermine the comfortable conviction that all phenomena are within the rational spectrum.

Occasionally, and under circumstances only partly understood, the proximity sense will emerge fully developed in a modern man. In many ways, Nicholai Hel was characteristic of those few who have flourishing proximity systems. All of his life had been intensely mental and internal. He had been a mystic and had experienced ecstatic transportation, and therefore was not uncomfortable with the extralogical. Gō had trained his intellect to conceive in terms of liquid permutations, rather than the simple problem/solution grid of Western cultures. Then a shocking event in his life had left him isolated within himself for a protracted period of time. All of these factors are consonant with those characterizing that one person in several million who exist in our time with the additional gift (or burden) of proximity sense.

This primordial perception system developed so slowly and regularly in Nicholai that he was unaware of it for fully a year. His prison existence was measured off in so many short, redundant bits that he had no sense of the passage of time outside the prison walls. He never dwelt upon himself, and he was never bored. In seeming contradiction of physical laws, time is heavy only when it is empty.

His conscious recognition of his gift was occasioned by a visit by Mr. Hirata. Nicholai was working over his books when he lifted his head and said aloud to himself (in German, for it was Friday), "That's odd. Why is Mr. Hirata coming to visit me?" Then he looked at his improvised calendar and realized that, indeed, six months had passed since Mr Hirata's last visit.

Several minutes later, he broke off from his study again to wonder who this stranger with Mr. Hirata was, because the person whose approach he sensed was not one of the regular guards. each of whom had a characteristic forepresence that Nicholai recognized.

Shortly later, the cell door was unlocked, and Mr. Hirata entered, accompanied by a young man who was in training for social work within the prison system, and who diffidently stood apart while the older man ran routinely through his list of questions and meticulously checked off each response on his clipboard sheet.

In response to the final catch-all question, Nicholai requested more paper and ink, and Mr. Hirata pulled in his neck and sucked air between his teeth to indicate the overwhelming difficulty of such a request. But there was something in his attitude that left Nicholai confident that his request would be fulfilled.

When Mr. Hirata was preparing to leave, Nicholai asked him, "Excuse me, sir. Did you pass near my cell about ten minutes ago?"

"Ten minutes ago? No. Why do you ask?"

"You didn't pass near my cell? Well then, did you think about me?"

The two prison officials exchanged glances. Mr. Hirata had informed his apprentice of this prisoner's precarious mental condition bordering on the suicidal. "No," the senior man began, "I don't believe I—ah, a moment! Why yes! Just before entering this wing, I spoke to the young man here about you."

"Ah," Nicholai said. "That explains it, then."

Uneasy glances were exchanged. "Explains what?"

Nicholai realized that it would be both difficult and unkind to introduce something so abstract and ethereal as the proximity sense to a civil service mentality, so he shook his head and said, "Nothing. It's not important."

Mr. Hirata shrugged and departed.

For the rest of that day and all of the next, Nicholai contemplated this ability he had discovered in himself to intercept parasensually the physical proximity and directed concentration of people. During his twenty minutes of exercise in the narrow court beneath a rectangle of stormy sky, he closed his eyes as he walked and tested if he could concentrate on some feature of the walls and know when he had approached it. He discovered that he could and, in fact, that he could spin around with his eyes closed to disorient himself and still concentrate on a crack in the wall or an oddly shaped stone and walk directly to it, then reach out and touch within several inches of it. So this proximity sense worked to some degree with inanimate objects as well. While doing this, he felt a flow of human concentration directed at him, and he knew, although he could not see past the sky-reflecting glass of the guard tower, that his antics were being observed and commented on by the men there. He could distinguish between the qualities of their intercepted concentration and tell that they were two in number, a strong-willed man and a man with weaker will—or who was, perhaps, relatively indifferent to the carryings-on of a crazed inmate.

Back in his cell, he pondered this gift further. How long had he had it? Where did it come from? What were its potential uses? So far as he remembered at first, it had developed during this last year in prison. And so slowly had it formed that he couldn't recall its coming. For some time now he had known, without thinking anything of it, when the guards were approaching his cell, and whether it was the short one with the wall eyes, or the Polynesian-looking one who probably had Ainu blood. And he had known which of the trustees was bringing his breakfast almost immediately upon waking.

But had there been traces of it before prison? Yes. Yes, he realized with dawning memory. There had always been modest, vestigial signals from his proximity system. Even as a child, he had always known immediately upon entering if a house was empty or occupied. Even in silence, he had always known whether his mother had remembered or forgotten some duty or chore for him. He could feel the lingering charge in the air of a recent argument or lovemaking in any room he entered. But he had considered these to be common experiences shared by everyone. To a degree, he was right. Many children, and a few adults, occasionally sense such vibrant impalpables through the remnants of their proximity systems, although they explain them away with such terms as "mood," or "edgyness," or "intuition." The only uncommon thing about Nicholai's contact with his proximity system was its consistency. He had always been sensitive to its messages.

It was during his experiences of caving with his Japanese friends that his paraperceptive gift first manifested itself boldly, although at the time he gave it neither consideration nor name. Under the special conditions of total dark, of concentrated background fear, of extreme physical effort, Nicholai's primitive central cortex powers cut into his sensory circuit. Deep in an unknown labyrinth with his companions, wriggling along a fault with millions of tons of rock inches above his spine, exertion throbbing in his temples, he had only to close his eyes (in order to be rid of the overriding impulse of the sensory system to pour energy out through the eyes, even in total darkness) and he could reach out with his proximity sense and tell, with unverifiable assurance, in which direction lay empty space, and in which heavy rock. His friends at first joked about his "hunches." One night as they sat in bivouac at the entrance of a cave system they had been exploring that day, the sleepy conversation drifted around to Nicholai's uncanny ability to orient himself. One young man put forth the conjecture that, without knowing it, Nicholai was reading subtle echoes from his breathing and scuffling and perhaps smelling differences in the subterranean air, and from these slight but certainly not mystical signals he could make his famous "hunches." Nicholai was willing to accept this explanation; he didn't really care much.

One of the team who was learning English to the end of getting a better job with the Occupation Forces slapped Nicholai on the shoulder and growled, "Clever, these Occidentals, at *orienting* themselves."

And another, a wry boy with a monkey face who was the clown of the group, said that it was not a bit odd that Nicholai should be able to see in the dark. He was, after all, a man of the twilight!

The tone of this statement signaled that it was meant to be a joke, but there was silence around the campfire for some seconds, as they tried to unravel the tortuous and oblique pun that was the common stock of the monkey-faced one's humor. And as it dawned on each in turn, there were groans and supplications to spare them, and one lad threw his cap at the offending wit.*

During the day and a half in his cell devoted to an examination of this proximity sense, Nicholai discovered several things about its nature. In the first place, it was not a simple sense, like hearing or sight. A better analogy might be the sense of touch, that complicated constellation of reactions that includes sensitivity to heat and pressure, headache and nausea, the elevator feelings of rising or falling, and balance controls through

* The pun was almost Shakespearean in its sophomoric obliquity. It was formed on the fact that Japanese friends called Nicholai "Nikko" to avoid the awkward *l*. And the most convenient Japanese pronunciation of Hel is *heru*.

189

the liquid of the middle ear—all of which are lumped up rather inadequately under the label of "touch." In the case of the proximity sense, there are two bold classes of sensory reaction, the qualitative and the quantitative; and there are two broad divisions of control, the active and the passive. The quantitative aspect deals largely with simple proximity, the distance and direction of animate and inanimate objects. Nicholai soon learned that the range of his intercepts was quite limited in the case of the inanimate, passive object—a book, a stone, or a man who was daydreaming. The presence of such an object could be passively sensed at no more than four or five meters, after which the signals were too weak to be felt. If, however, Nicholai concentrated on the object and built a bridge of force, the effective distance could be roughly doubled. And if the object was a man (or in some cases, an animal) who was thinking about Nicholai and sending out his own force bridge, the distance could be doubled again. The second aspect of the proximity sense was qualitative, and this was perceptible only in the cases of a human object. Not only could Nicholai read the distance and direction of an emitting source, but he could feel, through the sympathetic vibrations of his own emotions, the quality of emissions: friendly, antagonistic, threatening, loving, puzzled, angry, lustful. As the entire system was generated by the central cortex, the more primitive emotions were transmitted with greatest distinction: fear, hate, lust.

Having discovered these sketchy facts about his gifts, Nicholai turned his mind away from them and applied himself again to his studies and to the task of keeping his languages fresh. He recognized that, so long as he was in prison, the gifts could serve little purpose beyond that of a kind of parlor game. He had no way to foresee that, in later years, his highly developed proximity sense would not only assist him in earning worldwide reputation as a foremost cave explorer, but would serve him as both weapon and armor in his vocation as professional exterminator of international terrorists.

PART TWO

Sabaki

Washington

Mr. Diamond glanced up from the rear-projected roll down and spoke to the First Assistant. "Okay, break off here and jump ahead on the time line. Give us a light scan of his counterterrorist activities from the time he left prison to the present."

"Yes, sir. It will take just a minute to reset."

With the help of Fat Boy and the sensitive manipulations of the First Assistant, Diamond had introduced his guests to the broad facts of Nicholai Hel's life up to the middle of his term of imprisonment, occasionally providing a bit of amplification or background detail from his own memory. It had taken only twenty-two minutes to share this information with them because Fat Boy was limited to recorded incidents and facts; motives, passions, and ideals being alien to its vernacular.

Throughout the twenty-two minutes, Darryl Starr had slouched in his white plastic chair, yearning for a cigar, but not daring to light up. He assumed glumly that the details of this gook-lover's life were being inflicted on him as a kind of punishment for screwing up the Rome hit by letting the girl get away. In an effort to save face, he had assumed an attitude of bored resignation, sucking at his teeth and occasionally relieving himself of a fluttering sigh. But something disturbed him more than being punished like a recalcitrant schoolboy. He sen ed that Diamond's interest in Nicholaï Hel went beyond professionalism. There was something personal in it, and Starr's years of experience in the trenches of CIA operations made him wary of contaminating the job at hand with personal feelings.

As became the nephew of an important man and a CIA trainee-in-terror, the PLO goatherd at first adopted an expression of strictest attention to the information rear-projected on the glass conference table, but soon his concentration strayed to the taut pink skin of Miss

Swivven's calves, at which he grinned occasionally in his version of seductive gallantry.

The Deputy had responded to each bit of information with a curt nod of his head meant to create the impression that the CIA was current with all this information, and that he was merely ticking it off mentally. In fact, CIA did not have access to Fat Boy, although the Mother Company's biographic computer system had long ago consumed and digested everything in the tape banks of CIA and NSA.

For his part, Mr. Able had maintained a facade of thin boredom and marginal politeness, although he had been intrigued by certain episodes in Hel's biography, particularly those that revealed mysticism and the rare gift of proximity sense, for this refined man's tastes ran to the occult and exotic, which appetites were manifest in his sexual ambiguities.

A muted bell rang in the adjoining machine room, and Miss Swivven rose to collect the telephotos of Nicholai Hel that Mr. Diamond had requested. There was silence in the conference room for a minute, save for the hum and click of the First Assistant's console, where he was probing Fat Boy's international memory banks and recording certain fragments in his own short-term storage unit. Mr. Diamond lighted a cigarette (he permitted himself four a day) and turned his chair to look out on the spotlighted Washington Monument beyond the window, as he tapped his lips meditatively with his knuckle.

Mr. Able sighed aloud, straightened the crease of one trouser leg elegantly, and glanced at his watch. "I do hope this isn't going to take much longer. I have plans for this evening." Visions of that senator's Ganymede son had been in and out of his mind all evening.

"Ah," Diamond said, "here we are." He held out his hand for the photographs Miss Swivven was bringing from the machine room and leafed through them quickly. "They're in chronological order. This first is a blowup of his identification picture taken when he started working for Sphinx/FE Cryptography."

He passed it on to Mr. Able, who examined the photograph, grainy with excessive enlargement. "Interesting face. Haughty. Fine. Stern."

194

He pushed the picture across to the Deputy, who glanced at it briefly as though he were already familiar with it, then gave it to Darryl Starr.

"Shee-it," Starr exclaimed. "He looks like a kid! Fifteen-sixteen years old!"

"His appearance is misleading," Diamond said. "At the time this picture was taken he could have been as old as twenty-three. The youthfulness is a family trait. At this moment, Hel is somewhere between fifty and fifty-three, but I have been told that he looks like a man in his midthirties."

The Palestinian goatherd reached for the photograph, but it was passed back to Mr. Able, who looked at it again and said, "What's wrong with the eyes? They look odd. Artificial."

Even in black and white, the eyes had an unnatural transparency, as though they were underexposed.

"Yes," Diamond said, "his eyes are strange. They're a peculiar bright green, like the color of antique bottles. It's his most salient recognition feature."

Mr. Able looked obliquely at Diamond. "Have you met this man personally?"

"I . . . I have been interested in him for years," Diamond said evasively, as he passed along the second photograph.

Mr. Able winced as he looked at the picture. It would have been impossible to recognize this as the same man. The nose had been broken and was pushed to the left. There was a high ridge of scar tissue along the right cheek, and another diagonally across the forehead, bisecting the eyebrow. The lower lip had been thickened and split, and there was a puffy knob below the left cheekbone. The eyes were closed, and the face at rest.

Mr. Able pushed it over to the Deputy gingerly, as though he did not want to touch it.

The Palestinian held out his hand, but the picture was passed on to Starr. "Shit-o-dear! Looks like he went to Fistcity against a freight train!"

"What you see there," Diamond explained, "is the effect of a vigorous interrogation by Army Intelligence. The picture was taken some three years after the beating, while the subject was anesthetized in preparation

195

for plastic surgery. And here he is a week after the operation." Diamond slid the next picture along the conference table.

The face was still a little puffy in result of recent surgery, but all signs of the disfigurement were erased, and a general tightening-up had even removed the faint lines and marks of age.

"And how old was he at this time?" Mr. Able asked.

"Between twenty-four and twenty-eight."

"Amazing. He looks younger than in the first photograph."

The Palestinian tried to turn his head upside down to see the picture as it passed by him.

"These are blowups of passport photos. The Costa Rican one dates from shortly after his plastic surgery, and the French one the year after that. We also believe he has an Albanian passport, but we have no copy of it."

Mr. Able quickly shuffled through the passport photos which, true to their kind, were overlit and of poor quality. One feature caught his attention, and he turned back to the French picture. "Are you sure this is the same man?"

Diamond took the picture back and glanced at it. "Yes, this is Hel."

"But the eyes—"

"I know what you mean. Because the peculiar color of his eyes would blow any disguise, he has several pairs of noncorrective contact lenses that are clear in the center but colored in the iris."

"So he can have whatever color eyes he wants to have. Interesting."

"Oh yes. Hel runs to the ingenious."

The OPEC man smiled. "That's the second time I have detected a hint of admiration in your voice."

Diamond looked at him coldly. "You're mistaken."

"Am I? I see. Are these the most recent pictures you have of the ingenious—but not admired—Mr. Hel?"

Diamond took up the remaining sheaf of photographs and tossed them onto the conference table. "Sure. We have plenty. And they're typical examples of CIA efficiency."

The Deputy's eyebrows arched in martyred resignation.

Mr. Able leafed through the pictures with a puzzled frown, then pushed them toward Starr.

The Palestinian leapt up and slapped his hand down on the stack, then grinned sheepishly as everyone glared at his surprisingly rude gesture. He pulled the photographs over to him and examined them carefully.

"I don't understand," he admitted. "What is this?"

In each of the pictures, the central figure was blurred. They had been taken in a variety of settings—cafés, city streets, the seashore, the bleachers of a jai-alai match, an airport terminal—and all had the image compression characteristic of a telephoto lens; but in not one of them was it possible to recognize the man being photographed, for he had suddenly moved at the instant of the shutter click.

"This really is something I do not understand," the goatherd confessed, as though that were remarkable. "It is something that my comprehension does not . . . comprehend."

"It appears," Diamond explained, "that Hel cannot be photographed unless he wants to be, although there's reason to believe he's indifferent about CIA's efforts to keep track of him and record his actions."

"Then why does he spoil each photograph?" Mr. Able asked.

"By accident. It has to do with this proximity sense of his. He can feel concentration being focused on him. Evidently the feeling of being tracked by a camera lens is identical with that of being sighted through the scope of a rifle, and the moment of releasing the shutter feels just like that of squeezing a trigger."

"So he ducks at the instant the picture is being taken," Mr. Able realized. "Amazing. Truly amazing."

"Is that admiration I detect?" Diamond asked archly.

Mr Able smiled and tipped his head, granting the touch. "One thing I must ask. The Major who figured in the rather brutal interrogation of Hel was named Diamond. I am aware, of course, of the penchant of your people for identifying themselves with precious stones and metals—the mercantile world is richly ornamented with Pearls and Rubys and Golds—but never-

197

theless the coincidence of names here makes me uncomfortable. Coincidence, after all, is Fate's major weapon."

Diamond tapped the edges of the photographs on his desk to align them and set them aside, saying offhandedly, "The Major Diamond in question was my brother."

"I see," Mr. Able said.

Darryl Starr glanced uneasily toward Diamond, his worries about personal involvement confirmed.

"Sir?" the First Assistant said. "I'm ready with the printout of Hel's counterterrorist activities."

"All right. Bring it up on the table. Just surface stuff. No details. I only want to give these gentlemen a feeling for what we're facing."

Although Diamond had requested a shallow probe of Hel's known counterterrorist activities, the first outline to appear on the conference table was so brief that Diamond felt called upon to fill in. "Hel's first operation was not, strictly speaking, counterterrorist. As you see, it was a hit on the leader of a Soviet Trade Commission to Peking, not long after the Chinese communists had firmed up their control over that country. The operation was so inside and covert that most of the tapes were degaussed by CIA before the Mother Company began requiring them to give dupes of everything to Fat Boy. In bold, it went like this: the American intelligence community was worried about a Soviet/Chinese coalition, despite the fact that there were many grounds for dispute between them—matters of boundaries, ideology, unequal industrial development, racial mistrust. The Think Tank boys came up with a plan to exploit their underlying differences and break up any developing union. They proposed to send an agent into Peking to kill the head of the Soviet commission and plant incriminating directives from Moscow. The Chinese would think the Russians had sacrificed one of their own to create an incident as an excuse for breaking off the negotiations. The Soviets, knowing better, would think the Chinese had made the hit for the same reason. And when the Chinese brought out the incriminating directives as evidence of Russian duplicity, the Soviets would claim that Peking had manufactured the documents to justify their cowardly attack. The Chinese, knowing perfectly well that this was not the case, would be confirmed in their belief that the whole thing was a Russian plot.

"That the plan worked is proved by the fact that Sino-Soviet relations never did take firm root and are today characterized by mistrust and hostility, and Western bloc powers are able to play one of them off against the other and prevent what would be an overwhelming alliance.

"The little stumbling block to the ingenious plot of the Think Tank boys was finding an agent who knew enough Chinese to move through that country under cover, who could pass for a Russian when the necessity arose, and who was willing to take on a job that had slight chance of success, and almost no chance for escape after the hit was made. The operative had to be brilliant, multilingual, a trained killer, and desperate enough to accept an assignment that offered not one chance in a hundred of survival.

"CIA ran a key-way sort, and they found only one person among those under their control who fit the description . . ."

Japan

It was early autumn, the fourth autumn Hel had passed in his cell in Sugamo Prison. He knelt on the floor before his desk/bed, lost in an elusive problem of Basque grammar, when he felt a tingling at the roots of the hair on the nape of his neck. He lifted his head and concentrated on the projections he was intercepting. This person's approaching aura was alien to him. There were sounds at the door, and it swung open. A smiling guard with a triangular scar on his forehead entered, one Nicholai had never seen or felt before

The guard cleared his throat. "Come with me, please."

Hel frowned. The *O . . . nasai* form? Respect language from a guard to a prisoner? He carefully arranged his notes and closed the book before rising. He instructed himself to be calm and careful. There could be hope in this unprecedented rupture of routine . . . or danger. He rose and preceded the guard out of the cell.

"Mr. Hel? Delighted to make your acquaintance." The polished young man rose to shake Hel's hand as he entered the visitors' room. The contrast between his close-fitting Ivy League suit and narrow tie and Hel's crumpled gray prison uniform was no greater than that between their physiques and temperaments. The hearty CIA agent was robust and athletic, capable of the first-naming and knee-jerk congeniality that marks the American salesman. Hel, slim and wiry, was reserved and distant. The agent, who was noted for winning immediate confidences, was a creature of words and reason. Hel was a creature of meaning and undertone. It was the battering man and the rapier.

The agent nodded permission for the guard to leave. Hel sat on the edge of his chair, having had nothing but his steel cot to sit on for three years, and having lost the facility for sitting back and relaxing. After all that time of not hearing himself addressed in social speech, he found the urbane chat of the agent not so much disturbing as irrelevant.

"I've asked them to bring up a little tea," the agent said, smiling with a gruff shagginess of personality that he had always found so effective in public relations. "One thing you've got to hand to these Japanese, they make a good cup of tea—what my limey friends call a 'nice cuppa.' " He laughed at his failure to produce a recognizable cockney accent.

Hel watched him without speaking, taking some pleasure in the fact that the American was caught off balance by the battered appearance of his face, at first glancing away uneasily, and subsequently forcing himself to look at it without any show of disgust.

"You're looking pretty fit, Mr. Hel. I had expected that you would show the effects of physical inactivity. Of course, you have one advantage. You don't overeat. Most people overeat, if you want my opinion. The old human body would do better with a lot less food than we give it. We sort of clog up the tubes with chow, don't you agree? Ah, here we are! Here's the tea."

The guard entered with a tray on which there was a thick pot and two handleless Japanese cups. The agent poured clumsily, like a friendly bear, as though gracelessness were proof of virility. Hel accepted the cup, but he did not drink.

"Cheers," the agent said, taking his first sip. He shook his head and laughed. "I guess you don't say 'cheers' when you're drinking tea. What do you say?"

Hel set his cup on the table beside him. "What do you want with me?"

Trained in courses on one-to-one persuasion and small-group management, the agent believed he could sense a cool tone in Hel's attitude, so he followed the rules of his training and flowed with the ambience of the feedback. "I guess you're right. It would be best to get right to the point. Look, Mr. Hel, I've been reviewing your case, and if you ask me, you got a raw deal. That's my opinion anyway."

Hel let his eyes settle on the young man's open, frank face. Controlling impulses to reach out and break

201

it, he lowered his eyes and said, "That is your opinion, is it?"

The agent folded up his grin and put it away. He wouldn't beat around the bush any longer. He would tell the truth. There was an adage he had memorized during his persuasion courses: Don't overlook the truth; properly handled, it can be an effective weapon. But bear in mind that weapons get blunted with overuse.

He leaned forward and spoke in a frank, concerned tone. "I think I can get you out of here, Mr. Hel."

"At what cost to me?"

"Does that matter?"

Hel considered this for a moment. "Yes."

"Okay. We need a job done. You're capable of doing it. We'll pay you with your freedom."

"I have my freedom. You mean you'll pay me with my liberty."

"Whatever."

"What kind of liberty are you offering?"

"What?"

"Liberty to do what?"

"I don't think I follow you there. Liberty, man. Freedom. You can do what you want, go where you want?"

"Oh, I see. You are offering me citizenship and a considerable amount of money as well."

"Well . . . no. What I mean is . . . Look, I'm authorized to offer you your freedom, but no one said anything about money or citizenship."

"Let me be sure I understand you. You are offering me a chance to wander around Japan, vulnerable to arrest at any moment, a citizen of no country, and free to go anywhere and do anything that doesn't cost money. Is that it?"

The agent's discomfort pleased Hel. "Ah . . . I'm only saying that the matter of money and citizenship hadn't been discussed."

"I see." Hel rose. "Why don't you return when you have worked out the details of your proposal."

"Aren't you going to ask about the task we want you to perform?"

"No. I assume it to be maximally difficult. Very

dangerous. Probably involving murder. Otherwise, you wouldn't be here."

"Oh, I don't think I'd call it murder, Mr. Hel. I wouldn't use that word. It's more like . . . like a soldier fighting for his country and killing one of the enemy."

"That's what I said: murder."

"Have it your own way then."

"I shall. Good afternoon."

The agent began to have the impression that he was being handled, while all of his persuasion training had insisted that he do the handling. He fell back upon his natural defense of playing it for the hale good fellow. "Okay, Mr. Hel. I'll have a talk with my superiors and see what I can get for you. I'm on your side in this, you know. Hey, know what? I haven't even introduced myself. Sorry about that."

"Don't bother. I am not interested in who you are."

"All right. But take my advice, Mr. Hel. Don't let this chance get away. Opportunity doesn't knock twice, you know."

"Penetrating observation. Did you make up the epigram?"

"I'll see you tomorrow."

"Very well. And ask the guard to knock on my cell door twice. I wouldn't want to confuse him with opportunity."

Back in CIA Far East Headquarters in the basement of the Dai Ichi Building, Hel's demands were discussed. Citizenship was easy enough. Not American citizenship, of course. That high privilege was reserved for defecting Soviet dancers. But they could arrange citizenship of Panama or Nicaragua or Costa Rica—any of the CIA control areas. It would cost a bit in local baksheesh, but it could be done.

About payment they were more reluctant, not because they had any need to economize within their elastic budget, but a Protestant respect for lucre as a sign of God's grace made them regret seeing it wasted. And wasted it would probably be, as the mathematical likelihood of Hel's returning alive was slim. Another fiscal consideration was the expense they would be put to in transporting Hel to the United States for cosmetic surgery, as he had no chance of getting to Peking with a memorable face like that. Still, they decided at last, they really had no choice. Their key-way sort had delivered only one punch card for a man qualified to do the job.

Okay. Make it Costa Rican citizenship and 100 K.

Next problem . . .

But when they met the next morning in the visitor's room, the American agent discovered that Hel had yet another request to make. He would take the assignment on only if CIA gave him the current addresses of the three men who had interrogated him: the "doctor," the MP sergeant, and Major Diamond.

"Now, wait a minute, Mr. Hel. We can't agree to that sort of thing. CIA takes care of its own. We can't offer them to you on a platter like that. Be reasonable. Let bygones be bygones. What do you say?"

Hel rose and asked that the guard conduct him back to his cell.

The frank-faced young American sighed and shook his head. "All right. Let me call the office for an okay. Okay?"

Washington

". . . and I assume Mr. Hel was successful in his enterprise," Mr. Able said. "For, if he were not, we wouldn't be sitting about here concerning ourselves with him."

"That's correct," Diamond said. "We have no details, but about four months after he was introduced into China through Hong Kong, we got word that he had been picked up by a bush patrol of the Foreign Legion in French Indo-China. He was in pretty bad shape . . . spent a couple of months in a hospital in Saigon . . . then he disappeared from our observation for a period before emerging as a free-lance counterterrorist. We have him associated with a long list of hits against terrorist groups and individuals, usually in the pay of governments through their intelligence agencies." He spoke to the First Assistant. "Let's run through them at a high scan rate."

Superficial details of one extermination action after another flashed up on the surface of the conference table as Nicholai Hel's career from the early fifties to the mid-seventies was laid out by Fat Boy. Occasionally one or another of the men would ask for a freeze, as he questioned Diamond about some detail.

"Jesus H. Christ!" Darryl Starr said at one point. "This guy really works both sides of the street! In the States he's hit both Weathermen and tri-K's; in Belfast he's moved against both parts of the Irish stew; he seems to have worked for just about everybody except the A-rabs, Junta Greeks, the Spanish, and the Argentines. And did you eyeball the weapons used in the hits? Along with the conventional stuff of handguns and nerve-gas pipes, there were such weirdo weapons as a pocket comb, a drinking straw, a folded sheet of paper, a door key, a light bulb . . . This guy'd strangle you with your own skivvies, if you wasn't careful!"

"Yes," Diamond said. "That has to do with his

Naked/Kill training. It has been estimated that, for Nicholai Hel, the average Western room contains just under two hundred lethal weapons."

Starr shook his head and sucked his teeth aloud. "Gettin' rid of a fella like that would be hardern' snapping snot off a fingernail."

Mr. Able paled at the earthy image.

The PLO goatherd shook his head and tished. "I cannot understand these sums so extravagant he receives for his servicing. In my country a man's life can be purchased for what, in dollars, would be two bucks thirty-five cents."

Diamond glanced at him tiredly. "That's a fair price for one of your countrymen. The basic reason governments are willing to pay Hel so much for exterminating terrorists is that terrorism is the most economical means of warfare. Consider the cost of mounting a force capable of protecting every individual in a nation from attack in the street, in his home, in his car. It costs millions of dollars just to search for the victim of a terrorist kidnapping. It's quite a bargain if the government can have the terrorist exterminated for a few hundred thousand, and avoid the antigovernment propaganda of a trial at the same time." Diamond turned to the First Assistant. "What is the average fee Hel gets for a hit?"

The First Assistant posed the simple question to Fat Boy. "Just over quarter of a million, sir. That's in dollars. But it seems he has refused to accept American dollars since 1963."

Mr. Able chuckled. "An astute man. Even if one runs all the way to the bank to change dollars for real money, their plunging value will cost him some fiscal erosion."

"Of course," the First Assistant continued, "that average fee is skewed. You'd get a better idea of his pay if you used the mean."

"Why is that?" the Deputy asked, pleased to have something to say.

"It seems that he occasionally takes on assignments without pay."

"Oh?" Mr. Able said. "That's surprising. Considering his experiences at the hands of the Occupation

Forces and his desire to live in a style appropriate to his tastes and breeding, I would have assumed he worked for the highest bidder."

"Not quite," Diamond corrected. "Since 1967 he has taken on assignments for various Jewish militant groups without pay—some kind of twisted admiration for their struggle against larger forces."

Mr. Able smiled thinly.

"Take another case," Diamond continued. "He has done services without pay for ETA-6, the Basque Nationalist organization. In return, they protect him and his château in the mountains. That protection, by the way, is very effective. We have three known incidents of men going into the mountains to effect retribution for some action of Hel's, and in each case the men have simply disappeared. And every once in a while Hel takes on a job for no other reason than his disgust at the actions of some terrorist group. He did one like that not too long ago for the West German government. Flash that one up, Llewellyn."

The men around the conference table scanned the details of Hel's penetration into a notorious group of German urban terrorists that led to the imprisonment of the man after whom the group was named and the death of the woman.

"He was involved in that?" Mr. Able asked with a slight tone of awe.

"That was one heavy number," Starr admitted. "I shit thee not!"

"Yes, but his highest pay for a single action was in the United States," Diamond said. "And interestingly enough, it was a private individual who footed the bill. Let's have that one, Llewellyn."

"Which one is that, sir?"

"Los Angeles—May of seventy-four."

As the rear-projection came up, Diamond explained, "You'll remember this. Five members of a gang of urban vandals and thieves calling themselves the Symbiotic Maoist Falange were put away in an hour-long firefight in which three hundred fifty police SWAT forces, FBI men, and CIA advisers poured thousands of rounds into the house in which they were holed up."

"What did Hel have to do with that?" Starr asked.

"He had been hired by a certain person to locate the guerrillas and put them away. A plan was worked out in which the police and FBI were to be tipped off, the whole thing timed so they would arrive after the wet work was done, so they could collect the glory . . . and responsibility. Unfortunately for Hel, they arrived half an hour too early, and he was in the house when they surrounded it and opened fire, along with gas- and fire-bombing. He had to break through the floor and hide in the crawl space while the place burned down around him. In the confusion of the last minute, he was able to get out and join the mob of officers. Evidently he was dressed as a SWAT man—flack vest, baseball cap, and all."

"But as I recall," Mr. Able said, "there were reports of firing from within the house during the action."

"That was the released story. Fortunately, no one ever stopped to consider that, although two submachine guns and an arsenal of handguns and shotguns was found in the charred wreckage, not one of the three hundred fifty police (and God knows how many onlookers) was so much as scratched after an hour of firing."

"But it seems to me that I remember seeing a photograph of a brick wall with chips out of it from bullets."

"Sure. When you surround a building with over three hundred gunhappy heavies and open fire, a fair number of slugs are going to pass in one window and out another."

Mr. Able laughed. "You're saying the police and FBI and CIA were firing on themselves?"

Diamond shrugged. "You don't buy geniuses for twenty thousand a year."

The Deputy felt he had to come to the defense of his organization. "I should remind you that CIA was there purely in an advisory capacity. We are prohibited by law from doing domestic wet work."

Everyone looked at him in silence, until Mr. Able broke it with a question for Diamond: "Why did this individual go to the expense of having Mr. Hel do the hit, when the police were only too willing?"

"The police might have taken a prisoner. And that prisoner might have testified in a subsequent trial."

"Ah, yes. I see."

Diamond turned to the First Assistant. "Pick up the scan rate and just skim the rest of Hel's known operations."

In rapid chronological order, sketches of action after action flashed up on the tabletop. San Sebastian, sponsor ETA-6; Berlin, sponsor German government; Cairo, sponsor unknown; Belfast, sponsor IRA; Belfast, sponsor UDA; Belfast, sponsor British government—and on and on. Then the record suddenly stopped.

"He retired two years ago," Diamond explained.

"Well, if he is retired . . ." Mr. Able lifted his palms in a gesture that asked what they were so worried about.

"Unfortunately, Hel has an overdeveloped sense of duty to friends. And Asa Stern was a friend."

"Tell me. Several times this word 'stunt' came up on the printout. I don't understand that."

"It has to do with Hel's system for pricing his services. He calls his actions 'stunts'; and he prices them the same way movie stunt men do, on the basis of two factors: the difficulty of the job, and the danger of failure. For instance, if a hit is hard to accomplish for reasons of narrow access to the mark or difficult penetration into the organization, the price will be higher. But if the consequences of the act are not too heavy because of the incompetence of the organization against which the action is performed, the price is lower (as in the case of the IRA, for instance, or CIA). Or take a reverse case of that: Hel's last stunt before retirement. There was a man in Hong Kong who wanted to get his brother out of Communist China. For someone like Hel, this wasn't too difficult, so you might imagine the fee would be relatively modest. But the price of capture would have been death, so that adjusted the fee upward. See how it goes?"

"How much did he receive for that particular . . . stunt?"

"Oddly enough, nothing—in money. The man who hired him operates a training academy for the most expensive concubines in the world. He buys baby girls from all over the Orient and educates them in tact and

209

social graces. Only about one in fifty develop into beautiful and skillful enough products to enter his exclusive trade. The rest he simply equips with useful occupations and releases at the age of eighteen. In fact, all the girls are free to leave whenever they want, but because they get fifty percent of their yearly fee—between one and two hundred thousand dollars—they usually continue to work for him for ten or so years, then they retire in the prime of life with five hundred thousand or so in the bank. This man had a particularly stellar pupil, a woman of about thirty who went on the market for quarter-of-a-mil per year. In return for getting the brother out, Hel took two years of her service. She lives with him now at his château. Her name is Hana—part Japanese, part Negro, part Cauc. As an interesting sidelight, this training academy passes for a Christian orphanage. The girls wear dark-blue uniforms, and the women who train them wear nuns' habits. The place is called the Orphanage of the Passion."

Starr produced a low whistle. "You're telling me that this squack of Hel's gets a quarter of a million a year? What'd that come to per screw, I wonder?"

"In your case," Diamond said, "about a hundred twenty-five thousand."

The PLO goatherd shook his head. "This Nicholai Hel must be very rich from the point of view of money, eh?"

"Not so rich as you might imagine. In the first place, his 'stunts' are expensive to set up. This is particularly true when he has to neutralize the government of the country in which the stunt takes place. He does this through the information brokerage of a man we have never been able to locate—a man known only as the Gnome. The Gnome collects damaging facts about governments and political figures. Hel buys this information and uses it as blackmail against any effort on the part of the government to hamper his actions. And this information is very expensive. He also spends a lot of money mounting caving expeditions in Belgium, the Alps, and his own mountains. It's a hobby of his and an expensive one. Finally, there's the matter of his château. In the fifteen years since he bought it, he has spent a little over two million in restoring it to its original

210

condition, importing the last of the world's master stonemasons, wood carvers, tile makers, and what not. And the furniture in the place is worth a couple of million more."

"So," Mr. Able said, "he lives in great splendor, this Hel of yours."

"Splendor, I guess. But primitive. The château is completely restored. No electricity, no central heating, nothing modern except an underground telephone line that keeps him informed of the arrival and approach of any strangers."

Mr. Able nodded to himself. "So a man of eighteenth-century breeding has created an eighteenth-century world for himself in splendid isolation in the mountains. How interesting. But I am surprised he did not return to Japan and live in the style he was bred to."

"From what I understand, when he got out of prison and discovered to what degree the traditional ways of life and ethical codes of Japan had been 'perverted' by Americanism, he decided to leave. He has never been back."

"How wise. For him, the Japan of his memory will always remain what it was in gentler, more noble times. Pity he's an enemy. I would like your Mr. Hel."

"Why do you call him *my* Mr. Hel?"

Mr. Able smiled. "Does that irritate you?"

"Any stupidity irritates me. But let's get back to our problem. No, Hel is not as rich as you might imagine. He probably needs money, and that might give us an angle on him. He owns a few thousand acres in Wyoming, apartments in half a dozen world capitals, a mountain lodge in the Pyrenees, but there's less than half a million in his Swiss bank. He still has the expenses of his château and his caving expeditions. Even assuming he sells off the apartments and the Wyoming land, life in his château would be, by his standards, a modest existence."

"A life of . . . what was the word?" Mr. Able asked, smiling faintly to himself at the knowledge he was annoying Diamond.

"I don't know what you mean."

"That Japanese word for things reserved and under-stated?"

"Shibumi!"

"Ah, yes. So even without taking any more 'stunts,' your—I mean, *our* Mr. Hel would be able to live out a life of *shibumi*."

"I wouldn't be so sure," Starr interposed. "Not with nookie at a hundred K a throw!"

"Will you shut up, Starr," Diamond said.

Not quite able to follow what was going on here, the PLO goatherd had risen from the conference table and strayed to the window, where he looked down and watched an ambulance with a flashing dome light thread its way through the partially congealed traffic—as that ambulance did every night at precisely this time. Starr's colorful language had attracted his attention, and he was thumbing through his pocket English/Arabic dictionary, muttering, "Nookie . . . nookie . . ." when suddenly the Washington Monument and the wide avenue of cars vanished, and the window was filled with a blinding light.

The goatherd screamed and threw himself to the floor, covering his head in anticipation of the explosion.

Everyone in the room reacted characteristically. Starr leapt up and whipped out his Magnum. Miss Swivven slumped into a chair. The Deputy covered his face with a sheet of typing paper. Diamond closed his eyes and shook his head at these asses with which he was surrounded. Mr. Able examined his cuticles. And the First Assistant, absorbed in his technological intercourse with Fat Boy, failed to notice that anything had happened.

"Get off the floor, for chrissake," Diamond said. "It's nothing. The street-scene film has broken, that's all."

"Yes, but . . ." the goatherd babbled.

"You came down in the elevator. You must have known you were in the basement."

"Yes, but . . ."

"Did you think you were looking down from the Sixteenth Floor?"

"No, but . . ."

"Miss Swivven, shut the rear projector off and make a note to have it repaired." Diamond turned to Mr. Able. "I had it installed to create a better working environment, to keep the office from feeling shut up in the bowels of the earth."

"And you have been capable of fooling yourself?"

Starr snapped his gun back into its holster and glared at the window, as though to say it had been lucky . . . *this* time.

With ruminantial ambiguity, the goatherd grinned sheepishly as he got to his feet. "Boy-o-boy, that was a good one! I guess the joke was on me!"

Out in the machine room, Miss Swivven threw a switch, and the glaring light in the window went out, leaving a matte white rectangle that had the effect of sealing the room up and reducing its size.

"All right," Diamond said, "now you have some insight into the man we're dealing with. I want to talk a little strategy, and for that I would as soon have you two out of here." He pointed Starr and the PLO goatherd toward the exercise and sun room. "Wait in there until you're called."

Appearing indifferent to his dismissal, Star ambled toward the sun room, followed by the Arab who insisted on explaining again that he guessed the joke had been on him.

When the door closed behind them, Diamond addressed the two men at the conference table, speaking as though the First Assistant were not present, as indeed in many ways he was not.

"Let me lay out what I think we ought to do. First—"

"Just a moment, Mr. Diamond," Mr. Able interrupted. "I am concerned about one thing. Just what is your relationship to Nicholai Hel?"

"How do you mean?"

"Oh, come now! It is evident that you have taken a particular interest in this person. You are familiar with so many details that do not appear in the computer printout."

Diamond shrugged. "After all, he's a mauve-card man; and it's my job to keep current with—"

"Excuse me for interrupting you again, but I am not interested in evasions. You have admitted that the officer in charge of the interrogation of Nicholai Hel was your brother."

Diamond stared at the OPEC troubleshooter for a second. "That's right. Major Diamond was my brother. My older brother."

"You were close to your brother?"

"When our parents died, m' brother took care of me. He supported me while he was working his way through college. Even while he was working his way up through the OSS—a notoriously WASP organization—and later with CIA, he continued to—"

"Do spare us the domestic details. I would be correct to say that you were very close to him?"

Diamond's voice was tight. "Very close."

"All right. Now there is something you passed over rather quickly in your biographic sketch of Nicholai Hel. You mentioned that he required, as a part of his pay for doing the Peking assignment that got him out of prison, the current addresses of the three men involved in beating and torturing him during his interrogation. May I presume he did not want the addresses for the purpose of sending Christmas cards . . . or Hanukkah greetings?"

Diamond's jaw muscles rippled.

"My dear friend, if this affair is as serious as you seem to believe it is, and if you are seeking my assistance in clearing it up, then I must insist upon understanding everything that might bear upon the matter."

Diamond pressed his palms together and hooked the thumbs under his chin. He spoke from behind the fingers, his voice mechanical and atonic. "Approximately one year after Hel showed up in Indo-China, the 'doctor' who had been in charge of administering drugs during the interrogation was found dead in his abortion clinic in Manhattan. The coroner's report described the death as accidental, a freak fall which had resulted in one of the test tubes he was carrying shattering and going through his throat. Two months later, the MP sergeant who had administered the physical aspects of the interrogation and who had been transferred back to the United States died in an automobile accident. He had evidently fallen asleep at the wheel and driven his car off the road and over a cliff. Exactly three months later, Major Diamond—then Lieutenant Colonel Diamond—was on assignment in Bavaria. He had a skiing accident." Diamond paused and tapped his lips with his forefingers.

"Another freak accident, I suppose?" Mr. Able prompted.

"That's right. As best they could tell, he had taken a bad jump. He was found with a ski pole through his chest."

"Hm-m-m," Mr. Able said after a pause. "So this is the way CIA protects its own? It must be quite a satisfaction for you to have under your control the organization that gave away your brother's life as part of a fee."

Diamond looked across at the Deputy. "Yes. It has been a satisfaction."

The Deputy cleared his throat. "Actually, I didn't enter the Company until the spring of—"

"Tell me something," Mr. Able said. "Why haven't you taken retributive action against Hel before now?"

"I did once. And I will again. I have time."

"You did once? When was— Ah! Of course! Those policemen who surrounded that house in Los Angeles and opened fire half an hour before schedule! That was your doing?"

Diamond's nod had the quality of a bow to applause.

"So there is some revenge motive in all of this for you, it would seem."

"I'm acting in the best interest of the Mother Company. I have a message from the Chairman telling me that failure in this would be unacceptable. If Hel has to be terminated to assure the success of the Septembrists skyjacking then, yes, I shall take some personal satisfaction in that. It will be a life for a life, not, as in his case, three murders for one beating!"

"I doubt that he considered them murders. More likely he thought of them as executions. And if my guess is right, it was not the pain of the beatings that he was avenging."

"What, then?"

"The *indignity* of them. That's something you would have no way to understand."

Diamond puffed out a short laugh. "You really imagine you know Hel better than I do?"

"In some ways, yes—despite your years of studying him and his actions. You see, he and I—accepting our cultural differences—are of the same caste. You will never see this Hel clearly, squinting as you do across

215

the indefinite but impassable barrier of breeding—a great gulf fixed, as the Qoran or one of those books terms it. But let us not descend to personalities. Presumably you sent those two plebes from the room for some other reason than a desire to improve the quality of the company."

Diamond was stiffly silent for a moment, then he drew a short breath and said, "I have decided to pay a visit to Hel's place in the Basque country."

"This will be the first time you have met him face to face?"

"Yes."

"And you have considered the possibility that it may be more difficult to get out of those mountains than to get in?"

"Yes. But I believe I shall be able to convince Mr. Hel of the foolishness of attempting to assist Miss Stern. In the first place, there is no logical reason why he should take on this assignment for a misguided middle-class girl he doesn't even know. Hel has nothing but disgust for amateurs of all kinds, including amateurs in terror. Miss Stern may see herself as a noble soldier in the service of all that is right in the world, but I assure you that Hel will view her as a pain in the ass."

Mr. Able tilted his head in doubt. "Even assuming that Mr. Hel does look upon Miss Stern as a proctological nuisance (whether or not he reflects on the happy pun), there remains the fact that Hel was a friend of the late Asa Stern, and you have yourself said that he has strong impulses toward loyalty to friends."

"True. But there are fiscal pressures we can bring to bear. We know that he retired as soon as he had accumulated enough money to live out his life in comfort. Mounting a 'stunt' against our PLO friends would be a costly matter. It's probable that Hel is relying on the eventual sale of his Wyoming land for financial security. Within two hours, that land will no longer be his. All records of his having bought it will disappear and be replaced by proof that the land is held by the Mother Company." Diamond smiled. "By way of fringe benefit, there happens to be a little coal on that land that can be profitably stripped off. To complete his financial discomfort, two simple cables to Switzerland

216

from the Chairman will cause Hel's money held in a Swiss bank to vanish."

"And I imagine the money will turn up in Mother Company assets?"

"Part of it. The rest will be held by the banks as transactional costs. The Swiss are nothing if not frugal. It's a Calvinist principle that there is an entrance fee to heaven, to keep the riff-raff out. It is my intention to perform these fiscally punitive actions, regardless of Hel's decision to take or reject Miss Stern's job."

"A gesture in memory of your brother?"

"You may think of it that way, if you like. But it will also serve as a financial interdiction to Hel's being a nuisance to the Mother Company and to the nations whose interest you represent."

"What if money pressures alone are not sufficient to persuade him?"

"Naturally, I have a secondary line of action to address that contingency. The Mother Company will bring pressure upon the British government to spare no effort in protecting the Black Septembrists involved in the Munich Olympics debacle. It will be their task to make sure they are unmolested in their skyjacking of the Montreal plane. This will not require as much pressure as you might imagine because, now that the North Sea oil fields are producing, England's economic interests are more closely allied to those of OPEC than to those of the West."

Mr. Able smiled. "Frankly, I cannot imagine the MI-5 and MI-6 lads being an effective deterrent to Mr. Hel. The greater part of their energies are applied to writing imaginative memoirs of their daring exploits during the Second World War."

"True. But they will have a certain nuisance value. Also, we shall have the services of the French internal police to help us contain Hel within that country. And we are moving on another front. It is inconceivable that Hel would try to enter England to put the Septembrists away without first neutralizing the British police. I told you that he does this by buying blackmail material from an information broker known as the Gnome. For years the Gnome has evaded international efforts to locate and render him dysfunctional. Through the good services of Her communications subsidiaries, the Mother Company is beginning to close in on this man. We know that he lives somewhere near the city of Bayonne, and we're actively involved in tightening down on him. If we get to him before Hel does, we can interdict the use of blackmail leverage against the British police."

Mr. Able smiled. "You have a fertile mind, Mr. Diamond—when personal revenge is involved." Mr. Able turned suddenly to the Deputy. "Do you have something to contribute?"

Startled, the Deputy said, "Pardon me? What?"

"Never mind." Mr. Able glanced again at his watch. "Let's do get on with it. I assume you didn't ask me here so you could parade before me your array of tactics and interdictions. Obviously, you need my help in the unlikely event that all the machines you have set into motion fail, and Hel manages to put the Septembrists away."

"Exactly. And it is because this is a bit delicate that I wanted those two buffoons out of the room while we talked about it. I accept the fact that the nations you represent are committed to protecting the PLO, and therefore the Mother Company is, and therefore CIA is. But let's be frank among ourselves. We would all be happier if the Palestinian issue (and the Palestinians with it) would simply disappear. They're a nasty, ill-disciplined, vicious lot whom history happened to put in the position of a symbol of Arab unity. All right so far?"

Mr. Able waved away the obvious with his hand.

"Very well. Let's consider our posture, should everything fail and Hel manage to exterminate the Septembrists. All that would really concern us would be assuring the PLO that we had acted vigorously on its behalf. Considering their barbaric nature, I think they would be mollified if we took vengeance on their behalf by destroying Nicholai Hel and everything he possesses."

"Sowing the land with salt?" Mr. Able mused.

"Just so."

Mr. Able was silent for a time, his eyes lowered as he tickled his upper lip with his forefinger. "Yes, I believe we can rely on the PLO's sophomoric mentality

218

to that degree. They would accept a major act of revenge—provided it was lurid enough—as proof that we are devoted to their interests." He smiled to himself. "And do not imagine that it has escaped my notice that such an eventuality would allow you to slay two birds with one stone. You would solve the tactical problem at hand, and avenge your brother at one stroke. Is it possible that you would rather see all your devices fail and Nicholai Hel somehow break through and hit the Septembrists, freeing you to devise and execute a maximal punishment for him?"

"I shall do everything in my power to prevent the hit in the first instance. That would be best for the Mother Company, and Her interests take priority over my personal feelings." Diamond glanced toward the First Assistant. It was most likely that he reported directly to the Chairman on Diamond's devotion to the Company.

"That's it then," Mr. Able said, rising from the conference table. "If there is not further need for me, I shall return to the social event this business interrupted."

Diamond rang for Miss Swivven to escort Mr. Able out of the building.

The Deputy rose and cleared his throat. "I don't assume you'll be needing me?"

"Have I ever? But I'll expect you to keep yourself available to execute instructions. You may go."

Diamond directed the First Assistant to roll back the information on Nicholai Hel and be prepared to project it at a slow enough rate to accommodate the literacy of Starr and the PLO goatherd, who were returning from the exercise room, the Arab rubbing his inflamed eyes as he put his English/Arabic dictionary back into his pocket. "Goodness my gracious, Mr. Diamond! It is most difficult to read in that room. The lights along the walls are so bright!"

"I want you two to sit here and learn everything you're capable of about Nicholai Hel. I don't care if it takes all night. I've decided to bring you along when I visit this man—not because you'll be of any use, but because you're responsible for this screw-up, and I'm going to make you see it out to the end."

"That's mighty white of you," Starr muttered.

Diamond spoke to Miss Swivven as she reentered from the elevator. "Note the following. One: Hel's Wyoming land, terminate. Two: Swiss money, terminate. Three: The Gnome, intensify search for. Four: MI-5 and MI-6, alert and instruct. All right, Llewellyn, start the roll-down for our blundering friends here. And you two had better pray that Nicholai Hel has not already gone underground."

Gouffre Porte-de-Larrau

At that moment, Nicholai Hel was 393 meters underground, revolving slowly on the end of a cable half a centimeter thick. Seventy-five meters below him, invisible in the velvet black of the cave, was the tip of a vast rubble cone, a collection of thousands of years of debris from the natural shaft. And at the base of the rubble cone his caving partner was waiting for him to finish his eleventh descent down the twisting shaft that wound above him like a mammoth wood screw turned inside out.

The two Basque lads operating the winch at the edge of the *gouffre* almost four hundred meters above had set double friction clamps to hold the cable fast while they replaced a spent cable drum with a fresh one. This was the most unnerving moment of the descent—and the most uncomfortable. Unnerving, because Hel was now totally dependent on the cable, after ninety minutes of negotiating the narrow, twisting shaft with its bottlenecks, narrow ledges, tricky dihedrons, and tight passages down which he had to ease himself gingerly, never surrendering to gravity because the cable was slack to give him maneuvering freedom. Throughout the descent there was the constant irritation of keeping the cable from fouling or from becoming entangled with the telephone line that dangled beside it. But through all the problems of the shaft, some challenging and some only irritating, there was the constant comfort of the rock walls, close and visible in the beam of his helmet light, theoretically available for clinging to, should something go wrong with the cable or the winch.

But now he was out of the shaft and dangling just below the roof of the first great cave, the walls of which had receded beyond the throw of his helmet light, and he hung there in the infinite void; the combined weight of his body, of four hundred meters of cable, and of

221

the watertight container of food and equipment depending from two friction clamps four hundred meters above. Hel had full faith in the clamp-and-winch system; he had designed it himself and built it in his workshop. It was a simple affair, pedal-driven by the powerful legs of the Basque mountain lads above, and geared so low that descent was very slow. Sliding safety clamps were designed to bite into the cable and arrest it if it exceeded a certain rate of descent. The fulcrum was a tripod of aluminum tubes formed in an open tepee directly over the narrow entrance hole at the bottom of the *gouffre*. Hel trusted the mechanical system that prevented him from plummeting down through the dark onto the tip of that pile of rubble and boulders that filled about half of the first great cave, but all the same he muttered imprecations at the boys above to get on with it. He had to breathe orally, his mouth wide open, because he was hanging in the middle of a waterfall produced by the outflow of an underground stream into the shaft at meter point 370, making the last ninety-five meters a free descent through an icy spray that seeped up his arms, despite the tight rings of rubber at his wrists, and trickled up to shock his hot armpits. His helmet lamp was useless in the waterfall, so he turned it off and hung limp in the roar and echoing hiss of the water, his harness beginning to chafe his ribs and crotch. There was a certain advantage to his blindness. Inevitably, in the twisting, scrambling descent, the cable always got wound up, and when he gave his weight to the line and began the free descent through the roof of the first cave, he started to spin, slowly at first, then faster, then slowing down and pausing, then beginning to spin in the opposite direction. Had he been able to see the slant of the spray swirling around him, he would have felt the pangs of vertigo, but in the total dark there was only a sensation of "ballooning" as the speed of his spin tended to spread out his arms and legs.

Hel felt himself being drawn upward a short distance to loosen the safety clamps, then there was a stomach-clutching drop of several centimeters as his weight was transferred to the new cable drum, and he began a twisting descent through the waterfall, which soon broke up into thick mist. Eventually, he could make out a smear of light below where his caving partner awaited him, standing well aside from the line of fall of rock and water and, God forbid, possibly Hel.

The scrape of his dangling equipment container told Hel he had reached the tip of the rubble cone, and he pulled up his legs so as to make his first contact with the rock a sitting one, because the lads above would lock up with the first sign of slack, and it could be comically difficult to unharness oneself while standing tiptoe on the rim of a boulder.

Le Cagot scrambled over and helped with the unharnessing and unstrapping of equipment because Hel's legs and arms were numb with loss of circulation in the wet cold, and his fingers felt fat and insensitive as they fumbled with straps and buckles.

"So, Niko!" Le Cagot boomed, his basso voice reverberating in the cave. "You finally decided to drop in for a visit! Where have you been? By the Two Balls of Christ, I thought you had decided to give it over and go home! Come on. I have made some tea."

Le Cagot hoisted the container on his shoulder and started down the unstable rubble cone, picking his way quickly through familiarity, and avoiding loose stones that would precipitate an avalanche. Opening and closing his hands to restore circulation, Hel followed his partner's steps exactly because Le Cagot knew the treacherous and unstable rubble cone better than he. The gruff old Basque poet had been down here for two days, making base camp at the foot of the cone and taking little Theseus sorties into the small caves and galleries that gave out from the principal chamber. Most of these had run out into blocks and blank walls, or pinched out into cracks too narrow for penetration.

Le Cagot pawed around in the equipment container Hel had descended with. "What is this? You promised to bring a bottle of Izarra! Don't tell me you drank it on your way down! If you did this to me, Niko, then by the Epistolary Balls of Paul I shall have to do you hurt, though that would cause me some sadness, for you are a good man, despite your misfortune of birth." It was Le Cagot's conviction that any man so unlucky as not to be born Basque suffered from a tragic genetic flaw.

"It's in there somewhere," Hel said as he lay back on a flat rock and sighed with painful pleasure as his knotted muscles began to stretch and relax.

During the past forty hours, while Le Cagot had been making base camp and doing light peripheral explorations, Hel had made eleven trips up and down through the *gouffre* shaft, bringing down food, equipment, nylon rope, and flares. What he needed most of all now was a few hours of sleep, which he could take at any time in the constant blackness of a cave, despite the fact that, by outside time, it was shortly before dawn.

Nicholai Hel and Beñat Le Cagot had been a caving team for sixteen years, during which they had done most of the major systems in Europe, occasionally making news in the limited world of the speleologue with discoveries and new records of depth and distance. Over the years their division of duties had become automatic. Le Cagot, a bull of strength and endurance despite his fifty years, always went down first, sweeping up as he made his slow descent, clearing ledges and dihedrons of loose rock and rubble that could be knocked off by the cable and kill a man in the shaft. He always brought the battery telephone down with him and established some kind of base camp, well out of the line of fall for rock and water. Because Hel was more lithe and tactically more skillful, he made all the equipment trips when, as in the case of this new hole, the access shaft was sinuous and twisting, and gear could not be lowered without the guidance of an accompanying man. Usually this only entailed two or three trips. But this time they had discovered all the signs of a great network of caverns and galleries, the exploration of which would require a great deal of equipment, so Hel had had to make eleven chafing, grueling trips. And now that the job was over and his body was no longer sustained by the nervous energy of danger, fatigue was overtaking him, and his knotted muscles were slackening painfully.

"Do you know what, Niko? I have been giving a great problem the benefit of my penetrating and illuminating mind." Le Cagot poured himself a large portion of Izzara into the metal cap of a flask. After two days alone

224

in the dark cave, Le Cagot's gregarious personality was hungry for conversation which, for him, consisted of monologues delivered to an appreciative audience. "And here's what I have been thinking, Niko. I have decided that all cavers are mad, save of course for Basque cavers, in whom what is madness for others is a manifestation of bravery and thirst for adventure. Do you agree?"

Hel hum-grunted as he descended into a coma/sleep that seemed to soften the slab of stone beneath him.

"But, you protest, is it fair to say the caver is more crazy than the mountain climber? It is! And why? Because the caver faces the more dangerous friction. The climber confronts only the frictions of his body and strength. But the caver faces erosions of nerve and primordial fears. The primitive beast that lingers within man has certain deep dreads, beyond logic, beyond intelligence. He dreads the dark. He fears being underground, which place he has always called the home of evil forces. He fears being alone. He dreads being trapped. He fears the water from which, in ancient times, he emerged to become Man. His most primitive nightmares involve falling through the dark, or wandering lost through mazes of alien chaos. And the caver— crazy being that he is—volitionally chooses to face these nightmare conditions. That is why he is more insane than the climber, because the thing he risks at every moment is his sanity. This is what I have been thinking about, Niko . . . Niko? Niko? What, do you sleep while I am talking to you? Lazy bastard! I swear by the Perfidious Balls of Judas that not one man in a thousand would sleep while I am talking! You insult the poet in me! It is like closing your eyes to a sunset, or stopping your ears to a Basque melody. You know that, Niko? Niko? Are you dead? Answer yes or no. Very well, for your punishment, I shall drink your portion of the Izzara."

The shaft to the cave system they were preparing to explore had been discovered by accident the year before, but it had been kept secret because a part of the conical *gouffre* above it was in Spain, and there was a risk that the Spanish authorities might seal off the entrance as they had at Gouffre Pierre-Saint-Martin after the tragic fall and death of Marcel Loubens in 1952. During the winter, a team of young Basque lads had slowly shifted the boundary stones to put the *gouffre* well within France, moving twenty markers a little at a time so as to fool the Spanish border guards who checked the area routinely. This adjustment in borders seemed perfectly legitimate to them; after all, it was all Basque land, and they were not particularly interested in an arbitrary boundary established by the two occupying nations.

There was another reason for shifting the border. Since Le Cagot and the two Basque boys operating the winch were known activists in ETA, an arrival of Spanish border police while they were working the cave might end with their passing their lives in a Spanish prison.

Although the Gouffre Port-de-Larrau was rather distant from the vast field of funnel-shaped depressions that characterize the area around Pic d'Anie and earn it the name "the Gruyère of France," it had been visited occasionally by curious teams of cavers, each of which had been disappointed to find it "dry," its shaft clogged with boulders and rubble after a few meters down. In time the word spread amongst the tight community of deep cavers that there was no point in making the long climb up to Gouffre Port-de-Larrau, when there was so much better caving to be had in the vast *gouffre* field above Ste. Engrace, where the mountainsides and high plateaus were strewn with the conical depressions of *gouffres* formed by infalls of surface rock and earth into cave systems in the calciate rock below.

But a year ago, two shepherds tending flocks in the high grazing lands were sitting at the edge of Gouffre Port-de-Larrau, taking a lunch of fresh cheese, hard bread, and *xoritzo,* that strong red sausage, one bite of which will flavor a mouthful of bread. One of the lads thoughtlessly tossed a stone down toward the mouth of the *gouffre* and was surprised at the startled flight of two crows. It is well-known that crows make nests only over shafts of considerable depth, so it was puzzling that these birds had nested over the little dimple of Gouffre Larrau. In curiosity, they scrambled down the side of the funnel and dropped stones down the shaft. With the echoing and reechoing of the stones and the rubble they knocked off on their way down, it was impossible to tell how deep the shaft was, but one thing was sure: it was no longer a little dimple. Evidently the great earthquake of 1962 that had almost destroyed the village of Arrete had also cleared out some of the choke stones and rubble blocking the shaft.

When, two months later, the second transhumance brought the lads down to the valley, they informed Beñat Le Cagot of their discovery, knowing that the blustery poet of Basque separatism was also an avid caver. He swore them to secrecy and carried the news of the find to Nicholai Hel, with whom he lived in safety, whenever recent actions made remaining in Spain particularly unwise.

Neither Hel nor Le Cagot allowed himself to become too excited over the find. They realized that chances were against finding any great cave system at the bottom of the shaft—assuming they got to the bottom. In all probability, the earthquake had cleared only the upper portions of the shaft. Or, as is often the case, they might find that centuries of infall down the *gouffre* had built up the rubble cone below until it rose to the roof of the cave and its tip actually entered the shaft, choking it off forever.

Despite all these protective doubts, they decided to make a preliminary light exploration immediately— just clearing their way down and taking a look—nothing major.

With autumn, bad weather came to the mountains, and that was an advantage, for it would diminish any inclinations toward energetic border patrolling on the part of the Spanish (the French being congenitally disinclined to such rigors). The heavy weather would, however, make hard work of bringing into those desolate mountains the winch, the cable drums, the battery phones, the fulcrum tripod, and all the equipment and food they would need for the survey.

Le Cagot sniffed and made light of these tasks, reminding Hel that smuggling contraband over those mountains was the traditional occupation of the Soultain Basque.

"Did you know that we once brought a piano over from Spain?"

"I heard something about that. How did you do it?"

"Ah-ha! Wouldn't the flat hats like to know! Actually, it was fairly simple. Another insurmountable problem that crumbled in the face of Basque ingenuity."

Hel nodded fatalistically. There was no way to avoid the story now, as various manifestations of Basque racial superiority constituted the principal theme of Le Cagot's conversation.

"Because, Niko, you are something of an honorary Basque—despite your ludicrous accent—I shall tell you how we got the piano over. But you must promise to guard the secret to the death. Do you promise?"

"Pardon me?" Hel had been attending to something else.

"I accept your promise. Here's how we did it. We brought the piano over note by note. It took eighty-eight trips. The fellow stumbled while carrying the middle C and dented it, and to this day that piano has two B-flats side by side. That is the truth! I swear it on the Hopeless Balls of Saint Jude! Why would I lie?"

Two and a half days spent bringing the gear up to the *gouffre,* a day taken to set it up and test it, and the work of exploration began. Hel and Le Cagot took turns down in the shaft, clearing rubble from the narrow ledges, chipping off sharp outcroppings that threatened to abrade the cable, breaking down the triangular wedges of boulders that blocked off the shaft. And any one of those wedges might have proved too firmly lodged to be broken down; any one of them might turn out to be the tip of the clogging rubble cone; and their exploration would come to an inglorious end.

The shaft turned out not to be a dead fall, but rather an inside-out screw which so twisted the cable that each time they came to a short free drop their first task was to put their body weight on the line and accept the dizzying spin and counterspin necessary to unwind the cable. In addition to breaking up clogs and sweeping rubble from ledges, they often had to chip away at the mother rock, particularly in "jugs" and bottlenecks, to make a relatively straight line of fall for the cable, so it would pay out without rubbing against edges of

228

stone, which friction would sooner or later scar and weaken the cable, the thickness of which was already minimal: a hundred percent safety limit when carrying Le Cagot's eighty-two kilos plus a gear container. In designing the pedal winch, Hel had chosen the lightest cable possible for two reasons: flexibility through cork-screw passages and weight. It was not so much the weight of the cable drums that concerned him; his real concern was the weight of the paid-out line. When a man is down three or four hundred meters, the weight of the cable in the shaft triples the work of the men working the winch.

As it was always black in the shaft, they soon lost any sense of diurnal time, and sometimes came up surprised to find it was night. Each man worked as long as his body strength would allow, to reduce the time wasted bringing one man back up and lowering the other. There were exciting times when a clog would break through, revealing ten meters of open shaft; and spirits, both at the end of the cable and above at the telephone headset, would soar. At other times, a jam of choke stone would be loosened only to collapse into the next obstruction a meter or two down, thickening the clog.

The young men working the winch were new to the task, and on one occasion they failed to set the friction safety clamps. Hel was working down below, pecking away at a four-stone pyramid clog with a short-handled pick. Suddenly the clog gave away under his feet. The cable above him was slack. He fell . . .

About thirty centimeters to the next clog.

For a fraction of a second, he was a dead man. And for a few moments he huddled in silence as the adrenaline spurt made his stomach flutter. Then he put on his headset and in his soft prison voice gave slow, clear instructions on the use of the clamps. And he returned to work.

When both Hel and Le Cagot were too worn of body, too scuffed of knuckle and knee, too stiff of forearm to make a fist around the pick handle, they would sleep, taking shelter in a shepherd's *artzain chola* shelter used during the summer pasturage on the flank of Pic d'Orhy, this highest of the Basque mountains. Too knotted and tense to find sleep quickly, they would chat while the wind moaned around the south flank of Pic d'Orhy. It was there that Hel first heard the adage that the Basque, wherever they roam in the world, always yearn with a low-grade romantic fever to return to the Eskual-herri.

Orhiko choria Orhin laket: "the birds of Orhy are happy only at Orhy."

The meanest and most desperate time was spent at a thick jam at meter point 365, where they had to work in a constant rain of icy seep water. They could hear the roar and hiss of an underground river that entered the shaft close below. From the sound, it was evident that the river fell a long way after entering the shaft, and the chances were that the water had kept the rest of the hole clear of rock jams.

When Hel came up after three hours of picking away at the heavy clog, he was pale and shivering with bone-deep cold, his lips purple with incipient hypothermia, the skin of his hands and face bleached and wrinkled from hours in the water. Le Cagot had a great laugh at his expense and told him to stand aside and see how the rock would tremble and retreat before the force of a Basque. But he wasn't long down in the hole before his voice came gasping and spitting over the head-phones, damning the clog, the cold rain, the stupid shaft, the mountain, the hobby of caving, and all of creation by the Vaporous Balls of the Holy Ghost! Then suddenly there was silence. His voice came up the line, breathless and hushed. "It's going to slip. Make sure the goddamned clamps are set. If I fall and destroy my magnificent body, I'll come back up and kick many asses!"

"Wait!" Hel shouted over the telephone. The line above was still slack to give Le Cagot work room.

There was a grunt as he delivered the last blow, then the cable tensed. For a time there was silence, then his voice came, strained and metallic: "That is it, my friends and admirers! We are through. And I am hanging in a goddamned waterfall." There was a pause. "By the way, my arm is broken."

Hel took a long breath and pictured the schematic of the shaft in his mind. Then he spoke into the mouthpiece in his calm, soft voice. "Can you make it up through the corkscrew one-handed?"

There was no answer from below.

"Beñat? Can you make it up?"

"Considering the alternative, I think I had better give it a try."

"We'll take it slow and easy."

"That would be nice."

On instructions from Hel, the lad began to pedal. The system was so low-geared that it was easy to maintain a slow pace, and for the first twenty meters there was no difficulty. Then Le Cagot entered the corkscrew that twisted up for almost eighty meters. He couldn't be pulled up through this; the niches and slits they had cut into the rock for the free passage of the pay line were only centimeters wide. Le Cagot would have to climb, sometimes locking himself in a wedging stance while he called for slack in the cable so that he could reach up and flick it out of a narrow slit. All this one-handed.

At first, Le Cagot's voice came over the line regularly, joking and humming, the predictable manifestations of his ebullient braggadocio. It was his habit to talk and sing constantly when underground. He claimed, as poet and egotist, to delight in the sound of his voice enriched with reverberation and echo. Hel had always known that the chatter served the additional purpose of filling the silence and pressing back the dark and loneliness, but he never mentioned this. Before long, the joking, singing, and swearing with which he showed off for those above and numbed his sense of danger began to be replaced by the heavy rasp of labored breathing. Occasionally there were tight dental grunts as a movement shocked waves of pain up his broken arm.

Up and down the cable went. A few meters up, then slack had to be given so Le Cagot could work out some cable jam. If he had both hands free, he could hold the line clear above him and come up fairly steadily.

The first lad at the pedal winch wore out, and they locked the pay line in the double clamps while the second boy took his place. The pedaling was easier now that more than half the weight of the cable was up in the drums, but still Le Cagot's progress was slow and

231

irregular. Two meters up; three meters of slack for clearing a foul; take up the slack; a meter up; two meters down; two and a half meters up.

Hel did not talk to Le Cagot over the phones. They were old friends, and Hel would not insult him by seeming to think he needed the psychological support of being "talked up." Feeling useless and worn with tension and with silly but unavoidable attempts to help Le Cagot up by means of sympathetic kinesodics and "body English," Hel stood beside the take-up drum, listening to Le Cagot's rasping breath over the line. The cable had been painted with red stripes every ten meters, so by watching them come slowly into the pulley blocks Hel could tell where Le Cagot was in the shaft. In his mind, he could see the features around Beñat; that little ledge where he could get a toehold; that snarled dihedron where the cable was sure to foul; that bottleneck in which his broken arm must take some punishment.

Le Cagot's breathing was coming in gulps and gasps. Hel marked the cable with his eye; Le Cagot would now be at the most difficult feature of the ascent, a double dihedron at meter point 44. Just below the double dihedron was a narrow ledge where one could get purchase for the first jackknife squeeze, a maneuver hard enough for a man with two good arms, consisting of chimney climbing so narrow in places that all one could get was a heel-and-knee wedge, so wide in others that the wedge came from the flats of the feet to the back of the neck. And all the time the climber had to keep the slack cable from cross-threading between the overhanging knobs above.

"Stop," said Le Cagot's abraded voice. He would be at the ledge, tilting back his head and looking up at the lower of the two dihedrons in the beam of his helmet lamp. "I think I'll rest here a moment."

Rest? Hel said to himself. On a ledge six centimeters wide?

Obviously that was the end. Le Cagot was spent. Effort and pain had drained him, and the toughest bit was still above him. Once past the double dihedron, his weight could be taken on the cable and he could be dragged up like a sack of millet. But he had to make that reflex dihedron on his own.

The boy working the pedals looked toward Hel, his black Basque eyes round with fear. Papa Cagot was a folk hero to these lads. Had he not brought to the world an appreciation of Basque poetry in his tours of universities throughout England and the United States, where involved young people applauded his revolutionary spirit and listened with hushed attention to verse they could never understand? Was it not Papa Cagot who had gone into Spain with this outlander, Hel, to rescue thirteen who were in prison without trial?

Le Cagot's voice came over the wire. "I think I'll stay here for a while." He was no longer panting and rasping, but there was a calm of resignation alien to his boisterous personality. "This place suits me."

Not sure exactly what he was going to do, Nicholai began to speak in his soft voice. "Neanderthals. Yes, they're probably Neanderthals."

"What are you talking about?" Le Cagot wanted to know.

"The Basque."

"That in itself is good. But what is this about Neanderthals?"

"I've been giving some study to the origin of the Basque race. You know the facts as well as I. Their language is the only pre-Aryan tongue to survive. And there is certain evidence that they are a race apart from the rest of Europe. Type O blood is found in only forty percent of Europeans, while it appears in nearly sixty percent of the Basque. And among the Eskualdun, Type B blood is almost unknown. All this suggests that we have a totally separate race, a race descended from some different primate ancestor."

"Let me warn you right now, Niko. This talk is taking a path I do not like!"

". . . then too there is the matter of skull shape. The round skull of the Basque is more closely related to Neanderthal man than the higher Cro-Magnon, from which the superior peoples of the world descend."

"Niko? By the Two Damp Balls of John the Baptist, you will end by making me angry!"

"I'm not saying that it's a matter of intelligence that

separates the Basque from the human. After all, they have learned a great deal at the feet of their Spanish masters—"

"Argh!"

"—no, it's more a physical thing. While they have a kind of flashy strength and courage—good for a quick screw or a bandit raid—the Basque are shown up when it comes to sticking power, to endurance—"

"Give me some slack!"

"Not that I blame them. A man is what he is. A trick of nature, a wrinkle in time has preserved this inferior race in their mountainous corner of the world where they have managed to survive because, let's face it, who else would want this barren wasteland of the Eskual-Herri?"

"I'm coming up, Niko! Enjoy the sunlight! It's your last day!"

"Bullshit, Beñat. Even *I* would have trouble with that double dihedron. And I have two good arms and don't suffer the blemish of being a Neanderthal."

Le Cagot did not answer. His heavy breathing alone came over the wire, and sometimes a tight nasal snort as his broken arm took a shock.

Twenty centimeters now, thirty then, the boy at the winch took up the slack, his attention riveted to the cable markings as they passed through the tripod blocks, swallowing in sympathetic pain with the inhuman gasping that filled his earphones. The second lad held the taut take-up cable in his hand, a useless gesture of assistance.

Hel took off his headphones and sat on the rim of the *gouffre*. There was nothing more he could do, and he did not want to hear Beñat go, if he went. He lowered his eyes and brought himself into middle-density meditation, narcotizing his emotions. He did not emerge until he heard a shout from the lad at the winch. Mark 40 meters was in the blocks. They could take him on the line!

Hel stood at the narrow crevice of the *gouffre* mouth. He could hear Le Cagot down there, his limp body scraping against the shaft walls. Notch by notch, the lads brought him out with infinite slowness so as not to hurt him. The sunlight penetrated only a meter or two into the dark hole, so it was only a few seconds between the appearance of Le Cagot's harness straps and the time he was dangling free, unconscious and ashen-faced, from the pulley above.

When he regained consciousness, Le Cagot found himself lying on a board bed in the shepherd's *artzain xola*, his arm in an improvised sling. While the lads made a brushwood fire, Hel sat on the edge of the bed looking down into his comrade's weatherbeaten face with its sunken eyes and its sun-wrinkled skin still gray with shock under the full rust-and-gray beard.

"Could you use some wine?" Hel asked.

"Is the pope a virgin?" Le Cagot's voice was weak and raspy. "You squeeze it for me, Niko. There are two things a one-armed man cannot do. And one of them is to drink from a *xahako*."

Because drinking from a goatskin *xahako* is a matter of automatic coordination between hand and mouth, Nicholai was clumsy and squirted some wine into Beñat's beard.

Le Cagot coughed and gagged on the inexpertly offered wine. "You are the worst nurse in the world, Niko. I swear it by the Swallowed Balls of Jonah!"

Hel smiled. "What's the other thing a one-handed man can't do?" he asked quietly.

"I can't tell you, Niko. It is bawdy, and you are too young."

In fact, Nicholai Hel was older than Le Cagot, although he looked fifteen years younger.

"It's night, Beñat. We'll bring you down into the valley in the morning. I'll find a veterinarian to set that arm. Doctors work only on Homo sapiens."

Then Le Cagot remembered. "I hope I didn't hurt you too much when I got to the surface. But you had it coming. As the saying is: *Nola neurtcen baituçu; Hala neurtuco çare çu.*"

"I'll survive the beating you gave me."

"Good." Le Cagot grinned. "You really are simple-minded, my friend. Do you think I couldn't see through your childish ploy? You thought to enrage me to give me strength to make it up. But it didn't work, did it?"

"No, it didn't work. The Basque mind is too subtle for me."

"It is too subtle for everybody but Saint Peter—who, by the way, was a Basque himself, although not many people know it. So, tell me! What does our cave look like?"

"I haven't been down."

"Haven't been down? *Alla Jainkoa!* But I didn't get to the bottom! We haven't properly claimed it for ourselves. What if some ass of a Spaniard should stumble into the hole and claim it?"

"All right. I'll go down at dawn."

"Good. Now give me some more wine. And hold it steady this time! Not like some boy trying to piss his name into a snowbank!"

The next morning Hel went down on the line. It was clear all the way. He passed through the waterfall and down to the place where the shaft opened into the great cave. As he hung, spinning on the cable while the lads above held him in clamps as they replaced drums, he knew they had made a real find. The cavern was so vast that his helmet light could not penetrate to the walls.

Soon he was on the tip of the rubble heap, where he tied off his harness to a boulder so he could find it again. After carefully negotiating the rubble heap, where stones were held in delicate balance and counterbalance, he found himself on the cave floor, some two hundred meters below the tip of the cone. He struck off a magnesium flare and held it away behind him so he would not be blinded by its light. The cave was vast—larger than the interior of a cathedral—and myriad arms and branches led off in every direction. But the flow of the underground river was toward France, so that would be the route of major exploration when they returned. Filled though he was with the natural curiosity of a veteran caver, Hel could not allow himself to investigate further without Le Cagot. That would be unfair. He picked his way up the rubble cone and found the tied-off cable.

Forty minutes later he emerged into the misty morning sunlight of the *gouffre*. After a rest, he helped the lads dismount the aluminum-tube triangle and the anchoring cables for the winch. They rolled several heavy boulders over the opening, partly to hide it from anyone who might wander that way, but also to block the entrance to protect next spring's sheep from falling in.

They scattered stone and pebbles to efface the marks of the winch frame and cable tie-offs, but they knew that most of the work of concealment would be done by the onset of winter.

Back in the *artzain xola,* Hel made his report to Le Cagot, who was enthusiastic despite his swollen arm throbbing with pain.

"Good, Niko. We shall come back next summer. Listen. I've been pondering something while you were down in the hole. We must give our cave a name, no? And I want to be fair about naming it. After all, you were the first man in, although we must not forget that my courage and skill opened the last of the chokes. So, taking all this into consideration, I have come up with the perfect name for the cave."

"And that is?"

"Le Cagot's Cave! How does that sound?"

Hel smiled. "God knows it's fair."

All that was a year ago. When the snow cleared from the mountain, they came up and began descents of exploration and mapping. And now they were ready to make their major penetration along the course of the underground river.

For more than an hour, Hel had slept on the rock slab, fully clothed and booted, while Le Cagot had passed the time talking to himself and the unconscious Hel, all the while sipping at the bottle of Izarra, taking turns. One drink for himself. The next on Niko's behalf.

When at last Hel began to stir, the hardness of the rock penetrating even the comatose sleep of his fatigue, Le Cagot interrupted his monologue to nudge his companion with his boot. "Hey! Niko? Going to sleep your life away? Wake up and see what you have done! You've drunk up half a bottle of Izarra, greedy bastard!"

Hel sat up and stretched his cramped muscles. His inactivity had permitted the cave's damp cold to soak in to the bone. He reached out for the Izarra bottle, and found it empty.

"I drank the other half," Le Cagot admitted. "But I'll make you some tea." While Beñat fiddled with the portable solid-fuel cooker, Hel got out of his harness and paratrooper jumpsuit specially modified with bands of elastic at the neck and wrists to keep water out. He peeled off his four thin sweaters that kept his body warmth in and replaced the innermost with a dry jersey made of loosely knitted fabric, then he put three of the damp sweaters on again. They were made of good Basque wool and were warm even when wet. All this was done by the light of a device of his own design, a simple connection of a ten-watt bulb to a wax-sealed automobile battery which, for all its primitive nature, had the effect of keeping at bay the nerve-eroding dark that pressed in from all sides. A fresh battery could drive the little bulb day and night for four days and, if necessary, could be sent up, now that they had widened the bottleneck and double dihedron, to be recharged from the pedal-driven magneto that kept their telephone battery fresh.

Hel tugged off his gaiters and boots. "What time is it?"

Le Cagot was carrying over a tin cup of tea. "I can't tell you."

"Why not?"

"Because if I turn over my wrist, I will pour out your tea, ass! Here. Take the cup!" Le Cagot snapped his fingers to shake off the burn. "*Now* I will look at my watch. The time at the bottom of Le Cagot's Cave—and perhaps elsewhere in the world—is exactly six thirty-seven, give or take a little."

"Good." Hel shuddered at the taste of the thin tisane Le Cagot always brewed as tea. "That gives us five or six hours to eat and rest before we follow the stream into that big sloping tunnel. Is everything laid out?"

"Does the devil hate the wafer?"

"Have you tested the Brunton compass?"

"Do babies shit yellow?"

"And you're sure there's no iron in the rock?"

"Did Moses start forest fires?"

"And the fluorescein is packed up?"

"Is Franco an asshole?"

238

"Fine then. I'm going to get into a bag and get some sleep."

"How can you sleep! This is the big day! Four times we have been down in this hole, measuring, map-making, marking. And each time we have resisted our desire to follow the river course, saving the greatest adventure for last. And now the time has come! Surely you cannot sleep! Niko? Niko? I'll be damned." Le Cagot shrugged and sighed. "There is no understanding these Orientals."

Between them, they would be carrying twenty pounds of fluorescein dye to dump into the underground river when at last they could follow it no longer, either because their way was blocked by infall, or the river disappeared down a siphon. They had estimated that the outfall of the river had to be into the Torrent of Holçarté, and during the winter, while Le Cagot was up to patriotic mischief in Spain, Hel had investigated the length of that magnificent gorge where the torrent had cut a channel two hundred meters deep into the rock. He found several outfalls of underground streams, but only one seemed to have the flow velocity and position to make it a likely candidate. In a couple of hours, two young Basque caving enthusiasts would make camp by the outfall, taking turns watching the stream. With the first trace of dye color in the water, they would mark the time with their watch, synchronized with Le Cagot's. From this timing, and from their dead-reckoning navigation through the cave system, Hel and Le Cagot would estimate if it was feasible to follow the stream underwater in scuba gear and accomplish that finale of any thorough exploration of a cave, a trip from the vertical shaft to the light and air of the outfall.

After five hours of deep sleep, Hel awoke as he always did, instantly and thoroughly, without moving a muscle or opening his eyes. His highly developed proximity sense reported to him immediately. There was only one person within aura range, and that person's vibrations were defuse, defocused, vulnerable. The person was daydreaming or meditating or asleep. Then he heard Le Cagot's baritone snoring.

Le Cagot was in his sleeping bag, fully dressed, only his long, tousled hair and rust-gray beard visible in the dim light of the ten-watt battery lamp. Hel got up and set the solid-fuel stove going with a popping blue flame. While the water was coming to a boil, he searched about in the food containers for his tea, a strong tannic *cha* which he brewed so long it had twice the caffeine of coffee.

A man who committed himself totally to all physical activities, Le Cagot was a deep sleeper. He did not even stir when Hel tugged his arm out of the bag to check the time. They should be moving out. Hel kicked the side of Beñat's sleeping bag, but he got no more response than a groan and a muttered curse. He kicked again, and Le Cagot turned over on his side and coiled up, hoping this tormentor would evaporate. When the water was starting to form pinpoint bubbles along the sides of the pan, Hel gave his comrade a third and more vigorous kick. The aura changed wavelengths. He was awake.

Without turning over, Le Cagot growled thickly, "There is an ancient Basque proverb saying that those who kick sleeping men inevitably die."

"Everybody dies."

"You see? Another proof of the truth of our folk wisdom."

"Come on, get up!"

"Wait a minute! Give me a moment to arrange the world in my head, for the love of Christ!"

"I'm going to finish this tea, then I'm setting off. I'll tell you about the cave when I get back."

"All right!" Le Cagot kicked his way angrily out of the sleeping bag and sat on the stone slab beside Hel, hunching moodily over his tea. "Jesus, Mary, Joseph and the Donkey! What kind of tea is this?"

"Mountain *cha.*"

"Tastes like horse piss."

"I'll have to take your word for that. I lack your culinary experience."

Hel drank off the rest of his tea, then he hefted the two packs and selected the lighter one. He took up his coil of Edelrid rope and a fat carabiner on which were threaded a ring of smaller carabiners. Then he made a quick check of the side pocket of his pack to make sure he had the standard assortment of pitons for various kinds of fissures. The last thing he did before setting off was to replace the batteries for his helmet lamp with fresh ones. This device was another of his own design, based on the use of the experimental Gerard/Simon battery, a small and powerful cylinder, eight of which could be fitted into the helmet between the crown and webbing. It was one of Hel's hobbies to design and make caving equipment in his workshop. Although he would never consider patenting or manufacturing these devices, he often gave prototypes to old caving friends as presents.

Hel looked down at Le Cagot, still hunched petulantly over his tea. "You'll find me at the end of the cave system. I'll be easy to recognize; I'll be the one with the victorious look on his face." And he started down the long corridor that was the river's channel.

"By the Rocky Balls of St. Peter, you have the soul of a slave-driver! You know that?" Le Cagot shouted after Hel, as he rapidly donned his gear, grumbling to himself, "I swear there's a trace of Falange blood in his veins!"

Shortly after entering the gallery, Hel paused and waited for Le Cagot to catch up. The entire performance of exhortation and grousing was part of the established heraldry of their relationship. Hel was the leader by virtue of personality, of route-finding skills granted him by his proximity sense, and of the physical dexterity of his lithe body. Le Cagot's bullish strength and endurance made him the best backup man in caving. From the first, they had fallen into patterns that allowed Le Cagot to save face and maintain his self-respect. It was Le Cagot who told the stories when they emerged from the caves. It was Le Cagot who constantly swore, bullied, and complained, like an ill-mannered child. The poet in Le Cagot had confected for himself the role of the *miles gloriosus,* the Falstaffian clown—but with a unique difference: his braggadocio was founded on a record of reckless, laughing courage in numberless guerrilla actions against the fascist who oppressed his people in Spain.

When Le Cagot caught up with Hel, they moved together down the slanting, rapidly narrowing cut, its floor and walls scrubbed clean by the action of the underground stream, revealing the formational structure of the cave system. The rock above was limestone, but the floor along which the stream ran was ancient foliate schist. For eons, soak water had penetrated the porous limestone to the depth of the impermeable schist, along which bed it flowed, seeking depth and ultimate outfall. Slowly the slightly acid seep water had dissolved the limestone immediately above the schist, making a water pipe for itself. And slowly it had eaten at the edges of the water pipe until it had undermined its structure and caused infalls, which rubble it patiently eroded by absorptions and scrubbing; and the rubble itself acted as an abrasive carried along in the current, aiding in the work of undermining, causing greater infalls and multiplying the effect: and so, by geometric progression in which effects were also causes, through hundreds of thousands of years the great cave system was developed. The bulk of the work was accomplished by the silent, minute, relentless work of scrubbing and dissolution, and only occasionally was this patient action punctuated by the high geological drama of major collapses, most of them triggered by the earthquakes common to this underground system of faults and fissures which found surface expression in a landscape of karst, the abrupt outcroppings and frequent funnel pits and *gouffres* that earned this region its caving reputation.

For more than an hour they inched along the corridor, descending gently, while the sides and roof of their tunnel slowly closed in on them until they were easing along a narrow ledge beside the rushing current, the bed of which was a deep vertical cut not more than two meters wide, but some ten meters deep. The roof continued to close down on them, and soon they were moving with difficulty, bent over double, their packs scraping the rock overhead. Le Cagot swore at the pain in his trembling knees as they pushed along the narrow ledge walking in a half-squat that tormented the muscles of their legs.

As the shaft continued to narrow, the same unspoken thought harried them both. Wouldn't it be a stupid irony if, after their work of preparation and building up supplies, this was all there was? If this sloping shaft came to an end at a swallow down which the river disappeared?

The tunnel began to curve slowly to the left. Then

suddenly their narrow ledge was blocked by a knob of rock that protruded out over the gushing stream. It was not possible for Hel to see around the knob, and he could not wade through the riverbed; it was too deep in this narrow cut, and even if it had not been, the possibility of a vertical swallow ahead in the dark was enough to deter him. There were stories of cavers who had stepped into swallows while wading through underground rivers. It was said that they were sucked straight down, one hundred, two hundred meters through a roaring column of water at the bottom of which their bodies were churned in some great "giant's caldron" of boiling foam and rock until they were broken up enough to be washed away. And months afterward bits of equipment and clothing were found in streams and torrents along the narrow valleys of the outfall rivers. These, of course, were campfire tales and mostly lies and exaggerations. But like all folk narratives, they reflected real dreads, and for most cavers in these mountains the nightmare of the sudden swallow is more eroding to the nerves than thoughts of falling while scaling walls, or avalanches, or even being underground during an earthquake. And it is not the thought of drowning that makes the swallow awful, it is the image of being churned to fragments in that boiling giant's caldron.

"Well?" Le Cagot asked from behind, his voice reverberating in the narrow tunnel. "What do you see?"

"Nothing."

"That's reassuring. Are you just going to stand there? I can't squat here forever like a Béarnais shepherd with the runs!"

"Help me get my pack off."

In their tight, stooped postures, getting Hel's pack off was not easy, but once he was free of it he could straighten up a bit. The cut was narrow enough that he could face the stream, set his feet, and let himself fall forward to the wall on the other side. This done, he turned carefully onto his back, his shoulders against one side of the cut, his Vibram boot cleats giving him purchase against the ledge. Wriggling sideward in this pressure stance, using shoulders and palms and the flats of his feet in a traverse chimney climb, he inched along under the projecting knob of rock, the stream roaring

243

only a foot below his buttocks. It was a demanding and chafing move, and he lost some skin from his palms, but he made slow progress.

Le Cagot's laughter echoed, filling the cave. "Ola! What if it suddenly gets wider, Niko? Maybe you had better lock up there and let me use you like a bridge. That way at least one of us would make it!" And he laughed again.

Mercifully, it didn't get wider. Once past the knob, the cut narrowed, and the roof rose overhead to a height beyond the beam of Hel's lamp. He was able to push himself back to the interrupted ledge. He continued to inch along it, still curving to the left. His heart sank when his lamp revealed ahead that the diaclase through which they had been moving came to an abrupt end at an infall of boulders, under which the river gurgled and disappeared.

When he got to the base of the infall *raillère* and looked around, he could see that he was at the bottom of a great wedge only a couple of meters wide where he stood, but extending up beyond the throw of his light. He rested for a moment, then began a corner climb at the angle of the diaclase and the blocking wall of rubble. Foot- and handholds were many and easy, but the rock was rotten and friable, and each stance had to be tested carefully, each hold tugged to make sure it would not come away in his hand. When he climbed a slow, patient thirty meters, he wriggled into a gap between two giant boulders wedged against one another. Then he was on a flat ledge from which he could see nothing in front or to the sides. He clapped his hands once and listened. The echo was late, hollow, and repeated. He was at the mouth of a big cave.

His return to the knob was rapid; he rappelled down the infall clog on a doubled line which he left in place for their ascent. From his side of the knob he called to Le Cagot, who had retreated a distance back up the tunnel to a narrow place where he could lock himself into a butt-and-heels stance and find some relief from the quivering fatigue of his half-squatting posture.

Le Cagot came back to the knob. "So? Is it a go?"

"There's a big hole."

"Fantastic!"

The packs were negotiated on a line around the knob, then Le Cagot repeated Hel's chimney traverse around that tight bit, complaining bitterly all the while and cursing the knob by the Trumpeting Balls of Joshua and the Two Inhospitable Balls of the Innkeeper.

Because Hel had left a line in place and had cleared out much of the rotten rock, the climb back up the scree clog was not difficult. When they were together on the flat slab just after the crawl between two counter-balanced boulders that was later to be known as the Keyhole, Le Cagot struck off a magnesium flare, and the stygian chaos of that great cavern was seen for the first time in the numberless millennia of its existence.

"By the Burning Balls of the Bush," Le Cagot said in an awed hush. "A climbing cave!"

It was an ugly sight, but sublime. The raw crucible of creation that was this "climbing" cave muted the egos of these two humanoid insects not quite two meters tall standing on their little flake of stone suspended between the floor of the cave a hundred meters below and the cracked and rotten dome more than a hundred meters above. Most caves feel serene and eternal, but climbing caves are terrible in their organic chaos. Everything here was jagged and fresh; the floor was lost far below in layers of house-size boulders and rubble; and the roof was scarred with fresh infalls. This was a cavern in the throes of creation, an adolescent cave, awkward and unreliable, still in the process of "climbing," its floor rising from infall and rubble as its roof regularly collapsed. It might soon (twenty thousand years, fifty thousand years) stabilize and become an ordinary cave. Or it might continue to climb up the path of its fractures and faults until it reached the surface, forming in its final infall the funnel-shaped indentation of the classic "dry" *gouffre*. Of course, the youth and instability of the cave was relative and had to be considered in geological time. The "fresh" scars on the roof could be as young as three years old, or as old as a hundred.

The flare fizzled out, and it was some time before they got their cave eyes back sufficiently to see by the dim light of their helmet lamps. In the spot-dancing black, Hel heard Le Cagot say, "I baptize this cave and christen it. It shall be called Le Cagot Cave!"

From the splattering sound, Hel knew Le Cagot was not wasting water on the baptism. "Won't that be confusing?" he asked.

"What do you mean?"

"The first cave has the same name."

"Hm-m-m. That's true. Well, then, I christen this place Le Cagot's Chaos! How's that?"

"Fine."

"But I haven't forgotten your contribution to this find, Niko. I have decided to name that nasty outcropping back there—the one we had to traverse—Hel's Knob. How's that?"

"I couldn't ask for more."

"True. Shall we go on?"

"As soon as I catch up." Hel knelt over his notebook and compass, and in the light of his helmet lamp scratched down estimates of distance and direction, as he had every hundred or so meters since they left base camp at the rubble heap. After replacing everything in its waterproof packet, he said, "All right. Let's go."

Moving cautiously from boulder to boulder, squeezing between cracks and joints, picking their way around the shoulders of massive, toppling rocks the size of barns, they began to cross the Chaos. The Ariadne's String of the underground river was lost to them beneath layers upon layers of boulders, seeping, winding, bifurcating and rejoining, weaving its thousand threads along the schist floor far below. The recentness of the infalls and the absence of weather erosion that so quickly tames features on the surface combined to produce an insane jumble of precariously balanced slabs and boulders, the crazy canting of which seemed to refute gravity and create a carnival fun house effect in which water appears to run up hill, and what looks level is dangerously slanted. Balance had to be maintained by feel, not by eye, and they had to move by compass because their sense of direction had been mutilated by their twisting path through the vertigo madness of the Chaos. The problems of pathfinding were quite the opposite of those posed by wandering over a featureless moonscape. It was the confusing abundance of salient features that overloaded and cloyed the memory. And the vast black void overhead pressed down on their subconsciouses, oppressed by that scarred, unseen dome pregnant with infall, one-ten-thousandth part of which could crush them like ants.

Some two hours and five hundred meters later they had crossed enough of the Chaos to be able to see the far end of the cave where the roof sloped down to join the tangle of jagged young fall stone. During the past half-hour, a sound had grown around them, emerging so slowly out of the background ambience of gurgle and hiss far below that they didn't notice it until they stopped to rest and chart their progress. The thousand strands of the stream below were weaving tighter and tighter together, and the noise that filled the cavern was compounded of a full range of notes from thin cymbal hiss to basso tympany. It was a waterfall, a big waterfall somewhere behind that meeting of roof and rubble that seemed to block off the cave.

For more than an hour, they picked back and forth along the rubble wall, squeezing into crevices and triangular tents formed of slabs weighing tons, but they could find no way through the tangle. There were no boulders at this newer end of the Chaos, only raw young slab, many of which were the size of village *frontons*, some standing on end, some flat, some tilted at unlikely angles, some jetting out over voids for three-fourths of their length, held up by the cantilevering weight of another slab. And all the while, the rich roar of the waterfall beyond this infall lured them to find a way through.

"Let's rest and collect ourselves!" Le Cagot shouted over the noise, as he sat on a small fragment of slab, tugged off his pack, and pawed around inside for a meal of hardtack, cheese, and *xoritzo*. "Aren't you hungry?"

Hel shook his head. He was scratching away at his notebook, making bold estimates of direction and even vaguer guesses of slope, as the clinometer of his Brunton compass had been useless in the wilderness of the Chaos.

"Could that be the outfall behind the wall?" Le Cagot asked.

"I don't think so. We're not much more than halfway

to the Torrent of Holçarté, and we must still be a couple of hundred meters too high."

"And we can't even get down to the water to dump the dye in. What a nuisance this wall is! What's worse, we just ran out of cheese. Where are you going?"

Hel had dropped off his pack and was beginning a free climb of the wall. "I'm going to take a look at the tip of the heap."

"Try a little to your left!"

"Why? Do you see something there?"

"No. But I'm sitting right in the line of your fall, and I'm too comfortable to move."

They had not given much thought to trying the top of the slab heap because, even if there was a way to squeeze through, it would bring them out directly above the waterfall, and it would probably be impossible to pass through that roaring cascade. But the base and flanks of the clog had produced no way through, so the tip was all that was left.

Half an hour later, Le Cagot heard a sound above him. He tilted back his head to direct the beam of his lamp toward it. Hel was climbing back down in the dark. When he reached the slab, he slumped down to a sitting position, then lay back on his pack, one arm over his face. He was worn out and panting with effort, and the lens of his helmet lamp was cracked from a fall.

"You're sure you won't have anything to eat?" Le Cagot asked.

His eyes closed, his chest heaving with great gulps of air, sweat running down his face and chest despite the damp cold of the cave, Hel responded to his companion's grim sense of humor by making the Basque version of the universal hand language of animosity. he tucked his thumb into his fist and offered it to Le Cagot. Then he let the fist fall and lay there panting. His attempts to swallow were painful; the dryness in his throat was sharp-edged. Le Cagot passed his *xahako* over, and Hel drank greedily, beginning with the tip touching his teeth, because he had no light, then pulling it farther away and directing the thin jet of wine to the back of his throat by feel. He kept pressure on the sac, swallowing each time the back of his throat filled, drinking for so long that Le Cagot began to worry about his wine.

"Well?" Le Cagot asked grudgingly. "Did you find a way through?"

Hel grinned and nodded.

"Where did you come out?"

"Dead center above the waterfall."

"Shit!"

"No, I think there's a way around to the right, down through the spray."

"Did you try it?"

Hel shrugged and pointed to the broken helmet lens. "But I couldn't make it alone. I'll need you to protect me from above. There's a good belaying stance."

"You shouldn't have risked trying, Niko. One of these days you'll kill yourself, then you'll be sorry."

When he had wriggled through the mad network of cracks that brought him out beside Hel on a narrow ledge directly above the roaring waterfall, Le Cagot was exuberant with wonder. It was a long drop, and the mist rose through the windless air, back up the column of water, boiling all about them like a steam bath with a temperature of 40°. All they could see through the mist was the head of the falls below and a few meters of slimy rock to the sides of their ledge. Hel led the way to the right, where the ledge narrowed to a few centimeters, but continued around the shoulder of the cave opening. It was a worn, rounded ledge, obviously a former lip of the waterfall. The cacophonous crash of the falls made sign language their only means of communication as Hel indicated to Le Cagot the "good" belaying stance he had found, an outcrop of rock into which Le Cagot had to squeeze himself with difficulty and pay out the defending line around Hel's waist as he worked his way down the edge of the falls. The natural line of descent would bring him through the mist, through the column of water, and—it was to be hoped—behind it. Le Cagot grumbled about this "good" stance as he fixed his body into the wedge and drove a covering piton into the limestone above him, complaining that a piton in limestone is largely a psychological decoration.

Hel began his descent, stopping each time he found

the coincidence of a foothold for himself and a crack in the rock to drive in a piton and thread his line through the carabiner. Fortunately, the rock was still well-toothed and offered finger- and toeholds; the change in the falls course had been fairly recent, and it had not had time to wear all the ledge smooth. The greatest problem was with the line overhead. By the time he had descended twenty meters and had laced the line through eight carabiners, it took dangerous effort to tug slack against the heavy friction of the soaked rope through so many snap links; the effort of pulling on the line lifted his body partially out of his footholds. And this weakening of his stance occurred, of course, just when Le Cagot was paying out line from above and was, therefore, least able to hold him, should he slip.

He inched down through the sheath of mist until the oily black-and-silver sheet of the waterfall was only a foot from his helmet lamp, and there he paused and collected himself for the diciest moment of the descent.

First he would have to establish a cluster of pitons, so that he could work independently of Le Cagot, who might blindly resist on the line and arrest Hel while he was under the falls, blinded by the shaft of water, feeling for holds he could not see. And he would be taking the weight of the falling water on his back and shoulders. He had to give himself enough line to move all the way through the cascade, because he would not be able to breathe until he was behind it. On the other hand, the more line he gave himself, the greater his drop would be if the water knocked him off. He decided to give himself about three meters of slack. He would have liked more to avoid the possibility of coming to the end of his slack while still under the column of water, but his judgment told him that three meters was the maximum length that would swing him back out of the line of the falls, should he fall and knock himself out for long enough to drown, if he was hanging in the falls.

Hel edged to the face of the metallic, glittering sheet of water until it was only inches away from his face, and soon he began to have the vertigo sensation that the water was standing still, and his body rising through the roar and the mist. He reached into the face of the

250

falls, which split in a heavy, throbbing bracelet around his wrist, and felt around for the deepest handhold he could find. His fingers wriggled their way into a sharp little crack, unseen behind the water. The hold was lower than he would have wished, because he knew the weight of the water on his back would force him down, and the best handhold would have been high, so the weight would have jammed his fingers in even tighter. But it was the only crack he could find, and his shoulder was beginning to tire from the pounding of the water on his outstretched arm. He took several deep breaths, fully exhaling each one because he knew that it is more the buildup of carbon dioxide in the lungs than the lack of oxygen that forces a man to gasp for air. The last breath he took deeply, stretching his diaphragm to its full. Then he let a third of it out, and he swung into the falls.

It was almost comic, and surely anticlimactic.

The sheet of falling water was less than twenty centimeters thick, and the same movement that swung him into it sent him through and behind the cascade, where he found himself on a good ledge below which was a book corner piled with rubble so easy that a healthy child could make the climb down.

It was so obvious a go that there was no point in testing it, so Hel broke back through the sheet of water and scrambled up to Le Cagot's perch where, shouting over the din of the falls into Beñat's ear, their helmets clicking together occasionally, he explained the happy situation. They decided to leave the line in place to facilitate the return, and down they went one after the other, until they were at the base of the rubble-packed book corner.

It was a peculiar phenomenon that, once they were behind the silver-black sheet of the falls, they could speak in almost normal volume, as the curtain of water seemed to block out sound, and it was quieter behind the falls than without. As they descended, the falls slowly broke up as a great quantity of its water spun off in the mist, and the weight of the cascade at the bottom was considerably less than it was above. Its mass was diffused, and passing through it was more like going through a torrential rainfall than a waterfall. They advanced cautiously through the blinding, frigid steam, over a slick rock floor scrubbed clean of rubble. As they pressed on, the mists thinned until they found themselves in the clear dark air, the noise of the falls receding behind them. They paused and looked around. It was beautiful, a diamond cave of more human dimensions than the awful Le Cagot's Chaos; a tourist cave, far beyond the access capacities of any tourist.

Although it was wasteful, their curiosity impelled them to scratch off another magnesium flare.

Breathtakingly beautiful. Behind them, billowing clouds of mist churning lazily in the suction of the falling water. All around and above them, wet and dripping, the walls were encrusted with aragonite crystals that glittered as Le Cagot moved the flare back and forth. Along the north wall, a frozen waterfall of flowstone oozed down the side and puddled like ossified taffy. To the east, receding and overlapping curtains of calcite drapery, delicate and razor-sharp, seemed to ripple in an unfelt spelean wind. Close to the walls, thickets of slender crystal stalactites pointed down toward stumpy stalagmites, and here and there the forest was dominated by a thick column formed by the union of these patient speleothems.

They did not speak until the glare sputtered orange and went out, and the glitter of the walls was replaced by dancing dots of light in their eyes as they dilated to accommodate the relatively feeble helmet lamps. Le Cagot's voice was uncharacteristically hushed when he said, "We shall call this Zazpiak Bat Cave."

Hel nodded. *Zazpiak bat:* "Out of seven, let there be one," the motto of those who sought to unite the seven Basque provinces into a Trans-Pyrenean republic. An impractical dream, neither likely nor desirable, but a useful focus for the activities of men who choose romantic danger over safe boredom, men who are capable of being cruel and stupid, but never small or cowardly. And it was right that the cuckoo-land dream of a Basque nation be represented by a fairyland cave that was all but inaccessible.

He squatted down and made a rough measurement back to the top of the waterfall with his clinometer, then he did a bit of mental arithmetic. "We're down almost to the level of the Torrent of Holçarté. The outfall can't be far ahead."

"Yes," Le Cagot said, "but where is the river? What have you done with it?"

It was true that the river had disappeared. Broken up by the falls, it had evidently sounded through cracks and fissures and must be running below them somewhere. There were two possibilities. Either it would emerge again within the cave somewhere before them, or the cracks around the base of the waterfall constituted its final swallow before its outfall into the gorge. This latter would be unfortunate, because it would deny them any hope of final conquest by swimming through to the open air and sky. It would also make the long vigil of the Basque lads camped at the outfall pointless.

Le Cagot took the lead as they advanced through Zazpiak Bat Cavern, as he always did when the going was reasonably easy. They both knew that Nicholai was the better rock tactician; it was not necessary for Le Cagot to admit it, or for Hel to accent it. The lead simply changed automatically with the nature of a cave's features. Hel led through shafts, down faces, around cornices; while Le Cagot led as they entered caves and dramatic features, which he therefore "discovered" and named.

As he led, Le Cagot was testing his voice in the cave, singing one of those whining, atonic Basque songs that demonstrate the race's ability to withstand aesthetic pain. The song contained that uniquely Basque onomatopoeia that goes beyond imitations of sounds, to imitations of emotional states. In the refrain of Le Cagot's song, work was being done sloppily *(kirrimarra)* by a man in confused haste *(tarrapatakan)*.

He stopped singing when he approached the end of the diamond cave and stood before a broad, low-roofed gallery that opened out like a black, toothless grin. Indeed, it held a joke.

Le Cagot directed his lamp down the passage. The slope increased slightly, but it was no more than 15°, and there was enough overhead space for a man to stand erect. It was an avenue, a veritable boulevard! And yet more interesting, it was probably the last feature of the cave system. He stepped forward . . . and fell with a clatter of gear.

The floor of the passage was thickly coated with clay marl, as slick and filthy as axle grease and flat on his back, Le Cagot was slipping down the incline, not moving very fast at first, but absolutely helpless to arrest his slide. He cursed and pawed around for a hold, but everything was coated with the slimy mess, and there were no boulders or outcroppings to cling to. His struggling did no more than turn him around so that he was going down backward, half-sitting, helpless, furious, and risible. His slide began to pick up speed. From back on the edge of the marl shaft, Hel watched the helmet light grow smaller as it receded, turning slowly like the beam of a lighthouse. There was nothing he could do. The situation was basically comic, but if there was a cliff at the end of the passage . . .

There was no cliff at the end of the passage. Hel had never known a marl chute at this depth. At a good distance away, perhaps sixty meters, the light stopped moving. There was no sound, no call for help. Hel feared that Le Cagot had been bashed against the side of the passage and was lying there broken up.

Then came a sound up through the passage, Le Cagot's voice roaring with fury and outrage, the words indistinct because of the covering reverberations, but carrying the tonalities of wounded dignity. One phrase in the echoing outpour was decipherable: ". . . by the Perforated Balls of Saint Sebastian!"

So Le Cagot was unhurt. The situation might even be funny, were it not that their only coil of rope had gone down with him, and not even that ox of Urt could throw a coil of line sixty meters uphill.

Hel blew out a deep sigh. He would have to go back through Zazpiak Bat Cavern, through the base of the waterfall, up the rubble corner, back out through the falls, and up that dicy climb through icy mists to retrieve the line they had left in place to ease their retreat. The thought of it made him weary.

But . . . He tugged off his pack. No point carrying it with him. He called down the marl passage, spacing his words out so they would be understood through the muffling reverberations.

"I'm . . . going . . . after . . . line!"

The dot of light below moved. Le Cagot was standing up. "Why . . . don't . . . you . . . do . . . that!" came the call back. Suddenly the light disappeared, and there was the echoing sound of a splash, followed by a medley of angry roaring, scrambling, sputtering, and swearing. Then the light reappeared.

Hel's laughter filled both the passage and the cave. Le Cagot had evidently fallen into the river which must have come back to the surface down there. What a beginner's stunt!

Le Cagot's voice echoed back up the marl chute: "I . . . may . . . kill . . . you . . . when . . . you . . . get . . . down . . . here!"

Hel laughed again and set off back to the lip of the falls.

Three-quarters of an hour later, he was back at the head of the marl chute, fixing the line into a healthy crack by means of a choke nut.

Hel tried at first to take a rope-controlled glissade on his feet, but that was not on. The marl was too slimy. Almost at once he found himself on his butt, slipping down feet first, a gooey prow bone of black marl building up at his crotch and oozing back over his hip. It was nasty stuff, an ignoble obstacle, formidable enough but lacking the clean dignity of a cave's good challenges: cliffs and rotten rock, vertical shafts and dicy siphons. It was a mosquito of a problem, stupid and irritating, the overcoming of which brought no glory. Marl chutes are despised by all cavers who have mucked about in them.

When Hel glissed silently to his side, Le Cagot was sitting on a smooth slab, finishing off a hardtack biscuit and a cut of *xoritzo*. He ignored Hel's approach, still sulky over his own undignified descent, and dripping wet from his dunking.

Hel looked around. No doubt of it, this was the end of the cave system. The chamber was the size of a small house, or of one of the reception rooms of his château at Etchebar. Evidently, it was sometimes filled with water —the walls were smooth, and the floor was free of rubble. The slab on which Le Cagot was taking his lunch covered two-thirds of the floor, and in the distant corner there was a neat cubic depression about five meters on each edge—a regular "wine cellar" of a sump constituting the lowest point of the entire cave system. Hel went to the edge of the Wine Cellar and directed his beam down. The sides were smooth, but it looked to be a fairly easy corner climb, and he wondered why Le Cagot hadn't climbed down to be the first man to the end of the cave.

"I was saving it for you," Le Cagot explained.

"An impulse toward fair play?"

"Exactly."

There was something very wrong here. Basque to the bone though he was, Le Cagot had been educated in France, and the concept of fair play is totally alien to the mentality of the French, a people who have produced generations of aristocrats, but not a single gentleman; a culture in which the legal substitutes for the fair; a language in which the only word for fair play is the borrowed English.

Still, there was no point in standing there and letting the floor of that final Wine Cellar go virgin. Hel looked down, scanning for the best holds.

. . . Wait a minute! That splash. Le Cagot had fallen into water. Where was it?

Hel carefully lowered his boot into the Wine Cellar. A few centimeters down, it broke the surface of a pool so clear it appeared to be air. The features of the rock below were so sharp that no one would suspect they were under water.

"You bastard," Hel whispered. Then he laughed. "And you climbed right down into it, didn't you?"

The instant he pulled up his boot, the ripples disappeared from the surface, sucked flat by a strong siphon action below. Hel knelt at the side of the sump and examined it with fascination. The surface was not still at all; it was drawn tight and smooth by the powerful current below. Indeed, it bowed slightly, and when he put in his finger, there was a strong tug and a wake of eddy patterns behind it. He could make out a triangular opening down at the bottom of the sump which must be the outflow of the river. He had met trick pools like these before in caves, pools into which the water entered without bubbles to mark its current, the water so purified of those minerals and microorganisms that give it its tint of color.

Hel examined the walls of their small chamber for signs of water line. Obviously, the outflow through that triangular pipe down there had to be fairly constant, while the volume of the underground river varied with rainfall and seep water. This whole chamber, and that marl chute behind them acted as a kind of cistern that accepted the difference between inflow and outflow. That would account for marl appearing this far underground. There were doubtless times when this chamber in which they sat was full of water which backed up through the long chute. Indeed, upon rare occasions of heavy rain, the waterfall back there probably dropped into a shallow lake that filled the floor of Zazpiak Cavern. That would explain the stubbiness of the stalagmites in that diamond cave. If they had arrived at some other time, say a week after heavy rains had seeped down, they might have found their journey ending in Zazpiak Cavern. They had planned all along to consider a scuba exploration to the outfall in some future run, should the timing on the dye test prove practicable. But if they had been stopped by a shallow lake in the cavern above, it would have been unlikely that Hel would ever find that marl chute under water, swim all the way down it, locate this Wine Cellar sump, pass out through the triangular opening, and make it through that powerful current to the outfall. They were lucky to have made their descent after a long dry spell.

"Well?" Le Cagot said, looking at his watch. "Shall we drop the dye in?"

"What time is it?"

"A little before eleven."

"Let's wait for straight up. It'll make calculation easier." Hel looked down through the invisible pane of water. It was difficult to believe that there at the bottom, among those clear features of the floor, a current of great force was rushing, sucking. "I wish I knew two things," he said.

"Only two?"

"I wish I knew how fast that water was moving. And I wish I knew if that triangular pipe was clear."

"Let's say we get a good timing—say ten minutes—

257

are you going to try swimming it next time we come down?"

"Of course. Even with fifteen minutes."

Le Cagot shook his head. "That's a lot of line, Niko. Fifteen minutes through a pipe like that is a lot of line for me to haul you back against the current if you run into trouble. No, I don't think so. Ten minutes is maximum. If it's longer than that, we should let it go. It's not so bad to leave a few of Nature's mysteries virgin."

Le Cagot was right, of course.

"You have any bread in your pack?" Hel asked.

"What are you going to do?"

"Cast it upon the waters."

Le Cagot tossed over a cut of his flute baguette; Hel set it gently on the surface of the sump water and watched its motion. It sank slowly, seeming to fall in slow motion through clear air, as it pulsed and vibrated with unseen eddies. It was an unreal and eerie sight, and the two men watched it fascinated. Then suddenly, like magic, it was gone. It had touched the current down there and had been snatched into the pipe faster than the eye could follow.

Le Cagot whistled under his breath. "I don't know, Niko. That looks like a bad thing."

But already Hel was making preliminary decisions. He would have to enter the pipe feet first with no fins because it would be suicidal to rush head first through that triangular pipe, in case he met a choking boulder inside there. That could be a nasty knock. Then too, he would want to be head first coming out if it was not a go, so he could help Le Cagot's weight on the safety line by pushing with his feet.

"I don't like it, Niko. That little hole there could kill your ass and, what is worse, reduce the number of my admirers by one. And remember, dying is a serious business. If a man dies with a sin on his soul, he goes to Spain."

"We have a couple of weeks to think it over. After we get out, we'll talk about it and see if it's worth dragging scuba gear down here. For all we know, the dye test will tell us the pipe's too long for a try. What time is it?"

"Coming up to the hour."

"Let's drop off the dye then."

The fluorescein dye they had carried down was in two-kilo bags. Hel tugged them out of their packs, and Le Cagot cut off the corners and lined them along the edge of the Wine Cellar sump. When the second hand swept to twelve, they pushed them all in. Bright green smoke seeped from the cuts as the bags dropped through the crystal water. Two of them disappeared instantly through the triangular pipe, but the other two lay on the bottom, their smoking streams of color rushing horizontally toward the pipe until the nearly empty bags were snatched away by the current. Three seconds later, the water was clear and still again.

"Niko? I have decided to christen this little pool Le Cagot's Soul."

"Oh?"

"Yes. Because it is clear and pure and lucid."

"And treacherous and dangerous?"

"You know, Niko, I begin to suspect that you are a man of prose. It is a blemish in you."

"No one's perfect."

"Speak for yourself."

The return to the base of the rubble cone was relatively quick. Their newly discovered cave system was, after all, a clean and easy one with no long crawls through tight passages and around breakdowns, and no pits to contend with, because the underground river ran along the surface of a hard schist bed.

The Basque boys dozing up at the winch were surprised to hear their voices over the headsets of the field telephones hours before they had expected them.

"We have a surprise for you," one lad said over the line.

"What's that?" Le Cagot asked.

"Wait till you get up and see for yourself."

The long haul up from the tip of the rubble cone to the first corkscrew shaft was draining for each of the men. The strain on the diaphragm and chest from hanging in a parachute harness is very great, and men have been known to suffocate from it. It was such a constriction of the diaphragm that caused Christ's death on the cross—a fact the aptness of which did not escape Le Cagot's notice and comment.

To shorten the torture of hanging in the straps and struggling to breathe, the lads at the low-geared winch pedaled heroically until the man below could take a purchase within the corkscrew and rest for a while, getting some oxygen back into his blood.

Hel came up last, leaving the bulk of their gear below for future explorations. After he negotiated the double dihedron with a slack cable, it was a short straight haul up to the cone point of the *gouffre,* and he emerged from blinding blackness . . . into blinding white.

While they had been below, an uncommon atmospheric inversion had seeped into the mountains, creating that most dangerous of weather phenomena: a whiteout.

For several days, Hel and his mountaineer companions had known that conditions were developing toward a whiteout because, like all Basques from Haute Soule, they were constantly if subliminally attuned to the weather patterns that could be read in the eloquent Basque sky as the dominant winds circled in their ancient and regular boxing of the compass. First *Ipharra,* the north wind, sweeps the sky clear of clouds and brings a cold, greenish-blue light to the Basque sky, tinting and hazing the distant mountains. *Ipharra* weather is brief, for soon the wind swings to the east and becomes the cool *Iduzki-haizea,* "the sunny wind," which rises each morning and falls at sunset, producing the paradox of cool afternoons with warm evenings. The atmosphere is both moist and clear, making the contours of the countryside sharp, particularly when the sun is low and its oblique light picks out the textures of bush and tree; but the moisture blues and blurs details on the distant mountains, softening their outlines, smudging the border between mountain and sky. Then one morning one looks out to find that the atmosphere has become crystalline, and distant mountains have lost their blue haze, have closed in around the valley, their razor outlines acid-etched into the ardent blue of the sky. This is the time of *Hego-churia,* "the white southeast wind." In autumn, *Hego-churia* often dominates the weather for weeks on end, bringing the Pays Basque's grandest season. With a kind of karma justice, the glory of *Hego-churia* is followed by the fury

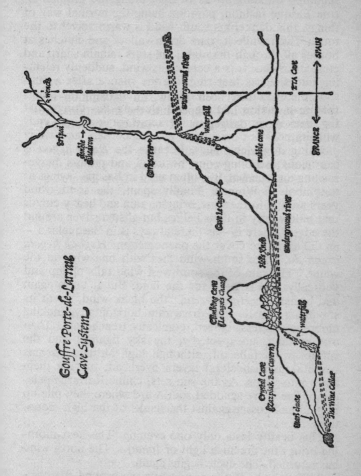

Gouffre Porte-de-Larrak
Cave System

SPAIN ← → FRANCE

ETA Cave

Winch

Sulpai

Bottle
Glaciarus

underground river

waterfall

Crossroads

Cave Le Cayol

rubble cone

underground river

Halb Knob

Climbing Cave
(Le Cage's Chaos)

Crystal Cave
(Razz pink Bat Cavern)

Short chute

waterfall

The Wine Cellar

of *Haize-hegoa,* the bone-dry south wind that roars around the flanks of the mountains, crashing shutters in the villages, ripping roof tiles off, cracking weak trees, scudding blinding swirls of dust along the ground. In true Basque fashion, paradox being the normal way of things, this dangerous south wind is warm velvet to the touch. Even while it roars down valleys and clutches at houses all through the night, the stars remain sharp and close overhead. It is a capricious wind, suddenly relenting into silences that ring like the silence after a gunshot, then returning with full fury, destroying the things that man makes, testing and shaping the things that God makes, shortening tempers and fraying nerve ends with its constant screaming around corners and reedy moaning down chimneys. Because the *Haize-hegoa* is capricious and dangerous, beautiful and pitiless, nerve-racking and sensual, it is often used in Basque sayings as a symbol of Woman. Finally spent, the south wind veers around to the west, bringing rain and heavy clouds that billow gray in their bellies but glisten silver around the edges. There is—as there always is in Basqueland— an old saying to cover the phenomenon: *Hegoak hegala urean du,* "The south wind flies with one wing in the water." The rain of the southwest wind falls plump and vertically and is good for the land. But it veers again and brings the *Haize-belza,* "the black wind," with its streaming squalls that drive rain horizontally, making umbrellas useless, indeed, comically treacherous. Then one evening, unexpectedly, the sky lightens and the surface wind falls off, although high altitude streams continue to rush cloud layers overhead, tugging them apart into wisps. As the sun sets, chimerical archipelagos of fleece are scudded southward where they pile up in gold and russet against the flanks of the high mountains.

This beauty lasts only one evening. The next morning brings the greenish light of *Ipharra.* The north wind has returned. The cycle begins again.

Although the winds regularly cycle around the compass, each with its distinctive personality, it is not possible to say that Basque weather is predictable; for in some years there are three or four such cycles, and in other years only one. Also, within the context of each prevailing wind there are vagaries of force and longevity. Indeed, sometimes the wind turns through a complete personality during a night, and the next morning it seems that one of the dominant phases has been skipped. Too, there are the balance times between the dominance of two winds, when neither is strong enough to dictate. At such times, the mountain Basque say, "There is no weather today."

And when there is no weather, no motion of wind in the mountains, then sometimes comes the beautiful killer: the whiteout. Thick blankets of mist develop, dazzling white because they are lighted by the brilliant sun above the layer. Eye-stinging, impenetrable, so dense and bright that the extended hand is a faint ghost and the feet are lost in milky glare, a major whiteout produces conditions more dangerous than simple blindness; it produces vertigo and sensory inversion. A man experienced in the ways of the Basque mountains can move through the darkest night. His blindness triggers off a compensating heightening of other senses; the movement of wind on his cheek tells him that he is approaching an obstacle; small sounds of rolling pebbles give him the slant of the ground and the distance below. And the black is never complete; there is always some skyglow picked up by widely dilated eyes.

But in a whiteout, none of these compensating sensory reactions obtains. The dumb nerves of the eyes, flooded and stung with light, persist in telling the central nervous system that they can see, and the hearing and tactile systems relax, slumber. There is no wind to offer subtle indications of distance, for wind and whiteout cannot coexist. And all sound is perfidious, for it carries far and crisp through the moisture-laden air, but seems to come from all directions at once, like sound under water.

And it was into a blinding whiteout that Hel emerged from the black of the cave shaft. As he unbuckled his parachute harness, Le Cagot's voice came from somewhere up on the rim of the *gouffre*.

"This is the surprise they told us about."

"How nice." When Hel scrambled up the *gouffre* side, he could dimly make out five forms hovering around the winch. He had to approach within a meter before he recognized the other two as the lads who had been camping down in Holçarté Gorge, waiting for the outfall of dye from the underground stream. "You climbed up through this?" Nicholai asked.

"It was forming as we came. We just made it."

"What is it like lower down?"

They were all mountain men here; they knew what he meant.

"It's grayer."

"Much?"

"Much."

If the sheet of mist was grayer below, passing down through it would be folly in this Swiss-cheese mountainside dotted with treacherous cracks and steep *gouffres*. They would have to climb upward and hope to break out of the mist before they ran out of mountain. It is always wisest to do so in a whiteout: it is difficult to fall *up* a mountain.

Alone, Hel could have made it down the mountain, despite the blinding mist with its sensory trickery. He could have relied on a combination of his proximity sense and intimate knowledge of the features of the mountain to move cautiously down over terrain hidden in the blinding haze. But he could not be responsible for Le Cagot and the four Basque lads.

Because it was impossible to see clearly farther than a meter and to see at all farther than three, they roped up, and Hel led a slow and careful ascent, picking the long and easy way around outcroppings of rock, across slides of scree, past the rims of deep *gouffres*. The blanket of mist did not thicken, but it grew ever more blindingly bright as they rose toward the sun. After three-quarters of an hour, Hel suddenly broke through into sunlight and taut blue skies, and the scene that greeted him was beautiful, and awful. In the absolute stillness of the mist layer, the motion of his body up through it created languorous swirls and billows that churned lazily behind him and down into which his rope passed to the next man only ten meters below, but hidden behind the milky wall. He was almost at eye level with a platform of dense white mist that stretched flat and stable for hundreds of kilometers, filling all the valleys below as though with a great snow. Through

264

this blanket of mist, the tops of the Basque Pyrenees stuck up, clear and sharp-edged in the ardent sunlight, like bits of mosaic tesserae set in a fleecy plaster. And above was the taut dark-blue sky peculiar to the Basque country. The stillness was so absolute that he could hear the squeak and surge of blood through his temples.

Then he heard another sound, Le Cagot's voice from below demanding, "Are we to stand here forever? By the Complaining Balls of Jeremiah, you should have relieved yourself before we started!" And when he broke through the layer of mist, he said, "Oh, I see. You were admiring the Basque spectacle all by yourself, while we dangled down there like bait on a line! You're a selfish man, Niko."

The sun was beginning to sink, so they moved around the flank of the mountain with some haste, to arrive at the highest of the *artzain xola* shelters before dark. When they got there, they found it already occupied by two old shepherds driven up from the other side of the mountain by the whiteout. Their heavy packs revealed them to be smugglers in a minor way. The Basque temperament is more comfortable with smuggling than with commerce; with poaching than with hunting. Socially condoned activities lack spice.

There was an exchange of greetings and wine, and the eight of the "fist" to the intruder, declaring that, if his will had power, that plane would fall from the sky like a wounded bird, littering Spain with the bodies of two hundred stupid vacationers on their way to Lisbon, and relieving the world of the burden of surplus population, for anyone who would fly through so perfect a moment was, by definition, an expendable being.

Le Cagot's gall up, he went on to extend his malediction to all those outlanders who defiled the mountains: the tourists, the back-packers, the hunters, and especially the skiers who bring vile machines into the mountains because they are too soft to walk up the hill, and who build ugly lodges and noisy après-ski amusements. The filthy shits! It was for dealing with loud-mouthed skiers and their giggling bunnies that God said, on the eighth day, let there also be handguns!

One of the old shepherds nodded sagely and agreed that outlanders were universally evil. *"Atzerri; otzerri."*

265

Following the ritual of conversation among strangers, Hel matched this ancient *dicton* with "But I suppose *chori bakhoitzari eder bere ohantzea.*"

"True," Le Cagot said. *"Zahar hitzak, zuhur hitzak."*

Hel smiled. These were the first words of Basque he had learned, years ago in his cell in Sugamo Prison. "With the possible exception," he said, "of that one."

The old smugglers considered this response for a moment, then both laughed aloud and slapped their knees. *"Hori phensatu zuenak, ongi afaldu zuen!"* (An Englishman with a clever story "dines out on it." Within the Basque culture, it is the listener who enjoys the feast.)

They sat in silence, drinking and eating slowly as the sun fell, drawing after it the gold and russet of the cloud layer. One of the young cavers stretched his legs out with a satisfied grunt and declared that this was the life. Hel smiled to himself, knowing that this would probably not be the life for this young man, touched as he was by television and radio. Like most of the Basque young, he would probably end up lured to the factories of the big cities, where his wife could have a refrigerator, and he could drink Coca-Cola in a café with plastic tables—the good life that was a product of the French Economic Miracle.

"It is the good life," Le Cagot said lazily. "I have traveled, and I have turned the world over in my hand, like a stone with attractive veining, and this I have discovered: a man is happiest when there is a balance between his needs and his possessions. Now the question is: how to achieve this balance. One could seek to do this by increasing his goods to the level of his appetites, but that would be stupid. It would involve doing unnatural things—bargaining, haggling, scrimping, working. Ergo? Ergo, the wise man achieves the balance by reducing his needs to the level of his possessions. And this is best done by learning to value the free things of life: the mountains, laughter, poetry, wine offered by a friend, older and fatter women. Now, me? I am perfectly capable of being happy with what I have. The problem is getting enough of it in the first place!"

"Le Cagot?" one of the old smugglers asked, as he

made himself comfortable in a corner of the *artzain xola*. "Give us a story to sleep on."

"Yes," said his companion. "Let it be of old things."

A true folk poet, who would rather tell a story than write one, Le Cagot began to weave fables in his rich basso voice, while the others listened or dozed. Everyone knew the tales, but the pleasure lay in the art of telling them. And Basque is a language more suited to storytelling than to exchanging information. No one can learn to speak Basque beautifully; like eye color or blood type, it is something one has to be born to. The language is subtle and loosely regulated, with its circumlocutory word orders, its vague declensions, its doubled conjugations, both synthetic and periphrastic, with its old "story" forms mixed with formal verb patterns. Basque is a song, and while outlanders may learn the words, they can never master the music.

Le Cagot told of the *Basa-andere,* the Wildlady who kills men in the most wonderful way. It is widely known that the *Basa-andere* is beautiful and perfectly formed for love, and that the soft golden hair that covers all her body is strangely appealing. Should a man have the misfortune to come upon her in the forest (she is always to be found kneeling beside a stream, combing the hair of her stomach with a golden comb), she will turn to him and fix him with a smile, then lie back and lift her knees, offering her body. Now, everyone knows that the pleasure from her is so intense that a man dies of it during climax, but still many and many have willingly died, their backs arched in the agony of unimaginable pleasure.

One of the old smugglers declared that he once found a man in the mountains who had died so, and in his dim staring eyes there was an awful mixture of fright and pleasure.

And the quietest of the young lads prayed that God would give him the strength to resist, should he ever come upon the *Basa-andere* with her golden comb. "You say she is all covered with golden hair, Le Cagot? I cannot imagine breasts covered with hair. Are the nipples visible then?"

Le Cagot sniffed and stretched out on the ground. "In truth, I cannot say from personal experience, child.

These eyes have never seen the *Basa-andere*. And I am glad of that, for had we met, that poor lady would at this moment be dead from pleasure."

The old man laughed and ripped up a turf of grass, which he threw at the poet. "Truly, Le Cagot, you are as full of shit as God is of mercy!"

"True," Le Cagot admitted. "So true. Have you ever heard me tell the story of . . ."

When dawn came the whiteout was gone, churned away by the night winds. Before they broke up, Hel paid the lads for their assistance and asked them to take apart the winch and tripod and bring them down to a barn in Larrau for storage, as they were already beginning to plan the next exploration into the cave, this time with wet suits and scuba gear, for the boys camping down by the fallout in the Gorge of Holçarté had marked the appearance of dye in the water at eight minutes after the hour. Although eight minutes is not a long time, it could indicate considerable distance, considering the speed of the water through that triangular pipe at the bottom of the Wine Cellar. But if the water pipe was not filled with obstructions or too narrow for a man, they might have the pleasure of exploring their cave from entrance shaft to outfall before they shared the secret of its existence with the caving fraternity.

Hel and Le Cagot trotted and glissaded down the side of the mountain to the narrow track on which they had parked Hel's Volvo. He delivered the door a mighty kick with his boot, as was his habit, and after examining the satisfying dent, they got in and drove down to the village of Larrau, where they stopped off to have a breakfast of bread, cheese, and coffee, after having splashed and scrubbed away most of the dried mud with which they were caked.

Their hostess was a vigorous widow with a strong ample body and a bawdy laugh who used two rooms of her house as a café/restaurant/tobacco shop. She and Le Cagot had a relationship of many years, for when things got too hot for him in Spain, he often crossed into France through the Forest of Irraty that abutted this village. Since time beyond memory, the Forest of Irraty had been both a sanctuary and an avenue for smugglers and bandits crossing from the Basque provinces under Spanish occupation to those under French. By ancient tradition, it is considered impolite—and dangerous—to seem to recognize anyone met in this forest.

When they entered the café, still wet from the pump in back, they were questioned by the half-dozen old men taking their morning wine. How had it gone up at the *gouffre?* Was there a cave under the hole?

Le Cagot was ordering breakfast, his hand resting proprietarily on the hip of the hostess. He did not have to think twice about guarding the secret of the new cave, for he automatically fell into the Basque trait of responding to direct questions with misleading vagueness that is not quite lying.

"Not all holes lead to caves, my friends."

The hostess's eyes glittered at what she took to be double entendre. She pushed his hand away with pleased coquetry.

"And did you meet Spanish border patrols?" an old man asked.

"No, I was not required to burden hell with more Fascist souls. Does that please you, Father?" Le Cagot addressed this last to the gaunt revolutionary priest sitting in the darkest corner of the café, who had turned his face away upon the entrance of Le Cagot and Hel. Father Xavier nurtured a smoldering hate for Le Cagot and a flaming one for Hel. Though he never faced danger personally, he wandered from village to village along the border, preaching the revolution and attempting to bind the goals of Basque independence to those of the Church—the Basque manifestation of that general effort on the part of God-merchants to diversify into social and political issues, now that the world was no longer a good market for hell-scare and soul-saving.

The priest's hatred (which he termed "righteous wrath") for Le Cagot was based on the fact that praise and hero worship that properly belonged to the ordained leaders of the revolution was being siphoned away by this blaspheming and scandalous man who had spent a part of his life in the Land of the Wolves, out of the Pays Basque. But at least Le Cagot was a native son. This Hel was a different matter. He was an outlander who never went to Mass and who lived with an Oriental woman. And it was galling to the priest that young Basque cavers, boys who should have chosen their idols from the ranks of the priesthood, told stories of his spelunking exploits and of the time he had crossed with Le Cagot into Spain and broken into a military prison in Bilbao to release ETA prisoners. This was the kind of man who could contaminate the revolution and divert its energies from the establishment of a Basque Theocracy, a last fortress of fundamentalist Catholicism in a land where Christian practices were primitive and deep, and where the key to the gates of heaven was a profound weapon of control.

Shortly after he bought his home in Etchebar, Hel began to receive unsigned threats and hate notes. Upon two occasions there were "spontaneous" midnight charivaris outside the château, and live cats bound in burning straw were thrown at the walls of the house, where they screamed in their death throes. Although Hel's experience had taught him to despise these fanatical Third World priests who incite children to their deaths for the purpose of linking the cause of social reform to the Church to save that institution from natural atrophy in the face of knowledge and enlightenment, he would nevertheless have ignored this kind of harassment. But he intended to make the Basque country his permanent home, now that the Japanese culture was infected with Western values, and he had to put an end to these insults because the Basque mentality ridicules those who are ridiculed. Anonymous letters and the mob frenzy of the charivari are manifestations of cowardice, and Hel had an intelligent fear of cowards, who are always more dangerous than brave men, when they outnumber you or get a chance to strike from behind, because they are forced to do maximal damage, dreading as they do the consequences of retaliation, should you survive.

Through Le Cagot's contacts, Hel discovered the author of these craven acts, and a couple of months later he came across the priest in the back room of a café in Ste. Engrace, where he was eating a free meal in silence, occasionally glaring at Nicholai, who was taking a glass of red with several men of the village—men who had previously been sitting at the priest's table, listening to his wisdom and cant.

When the men went off to work, Hel joined the priest at his table. Father Xavier started to rise, but Hel gripped his forearm and returned him to his chair. "You are a good man, Father," he said in his prison whisper. "A saintly man. In fact, at this moment you are closer to heaven than you know. Finish your food and listen well. There will be no more anonymous letters, no more charivaris. Do you understand?"

"I'm afraid I don't—"

"Eat."

"What?"

"Eat!"

Father Xavier pushed another forkful of piperade into his mouth and chewed sullenly.

"Eat faster, Father. Fill your mouth with food you have not earned."

The priest's eyes were damp with fury and fear, but he shoveled forkful after forkful into his mouth and swallowed as rapidly as he could.

"If you choose to stay in this corner of the world, Father, and if you do not feel prepared to join your God, then this is what you will do. Each time we meet in a village, you will leave that village immediately. Each time we meet on the trails, you will step off the track and turn your back as I pass. You can eat faster than that!"

The priest choked on his food, and Hel left him gasping and gagging. That evening, he told the story to Le Cagot with instructions to make sure it got around. Hel considered public humiliation of this coward to be necessary.

"Hey, why don't you answer me, Father Esteka?" Le Cagot asked.*

The priest rose and left the café, as Le Cagot called after him, "Hola! Aren't you going to finish your piperade?"

Because they were Catholic, the old men in the café

* *Esteka* is Basque for "sexual deficiency."

271

could not laugh; but they grinned, because they were Basque.

Le Cagot patted the hostess's bottom and sent her after their food. "I don't think we have made a great friend there, Niko. And he is a man to be feared." Le Cagot laughed. "After all, his father was French and very active in the Resistance."

Hel smiled. "Have you ever met one who was not?"

"True. It is astonishing that the Germans managed to hold France with so few divisions, considering that everyone who wasn't draining German resources by the clever maneuver of surrendering en masse and making the Nazi's feed them was vigorously and bravely engaged in the Resistance. Is there a village without its Place de la Resistance? But one has to be fair; one has to understand the Gallic notion of resistance. Any hotelier who overcharged a German was in the Resistance. Each whore who gave a German soldier the clap was a freedom fighter. All those who obeyed while viciously withholding their cheerful morning *bonjours* were heroes of liberty!"

Hel laughed. "You're being a little hard on the French."

"It is history that is hard on them. I mean real history, not the *verité à la cinquième République* that they teach in their schools. The truth be known, I admire the French more than any other foreigners. In the centuries they have lived beside the Basque, they have absorbed certain virtues—understanding, philosophic insight, a sense of humor—and these have made them the best of the 'others.' But even I am forced to admit that they are a ridiculous people, just as one must confess that the British are bungling, the Italians incompetent, the Americans neurotic, the Germans romantically savage, the Arabs vicious, the Russians barbaric, and the Dutch make cheese. Take the particular manifestation of French ridiculousness that makes them attempt to combine their myopic devotion to money with the pursuit of phantom *gloire*. The same people who dilute their burgundy for modest profit willingly spend millions of francs on the atomic contamination of the Pacific Ocean in the hope that they will be thought to be the technological equals of the Americans. They see themselves as the feisty David against the grasping Goliath. Sadly for their image abroad, the rest of the world views their actions as the ludicrous egotism of the amorous ant climbing a cow's leg and assuring her that he will be gentle."

Le Cagot looked down at the tabletop thoughtfully. "I cannot think of anything further to say about the French just now."

The widow had joined them at table, sitting close to Le Cagot and pressing her knee against his. "Hey, you have a visitor down at Etchehelia," she told Hel, using the Basque name for his château. "It is a girl. An outsider. Arrived yesterday evening."

Hel was not surprised that this news was already in Larrau, three mountains and fifteen kilometers from his home. It had doubtless been common knowledge in all the local villages within four hours of the visitor's arrival.

"What do you know about her?" Hel asked.

The widow shrugged and tucked down the corners of her mouth, indicating that she knew only the barest facts. "She took coffee *chez* Jaureguiberry and did not have money to pay. She walked all the way from Tardets to Etchebar and was seen from the hills several times. She is young, but not too young to bear. She wore short pants that showed her legs, and it is said that she has a plump chest. She was received by your woman, who paid her bill with Jaureguiberry. She has an English accent. And the old gossips in your village say that she is a whore from Bayonne who was turned out from her farm for sleeping with the husband of her sister. As you see, very little is known of her."

"You say she is young with a plump chest?" Le Cagot asked. "No doubt she is seeking me, the final experience."

The widow pinched his thigh.

Hel rose from the table. "I think I'll go home and take a bath and a little sleep. You coming?"

Le Cagot looked at the widow sideways. "What do you think? Should I go?"

"I don't care what you do, old man."

But as he started to rise, she tugged him back by his belt.

"Maybe I'll stay a while, Niko. I'll come back this evening and take a look at your girl with the naked legs and the big boobs. If she pleases me, I may bless you with an extension of my visit. Ouch!"

Hel paid and went out to his Volvo, which he kicked in the rear fender, then drove away toward his home.

Château d'Etchebar

After parking in the square of Etchebar (he did not permit automobiles on his property) and giving the roof a parting bash with his fist, Hel walked down the private road to his château feeling, as he always did upon returning home, a paternal affection for this perfect seventeenth-century house into which he had put years of devotion and millions of Swiss francs. It was the thing he loved most in the world, a physical and emotional fortress against the twentieth century. He paused along the path up from the heavy gates to pat the earth in around a newly planted shrub, and as he was doing this he felt the approach of that vague and scattered aura that could only be Pierre, his gardener.

"*Bonjour, M'sieur*," Pierre greeted in his singsong way, as he recognized Hel through the haze of his regularly spaced glasses of red that began with his rising at dawn.

Hel nodded. "I hear we have a guest, Pierre."

"It is so. A girl. She still sleeps. The women have told me that she is a whore from——"

"I know. Is Madame awake?"

"To be sure. She was informed of your approach twenty minutes ago." Pierre looked up into the sky and nodded sagely. "Ah, ah, ah," he said, shaking his head. Hel realized that he was preparing to make a weather prediction, as he did every time they met on the grounds. All the Basque of Haute Soule believe they have special genetic gifts for meteorological prognostication based upon their mountain heritage and the many folk adages devoted to reading weather signs. Pierre's own predictions, delivered with a quiet assurance that was never diminished by his unvarying inaccuracy, had constituted the principal topic of his conversation with M'sieur Hel for fifteen years, ever since the village drunk had been elevated to the rank

275

of the outlander's gardener and his official defender from village gossip.

"Ah, M'sieur, there will be rain before this day is out," Pierre chanted, nodding to himself with resigned conviction. "So there is no point in my setting out these flowers today."

"Is that so, Pierre?" How many hundreds of times had they had this conversation?

"Yes, it is so. Last night at sunset there was red and gold in the little clouds near the mountains. It is a sure sign."

"Oh? But doesn't the saying go the other way? Isn't it *arrats gorriak eguraldi?*"

"That is how the saying goes, M'sieur. However . . ." Pierre's eyes glittered with conspiratorial slyness as he tapped the side of his long nose. ". . . everything depends on the phase of the moon."

"Oh?"

Pierre closed his eyes and nodded slowly, smiling benevolently on the ignorance of all outlanders, even such basically good men as M'sieur Hel. "When the moon is ascending, the rule is as you have said; but when the moon is descending, it is the other way."

"I see. Then when the moon is descending it is: *Goiz gorriak dakarke uri?*"

Pierre frowned, uncomfortable about being forced to a firm prediction. He considered for a moment before answering. "That varies, M'sieur."

"I'm sure it does."

"And . . . there is an additional complication."

"You're going to tell me about it."

Pierre glanced about uneasily and shifted to French, to avoid the risk of offending the earth spirits who, of course, understand only Basque. *"Vous voyez, M'sieur, de temps en temps, la lune se trompe!"*

Hel drew a long breath and shook his head. "Good morning, Pierre."

"Good morning, M'sieur." Pierre tottered down the path to see if there was something else requiring his attention.

His eyes closed and his mind afloat, Hel sat neck-deep in the Japanese wooden tub filled with water so

276

hot that lowering himself into it had been an experience on the limen between pain and pleasure. The servants had fired up the wood-stoked water boiler as soon as they heard that M. Hel was approaching from Larrau, and by the time he had scrubbed himself thoroughly and taken a shock shower in icy water, his Japanese tub was full, and the small bathing room was billowing with dense steam.

Hana dozed across from him, sitting on a higher bench that allowed her to sit neck-deep too. As always when they bathed together, their feet were in casual embrace.

"Do you want to know about the visitor, Nicholai?"

Hel shook his head slowly, not willing to interrupt his comatose relaxation. "Later," he muttered.

After a quarter of an hour, the water cooled enough that it was possible to make a movement in the tub without discomfort. He opened his eyes and smiled sleepily at Hana. "One grows old, my friend. After a couple of days in the mountains, the bath becomes more a medical necessity than a pleasure."

Hana smiled back and squeezed his foot between hers. "Was it a good cave?"

He nodded. "An easy one, really. A walk-in cave with no long crawls, no siphons. Still, it was just about all the work my body could handle."

He climbed the steps on the side of the tub and slid back the padded panel that closed the bathing room off from the small Japanese garden he had been perfecting for the past fifteen years, and which he assumed would be acceptable in another fifteen. Steam billowed past him into the cool air, which felt bracing on his skin, still tight and tingling from the heat. He had learned that a hot tub, twenty minutes of light meditation, an hour of lovemaking, and a quick shower replenished his body and spirit better than a night's sleep; and this routine was habitual with him upon returning from a caving bash or, in the old days, from a counterterrorist stunt.

Hana left the tub and put a lightly padded kimono over her still-wet body. She helped him into his bathing kimono, and they walked across the garden, where he stopped for a moment to adjust a sounding stone in the stream leading from the small pond because the water was low and the sound of it was too treble to please him. The bathing room with its thick plank walls was half hidden in a stand of bamboo that bordered the garden on three sides. Across from it was a low structure of dark wood and sliding paper panels that contained his Japanese room, where he studied and meditated, and his "gun room," where he kept the implements of the trade from which he had recently retired. The fourth side of the garden was closed off by the back of his château, and both of the Japanese buildings were freestanding, so as to avoid breaking the mansard perfection of its marble facade. He had worked through all of one summer, building the Japanese structures with two craftsmen he brought from Kyushu for the purpose, men old enough to remember how to work in wood-and-wedge.

Kneeling at a low lacquered table, facing out toward the Japanese garden, they took a light meal of melon balls (warm, to accent the musky flavor), tart plums (glaucous, icy, and full of juice), unflavored rice cakes, and a half glass of chilled Irouléguy.

The meal done, Hana rose from the table. "Shall I close the panels?"

"Leave one ajar, so we can see the garden."

Hana smiled. Nicholai and his garden . . . like a father with a delicate but willful child. The garden was the most important of his possessions, and often, after a trip, he would return home unannounced, change clothes, and work in the garden for hours before anyone knew he was home. To him, the garden with its subtle articulations was a concrete statement of *shibumi,* and there was an autumnal correctness to the fact that he would probably not live to see its full statement.

She let her kimono fall away. "Shall we have a wager?"

He laughed. "All right. The winner receives . . . let's see. How about one half-hour of the Delight of the Razor?"

"Fine. I am sure I shall enjoy it very much."

"That sure of yourself?"

"My good friend, you have been off in the mountains for three days. Your body has been manufacturing love, but there has been no outlet. You are at a great disadvantage in the wager."

"We shall see."

With Hana and Nicholai, the foreplay was as much mental as physical. They were both Stage IV lovemakers, she by virtue of her excellent training, he because of the mental control he had learned as a youth, and his gift of proximity sense, which allowed him to eavesdrop on his partner's sensations and know precisely where she was in relation to climax contractions. The game was to cause the other to climax first, and it was played with no holds or techniques barred. To the winner went the Delight of the Razor, a deeply relaxing thrill massage in which the skin of the arms, legs, chest, back, stomach, and pubes is lightly brushed with a keenly honed razor. The tingling delight, and the background fear of a slip, combine to require the person receiving the massage to relax completely as the only alternative to unbearable tension and pleasure. Typically, the Delight of the Razor begins with the extremities, sweeping waves of thrill inward as the razor approaches the erogenous areas, which become ardent with pleasure and the shadow of fear. There are subtleties of technique when the razor comes to these zones that are dangerous to describe.

The Delight of the Razor culminates in quick oral lovemaking.

Whichever of them won the wager by making the other climax first would receive the Delight of the Razor, and there was a special cachet to their way of playing the game. They knew one another well enough to bring both of them to the threshold of climax quickly, and the game was played out there, on the teetering edge of pleasure and control.

It was not until after he got away from Sugamo Prison and began his life in the West that Hel's sexual experience took on form and articulation. Before that there had been only amateur play. His relationship with Mariko had not been physical in essence; it had been youthful affection, and their bungling sexual experiences had been nothing more than a physical footnote to their gentle and uncertain affection.

With the Tanaka sisters, Hel entered Stage I lovemaking, that healthy and simplistic stage of sexual curiosity during which strong young animals brimming with the impulse to continue their species exercise themselves on one another's bodies. Although plebeian and monotonic, Stage I is wholesome and honest, and Hel enjoyed his time spent in that rank, regretting only that so many people are sensationally crippled by their cultures and can accept the strong, sweaty lovemaking of Stage I only when disguised as romance, love, affection, or even self-expression. In their confusion, they build relationships upon the sand of passion. Hel considered it a great pity that mass man had come into contact with romantic literature, which created expectations beyond the likelihood of fulfillment and contributed to that marital delinquency characteristic of Western sexual adolescents.

During his brief sojourn in Stage II—the use of sex as psychological aspirin, as social narcosis, a kind of bloodletting to reduce fevers and pressures—Hel began to have glimpses of the fourth level of sexual experience. Because he realized that sexual activity would be a significant part of his life, and because he detested amateurism in all its forms, he undertook to prepare himself. He received professional tactical training in Ceylon and in the exclusive bordellos of Madagascar, where he lived for four months, learning from women of every race and culture.

Stage III, sexual gourmandizing, is the highest stage ever reached by Westerners and, indeed, by most Orientals. Hel moved through this stage leisurely and with high appetite because he was young, his body strong and taut, and his imagination fertile. He was in no danger of getting bogged down in the sexual black masses of artificial stimulation with which the nastier-than-thou jetsetters and the soft intellectuals of the literary and filmmaking worlds seek to compensate for callused nerve ends and imaginations by roiling among one another's tepid flesh and lubricating fluids.

Even while in the sexual smorgasbord of Stage III, Hel began to experiment with such refined tactics as climax hovering and mental intercourse. He found it amusing to associate sexual techniques with Gō nomenclature. Such terms as *aji keshi, ko, furikawari,* and *hane* lent themselves easily as illuminating images; while others, such as *kaketsugi, nozoki,* and *yosu-miru,* could be applied to lovemaking only with a liberal and procrustean view of metaphor.

By the age of thirty, Hel's sexual interests and capacities led him naturally to Stage IV, the final "game phase," in which excitation and climax are relatively trivial terminal gestures in an activity that demands all the mental vigor and reserve of championship Gō, the training of a Ceylonese whore, and the endurance and agility of a gifted grade VI rock climber. The game of his preference was an invention of his own which he called *"kikashi* sex." This could only be played with another Stage IV lovemaker, and only when both were feeling particularly strong. The game was played in a small room, about six *tatami*. Both players dressed in formal kimonos and knelt facing one another, their backs against opposite walls. Each, through concentration alone, was required to come to the verge of climax and to hover there. No contact was permitted, only concentration and such gestures as could be made with one hand.

The object of the game was to cause climax before climaxing yourself, and it was best played while it was raining.

In time, he abandoned *kikashi* sex as being somewhat too demanding, and also because it was a lonely and selfish experience, lacking the affection and caressing of afterplay that decorates the best of lovemaking.

Hana's eyes were squeezed shut with effort, and her lips were stretched over her teeth. She tried to escape from the involute position in which he held her, but he would not release her.

"I thought we agreed that you weren't permitted to do that!" she pled.

"I didn't agree to anything."

"Oh, Nikko . . . I can't! . . . I can't hold on! Damn you!"

She arched her back and emitted a squeak of final effort to avoid climaxing.

Her delight infected Hel, who relinquished his control to allow himself to climax just after she did. Then suddenly his proximity sense sounded the alarm. She was faking! Her aura was not dancing, as it would at climax. He tried to void his mind and arrest his climax, but it was too late. He had broken over the rim of control.

"You devil!" he shouted as he came.

She was laughing as she climaxed a few seconds later.

She lay on her stomach, humming sleepily in appreciation as he slowly inched the razor over her buttock, a perfect object blending the fineness of her Japanese blood with the useful shape of her Black. He kissed it gently and continued the Delight.

"In two months your tenure with me is over, Hana."

"Hmm-hmm." She did not want to break her languor by speaking.

"Have you considered my suggestion that you stay on with me?"

"Hmm-hmm."

"And?"

"Unh-nh-nh-nh-nh." The prolonged sound through slack lips meant, "Don't make me talk."

He chuckled and turned her over onto her back, continuing the thrill massage with close attention to technique and detail. Hana was in a perfect state. She was in her midthirties, the youngest a woman can be and still possess the training and experience of a grand lover. Because of the excellent care she took of her body and because of the time-annihilating effects of her ideal blend of Oriental, Black, and Caucasian strains, she would be in her prime for another fifteen years. She was a delight to look at, and to work on. Her greatest quality lay in her ability to receive pleasure completely and graciously.

When the Delight of the Razor had closed to her centers and had rendered her moist and passive, he concluded the event with its classic quick finish. And for a time they lay together in that comfortable lover's twine that knows how to deal with the extra arm.

"I *have* thought about staying on, Nikko," she said, her voice buzzing against his chest. "There are many reasons that might prompt me to do so. This is the most beautiful spot in the world. I shall always be grateful to you for showing me this corner of the Basque country. And certainly you have constructed a life of *shibumi* luxury here that is attractive. And there is you, so quiet and stern when you deal with the outside world, so boyish in lovemaking. You are not without a certain charm."

"Thank you."

"And I must also confess that it is much rarer to find a well-trained man than an accomplished woman. But . . . it is lonely here. I know that I am free to go to Bayonne or Paris whenever I wish—and I have a good time when I do go—but day to day, despite your attention and the delights of your conversation, and despite the bawdy energy of our friend Le Cagot, it is lonely for a woman whose interests and appetites have been so closely honed as mine have been."

"I understand that."

"It is different for you, Nikko. You are a recluse by nature. You despise the outside world, and you don't need it. I too find that most of the people out there either bore or annoy me. But I am not a recluse by nature, and I have a vivid curiosity. Then too . . . there is another problem."

"Yes?"

"Well, how shall I put this? Personalities such as yours and mine are meant to dominate. Each of us should function in a large society, giving flavor and texture to the mass. The two of us together in one place is like a wasteful concentration of spice in one course of an otherwise bland meal. Do you see what I mean?"

"Does that mean that you have decided to leave when your tenure is up?"

She blew a jet of breath over the hairs of his chest. "It means that I have not yet made up my mind." She was silent for a time, then she said, "I suppose I would really prefer to have the best of both worlds, spending half of every year here, resting and learning with you, and half of each year out there, stunning my audience."

"I see nothing wrong with that."

She laughed. "It would mean that you would have to make do for six months each year with the bronzed,

283

long-legged, mindless nymphs of the Côte Basque. Actresses and models and that sort. Could you do that?"

"As easily as you could make do with round-armed lads possessing excellent muscle tone and honest, empty eyes. For both of us, it would be like subsisting on hors d'oeuvres. But why not? There is some amusement in hors d'oeuvres, though they cloy without nourishing."

"Let me think about it, Nikko. It is an attractive idea." She raised herself onto one elbow and looked down into his half-closed, amused eyes. "Then too, freedom is also attractive. Maybe I won't make any decision at all."

"That's a kind of decision."

They dressed and went to shower beneath the perforated copper cask designed for the purpose by the first enlightened owner of the château nearly three hundred years before.

It was not until they were taking tea in the cream-and-gold east salon that Hel asked about the visitor.

"She is still asleep. When she arrived yesterday evening, she was desperate. She had walked from the village after flying in to Pau from Rome and hitchhiking to Tardets. Although she tried to chat and follow the forms of politeness, I could tell from the first that she was very distraught. She began weeping while she was taking tea. Weeping without knowing she was doing it. I gave her something to calm her and put her to bed. But she awoke during the night with nightmares, and I sat on the edge of her bed, stroking her hair and humming to her, until she was calm and dropped off again."

"What is her problem?"

"She talked about it while I stroked her hair. There was a nasty business at the airport in Rome. Two of her friends were shot and killed."

"Shot by whom?"

"She didn't say. Perhaps she didn't know."

"Why were they shot?"

"I have no idea."

"Did she tell you why she came to our home?"

"Evidently all three of them were on their way here. She had no money, only her plane ticket."

"Did she give you her name?"

284

"Yes. Hannah Stern. She said her uncle was a friend of yours."

Hel set his cup down, closed his eyes, and pushed out a long nasal sigh. "Asa Stern was a friend. He's dead. I am indebted to him. There was a moment when, without his help, I would have died."

"And this indebtedness, does it extend to the girl as well?"

"We'll see. Did you say the blow-away in Rome International happened yesterday afternoon?"

"Or morning. I am not sure which."

"Then it should be on the news at noon. When the girl wakes up, please have her come and see me. I'll be in the garden. Oh, and I think Le Cagot will take dinner with us—if he finishes his business in Larrau in time."

Hel worked in the garden for an hour and a half, trimming, controlling, striving for modest and subtle effects. He was not an artist, but he was sensitive; so while his garden, the major statement of his impulse to create, lacked *sabi,* it had the *shibui* features that separate Japanese art from the mechanical dynamics of Western art and the florid hyperbole of Chinese. There was that sweet melancholy, that forgiving sadness that characterizes the beautiful in the Japanese mind. There was intentional imperfection and organic simplicity that created, then satisfied, aesthetic tensions, functioning rather as balance and imbalance function in Western art.

Just before noon, a servant brought out a battery radio, and Hel listened in his gun room for the twelve o'clock broadcast of BBC World Service. The news reader was a woman whose distinctive voice has been a source of amusement for the international Anglophone community for years. To that peculiar pronunciation that is BBC's own, she adds a clipped, half-strangled sound which the world audience has long taken to be the effect of an uncomfortable suppository, although there is lively dispute and extensive wagering between those who maintain that the suppository is made of sandpaper and those who promote the ice-cube theory.

Buried among the trivia of collapsing governments, the falling dollar, and Belfast bombings was a descrip-

285

tion of the atrocity at Rome International. Two Japanese men, subsequently identified from papers on their persons as Red Army members working in behalf of the Black Septembrists, opened fire with automatic weapons, killing two young Israeli men, whose identities are being withheld. The Red Army assassins were themselves killed in an exchange of gunfire with Italian police and special agents, as were several civilian bystanders. And now for news of a lighter note . . .

"Mr. Hel?"

He switched off the radio and beckoned to the young woman standing in the doorway of the gun room. She was wearing fresh khaki walking shorts and a short-sleeved shirt with three top buttons open. As hors d'oeuvres go, she was a promising morsel: long strong legs, slim waist, aggressive bosom, reddish hair fluffy from recent washing. More soubrette than heroine, she was in that brief desirable moment between coltishness and *zaftig*. But her face was soft and without lines of experience, giving the strain she was under the look of petulance.

"Mr. Hel?" she said again, her tone uncertain.

"Come in and sit down, Miss Stern."

She took a chair beneath a rack of metal devices she did not recognize to be weapons and smiled faintly. "I don't know why, but I thought of you as an older man. Uncle Asa spoke of you as a friend, a man of his own age."

"We were of an age; we shared an era. Not that that's pertinent to anything." He looked at her flatly, evaluating her. And finding her wanting.

Uncomfortable under the expressionless gaze of his bottle-green eyes, she sought the haven of small talk. "Your wife—Hana, that is—has been very kind to me. She sat up with me last night and—"

He cut her off with a gesture. "Begin by telling me about your uncle. Why he sent you here. After that, give me the details of the events at Rome International. Then tell me what your plans are and what they have to do with me."

Surprised by his businesslike tone, she took a deep breath, gathered her thoughts, and began her story, characteristically enough, with herself. She told him

286

that she had been raised in Skokie, had attended North-western University, had taken an active interest in political and social issues, and had decided upon graduation to visit her uncle in Israel—to find her roots, discover her Jewishness.

Hel's eyelids drooped at this last, and he breathed a short sigh. With a rolling motion of his hand he gestured her to get on with it.

"You knew, of course, that Uncle Asa was committed to punishing those who committed the Munich murders."

"That was on the grapevine. We never spoke of such things in our letters. When I first heard of it, I thought your uncle was foolish to come out of retirement and attempt something like that with his old friends and contacts either gone or decayed into politics. I could only assume it was the desperate act of a man who knew he was in his final illness."

"But he first organized our cell a year and a half ago, and he didn't become sick until a few months ago."

"That is not true. Your uncle has been ill for several years. There were two brief remissions. At the time you say he organized your cell, he was combating pain with drugs. That might account for his crepuscular thinking."

Hannah Stern frowned and looked away. "You don't sound as though you held my uncle in much esteem."

"On the contrary, I liked him very much. He was a brilliant thinker and a man of generous spirit—a man of *shibumi.*"

"A man of . . . what?"

"Never mind. Your uncle never belonged in the business of terror. He was emotionally unequipped for it—which of course says a good deal in his favor as a human being. In happier times, he would have lived the gentle life of a teacher and scholar. But he was passionate in his sense of justice, and not only for his own people. The way things were twenty-five years ago, in what is now Israel, passionate and generous men who were not cowards had few options open to them."

Hannah was not used to Hel's soft, almost whispered prison voice, and she found herself leaning close to hear his words.

"You are wrong to imagine that I did not esteem

287

your uncle. There was a moment in Cairo sixteen years ago when he risked his safety, possibly his life, to help me. What is more significant, he also risked the success of a project he was devoted to. I had been shot in the side. The situation was such that I could not seek medical assistance. When I met him, I had gone two days with a wad of blood-soaked cloth under my shirt, wandering in the back streets because I didn't dare try a hotel. I was dazed with fever. No, I esteem him a great deal. And I am in his debt." Hel had said this in a soft monotone, without the histrionics she would have associated with sincerity. He told her these things because he thought that, in fairness to the uncle, she had a right to know the extent of his debt of honor. "Your uncle and I never met again after that business in Cairo. Our friendship grew through years of exchanging letters that both of us used as outlets for testing ideas, for sharing our attitudes toward books we were reading, for complaining about fate and life. We enjoyed that freedom from embarrassment one only finds in talking to a stranger. We were very close strangers." Hel wondered if this young woman could understand such a relationship. Deciding she could not, he focused in on the business at hand. "All right, after his son was killed in Munich, your uncle formed a cell to aid him in his mission of punishment. How many people, and where are they now?"

"I am the only one left."

"*You* were within the cell?"

"Yes. Why? Does that seem—"

"Never mind." Hel was convinced now that Asa Stern had been acting in dazed desperation, to introduce this soft college liberal into an action cell. "How large was the cell?"

"We were five. We called ourselves the Munich Five."

His eyelids drooped again. "How theatrical. Nothing like telegraphing the stunt."

"I beg your pardon?"

"Five in the cell? Your uncle, you, the two hit in Rome—who was the fifth member? David O. Selznik?"

"I don't understand what you mean. The fifth man was killed in a café bombing in Jerusalem. He and I were . . . we were . . ." Her eyes began to shine with tears.

"I'm sure you were. It's a variation of the summer vacation romance: one of the fringe benefits of being a committed young revolutionary with all humanity as your personal flock. All right, tell me how far you had got before Asa died."

Hannah was confused and hurt. This was nothing like the man her uncle had described, the honest professional who was also a gentle man of culture, who paid his debts and refused to work for the uglier of the national and commercial powers. How could her uncle have been fond of a man who showed so little human sympathy? Who was so lacking in understanding?

Hel, of course, understood only too well. He had several times had to clean up after these devoted amateurs. He knew that when the storm broke, they either ran or, from equally cowardly impulses, shot up everything in sight.

Hannah was surprised to find that no tears came, their flow cauterized by Hel's cold adherence to fact and information. She sniffed and said, "Uncle Asa had sources of information in England. He learned that the last remaining two of the Munich murderers were with a group of Black Septembrists planning to hijack a plane departing from Heathrow."

"How large a group?"

"Five or six. We were never sure."

"Had you identified which of them were involved in Munich?"

"No."

"So you were going to put all five of them under?" She nodded.

"I see. And your contacts in England? What is their character and what are they going to do for you?"

"They are urban guerrillas working for the freedom of Northern Ireland from English domination."

"Oh, God."

"There is a kind of brotherhood among all freedom fighters, you know. Our tactics may be different, but our ultimate goals are the same. We all look forward to a day when—"

"Please," he interrupted. "Now, what were these IRA's going to do for you?"

"Well . . . they were keeping watch on the Septembrists. They were going to house us when we arrived in London. And they were going to furnish us with arms."

" 'Us' being you and the two who got hit in Rome?"

"Yes."

"I see. All right, now tell me what happened in Rome. BBC identifies the stuntmen as Japanese Red Army types acting for the PLO. Is that correct?"

"I don't know."

"Weren't you there?"

"Yes! I was there!" She controlled herself. "But in the confusion . . . people dying . . . gunfire all around me . . ." In her distress, she rose and turned her back on this man she felt was intentionally tormenting her, testing her. She told herself that she mustn't cry, but tears came nonetheless. "I'm sorry. I was terrified. Stunned. I don't remember everything." Nervous and lacking something to do with her hands, she reached out to take a simple metal tube from the rack on the wall before her.

"Don't touch that!"

She jerked her hand away, startled to hear him raise his voice for the first time. A shot of righteous anger surged through her. "I wasn't going to hurt your toys!"

"They might hurt you." His voice was quiet and modulated again. "That is a nerve gas tube. If you had turned the bottom half, you would be dead now. And what is more important, so would I."

She grimaced and retreated from the weapons rack, crossing to the open sliding door leading to the garden, where she leaned against the sill to regain something of her composure.

"Young woman, I intend to help you, if that is possible. I must confess that it may not be possible. Your little amateur organization has made every conceivable mistake, not the least of which was aligning yourselves with IRA dummies. Still, I owe it to your uncle to hear you out. Perhaps I can protect you and get you back to the bourgeois comfort of your home, where you can express your social passions by campaigning against litter in national parks. But if I am to help you at all, I have to know how the stones lie on the board. So I want you to save your passion and theatrics for your memoirs and answer my questions as fully and as succinctly as you can. If you're not prepared to do that just now, we can chat again later. But it is possible that I may have to move quickly. Typically in patterns like this, after a spoiling raid (and that's probably what the Rome International number was) time favors the other fellows. Shall we talk now, or shall we go take luncheon?"

Hannah slid down to the *tatami* floor, her back against the sill, her profile cameoed against the sunlit garden. After a moment, she said, "I'm sorry. I've been through a lot."

"I don't doubt that. Now tell me about the Rome hit. Facts and impressions, not emotions."

She looked down and drew little circles on her tanned thigh with her fingernail, then she pulled up her knees and hugged them to her breast. "All right. Avrim and Chaim went through passport check ahead of me. I was slowed down by the Italian officer, who was sort of flirting and ogling my breasts. I suppose I should have kept my shirt buttoned all the way up. Finally, he stamped my passport, and I started out into the terminal. Then the gunshots broke out. I saw Avrim run . . . and fall . . . the side of his head all . . . all. Wait a minute." She sniffed and drew several deep, controlling breaths. "I started to run too . . . everyone was running and screaming . . . an old man with a white beard was hit . . . a child . . . a fat old woman. Then there were gunshots coming from the other side of the terminal and from the overhanging mezzanine, and the Oriental gunmen were hit. Then suddenly there was no more gunfire, only screams, and people all around, bleeding and hurt. I saw Chaim lying against the lockers, his legs all wrong and crooked. He had been shot in the face. So I . . . I just walked away. I just walked away. I didn't know what I was doing, where I was going. Then I heard the announcement on the loudspeaker for the plane for Pau. And I just kept walking straight ahead until I came to the departure gate. And . . . and that's all."

"All right. That's fine. Now tell me this. Were you a target?"

"What?"

"Was anyone shooting specifically at you?"

"I don't know! How *could* I know?"

"Were the Japanese using automatic weapons?"

"What?"

"Did they go rat-a-tat, or bang! bang! bang!"

She looked up at him sharply. "I know what an automatic weapon is! We used to practice with them out in the mountains!"

"Rat-a-tat or bang bang?"

"They were machine guns."

"And did anyone standing close to you go down?"

She thought hard, squeezing her knees to her lips. "No. No one standing close to me."

"If professionals using automatic weapons didn't drop anyone near you, then you were not a target. It is possible they didn't identify you as being with your two friends. Particularly as you left the check-through line some time after them. All right, please turn your mind to the shots that came from the mezzanine and blew away the Japanese hitmen. What can you tell me about them?"

She shook her head. "Nothing. I don't remember anything. The guns were not automatics." She looked at Hel obliquely. "They went bang bang."

He smiled. "That's the way. Humor and anger are more useful just now than the wetter emotions. Now, the radio report said something about 'special agents' being with the Italian police. Can you tell me anything about them?"

"No. I never saw the people firing from the mezzanine."

Hel nodded and bowed his head, his palms pressed together and the forefingers lightly touching his lips. "Give me a moment to put this together." He fixed his eyes on the weave pattern of the *tatami*, then defocused as he reviewed the information in hand.

Hannah sat on the floor, framed in the doorway, and gazed out on the Japanese garden where sunlight reflected from the small stream glittered through bamboo leaves. Typical of her class and culture, she lacked the inner resources necessary to deal with the delights of silence, and soon she was uncomfortable. "Why aren't there any flowers in your . . ."

He lifted his hand to silence her without looking up. Four minutes later he raised his head. "What?"

"Pardon me?"

"Something about flowers."

"Oh, nothing important. I just wondered why you didn't have any flowers in your garden."

"There are three flowers."

"Three varieties?"

"No. Three flowers. One to signal each of the seasons of bloom. We are between seasons now. All right, let's see what we know or can assume. It's pretty obvious that the raid in Rome was organized either by PLO or by the Septembrists, and that they had learned of your intentions—probably through your London-based IRA comrades, who would sell their mothers into Turkish seraglios if the price was right (and if any self-respecting Turk would use them). The appearance of Japanese Red Army fanatics would seem to point to Septembrists, who often use others to do their dangerous work, having little appetite for personal risk. But things get a little complicated at this point. The stunt men were disposed of within seconds, and by men stationed in the mezzanine. Probably not Italian police, because the thing was done efficiently. The best bet is that the tip-off was tipped off. Why? The only reason that comes quickly to mind is that no one wanted the Japanese stunt men taken alive. And why? Possibly because they were not Red Army dum-dums at all. And that, of course, would bring us to CIA. Or to the Mother Company, which controls CIA, and everything else in American government, for that matter."

"What is the Mother Company? I've never heard of them."

"Few Americans have. It is a control organization of the principal international oil and energy companies. They've been in bed with the Arabs forever, using those poor benighted bastards as pawns in their schemes of induced shortages and profiteering. The Mother Company is a wiry opponent; they can't be got at through nationalistic pressures. Although they put up a huge media front of being loyal American (or British or German or Dutch) companies, they are in fact international infragovernments whose only patriotism is profit. Chances are that your father owns stock in them, as do half the dear gray-haired ladies of your country."

Hannah shook her head. "I can't feature CIA taking sides with the Black Septembrists. The United States supports Israel; they're allies."

"You underestimate the elastic nature of your country's conscience. They have made a palpable shift since the oil embargo. American devotion to honor varies inversely with its concern for central heating. It is a property of the American that he can be brave and self-sacrificing only in short bursts. That is why they are better at war than at responsible peace. They can face danger, but not inconvenience. They toxify their air to kill mosquitoes. They drain their energy sources to provide themselves with electric carving knives. We must never forget that there was always Coca-Cola for the soldiers in Viet Nam."

Hannah felt a chauvinistic sting. "Do you think it's fair to generalize like that about a people?"

"Yes. Generalization is flawed thinking only when applied to individuals. It is the most accurate way to describe the mass, the Wad. And yours is a democracy, a dictatorship of the Wad."

"I refuse to believe that Americans were involved in the blood and horror of what went on in that airport. Innocent children and old men . . ."

"Does the sixth of August mean anything to you?"

"Sixth of August? No. Why?" She gripped her legs closer to her chest.

"Never mind." Hel rose. "I have to think this out a bit. We'll talk again this afternoon."

"Do you intend to help me?"

"Probably. But probably not in any style you have in mind. By the way, can you stand a bit of avuncular advice?"

"What would that be?"

"It is a sartorial indiscretion for a young lady so

lavishly endowed with pubic hair as you to wear shorts that brief, and to sit in so revealing a posture. Unless, of course, it is your intention to prove that your red hair is natural. Shall we take lunch?"

Lunch was set at a small round table in the west reception room giving out onto the rolling green and allée that descended to the principal gates. The *porte fenêtres* were open, and the long curtains billowed lazily with cedar-scented breezes. Hana had changed to a long dress of plum-colored silk, and when Hel and Hannah entered, she smiled at them as she put the finishing touches to a centerpiece of delicate bell-shaped flowers. "What perfect timing. Lunch was just this minute set." In fact, she had been awaiting them for ten minutes, but one of her charms was making others feel socially graceful. A glance at Hannah's face told her that things had gone distressingly for her during the chat with Hel, so Hana took the burden of civilized conversation upon herself.

As Hannah opened her starched linen napkin, she noticed that she had not been served the same things as Hana and Hel. She had a bit of lamb, chilled asparagus in mayonnaise, and rice pilaf, while they had fresh or lightly sauteed vegetables with plain brown rice.

Hana smiled and explained. "Our age and past indiscretions require that we eat a little cautiously, my dear. But we do not inflict our spartan regimen on our guests. In fact, when I am away from home, in Paris for instance, I go on a spree of depraved eating. Eating for me is what you might call a managed vice. A vice particularly difficult to control when one is living in France where, depending on your point of view, the food is either the world's second best or the world's very worst."

"What do you mean?" Hannah asked.

"From a sybaritic point of view, French food is second only to classic Chinese cuisine. But it is so handled, and sauced, and prodded, and chopped, and stuffed, and seasoned as to be a nutritive disaster. That is why no people in the West have so much delight with eating as the French, or so much trouble with their livers."

"And what do you think about American food?"

Hannah asked, a wry expression on her face, because she was of that common kind of American abroad who seeks to imply sophistication by degrading everything American.

"I couldn't really say; I have never been in America. But Nicholai lived there for a time, and he tells me that there are certain areas in which American cooking excels."

"Oh?" Hannah said, looking archly at Hel. "I'm surprised to hear that Mr. Hel has anything good to say about America or Americans."

"It's not Americans I find annoying; it's Americanism: a social disease of the postindustrial world that must inevitably infect each of the mercantile nations in turn, and is called 'American' only because your nation is the most advanced case of the malady, much as one speaks of Spanish flu, or Japanese Type-B encephalitis. Its symptoms are a loss of work ethic, a shrinking of inner resources, and a constant need for external stimulation, followed by spiritual decay and moral narcosis. You can recognize the victim by his constant efforts to get in touch with himself, to believe his spiritual feebleness is an interesting psychological warp, to construe his fleeing from responsibility as evidence that he and his life are uniquely open to new experience. In the latter stages, the sufferer is reduced to seeking that most trivial of human activities: fun. As for your food, no one denies that the Americans excel in one narrow rubric: the snack. And I suspect there's something symbolic in that."

Hana disapproved of Hel's ingracious tone, so she took control of the dinner talk as she brought Hannah's plate to the sideboard to replenish it. "My English is imperfect. There is more than one asparagus here, but the word 'asparaguses' sounds awkward. Is it one of those odd Latin plurals, Nicholai? Does one say asperagae, or something like that?"

"One would say that only if he were that overinformed/undereducated type who attends concerti for celli and afterward orders cups of capuccini. Or, if he is American, dishes of raspberry Jell-I."

"*Arrêtes un peu et sois sage,*" Hana said with a slight

296

shake of her head. She smiled at Hannah. "Isn't he a bore on the subject of Americans? It's a flaw in his personality. His sole flaw, he assures me. I've been wanting to ask you, Hannah, what did you read at university?"

"What did I read?"

"What did you major in," Hel clarified.

"Oh. Sociology."

He might have guessed it. Sociology, that descriptive pseudo-science that disguises its uncertainties in statistical mists as it battens on the narrow gap of information between psychology and anthropology. The kind of nonmajor that so many Americans use to justify their four-year intellectual vacations designed to prolong adolescence.

"What did you study in school?" Hannah asked her hostess thoughtlessly.

Hana smiled to herself. "Oh . . . informal psychology, anatomy, aesthetics—that sort of thing."

Hannah applied herself to the asparagus, asking casually, "You two aren't married, are you? I mean . . . you joked the other night about being Mr. Hel's concubine."

Hana's eyes widened in rare astonishment. She was not accustomed to that inquisitive social gaucherie that Anglo-Saxon cultures mistake for admirable frankness. Hel opened his palm toward Hana, gesturing her to answer, his eyes wide with mischievous innocence.

"Well . . ." Hana said, ". . . in fact, Mr. Hel and I are not married. And in fact I am his concubine. Will you take dessert now? We have just received our first shipment of the magnificent cherries of Itxassou, of which the Basque are justly proud."

Hel knew Hana was not going to get off that easily, and he grinned at her as Miss Stern pursued, "I don't think you mean concubine. In English, concubine means someone who is hired for . . . well, for her sexual services. I think you mean 'mistress.' And even mistress is sort of old-fashioned. Nowadays people just say they are living together."

Hana looked at Hel for help. He laughed and interceded for her. "Hana's English is really quite good. She was only joking about the asparagus. She knows the difference among a mistress, a concubine, and a wife. A mistress is unsure of her wage, a wife has none; and they are both amateurs. Now, do try the cherries."

Hel sat on a stone bench in the middle of the cutting gardens, his eyes closed and his face lifted to the sky. Although the mountain breeze was cool, the thin sunlight penetrated his *yukata* and made him warm and drowsy. He hovered on the delicious verge of napping until he intercepted the approaching aura of someone who was troubled and tense.

"Sit down, Miss Stern," he said, without opening his eyes. "I must compliment you on the way you conducted yourself at lunch. Not once did you refer to your problems, seeming to sense that in this house we don't bring the world to our table. To be truthful, I hadn't expected such good form from you. Most people of your age and class are so wrapped up in themselves —so concerned with what they're 'into'—that they fail to realize that style and form are everything, and substance a passing myth." He opened his eyes and smiled as he made a pallid effort to imitate the American accent: "It ain't what you do, it's how you do it."

Hannah perched on the marble balustrade before him, her thighs flattened by her weight. She was barefoot, and she had not heeded his advice about changing into less revealing clothes. "You said we should talk some more?"

"Hm-m-m. Yes. But first let me apologize for my uncivil tone, both during our little chat and at lunch. I was angry and annoyed. I have been retired for almost two years now, Miss Stern. I am no longer in the profession of exterminating terrorists; I now devote myself to gardening, to caving, to listening to the grass grow, and to seeking a kind of deep peace I lost many years ago—lost because circumstances filled me with hate and fury. And then you come along with a legitimate claim to my assistance because of my debt to your uncle, and you threaten me with being pressed back into my profession of violence and fear. And fear is a good part of why I was annoyed with you. There is a certain amount of antichance in my work. No matter how well-trained one is, how careful, how coolheaded, the odds regularly build up over the years; and there comes a time when luck and antichance weigh heavily against you. It's not that I've been lucky in my work—I mistrust luck—but I have never been greatly hampered by bad luck. So there's a lot of bad luck out there waiting for its turn. I've tossed up the coin many times, and it has come down heads. There are more than twenty years' worth of tails waiting their turn. So! What I wanted to explain was the reason I have been impolite to you. It's fear mostly. And some annoyance. I've had time to consider now. I think I know what I should do. Fortunately, the proper action is also the safest."

"Does that mean you don't intend to help me?"

"On the contrary. I am going to help you by sending you home. My debt to your uncle extends to you, since he sent you to me; but it does not extend to any abstract notion of revenge or to any organization with which you are allied."

She frowned and looked away, out toward the mountains. "Your view of the debt to my uncle is a convenient one for you."

"So it turns out, yes."

"But . . . my uncle gave the last years of his life to hunting down those killers, and it would make that all pretty pointless if I didn't try to do something."

"There's nothing you can do. You lack the training, the skill, the organization. You didn't even have a plan worthy of the name."

"Yes, we did."

He smiled. "All right. Let's take a look at your plan. You said that the Black Septembrists were intending to hijack a plane from Heathrow. Presumably your group was going to hit them at that time. Were you going to take them on the plane, or before they boarded?"

"I don't know."

"You don't know?"

"Avrim was the leader after Uncle Asa died. He told us no more than he thought we had to know, in case one of us was captured or something like that. But I don't believe we were going to meet them on the plane. I think we were going to execute them in the terminal."

"And when was this to take place?"

"The morning of the seventeenth."

299

"That's six days away. Why were you going to London so soon? Why expose yourself for six days?"

"We weren't going to London. We were coming here. Uncle Asa knew we didn't have much chance of success without him. He had hoped he would be strong enough to accompany us and lead us. The end came too fast for him."

"So he sent you here? I don't believe that."

"He didn't exactly send us here. He had mentioned you several times. He said that if we got into trouble we could come to you and you would help."

"I'm sure he meant that I would help you get away after the event."

She shrugged.

He sighed. "So you three youngsters were going to pick up your arms from your IRA contacts in London, loiter around town for six days, take a taxi out to Heathrow, stroll into the terminal, locate the targets in the waiting area, and blow them away. Was that your plan?"

Her jaw tightened, and she looked away. It did sound silly, put like that.

"So, Miss Stern, notwithstanding your disgust and horror over the incident at Rome International, it turns out that you were planning to be responsible for the same kind of messy business—a stand-up blow-away in a crowded waiting room. Children, old women, and bits thereof flying hither and yon as the dedicated young revolutionaries, eyes flashing and hair floating, shoot their way into history. Is that what you had in mind?"

"If you're trying to say we are no different from those killers who murdered young athletes in Munich or who shot my comrades in Rome—!"

"The differences are obvious! *They* were well organized and professional!" He cut himself off short. "I'm sorry. Tell me this: what are your resources?"

"Resources?"

"Yes. Forgetting your IRA contacts—and I think we can safely forget them—what kind of resources were you relying on? Were the boys killed in Rome well trained?"

"Avrim was. I don't think Chaim had ever been involved in this sort of thing before."

"And money?"

"Money? Well, we were hoping to get some from you. We didn't need all that much. We had hoped to stay here for a few days—talk to you and get advice and instructions. Then fly directly to London, arriving the day before the operation. All we needed was air fare and a little more."

Hel closed his eyes. "My dear, dumb, lethal girl. If I were to undertake something like you people had in mind, it would cost between a hundred and a hundred-fifty-thousand dollars. And I am not speaking of my fee. That would be only the setup money. It costs a lot to get in, and often even more to get out. Your uncle knew that." He looked out over the horizon line of mountain and sky. "I'm coming to realize that what he had put together was a suicide raid."

"I don't believe that! He would never lead us into suicide without telling us!"

"He probably didn't intend to have you up front. Chances are he was going to use you three children as backups, hoping he could do the number himself, and you three would be able to walk away in the confusion. Then too . . ."

"Then too, what?"

"Well, we have to realize that he had been on drugs for a long time to manage his pain. Who knows what he was thinking; who knows how much he had left to think with toward the end?"

She drew up one knee and hugged it to her chest, revealing again her erubescence. She pressed her lips against her knee and stared over the top of it across the garden. "I don't know what to do."

Hel looked at her through half-closed eyes. Poor befuddled twit, seeking purpose and excitement in life, when her culture and background condemned her to mating with merchants and giving birth to advertising executives. She was frightened and confused, and not quite ready to give up her affair with danger and significance and return to a life of plans and possessions. "You really don't have much choice. You'll have to go home. I shall be delighted to pay your way."

"I can't do that."

"You can't do anything else."

For a moment, she sucked lightly on her knee. "Mr. Hel—may I call you Nicholai?"

"Certainly not."

"Mr. Hel. You're telling me that you don't intend to help me, is that it?"

"I am helping you when I tell you to go home."

"And if I refuse to? What if I go ahead with this on my own?"

"You would fail—almost surely die."

"I know that. The question is, could you let me try to do it alone? Would your sense of debt to my uncle allow you to do that?"

"You're bluffing."

"And if I'm not?"

Hel glanced away. It was just possible that this bourgeois muffin was dumb enough to drag him into it, or at least to make him decide how far loyalty and honor went. He was preparing to test her, and himself, when he felt an approaching presence he recognized as Pierre's, and he turned to see the gardener shuffling toward them from the château.

"Good afternoon, 'sieur, m'selle. It must be pleasant to have the leisure to sun oneself." He drew a folded sheet of paper from the pocket of his blue worker's smock and handed it to Hel with great solemnity, then he explained that he could not stay for there were a thousand things to be done, and he went on toward the garden and his gatehouse, for it was time to soften his day with another glass.

Hel read the note.

He folded it and tapped it against his lips. "It appears, Miss Stern, that we may not have all the freedom of option we thought. Three strangers have arrived in Tardets and are asking questions about me and, more significantly, about you. They are described as Englishmen or *Amérlos*—the village people wouldn't be able to distinguish those accents. They were accompanied by French Special Police, who are being most cooperative."

"But how could they know I am here?"

"A thousand ways. Your friends, the ones who were killed in Rome, did they have plane tickets on them?"

302

"I suppose so. In fact, yes. We each carried our own tickets. But they were not to here; they were to Pau."

"That's close enough. I am not completely unknown." Hel shook his head at this additional evidence of amateurism. Professionals always buy tickets to points well past their real destinations, because reservations go into computers and are therefore available to government organizations and to the Mother Company.

"Who do you think the men are?" she asked.

"I don't know."

"What are you going to do?"

He shrugged. "Invite them to dinner."

After leaving Hannah, Hel sat for half an hour in his garden, watching the accumulation of heavy-bellied storm clouds around the shoulders of the mountains and considering the lie of the stones on the board. He came to two conclusions at about the same time. It would rain that night, and his wisest course would be to rush the enemy.

From the gun room he telephoned the Hôtel Dabadie where the Americans were staying. A certain amount of negotiation was required. The Dabadies would send the three *Amérlos* up to the château for dinner that evening, but there was the problem of the dinners they had prepared for their guests. After all, a hotel makes its money on its meals, not its rooms. Hel assured them that the only fair and proper course would be to include the uneaten dinners in their bill. It was, God knows, not the fault of the Dabadies that the strangers decided at the last moment to dine with M. Hel. Business is business. And considering that waste of food is abhorrent to God, perhaps it would be best if the Dabadies ate the dinners themselves, inviting the abbé to join them.

He found Hana reading in the library, wearing the quaint little rectangular glasses she needed for close work. She looked over the top of them as he entered. "Guests for dinner?" she asked.

He caressed her cheek with his palm. "Yes, three. Americans."

"How nice. With Hannah and Le Cagot, that will make quite a dinner party."

"It will that."

303

She slipped in a bookmark and closed the volume. "Is this trouble, Nikko?"

"Yes."

"It has something to do with Hannah and her problems?"

He nodded.

She laughed lightly. "And just this morning you invited me to stay on with you for half of each year, trying to entice me with the great peace and solitude of your home."

"It will be peaceful soon. I have retired, after all."

"Can one? Can one completely retire from such a trade as yours? Ah well, if we are to have guests, I must send down to the village. Hannah will need some clothes. She cannot take dinner in those shorts of hers, particularly considering her somewhat cavalier attitude toward modest posture."

"Oh? I hadn't noticed."

A greeting bellow from the allée, a slamming of the salon *porte fenêtre* that rattled the glass, a noisy search to find Hana in the library, a vigorous hug with a loud smacking kiss on her cheek, a cry for a little hospitality in the form of a glass of wine, and all the household knew that Le Cagot had returned from his duties in Larrau. "Now, where is this young girl with the plump breasts that all the valley is talking about? Bring her on. Let her meet her destiny!"

Hana told him that the young woman was napping, but that Nicholai was working in the Japanese garden.

"I don't want to see him. I've had enough of his company for the last three days. Did he tell you about my cave? I practically had to drag your man through it. Sad to confess, he's getting old, Hana. It's time for you to consider your future and to look around for an ageless man—perhaps a robust Basque poet?"

Hana laughed and told him that his bath would be ready in half an hour. "And after that you might choose to dress up a bit; we're having guests for dinner."

"Ah, an audience. Good. Very well, I'll go get some wine in the kitchen. Do you still have that young Portuguese girl working for you?"

"There are several."

304

"I'll go sample around a bit. And wait until you see me dressed up! I bought some fancy clothes a couple of months ago, and I haven't had a chance to show them off yet. One look at me in my new clothes, and you'll melt, by the Balls . . ."

Hana cast a sidelong glance at him, and he instantly refined his language.

". . . by the Ecstasy of Ste. Therese. All right, I'm off to the kitchen." And he marched through the house, slamming doors and shouting for wine.

Hana smiled after Le Cagot. From the first he had taken to her, and his gruff way of showing his approval was to maintain a steady barrage of hyperbolic gallantry. For her part, she liked his honest, rough ways, and she was pleased that Nicholai had a friend so loyal and entertaining as this mythical Basque. She thought of him as a mythic figure, a poet who had constructed an outlandish romantic character, and who spent the rest of his life playing the role he had created. She once asked Hel what had happened to make the poet protect himself within this opéra-bouffe, picaresque facade of his. Hel could not give her the details; to do so would betray a confidence, one Le Cagot was unaware he had invested, because the conversation had taken place one night when the poet was crushed by sadness and nostalgia, and very drunk. Many years ago, the sensitive young poet who ultimately assumed the persona of Le Cagot had been a scholar of Basque literature, and had taken a university post in Bilbao. He married a beautiful and gentle Spanish Basque girl, and they had a baby. One night, for vague motives, he joined a student demonstration against the repression of Basque culture. His wife was with him, although she had no personal interest in politics. The federal police broke up the demonstration with gunfire. The wife was killed. Le Cagot was arrested and spent the next three years in prison. When he escaped, he learned that the baby had died while he was in jail. The young poet drank a great deal and participated in pointless and terribly violent anti-government actions. He was arrested again; and when he again escaped, the young poet no longer existed. In his place was Le Cagot, the invulnerable caricature who became a folk legend for his patriotic verse, his participation in

Basque Separatist causes, and his bigger-than-life personality, which brought him invitations to lecture and read his poetry in universities throughout the Western world. The name he gave to his persona was borrowed from the Cagots, an ancient pariah race of untouchables who had practiced a variant of Christianity which brought down upon them the rancor and hatred of their Basque neighbors. The Cagots sought relief from persecution through a request to Pope Leo X in 1514, which was granted in principle, but the restrictions and indignities continued to the end of the nineteenth century, when they ceased to exist as a distinct race. Their persecution took many forms. They were required to wear on their clothing the distinctive sign of the Cagot in the shape of a goose footprint. They could not walk barefooted. They could not carry arms. They could not frequent public places, and even in entering church they had to use a low side door constructed especially for the purpose, which door is still to be seen in many village churches. They could not sit near others at Mass, or kiss the cross. They could rent land and grow food, but they could not sell their produce. Under pain of death, they could not marry or have sexual relations outside their race.

All that remained for the Cagots were the artisan trades. For many centuries, both by restriction and privilege, they were the land's only woodcutters, carpenters, and joiners. Later, they also became the Basque masons and weavers. Because their misshapen bodies were considered funny, they became the strolling musicians and entertainers of their time, and most of what is now called Basque folk art and folklore was created by the despised Cagots.

Although it was long assumed that the Cagots were a race apart, propagated in Eastern Europe and driven along before the advancing Visigoths until they were deposited, like moraine rubble before a glacier, in the undesirable land of the Pyrenees, modern evidence suggests they were isolated pockets of Basque lepers, ostracized at first for prophylactic reasons, physically diminished in result of their disease, eventually taking on distinguishable characteristics because of enforced intermarriage. This theory goes a long way toward explaining the various limitations placed upon their freedom of action.

Popular tradition has it that the Cagots and their descendants had no earlobes. To this day, in the more traditional Basque villages, girls of five and six years of age have their ears pierced and wear earrings. Without knowing the source of the tradition, the mothers respond to the ancient practice of demonstrating that their girls have lobes in which to wear earrings.

Today the Cagots have disappeared, having either withered and grown extinct, or slowly merged with the Basque population (although this last suggestion is a risky one to advance in a Basque bar), and their name has all but fallen from use, save as a pejorative term for bent old women.

The young poet whose sensitivity had been cauterized by events chose Le Cagot as his pen name to bring attention to the precarious situation of contemporary Basque culture, which is in danger of disappearing, like the suppressed bards and minstrels of former times.

A little before six, Pierre tottered down to the square of Etchebar, the cumulative effect of his day's regularly spaced glasses of wine having freed him from the tyranny of gravity to such a degree that he navigated toward the Volvo by means of tacking. He had been sent to pick up two ensembles which Hana had ordered by telephone after asking Hannah for her sizes and translating them into European standards. After the dresses, Pierre was to collect three dinner guests from the Hôtel Dabadie. Having twice missed the door handle, Pierre pulled down the brim of his beret and focused all of his attention on the not-inconsiderable task of getting into the car, which he eventually accomplished, only to slap his forehead as he remembered an omission. He struggled out again and delivered a glancing kick to the rear fender in imitation of M'sieur Hel's ritual, then he found his way to the driver's seat again. With his native Basque mistrust for things mechanical, Pierre limited his gear options to reverse and low, in which he drove with the throttle wide open, using all the road and both verges. Such sheep, cows, men, and wobbly Solex mopeds as suddenly appeared before his bumper he managed to avoid by twisting the wheel sharply, then seeking the road again by feel. He abjured the effete practice of using the foot brake, and even the emergency brake he viewed as a device only for parking. As he always stopped without depressing the clutch, he avoided the nuisance of having to turn off the engine, which always bucked and died as he reached his destination and hauled back on the brake lever. Fortunately for the peasants and villagers between the château and Tardets, the sound of the Volvo's loosened body clattering and clanking and the roar of its engine at full speed in low gear preceded Pierre by half a kilometer, and there was usually time to scurry behind trees or jump over stone walls. Pierre felt a justified pride in his driving skills, for he had never been involved in an accident. And this was all the more notable considering the wild and careless drivers all around him, whom he frequently observed swerving into ditches and up on sidewalks, or crashing into one another as he roared through stop signs or up one-way streets. It was not so much the maladroit recklessness of these other drivers that disturbed Pierre as their blatant rudeness, for often they had shouted vulgar things at him, and he could not count the number of times he had seen through his rearview mirror a finger, a fist, or even a whole forearm, throwing an angry *figue* at him.

Pierre brought the Volvo to a bucking and coughing stop in the center of the Place of Tardets and clawed his way out. After bruising his toe against the battered door, he set about his commissions, the first of which was to share a hospitable glass with old friends.

No one thought it odd that Pierre always delivered a kick to the car upon entering or leaving, as Volvo-bashing was a general practice in southwestern France, and could even be encountered as far away as Paris. Indeed, carried to cosmopolitan centers around the world by tourists, Volvo-bashing was slowly becoming a cult activity throughout the world, and this pleased Nicholai Hel, since he had begun it all.

Some years before, seeking a car-of-all-work for the château, Hel had followed the advice of a friend and purchased a Volvo on the assumption that a car so expensive, lacking in beauty, comfort, speed, and fuel economy must have something else to recommend it. And he was assured that this something else was durability and service. His battle with rust began on the third day; and little errors of construction and design and set-up (misaligned wheels that wore out his tires within five thousand kilometers, a windshield wiper that daintily avoided contact with the glass, a rear hatch catch so designed as to require two hands to close it, so that loading and unloading was a burlesque of inefficient motion) required that he return the automobile frequently to the dealer some 150 kilometers away. It was the dealer's view that these problems were the manufacturer's and the manufacturer's view that the responsibility lay with the dealer; and after months of receiving polite but vague letters of disinterested condolence from the company, Hel decided to bite the bullet and set the car to the brutish tasks of transporting sheep and bringing equipment up rough mountain roads, hoping that it would soon fall apart and justify his purchase of a vehicle with a more reliable service infrastructure. Sadly, while he had found no truth in the company's reputation for service, there was some basis for the car's claim to durability and, while it always ran poorly, it always ran. Under other circumstances, Hel would have viewed durability as a virtue in a machine, but he could find little consolation in the threat that his problems would go on for years.

Having observed Pierre's skills as a chauffeur, Hel thought to shorten his torment by allowing Pierre to drive the car whenever he chose. But this plot was foiled because ironic fate shielded Pierre from accidents. So Hel came to accept his Volvo as one of the comic burdens of life, but he allowed himself to vent his frustration by kicking or bashing the car each time he got in or out.

It was not long before his caving associates fell into the practice of bashing his Volvo whenever they passed it, at first as a joke and later by habit. Soon they and the young men they traveled with began to bash any Volvo they passed. And in the illogical way of fads, Volvo-bashing began to spread, here taking on an anti-Establishment tone, there a quality of youthful exuberance; here as an expression of antimaterialism, there as a manifestation of in-cult with-itness.

Even owners of Volvos began to accept the bashing craze, for it proved that they traveled in circles of the internationally aware. And there were cases of owners secretly bashing their own Volvos, to gain unearned reputations as cosmopolites. There were persistent, though probably apocryphal, rumors that Volvo was planning to introduce a prebashed model in its efforts to attract the smart set to an automobile that had sacrificed everything to passenger safety (despite their use of Firestone 500 tires on many models) and primarily appealed to affluent egotists who assumed that the continuance of their lives was important to the destiny of Man.

After his shower, Hel found laid out in the dressing room his black broadcloth Edwardian suit, which had been designed to protect either guests in simple business suits or those in evening wear from feeling under- or overdressed. When he met Hana at the top of the principal staircase, she was in a long dress of Cantonese style that had the same social ambiguity as his suit.

"Where's Le Cagot?" he asked as they went down to a small salon to await their guests. "I've felt his presence several times today, but I haven't heard or seen him."

"I assume he is dressing in his room." Hana laughed lightly. "He told me that I would be so taken by his new clothes that I would swoon amorously into his arms."

"Oh, God." Le Cagot's taste in clothes, as in most things, ran to operatic overstatement. "And Miss Stern?"

"She has been in her room most of the afternoon. You evidently gave her rather a bad time during your chat."

"Hm-m-m."

"She'll be down shortly after Pierre returns with clothes for her. Do you want to hear the menu?"

"No, I'm sure it's perfect."

"Not that, but adequate. These guests give us a chance to be rid of the roebuck old M. Ibar gave us. It's been hanging just over a week, so it should be ready. Is there something special I should know about our guests?"

"They are strangers to me. Enemies, I believe."

"How should I treat them?"

"Like any guest in our house. With that particular charm of yours that makes all men feel interesting and important. I want these people to be off balance and unsure of themselves. They are Americans. Just as you or I would be uncomfortable at a barbecue, they suffer from social vertigo at a proper dinner. Even their *gratin,* the jetset, are culturally as bogus as airlines cuisine."

"What on earth is a 'barbecue'?"

"A primitive tribal ritual featuring paper plates, elbows, flying insects, encrusted meat, hush puppies, and beer."

"I daren't ask what a 'hush puppy' is."

"Don't."

They sat together in the darkening salon, their fingers touching. The sun was down behind the mountains, and through the open *porte fenêtres* they could see a silver gloaming that seemed to rise from the ground of the park, its dim light filling the space beneath the black-green pines, the effect rendered mutable and dear by the threat of an incoming storm.

"How long did you live in America, Nikko?"

"About three years, just after I left Japan. In fact, I still have an apartment in New York."

"I've always wanted to visit New York."

"You'd be disappointed. It's a frightened city in which everyone is in hot and narrow pursuit of money: the bankers, the muggers, the businessmen, the whores. If you walk the streets and watch their eyes, you see two things: fear and fury. They are diminished people hovering behind triple-locked doors. They fight with men they don't hate, and make love to women they don't like. Asea in a mongrel society, they borrow orts and leavings from the world's cultures. Kir is a popular drink among those desperate to be 'with it,' and they affect Perrier, although they have one of the world's great waters in the local village of Saratoga. Their best French restaurants offer what we would think of as thirty-franc meals for ten times that much, and the service is characterized by insufferable snottiness on the

311

part of the waiter, usually an incompetent peasant who happens to be able to read the menu. But then, Americans enjoy being abused by waiters. It's their only way of judging the quality of the food. On the other hand, if one must live in urban America—a cruel and unusual punishment at best—one might as well live in the real New York, rather than in the artificial ones farther inland. And there are some good things. Harlem has real tone. The municipal library is adequate. There is a man named Jimmy Fox who is the best barman in North America. And twice I even found myself in conversation about the nature of *shibui*—not *shibumi*, of course. It's more within the range of the mercantile mind to talk of the characteristics of the beautiful than to discuss the nature of Beauty."

She struck a long match and lighted a lamp on the table before them. "But I remember you mentioning once that you enjoyed your home in America."

"Oh, that was not New York. I own a couple of thousand hectares in the state of Wyoming, in the mountains."

"Wy-om-ing. Romantic-sounding name. Is it beautiful?"

"More sublime, I would say. It's too ragged and harsh to be beautiful. It is to this Pyrenees country what an ink sketch is to a finished painting. Much of the open land of America is attractive. Sadly, it is populated by Americans. But then, one could say a similar thing of Greece or Ireland."

"Yes, I know what you mean. I've been to Greece. I worked there for a year, employed by a shipping magnate."

"Oh? You never mentioned that."

"There was nothing really to mention. He was very rich and very vulgar, and he sought to purchase class and status, usually in the form of spectacular wives. While in his employ, I surrounded him with quiet comfort. He made no other demands of me. By that time, there were no other demands he could make."

"I see. Ah—here comes Le Cagot."

Hana had heard nothing, because Le Cagot was sneaking down the stairs to surprise them with his sartorial splendor. Hel smiled to himself because Le

Cagot's preceding aura carried qualities of boyish mischief and ultra-sly delight.

He appeared at the door, his bulk half-filling the frame, his arms in cruciform to display his fine new clothes. "Regard! Regard, Niko, and burn with envy!"

Obviously, the evening clothes had come from a theatrical costumer. They were an eclectic congregation, although the *fin-de-siècle* impulse dominated, with a throat wrapping of white silk in place of a cravat, and a richly brocaded waistcoat with double rows of rhinestone buttons. The black swallowtail coat was long, and its lapels were turned in gray silk. With his still-wet hair parted in the middle and his bushy beard covering most of the cravat, he had something the appearance of a middle-aged Tolstoi dressed up as a Mississippi riverboat gambler. The large yellow rose he had pinned to his lapel was oddly correct, consonant with this amalgam of robust bad taste. He strode back and forth, brandishing his long *makila* like a walking stick. The *makila* had been in his family for generations, and there were nicks and dents on the polished ash shaft and a small bit missing from the marble knob, evidences of use as a defensive weapon by grandfathers and great-grandfathers. The handle of a *makila* unscrews, revealing a twenty-centimeter blade designed for foining, while the butt in the left hand is used for crossed parries, and its heavy marble knob is an effective clubbing weapon. Although now largely decorative and ceremonial, the *makila* once figured importantly in the personal safety of the Basque man alone on the road at night or roving in the high mountains.

"That is a wonderful suit," Hana said with excessive sincerity.

"Is it not? Is it not?"

"How did you come by this . . . suit?" Hel asked.

"It was given to me."

"In result of your losing a bet?"

"Not at all. It was given to me by a woman in appreciation for . . . ah, but to mention the details would be ungallant. So, when do we eat? Where are these guests of yours?"

"They are approaching up the allée right now," Hel said, rising and crossing toward the central hall.

313

Le Cagot peered out through the *porte fenêtre,* but he could see nothing because evening and the storm had pressed the last of the gloaming into the earth. Still, he had become used to Hel's proximity sensitivity, so he assumed there was someone out there.

Just as Pierre was reaching for the handle of the pull bell, Hel opened the door. The chandeliers of the hall were behind him, so he could read the faces of his three guests, while his own was in shadow. One of them was obviously the leader; the second was a gunny CIA type, Class of '53; and the third was an Arab of vague personality. All three showed signs of recent emotional drain resulting from their ride up the mountain road without headlights, and with Pierre showing off his remarkable driving skills.

"Do come in," Hel said, stepping from the doorway and allowing them to pass before him into the reception hall, where they were met by Hana who smiled as she approached.

"It was good of you to accept our invitation on such short notice. I am Hana. This is Nicholai Hel. And here is our friend, M. Le Cagot." She offered her hand.

The leader found his aplomb. "Good evening. This is Mr. Starr. Mr. . . . Haman. And I am Mr. Diamond." The first crack of thunder punctuated his last word.

Hel laughed aloud. "That must have been embarrassing. Nature seems to be in a melodramatic mood."

PART THREE

Seki

Château d'Etchebar

From the moment they had the heart-squeezing experience of driving with Pierre in the battered Volvo, the three guests never quite got their feet on firm social ground. Diamond had expected to get down to cases immediately with Hel, but that clearly was not on. While Hana was conducting the party to the blue-and-gold salon for a glass of Lillet before dinner, Diamond held back and said to Hel, "I suppose you're wondering why—"

"After dinner."

Diamond stiffened just perceptibly, then smiled and half-bowed in a gesture he instantly regretted as theatrical. That damned clap of thunder!

Hana refilled glasses and handed around canapés as she guided the conversation in such a way that Darryl Starr was soon addressing her as "Ma'am" and feeling that her interest in Texas and things Texan was a veiled fascination with him; and the PLO trainee called Haman grinned and nodded with each display of concern for his comfort and well-being. Even Diamond soon found himself recounting impressions of the Basque country and feeling both lucid and insightful. All five men rose when Hana excused herself, saying that she had to attend to the young lady who would be dining with them.

There was a palpable silence after she left, and Hel allowed the slight discomfort to lie there, as he watched his guests with distant amusement.

It was Darryl Starr who found a relevant remark to fill the void. "Nice place you got here."

"Would you like to see the house?" Hel asked.

"Well . . . no, don't trouble yourself on my account."

Hel said a few words aside to Le Cagot, who then crossed to Starr and with gruff bonhomie pulled him from his chair by his arm and offered to show him the garden and the gun room. Starr explained that he was

317

comfortable where he was, thank you, but Le Cagot's grin was accompanied by painful pressure around the American's upper arm.

"Indulge my whim in this, my good friend," he said. Starr shrugged—as best he could—and went along.

Diamond was disturbed, torn between a desire to control the situation and an impulse, which he recognized to be childish, to demonstrate that his social graces were as sophisticated as Hel's. He realized that both he and this event were being managed, and he resented it. For something to say, he mentioned, "I see you're not having anything to drink before dinner, Mr. Hel."

"That's true."

Hel did not intend to give Diamond the comfort of rebounding conversational overtures; he would simply absorb each gesture and leave the chore of initiation constantly with Diamond, who chuckled and said, "I feel I should tell you that your driver is a strange one."

"Oh?"

"Yes. He parked the car out in the village square and we had to walk the rest of the way. I was sure the storm would catch us."

"I don't permit automobiles on my grounds."

"Yes, but after he parked the car, he gave the front door a kick that I'm sure must have dented it."

Hel frowned and said, "How odd. I'll have to talk to him about that."

At this point, Hana and Miss Stern joined the men, the young woman looking refined and desirable in a summer tea dress she had chosen from those Hana had bought for her. Hel watched Hannah closely as she was introduced to the two men, grudgingly admiring her control and ease while confronting the people who had engineered the killing of her comrades in Rome. Hana beckoned her to sit beside her and managed immediately to focus the social attention on her youth and beauty, guiding her in such a way that only Hel could sense traces of the reality vertigo the girl was feeling. At one moment, he caught her eyes and nodded slightly in approval of aplomb. There was some bottom to this girl after all. Perhaps if she were in the company of a woman like Hana for four or five years ... who knows?

There was a gruff laugh from the hall and Le Cagot reentered, his arm around Starr's shoulders. The Texan looked a bit shaken and his hair was tousled, but Le Cagot's mission was accomplished; the shoulder holster under Starr's left armpit was now empty.

"I don't know about you, my friends," Le Cagot said in his accented English with the overgrowled *r* of the Francophone who has finally conquered that difficult consonant, "but I am ravenous! *Bouffons!* I could eat for four!"

The dinner, served by the light of two candelabra on the table and lamps in wall sconces, was not sumptuous, but it was good: trout from the local *gave,* roebuck with cherry sauce, garden vegetables cooked in the Japanese style, the courses separated by conversation and appropriate ices, finally a salad of greens before dessert of fruit and cheeses. Compatible wines accompanied each entrée and *relevé,* and the particular problem of game in a fruit sauce was solved by a fine pink wine which, while it could not support the flavors, did not contradict them either. Diamond noted with slight discomfort that Hel and Hana were served only rice and vegetables during the early part of the meal, though they joined the others in salad. Further, although their hostess drank wine with the rest of them, Hel's glass was little more than moistened with each bottle, so that in total he drank less than a full glass.

"You don't drink, Mr. Hel?" he asked.

"But I do, as you see. It is only that I don't find two sips of wine more delicious than one."

Fadding with wines and waxing pseudopoetic in their failure to describe tastes lucidly is an affectation of socially mobile Americans, and Diamond fancied himself something of an authority. He sipped, swilled and examined the pink that accompanied the roebuck, then said, "Ah, there are Tavels, and there are Tavels."

Hel frowned slightly. "Ah ... that's true, I suppose."

"But this *is* a Tavel, isn't it?"

When Hel shrugged and changed the subject diplomatically, the nape of Diamond's neck horripilated with embarrassment. He had been so sure it was Tavel.

Throughout dinner, Hel maintained a distant silence, his eyes seldom leaving Diamond, though they appeared to focus slightly behind him. Effortlessly, Hana evoked jokes and stories from each of the guests in turn, and her delight and amusement was such that each felt he had outdone himself in cleverness and charm. Even Starr, who had been withdrawn and petulant after his rough treatment at Le Cagot's hands, was soon telling Hana of his boyhood in Flatrock, Texas, and of his adventures fighting against the gooks in Korea.

At first Le Cagot attended to the task of filling himself with food. Soon the ends of his wrapped cravat were dangling, and the long swallowtailed coat was cast aside, so by the time he was ready to dominate the party and hold forth at his usual length with vigorous and sometimes bawdy tales, he was down to his spectacular waistcoat with its rhinestone buttons. He was seated next to Hannah, and out of the blue he reached over, placed his big warm hand on her thigh, and gave it a friendly squeeze. "Tell me something in all frankness, beautiful girl. Are you struggling against your desire for me? Or have you given up the struggle? I ask you this only that I may know how best to proceed. In the meantime, eat, eat! You will need your strength. So! You men are from America, eh? Me, I was in America three times. That's why my English is so good. I could probably pass for an American, eh? From the point of view of accent, I mean."

"Oh, no doubt of it," Diamond said. He was beginning to realize how important to such men as Hel and Le Cagot was the heraldry of sheer style, even when faced by enemies, and he wanted to show that he could play any game they could.

"But of course once people saw the clear truth shining in my eyes, and hear the music of my thoughts, the game would be up! They would know I was not an American."

Hel concealed a slight smile behind a finger.

"You're hard on Americans," Diamond said.

"Maybe so," Le Cagot admitted. "And maybe I am being unjust. We get to see only the dregs of them here: merchants on vacation with their brassy wives, military men with their papier-mâché, gum-chewing women, young people seeking to 'find themselves,' and worst of all, academic drudges who manage to convince granting agencies that the world would be improved if they were beshat upon Europe. I sometimes think that America's major export product is bewildered professors on sabbaticals. Is it true that everyone in the United States over twenty-five years of age has a Ph.D?" Le Cagot had the bit well between his teeth, and he began one of his tales of adventure, based as usual on a real event, but decorated with such improvements upon dull truth as occurred to him as he went along. Secure in the knowledge that Le Cagot would dominate things for many minutes, Hel let his face freeze in a politely amused expression while his mind sorted out and organized the moves that would begin after dinner.

Le Cagot had turned to Diamond. "I am going to shed some light upon history for you, American guest of my friend. Everyone knows that the Basque and the Fascists have been enemies since before the birth of history. But few know the real source of this ancient antipathy. It was our fault, really. I confess it at last. Many years ago, the Basque people gave up the practice of shitting by the roadside, and in doing this we deprived the Falange of its principal source of nourishment. And that is the truth, I swear it by Methuselah's Wrinkled B—"

"Beñat?" Hana interrupted, indicating the young girl with a nod of her head.

"—by Methuselah's Wrinkled *Brow*. What's wrong with you?" he asked Hana, his eyes moist with hurt. "Do you think I have forgotten my manners?"

Hel pushed back his chair and rose. "Mr. Diamond and I have a bit of business to attend to. I suggest you take your cognac on the terrace. You might just have time before the rain comes."

As they stepped down from the principal hall to the Japanese garden, Hel took Diamond by the arm. "Allow me to guide you; I didn't think to bring a lantern."

"Oh? I know about your mystic proximity sense, but I didn't know you could see in the dark as well."

"I can't. But we are on my ground. Perhaps you would be well advised to remember that."

321

Hel lighted two spirit lamps in the gun room and gestured Diamond toward a low table on which there was a bottle and glasses. "Serve yourself. I'll be with you in a moment." He carried one of the lamps to a bookcase filled with pull drawers of file cards, some two hundred thousand cards in all. "May I assume that Diamond is your real name?"

"It is."

Hel searched for the proper key card containing all cross references to Diamond. "And your initials are?"

"Jack O." Diamond smiled to himself as he compared Hel's crude card file with his own sophisticated information system, Fat Boy. "I didn't see any reason to use an alias, assuming that you would see a family resemblance between me and my brother."

"Your brother?"

"Don't you remember my brother?"

"Not offhand." Hel muttered to himself as he fingered through a drawer of cards. As the information on Hel's cards was in six languages, the headings were arranged phonetically. "D. D-A, D-AI diphthong, D-AI-M . . . ah, here we are. Diamond, Jack O. Do have a drink, Mr. Diamond. My filing system is a bit cumbersome, and I haven't been called on to use it since my retirement."

Diamond was surprised that Hel did not even remember his brother. To cover his temporary confusion, he picked up the bottle and examined the label. "Armagnac?"

"Hm-m-m." Hel made a mental note of the cross-reference indices and sought those cards. "We're close to the Armagnac country here. You'll find that very old and very good. So you are a servant of the Mother Company, are you? I can therefore assume that you already have a good deal of information about me from your computer. You'll have to give me a moment to catch up with you."

Diamond carried his glass with him and wandered about the gun room, looking at the uncommon weapons in cases and racks along the walls. Some of these he recognized: the nerve-gas tube, air-driven glass sliver projectors, dry-ice guns, and the like. But others were foreign to him: simple metal disks, a device that seemed

322

to be two short rods of hickory connected by a metal link, a thimblelike cone that slipped over the finger and came to a sharp point. On the table beside the Armagnac bottle he found a small, French-made automatic. "A pretty common sort of weapon among all this exotica," he said.

Hel glanced up from the card he was reading. "Oh yes, I noticed that when we came in. It's not mine, actually. It belongs to your man, the bucolic tough from Texas. I thought he might feel more relaxed without it."

"The thoughtful host."

"Thank you." Hel set aside the card he was reading and pulled open another drawer in search of the next. "That gun tells us rather a lot. Obviously, you decided not to travel armed because of the nuisance of boarding inspections. So your lad was given the gun after he got here. Its make tells us he received the gun from French police authorities. That means you have them in your pocket."

Diamond shrugged. "France needs oil too, just like every other industrial country."

"Yes. *Ici on n'a pas d'huile, mais on a des idées.*"

"Meaning?"

"Nothing really. Just a slogan from French internal propaganda. So I see here that the Major Diamond from Tokyo was your brother. That's interesting—mildly interesting, anyway." Now that he considered it, Hel found a certain resemblance between the two, the narrow face, the intense black eyes set rather close together, the falciform nose, the thin upper lip and heavy, bloodless lower, a certain intensity of manner.

"I thought you would have guessed that when you first heard my name."

"Actually, I had pretty much forgotten him. After all, our account was settled. So you began working for the Mother Company in the Early Retirement Program, did you? That is certainly consonant with your brother's career."

Some years before, the Mother Company had discovered that its executives after the age of fifty began to be notably less productive, just at the time the Company was paying them the most. The problem was presented to Fat Boy, who offered the solution of orga-

323

nizing an Early Retirement Division that would arrange for the accidental demise of a small percentage of such men, usually while on vacation, and usually of apparent stroke or heart attack. The savings to the Company were considerable. Diamond had risen to the head of this division before being promoted to conducting Mother Company's control over CIA and NSA.

". . . so it appears that both you and your brother found a way to combine native sadism with the comforting fringe benefits of working for big business, he for the army and CIA, you for the oil combines. Both products of the American Dream, the mercantile mumpsimus. Just bright young men trying to get ahead."

"But at least neither of us ended up as hired killers."

"Rubbish. Any man is a killer who works for a company that pollutes, strip-mines, and contaminates the air and water. The fact that you and your unlamented brother killed from institutional and patriotic ambush doesn't mean you're not killers—it only means you're cowards."

"You think a coward would walk into your lair as I have done?"

"A certain kind of coward would. A coward who was afraid of his cowardice."

Diamond laughed thinly. "You really hate me, don't you."

"Not at all. You're not a person, you're an organization man. One couldn't hate you as an individual; one could only hate the phylum. At all events, you're not the sort to evoke such intense emotions as hate. Disgust might be closer to the mark."

"Still, for all the disdain of your breeding and private education, it is people like me—what you sneeringly call the merchant class—who hire you and send you out to do their dirty work."

Hel shrugged. "It has always been so. Throughout all history, the merchants have cowered behind the walls of their towns, while the paladins did battle to protect them, in return for which the merchants have always fawned and bowed and played the lickspittle. One cannot really blame them. They are not bred to courage. And, more significantly, you can't put bravery in the bank." Hel read the last information card quickly and

324

tossed it on the stack to be refiled later. "All right, Diamond. Now I know who you are and what you are. At least, I know as much about you as I need to, or choose to."

"I assume your information came from the Gnome?"

"Much of it came from the person you call the Gnome."

"We would give a great deal to know how that man came by his intelligence."

"I don't doubt it. Of course, I wouldn't tell you if I knew. But the fact is, I haven't the slightest idea."

"But you do know the identity and location of the Gnome."

Hel laughed. "Of course I do. But the gentleman and I are old friends."

"He's nothing more or less than a blackmailer."

"Nonsense. He is an artisan in the craft of information. He has never taken money from a man in return for concealing the facts he collects from all over the world."

"No, but he provides men like you with the information that protects you from punishment by governments, and for that he makes a lot of money."

"The protection is worth a great deal. But if it will set your mind at rest, the man you call the Gnome is very ill. It is doubtful that he will live out the year."

"So you will soon be without protection?"

"I shall miss him as a man of wit and charm. But the loss of protection is a matter of little importance to me. I am, as Fat Boy must have informed you, fully retired. Now what do you say we get on with our little business."

"Before we start, I have a question I want to ask you."

"I have a question for you as well, but let's leave that for later. So that we don't waste time with exposition, allow me to give you the picture in a couple of sentences, and you may correct me if I stray." Hel leaned against the wall, his face in the shadows and his soft prison voice unmodulated. "We begin with Black Septembrists murdering Israeli athletes in Munich. Among the slain was Asa Stern's son. Asa Stern vows to have vengeance. He organizes a pitiful little amateur cell to

325

this end—don't think badly of Mr. Stern for the paucity of this effort; he was a good man, but he was sick and partially drugged. Arab intelligence gets wind of this effort. The Arabs, probably through an OPEC representative, ask the Mother Company to erase this irritant. The Mother Company turns the task over to you, expecting you to use your CIA bully boys to do the job. You learn that the revenge cell—I believe they called themselves the Munich Five—was on its way to London to put the last surviving members of the Munich murder away. CIA arranges a spoiling action in Rome International. By the way, I assume those two fools back in the house were involved in the raid?"

"Yes."

"And you're punishing them by making them clean up after themselves?"

"That's about it."

"You're taking the risks, Mr. Diamond. A foolish associate is more dangerous than a clever opponent."

"That's my concern."

"To be sure. All right, your people do a messy and incomplete job in Rome. Actually, you should be grateful they did as well as they did. With a combination of Arab Intelligence and the CIA competence, you're lucky they didn't go to the wrong airport. But that, as you have said, is your concern. Somehow, probably when the raid was evaluated in Washington, you discovered that the Israeli boys were not going to London. They carried airline tickets for Pau. You also discovered that one of the cell members, the Miss Stern with whom you just took dinner, had been overlooked by your killers. Your computer was able to relate me to Asa Stern, and the Pau destination nailed it down. Is that it?"

"That roughly is it."

"All right. So much for catching up. The ball, I believe, is in your court."

Diamond had not yet decided how he would present his case, what combination of threat and promise would serve to neutralize Nicholai Hel. To gain time, he pointed to a pair of odd-looking pistols with curved handles like old-fashioned dueling weapons and double nine-inch barrels that were slightly flared at the ends. "What are these?"

"Shotguns, in a way of speaking."

"Shotguns?"

"Yes. A Dutch industrialist had them made for me. A gift in return for a rather narrow action involving his son who was held captive on a train by Moluccan terrorists. Each gun, as you see, has two hammers which drop simultaneously on special shotgun shells with powerful charges that scatter loads of half-centimeter ball bearings. All the weapons in this room are designed for a particular situation. These are for close work in the dark, or for putting away a roomful of men on the instant of break-in. At two meters from the barrel, they lay down a spread pattern a meter in diameter." Hel's bottle-green eyes settled on Diamond. "Do you intend to spend the evening talking about guns?"

"No. I assume that Miss Stern has asked you to help her kill the Septembrists now in London?"

Hel nodded.

"And she took it for granted that you would help, because of your friendship for her uncle?"

"She made that assumption."

"And what do you intend to do?"

"I intend to listen to your proposal."

"My proposal?"

"Isn't that what merchants do? Make proposals?"

"I wouldn't exactly call it a proposal."

"What would you call it?"

"I would call it a display of deterrent action, partially already on line, partially ready to be brought on line, should you be so foolish as to interfere."

Hel's eyes crinkled in a smile that did not include his lips. He made a rolling gesture with his hand, inviting Diamond to get on with it.

"I'll confess to you that, under different conditions, neither the Mother Company nor the Arab interests we are allied with would care much one way or another what happened to the homicidal maniacs of the PLO. But these are difficult times within the Arab community, and the PLO has become something of a rallying banner, an issue more of public relations than of private taste. For this reason, the Mother Company is com-

327

mitted to their protection. This means that you will not be allowed to interfere with those who intend to hijack that plane in London."

"How will I be prevented?"

"Do you recall that you used to own several thousand acres of land in Wyoming?"

"I assume the tense is not a matter of grammatical carelessness."

"That's right. Part of that land was in Boyle County, the rest in Custer County. If you contact the county clerk offices, you will discover that there exists no record of your having purchased that land. Indeed, the records show that the land in question is now, and has been for many years, in the hands of one of Mother Company's affiliates. There is some coal under the land, and it is scheduled for strip-mining."

"Do I understand that if I cooperate with you, the land will be returned to me?"

"Not at all. That land, representing as it does most of what you have saved for your retirement, has been taken from you as a punishment for daring to involve yourself in the affairs of the Mother Company."

"May I assume you suggested this punishment?"

Diamond tipped his head to the side. "I had that pleasure."

"You are a vicious little bastard, aren't you. You're telling me that if I pull out of this affair, the land will be spared from strip-mining?"

Diamond pushed out his lower lip. "Oh, I'm afraid I couldn't make an arrangement like that. America needs all its natural energy to make it independent from foreign sources." He smiled at this repetition of the worn party line. "Then too, you can't put beauty in the bank." He was enjoying himself.

"I don't understand what you're doing, Diamond. If you intend to take the land and destroy it, no matter what I do, then what leverage does that give you over my actions?"

"As I said, taking your land was in the nature of a warning shot across your bow. And a punishment."

"Ah, I see. A personal punishment. From you. For your brother?"

"That's right."

"He deserved death, you know. I was tortured for three days. This face of mine is not completely mobile even now, after all the operations."

"He was my brother! Now, let's pass on to the sanctions and penalties you will incur, should you fail to cooperate. Under the key group KL443, Code Number 45-389-75, you had approximately one-and-a-half-million dollars in gold bullion in the Federal Bank of Zurich. That represented nearly all the rest of what you intended to retire on. Please note the past tense again."

Hel was silent for a moment. "The Swiss too need oil."

"The Swiss need oil too," Diamond echoed. "That money will reappear in your account seven days after the successful accomplishment of the hijacking by the Septembrists. So you see, far from interrupting their plans and killing some of their number, it would benefit you to do everything in your power to make sure they succeed."

"And presumably that money serves also as your personal protection."

"Precisely. Should anything happen to me or my friends while we are your guests, that money disappears, victim of an accounting error."

Hel was attracted to the sliding doors giving out on his Japanese garden. The rain had come, hissing in the gravel and vibrating the tips of black and silver foliage. "And that is it?"

"Not quite. We are aware that you probably have a couple of hundred thousand here and there as emergency funds. A psychological profile of you from Fat Boy tells us that it is just possible that you may put such things as loyalty to a dead friend and his niece ahead of all considerations of personal benefit. All part of being selectively bred and tutored in Japanese concepts of honor, don't you know. We are prepared for that foolish eventuality as well. In the first place, the British MI-5 and MI-6 are alerted to keep tabs on you and to arrest you the moment you set foot on their soil. To assist them in this task, the French Internal Security forces are committed to making sure you do not leave this immediate district. Descriptions of you have been distributed. If you are discovered in any village other than your own, you will be shot on sight. Now, I am familiar with your history of accomplishments in the face of improbable odds, and I realize that, for you, these forces we have put on line are more in the nature of nuisances than deterrents. But we are going through the motions nonetheless. The Mother Company must be *seen* to be doing everything in Her power to protect the London Septembrists. Should that protection fail—and I almost hope it does—then the Mother Company must be seen to mete out punishment—punishment of an intensity that will satisfy our Arab friends. And you know what those people are like. To satisfy their taste for revenge, we would be forced to do something very thorough and very . . . imaginative."

Hel was silent for a moment. "I told you at the outset of our chat that I had a question for you, merchant. Here it is. Why did you come here?"

"That should be obvious."

"Perhaps I didn't accent my question properly. Why did *you* come here? Why didn't you send a messenger? Why bring your face into my presence and run the risk of my remembering you?"

Diamond stared at Hel for a moment. "I'll be honest with you . . ."

"Don't break any habits on my account."

"I wanted to tell you about the loss of your land in Wyoming personally. I wanted to display in person the mass of punishment I have designed, if you are rash enough to disobey the Mother Company. It's something I owe my brother."

Hel's emotionless gaze settled on Diamond, who stood rigid with defiance, his eyes shining with a tear glaze that revealed the body fright within him. He had taken a dangerous plunge, this merchant. He had left the cover of laws and systems behind which corporate men hide and from which their power derives, and he had run the risk of showing his face to Nicholai Alexandrovitch Hel. Diamond was subconsciously aware of his dependent anonymity, of his role as a social insect clawing about in the frantic nests of profit and success. Like others of his caste, he found spiritual solace in the cowboy myth. At this moment, Diamond saw himself as a virile individualist striding bravely down the dusty street of a Hollywood back lot, his hand hovering an inch above the computer in his holster. It is revealing of the American culture that its prototypic hero is the cowboy: an uneducated, boorish, Victorian migrant agricultural worker. At base, Diamond's role was ludicrous: the Tom Mix of big business facing a *yojimbo* with a garden. Diamond possessed the most extensive computer system in the world; Hel had some file cards. Diamond had all the governments of the industrialized West in his pocket; Hel had some Basque friends. Diamond represented atomic energy, the earth's oil supply, the military/industrial symbiosis, the corrupt and corrupting governments established by the Wad to shield itself from responsibility; Hel represented *shibumi*, a faded concept of reluctant beauty. And yet, it was obvious that Hel had a considerable advantage in any battle that might be joined.

Hel turned his face away and shook his head slightly. "This must be embarrassing to be you."

During the silence, Diamond's fingernails had dug into his palms. He cleared his throat. "Whatever you think of me, I cannot believe that you will sacrifice the years remaining to you for one gesture that would be appreciated by no one but that middle-class dumpling I met at dinner. I think I know what you are going to do, Mr. Hel. You are going to consider this matter at length and realize at last that a handful of sadistic Arabs is not worth this home and life you have made for yourself here; you will realize that you are not honor-bound to the desperate hopes of a sick and drug-befuddled man; and finally you will decide to back off. One of the reasons you will do this is because you would consider it demeaning to make an empty gesture of courage to impress me, a man you despise. Now, I don't expect you to tell me that you're backing off right now. That would be too humiliating, too damaging to your precious sense of dignity. But that is what you will do at last. To be truthful, I almost wish you would persist in this matter. It would be a pity to see the punishments I have devised for you go unused. But, fortunately for you, the Chairman of the Mother Company is adamant that the Septembrists go unmolested. We are arranging what will be called the Camp David Peace Talks in the course of which Israel will be pressured into leaving her southern and eastern borders naked. As a by-product of these talks, the PLO will be dealt out of the Middle Eastern game. They have served their irritant purpose. But the Chairman wants to keep the Palestinians mollified until this coup comes off. You see, Mr. Hel, you're swimming in deep currents, involved with forces just a little beyond shotgun pistols and cute gardens."

Hel regarded Diamond in silence for a moment. Then he turned toward his garden. "This conversation is over," he said quietly.

"I see." Diamond took a card from his pocket. "I can be contacted at this number. I shall be back at my office within ten hours. When you tell me that you have decided not to interfere in this business, I shall initiate the release of your Swiss funds."

As Hel no longer seemed to be aware of his presence, Diamond put the card on the table. "There's nothing more for us to discuss at this time, so I'll be on my way."

"What? Oh, yes. I am sure you can find your way out, Diamond. Hana will serve you coffee before sending you and your lackeys back to the village. No doubt Pierre has been fortifying himself with wine for the past few hours and will be in good form to give you a memorable ride."

"Very well. But first . . . there was that question I had for you."

"Well?"

"That rosé I had with dinner. What was it?"

"Tavel, of course."

"I knew it!"

"No, you didn't. You almost knew it."

The arm of the garden extending toward the Japanese building had been designed for listening to rain. Hel worked for weeks each rainy season, barefoot and wearing only sodden shorts, as he tuned the garden. The gutters and downspouts had been drilled and shaped, plants moved and removed, gravel distributed, sounding stones arranged in the stream, until the blend of soprano hissing of rain through gravel, the basso drip onto broad-leaved plants, the reedy resonances of quivering bamboo leaves, the counterpoint of the gurgling stream, all were balanced in volume in such a way that, if one sat precisely in the middle of the *tatami*'d room, no single sound dominated. The concentrating listener could draw one timbre out of the background, or let it merge again, as he shifted the focus of his attention, much as the insomniac can tune in or out the ticking of a clock. The effort required to control the instrument of a well-tuned garden is sufficient to repress quotidian worries and anxieties, but this anodyne property is not the principal goal of the gardener, who must be more devoted to creating a garden than to using it.

Hel sat in the gun room, hearing the rain, but lacking the peace of spirit to listen to it. There was bad *aji* in this affair. It wasn't of a piece, and it was treacherously . . . personal. It was Hel's way to play against the patterns on the board, not against fleshy, inconsistent living opponents. In this business, moves would be made for illogical reasons; there would be human filters between cause and effect. The whole thing stank of passion and sweat.

He released a long sigh in a thin jet of breath. "Well?" he asked. "And what do you make of all this?"

There was no answer. Hel felt her aura take on a leporine palpitation between the urge to flee and fear of movement. He slid back the door panel to the tea room and beckoned with his finger.

Hannah Stern stood in the doorway, her hair wet with rain, and her sodden dress clinging to her body and legs. She was embarrassed at being caught eavesdropping, but defiantly unwilling to apologize. In her view, the importance of the matters at hand out-weighed any consideration of good form and rules of polite behavior. Hel might have told her that, in the long run, the "minor" virtues are the only ones that matter. Politeness is more reliable than the moist virtues of compassion, charity, and sincerity; just as fair play is more important than the abstraction of justice. The major virtues tend to disintegrate under the pressures of convenient rationalization. But good form is good form, and it stands immutable in the storm of circumstance.

Hel might have told her this, but he was not interested in her spiritual education, and he had no wish to decorate the unperfectible. At all events, she would probably have understood only the words, and if she were to penetrate to meanings, what use would be the barriers and foundations of good form to a woman whose life would be lived out in some Scarsdale or other?

"Well?" he asked again. "What did you make of all that?"

She shook her head. "I had no idea they were so . . . organized; so . . . cold-blooded. I've caused you a lot of trouble, haven't I."

"I don't hold you responsible for anything that has happened so far. I have long known that I have a karma debt. Considering the fact that my work has cut across the grain of social organization, a certain amount of bad luck would be expected. I've not had that bad luck, and so I've built up a karma debt; a weight of antichance against me. You were the vehicle for karma balance, but I don't consider you the cause. Do you understand any of that?"

She shrugged. "What are you going to do?"

The storm was passing, and the winds behind it blew in from the garden and made Hannah shudder in her wet dress.

"There are padded kimonos in that chest. Get out of those clothes."

"I'm all right."

"Do as I tell you. The tragic heroine with the sniffles is too ludicrous an image."

It was consonant with the too-brief shorts, the unbuttoned shirt front, and the surprise Hannah affected (believed she genuinely felt) when men responded to her as an object that she unzipped and stepped out of the wet dress before she sought out the dry kimono. She had never confessed to herself that she took social advantage of having a desirable body that appeared to be available. If she had thought of it, she would have labeled her automatic exhibitionism a healthy acceptance of her body—an absence of "hang-ups."

"What are you going to do?" she asked again, as she wrapped the warm kimono about her.

"The real question is what are you going to do. Do

334

you still intend to press on with this business? To throw yourself off the pier in the hopes that I will have to jump in after you?"

"Would you? Jump in after me?"

"I don't know."

Hannah stared out into the dark of the garden and hugged the comforting kimono to herself. "I don't know . . . I don't know. It all seemed so clear just yesterday. I knew what I had to do, what was the only just and right thing to do."

"And now . . . ?"

She shrugged and shook her head. "You'd rather I went home and forgot all about it, wouldn't you?"

"Yes. And that might not be as easy as you think, either. Diamond knows about you. Getting you safely home will take a little doing."

"And what happens to the Septembrists who murdered our athletes in Munich?"

"Oh, they'll die. Everyone does, eventually."

"But . . . if I just go home, then Avrim's death and Chaim's would be pointless!"

"That's true. They were pointless deaths, and nothing you might do would change that."

Hannah stepped close to Hel and looked up at him, her face full of confusion and doubt. She wanted to be held, comforted, told that everything would be just fine.

"You'll have to decide what you intend to do fairly quickly. Let's go back to the house. You can think things out tonight."

They found Hana and Le Cagot sitting in the cool of the wet terrace. The gusting wind had followed the storm, and the air was fresh and washed. Hana rose as they approached and took Hannah's hand in an unconscious gesture of kindness.

Le Cagot was sprawled on a stone bench, his eyes closed, his brandy glass loose in his fingers, and his heavy breathing occasionally rippling in a light snore.

"He dropped off right in the middle of a story," Hana explained.

"Hana," Hel said. "Miss Stern won't be staying with us after tonight. Would you see to having her things packed by morning? I'm going to take her up to the lodge." He turned to Hannah. "I have a mountain place. You can stay there, out of harm's way, while I consider how to get you back to your parents safely."

"I haven't decided that I *want* to go home."

Instead of responding, Hel kicked the sole of Le Cagot's boot. The burly Basque started and smacked his lips several times. "Where was I? Ah . . . I was telling you of those three nuns in Bayonne. Well, I met them—"

"No, you decided not to tell that one, considering the presence of ladies."

"Oh? Well, good! You see, little girl, a story like that would inflame your passions. And when you come to me, I want you to do so of your own will, and not driven by blinding lust. What happened to our guests?"

"They've gone. Probably back to the United States."

"I am going to tell you something in all frankness, Niko. I do not like those men. There is cowardice in their eyes; and that makes them dangerous. You must either invite a better class of guests, or risk losing my patronage. Hana, wonderful and desirable woman, do you want to go to bed with me?"

She smiled. "No, thank you, Beñat."

"I admire your self control. What about you, little girl?"

"She's tired," Hana said.

"Ah well, perhaps it's just as good. It would be a little crowded in my bed, what with the plump Portuguese kitchen maid. So! I hate to leave you without the color and charm of my presence, but the magnificent machine that is my body needs draining, then sleep. Good night, my friends." He grunted to his feet and started to leave, then he noticed Hannah's kimono. "What's this? What happened to your clothes? Oh, Niko, Niko. Greed is a vice. Ah well . . . good night."

Hana had gently stroked the tension from his back and shoulders as he lay on his stomach, and now she tugged his hair until he was half asleep. She placed her body over his, fitting her lap to his buttocks, her legs and arms over his, her warm weight protecting him, comforting, forcing him to relax. "This is trouble, isn't it?" she whispered.

336

He hummed in affirmation.

"What are you going to do?"

"I don't know," he breathed. "Get the girl away from here first. They may think that her death would cancel my debt to the uncle."

"You are sure they won't find her? There's no such thing as a secret in these valleys."

"Only the mountain men will know where she is. They're my people; and they don't talk to police, by habit and tradition."

"And what then?"

"I don't know. I'll think about it."

"Shall I bring you pleasure?"

"No. I'm too tense. Let me be selfish. Let me bring you pleasure."

Larun

Hel was awake at dawn and put in two hours of work on the garden before he took breakfast with Hana in the *tatami*'d room overlooking the newly raked sea gravel that flowed down to the edge of the stream. "In time, Hana, this will be an acceptable garden. I hope you are here to enjoy it with me."

"I have been giving that matter consideration, Nikko. The idea is not without its attractions. You were very thorough last night."

"I was working out some stresses. That's an advantage."

"If I were selfish, I would hope for such stresses always."

He chuckled. "Oh, will you telephone down to the village and arrange for the next flight back to the United States for Miss Stern? It will be Pau to Paris, Paris to New York, New York to Chicago."

"She is leaving us then?"

"Not just yet. I don't want her in the open. But the reservations will be stored in the airline's computer bank, and will be immediately available to Fat Boy. It will throw them off the track."

"And who is 'Fat Boy'?"

"A computer. The final enemy. It arms stupid men with information."

"You sound bitter this morning."

"I am. Even self-pitying."

"I had avoided that phrase, but it is the right one. And it's not becoming in a man like you."

"I know." He smiled. "No one in the world would dare correct me like that, Hana. You're a treasure."

"It's my role to be a treasure."

"True. By the way, where is Le Cagot? I haven't heard him thundering about."

"He went off an hour ago with Miss Stern. He's going

338

to show her some of the deserted villages. I must say she seemed to be in good spirits."

"The shallow recover quickly. You can't bruise a pillow. When will they be back?"

"By lunch surely. I promised Beñat a roast of *gigot*. You said you were taking Hannah to the lodge. When will you be leaving?"

"After twilight. I'm being watched."

"You intend to spend the night there with her?"

"Hm-m. I suppose so. I wouldn't want to come back down those roads in the dark."

"I know you don't like Hannah, but—"

"I don't like her type, thrill-seeking middle-class muffins tickling themselves with the thrill of terror and revolution. Her existence has already cost me a great deal."

"Do you intend to punish her while you're up there?"

"I hadn't thought about it."

"Don't be harsh. She's a good child."

"She is twenty-four years old. She has no right to be a child at that age. And she is not good. At best, she is 'cute.' "

Hel knew what Hana meant by "punishing" the girl. He had occasionally avenged himself on young women who had annoyed him by making love to them, using his tactical skills and exotic training to create an experience the woman could never approach again and would seek in vain through affairs and marriages for the rest of her life.

Hana felt no jealousy concerning Hannah; that would have been ridiculous. During the two years they had lived together, both she and Hel had been free to go off on little trips and seek sexual diversion, exercises of physical curiosity that kept their appetites in tone and made more precious, by comparison, what they had. Hana once chided him lightheartedly, complaining that he had the better of the arrangement, for a trained man can accomplish decent levels of exercise with a willing amateur; while even the most gifted and experienced woman has difficulty, with the gauche instrument of a bumbling man, achieving much beyond lust-scratching. Still, she enjoyed the occasional well-muscled young

339

man of Paris or the Côte d'Azure, primarily as objects of physical beauty: toys to cuddle.

They drove along the twisting valley road, already dark with descending evening. The mountains rising sharply to their left were featureless geometric shapes, while those to their right were pink and amber in the horizontal rays of the setting sun. When they started from Etchebar, Hannah had been full of chatter about the robust good time she had had that afternoon with Le Cagot, wandering through deserted villages in the uplands, where she had noticed that each church clock had had its hands removed by the departing peasants. Le Cagot had explained that removing the hands of the clocks was considered necessary, because there would be no one in the churches to keep the clock weights screwed up, and one could not allow God's clock to be inaccurate. The dour tone of primitive Basque Catholicism was expressed in a *memento mori* inscription on the tower of one deserted church: "Each hour wounds, the last kills."

She was silent now, awed by the desolate beauty of the mountains rising so abruptly from the narrow valley that they seemed to overhang. Twice, Hel frowned and glanced over at her to find her eyes soft and a calm smile on her lips. He had been attracted and surprised by the alpha saturation in her aura, uncommon and unexpected in a person he had dismissed as a peppy twit. It was the timbre of calm and inner peace. He was going to question her about her decision concerning the Septembrists, when his attention was arrested by the approach of a car from behind driving with only wing lights. It flashed through his mind that Diamond or his French police lackeys might have learned that he was moving her to a safer place, and his hands gripped the wheel as he recalled the features of the road, deciding where he would force the car to pass him, then knock it into the ravine that raced along to their left. He had taken an exhaustive course in offensive driving, in result of which he always drove heavy cars, like his damned Volvo, for just such emergencies as this.

The road was never straight, constantly curving and twisting as it followed the course of the river ravine.

There was no place a safe pass could be made, but that, of course, would not deter a French driver, whose adolescent impulse to pass is legendary. The car behind continued to close the distance until it was only a meter from his back bumper. It flashed its headlights and sounded its horn, then whipped around while they were in a tight blind curve.

Hel relaxed and slowed to let the car pass. The horn and the lights told him that this was not an assassination attempt. No professional would telegraph his move like that. It was just another childish French driver.

He shook his head paternally as the underpowered Peugeot strained its motor in its laboring effort to pass, the young driver's knuckles white on the steering wheel, his eyes bulging from their sockets in his effort to hold the road.

In his experience, Hel had found that only older North American drivers, with the long distances they habitually travel on good roads with competent machines, have become inured to the automobile as toy and as manhood metaphor. The French driver's infantile recklessness often annoyed him, but not so much as did the typical Italian driver's use of the automobile as an extension of his penis, or the British driver's use of it as a substitute.

For half an hour after leaving the valley road, they pulled up toward the mountains of Larun, over an unimproved road that writhed like a snake in its final agony. Some of the cutbacks were inside the turning radius of the Volvo, and negotiating them required two cuts and a bit of skidding close to the edge of loose gravel verges. They were never out of low gear, and they rose so steeply that they climbed out of the night that had pooled in the valley and into the zebra twilight of the high mountains: a blinding glare on the windshield when they turned toward the west, then blackness when outcroppings of rock blocked the setting sun.

Even this primitive road petered out, and they continued to ascend along faint ruts pressed into stubbly alpine meadows. The setting sun was now red and huge, its base flattened as it melted into the shimmering horizon. There were snow fields on the peaks above them glowing pink, then soon mauve, then purple against a black sky. The first stars glittered in the darkening east while the sky to the west was still hazy blue around the blood-red rim of the sinking sun.

Hel stopped the car by an outcropping of granite and set the hand brake. "We have to pack in from here. It's another two and a half kilometers."

"Up?" Hannah asked.

"Mostly up."

"God, this lodge of yours is certainly out of the way."

"That's its role." They got out and unloaded her pack from the car, experiencing the characteristic frustration of the Volvo's diabolic rear latch. They had walked twenty meters before it occurred to him to perform his satisfying ritual. Rather than go back, he picked up a jagged rock and hurled it, a lucky shot that hit a rear window and made a large cobweb of crackled safety glass.

"What was that all about?" Hannah asked.

"Just a gesture. Man against the system. Let's go. Stay close. I know the trail by feel."

"How long will I be up here all alone?"

"Until I decide what to do with you."

"Will you be staying tonight?"

"Yes."

They walked on for a minute before she said, "I'm glad."

He maintained a brisk pace because the light was draining fast. She was strong and young, and could stay with him, walking in silence, captured by the rapid but subtle color shifts of a mountain twilight. Again, as before down in the valley, he intercepted a surprising alpha tone in her aura—that rapid, midvolume signal that he associated with meditation and soul peace, and not at all with the characteristic signature timbres of young Westerners.

She stopped suddenly as they were crossing the last alpine meadow before the narrow ravine leading to the lodge.

"What is it?"

"Look. These flowers. I've never seen anything like them before." She bent close to the wiry-stalked bells of dusty gold, just visible in the groundglow.

He nodded. "They're unique to this meadow and to one other over there." He gestured westward, toward the Table of the Three Kings, no longer visible in the gloom. "We're just above twelve hundred here. Both here and over there, they grow only at twelve hundred. Locally they are called the Eye of Autumn, and most people have never seen them, because they bloom for only three or four days."

"Beautiful. But it's almost dark, and they're still open."

"They never close. Tradition has it that they live so short a time they dare not close."

"That's sad."

He shrugged.

They sat opposite one another at a small table, finishing supper as they looked out through the plate-glass wall that gave onto the steep, narrow gully that was the only access to the lodge. Normally, Hel would be uneasy sitting in front of a glass wall, his form lighted by an oil lamp, while all was dark beyond. But he knew that the double plate glass was bulletproof.

The lodge was built of local stone and was simple of design: one large room with a cantilevered sleeping balcony. When first they arrived, he had acquainted Hannah with its features. The stream that flowed from a permanent snowfield above passed directly under the lodge, so one could get water through a trap door without going outside. The four-hundred-liter oil tank that fueled the stove and space heater was encased in the same stone as the lodge, so that incoming gunfire could not rupture it. There was a boiler-plate shutter that closed over the only door. The larder was cut into the face of granite that constituted one wall of the lodge, and contained thirty days' supply of food. Set into the bulletproof plate-glass wall was one small pane that could be broken out to permit firing down into the tight ravine up which anyone approaching the lodge would have to pass. The walls of the ravine were smooth, and all covering boulders had been dislodged and rolled to the bottom.

"Lord, you could hold an army off forever!" she exclaimed.

"Not an army, and not forever; but it would be a costly position to take." He took a semiautomatic rifle with telescopic sights from its rack and gave it to her. "Can you use this weapon?"

"Well . . . I suppose so."

"I see. Well, the important thing is that you shoot if you see anyone approaching up the gully who is not carrying a *xahako*. It doesn't matter if you hit him or not. The sound of your fire will carry in these mountains, and within half an hour help will be here."

"What's a . . . ah . . ."

"A *xahako* is a wine skin like this one. The shepherds and smugglers in these hills all know you are here. They're my friends. And they all carry *xahakos*. An outlander wouldn't."

"Am I really in all that much danger?"

"I don't know."

"But why would they want to kill me?"

"I'm not sure they do. But it's a possibility. They might reason that my involvement would be over if you were dead, and there was nothing more I could do to repay my debt to your uncle. That would be stupid thinking, because if they killed you while you were in my protection, I would be forced to make a countergesture. But we are dealing here with merchant and military mentalities, and stupidity is their intellectual idiom. Now let's see if you can manage everything."

He rehearsed her in lighting the stove and space heater, in drawing water from the trap door over the stream, and in loading clips into the rifle. "By the way, remember to take one of these mineral tablets each day. The water running under the floor is snowmelt. It has no minerals, and in time it will leech the minerals out of your system."

"God, how long will I be here?"

"I'm not sure. A week. Maybe two. Once those Septembrists have accomplished their hijack, the pressure will be off you."

While he made supper from tinned foods in the larder, she had wandered about the lodge, touching things, thinking her own thoughts.

And now they sat across the round table by the glass wall, the candlelight reversing the shadows on her soft young face on which lines of character and experience had not yet developed. She had been silent throughout the meal, and she had drunk more wine than was her habit, and now her eyes were moist and vague. "I should tell you that you don't have to worry about me anymore. I know what I'm going to do now. Early this morning, I decided to go home and try my best to forget all this anger and . . . ugliness. It's not my kind of thing. More than that, I realize now that it's all—I don't know—all sort of unimportant." She played absently with the candle flame, passing her finger through it just quickly enough to avoid being burned. "A strange thing happened to me last night. Weird. But wonderful. I've been feeling the effects of it all day long."

Hel thought of the alpha timbres he had been intercepting.

"I couldn't sleep. I got up and wandered around your house in the dark. Then I went to the garden. The air was cool and there was no breeze at all. I sat by the stream, and I could see the dark flicker of the water. I was staring at it, not thinking of anything in particular, then all at once I . . . it was a feeling I almost remember having when I was a child. All at once, all the pressures and confusions and fears were gone. They dissolved away, and I felt light. I felt like I was transported somewhere else, someplace I've never been to, but I know very well. It was sunny and still, and there was grass all around me; and I seemed to understand everything. Almost as though I was . . . I don't know. Almost as though I was—ouch!" She snapped her hand back and sucked the singed finger.

He laughed and shook his head, and she laughed too. "That was a stupid thing to do," she said.

"True. I think you were going to say that it was almost as though you and the grass and the sun were all one being, parts of the same thing."

She stared at him, her finger still to her lips. "How did you know that?"

"It's an experience others have had. You said you remembered similar feelings when you were a child?"

"Well, not exactly remember. No, not remember at all. It's just that when I was there, I had the feeling that

345

this wasn't new and strange. It was something I had done before—but I don't actually remember doing it before. You know what I mean?"

"I think I do. You might have been participating in the atavistic—"

"I'll tell you what! I'm sorry, I don't mean to interrupt you. But I'll tell you what it's like. It's like the very best high on pot or something, when you're in a perfect mood and everything's going just right. It's not exactly like that, because you never get there with hooch, but it's where you think you're going. You know what I mean?"

"No."

"You never use pot or anything?"

"No. I've never had to. My inner resources are intact."

"Well. It was something like that."

"I see. How's your finger?"

"Oh, it's fine. The point is that, after the feeling had passed last night, I found myself sitting there in your garden, rested and clear-minded. And I wasn't confused any more. I knew there was no point in trying to punish the Septembrists. Violence doesn't get you anywhere. It's irrelevant. Now I think I just want to go home. Spend a little time getting in touch with myself. Then maybe—I don't know. See what's happening around me, maybe. Deal with that." She poured herself out another glass of wine and drank it down, then she put her hand on Hel's arm. "I guess I've been a lot of trouble to you."

"I believe the American idiom is 'a pain in the ass.'"

"I wish there were some way I could make it up to you."

He smiled at her obliquity.

She poured another glass of wine and said, "Do you think Hana minds your being here?"

"Why should she?"

"Well, I mean . . . do you think she minds our spending the night together?"

"What does that phrase signify to you?"

"What? Well . . . we'll be sleeping together."

"Sleeping together?"

"In the same place, I mean. You know what I mean."

346

He regarded her without speaking. Her experience of mystic transport, even if it was a unique event prompted by an overload of tension and desperation, rather than the function of a spirit in balance and peace, gave her a worthiness in his eyes. But this new acceptance was not free from a certain envy, that this vague-minded muffin should be able to achieve the state that he had lost years ago, probably forever. He recognized the envy to be adolescent and small on his part, but this recognition was not sufficient to banish the feeling.

She had been frowning into the candle flame, trying to sort out her emotions. "I should tell you something."

"Should you?"

"I want to be honest with you."

"Don't bother."

"No, I want to be. Even before I met you, I used to think about you . . . daydream, sort of. All the stories my uncle used to tell about you. I was really surprised at how young you are—how young you appear, that is. And I suppose if I analyzed my feelings, there's a sort of father projection. Here you are, the great myth in the flesh. I was scared and confused, and you protected me. I can see all the psychological impulses that would draw me toward you, can't you?"

"Have you considered the possibility that you're a randy young woman with a healthy and uncomplicated desire to climax? Or do you find that psychologically unsubtle?"

She looked at him and nodded. "You certainly know how to put a person down, don't you. You don't leave a person much to cover herself with."

"That's true. And perhaps it's uncivil of me. I'm sorry. Here is what I think is going on with you. You're alone, lonely, confused. You want to be cuddled and comforted. You don't know how to ask for that, because you're a product of the Western culture; so you negotiate for it, bartering sex for cuddling. It's not an uncommon negotiation for the Western woman to engage in. After all, she's limited to negotiating with the Western male, whose concept of social exchange is brittle and limited, and who demands earnest money in the form of sex, because that's the only part of the bargain he is comfortable with. Miss Stern, you may sleep with me tonight if you wish. I'll hold you and comfort you, if that's what you want."

Both gratitude and too much wine moistened her eyes. "I would like that, yes."

But the animal lurking within is seldom tethered by good intentions. When he awoke to her attentions and felt emanating from her the alpha/theta syncopation that attends sexual excitation, his response was not solely dictated by a desire to shield her from rejection.

She was exceptionally ripe and easy, all of her nerves close to the surface and desperately sensitive. Because she was young, there was a bit of difficulty keeping her lubricated, but beyond that mechanical nuisance he could hold her in climax without much effort.

Her eyes rolled back again and she pleaded, "No . . . please . . . I can't again! I'll die if I do again!" But her involuntary contractions rushed closer and closer together, and she was gasping in her fourth orgasm, which he prolonged until her fingernails were clawing frantically at the nap of the rug.

He recalled Hana's injunction against dimming Hannah's future experience by comparison, and he had no particular impulse to climax himself, so he brought her back down slowly, stroking and cooling her as the muscles of her buttocks, stomach, and thighs quivered with the fatigue of repeated orgasm, and she lay still on the pile of pillows, half-unconscious and feeling that her flesh was melting.

He washed in frigid meltwater, then went up to the overhanging balcony to sleep.

Some time later, he felt her approach silently. He made space for her and a nest in his arms and lap. As she dipped toward sleep, she said dreamily, "Nicholai?"

"Please don't call me by my first name," he murmured.

She was silent for a time. "Mr. Hel? Don't be scared by this, because it's just a passing thing. But at this moment, I am in love with you."

"Don't be foolish."

"Do you know what I wish?"

He did not answer.

"I wish it were morning and I could go out and pick you a bunch of flowers . . . those Eyes of Autumn we saw."

He chuckled and folded her in. "Good night, Miss Stern."

Etchebar

It was midmorning before Hana heard the splash of a slab of rock into the stream and came from the château to find Hel rearranging the sounding stones, his trouser legs rolled up, and his forearms dripping with water.

"Will I ever get this right, Hana?"

She shook her head. "Only you will ever know, Nikko. Is Hannah safely set up at the lodge?"

"Yes. I think the girls have heated the water by now. Do you feel like taking a bath with me?"

"Certainly."

They sat opposite one another, their feet in their habitual caress, their eyes closed and their bodies weightless.

"I hope you were kind to her," Hana murmured sleepily.

"I was."

"And you? How was it for you?"

"For me?" He opened his eyes. "Madame, do you have anything pressing on your schedule just now?"

"I'll have to consult my *carnet de bal,* but it is possible that I can accommodate you."

Shortly after noon, when he had reason to hope the local PTT would be functioning at least marginally, Hel placed a transatlantic call to the number Diamond had left with him. He had decided to tell the Mother Company that Hannah Stern had decided to return home, leaving the Septembrists unmolested. He assumed Diamond would take personal satisfaction in the thought that he had frightened Nicholai Hel off, but just as praise from such a source would not have pleased him, so scorn could not embarrass him.

It would be more than an hour before the viscous and senile French telephone system could place his call, and he chose to pass the interval inspecting the grounds. He felt lighthearted, well-disposed toward everything, enjoying that generalized euphoria that follows a close call with danger. For a whole constellation of impalpable reasons, he had dreaded getting involved in a business that was trammeled with personalities and passions.

He was wandering through the privet maze on the east lawns when he came across Pierre, who was in his usual vinous fog of contentment. The gardener looked up into the sky and pontificated. "Ah, M'sieur. Soon there will be a storm. The signs all insist on it."

"Oh?"

"Oh yes, there is no doubt. The little clouds of the morning have been herded against the flank of *ahuñe-mendi*. The first of the *ursoa* flew up the valley this afternoon. The *sagarra* turned its leaves over in the wind. These are sure signs. A storm is inevitable."

"That's too bad. We could have used a little rain."

"True, M'sieur. But look! Here comes M'sieur Le Cagot. How finely he dresses!"

Le Cagot was approaching across the lawn, still wearing the rumpled theatrical evening dress of two nights ago. As he neared, Pierre tottered away, explaining that there were many thousands of things that demanded his immediate attention.

Hel greeted Le Cagot. "I haven't seen you in a while, Beñat. Where have you been?"

"Bof. I've been up in Larrau with the widow, helping her put out the fire in her belly." Le Cagot was uneasy, his badinage mechanical and flat.

"One day, Beñat, that widow will have you in the trap, and you'll be . . . What is it? What's wrong?"

Le Cagot put his hands on Hel's shoulders. "I have hard news for you, friend. A terrible thing has happened. That girl with the plump breasts? Your guest? . . ."

Hel closed his eyes and turned his head to the side. After a silence he said quietly, "Dead?"

"I'm afraid so. A *contrabandier* heard the shots. By the time he got to your lodge, she was dead. They had shot her . . . many, many times."

Hel took a long, slow breath and held it for a mo-

351

ment; then he let it out completely, as he absorbed the first shock and avoided the flash of mind-fogging fury. Keeping his mind empty, he walked back toward the château, while Le Cagot followed, respecting his friend's armor of silence.

Hel had sat for ten minutes at the threshold of the *tatami*'d room, staring out over the garden, while Le Cagot slumped beside him. He refocused his eyes and said in a monotone, "All right. How did they get into the lodge?"

"They didn't have to. She was found in the meadow below the ravine. Evidently she was picking wild-flowers. There was a large bunch found in her hand."

"Silly twit," Hel said in a tone that might have been affectionate. "Do we know who shot her?"

"Yes. Early this morning, down in the village of Lescun, two outlanders were seen. Their descriptions are those of the *Amérlo* from Texas I met here and that little Arab snot."

"But how did they know where she was? Only our people knew that."

"There is only one way. Someone must have informed."

"One of *our* people?"

"I know. I know!" Le Cagot spoke between his teeth. "I have asked around. Sooner or later, I shall find out who it was. And when I do, by the Prophetic Balls of Joseph in Egypt, I swear that the blade of my *makila* will puncture his black heart!" Le Cagot was ashamed and furious that one of his own, a mountain Basque, had disgraced the race in this way. "What do you say, Niko? Shall we go get them, the *Amérlo* and the Arab?"

Hel shook his head. "By now they are on a plane bound for the United States. Their time will come."

Le Cagot smashed his fists together, breaking the skin over a knuckle. "But *why*, Niko! Why kill such a morsel? What harm could she do, the poor muffin?"

"They wanted to prevent me from doing something. They thought they could erase my debt to the uncle by killing the niece."

"They are mistaken, of course."

"Of course." Hel sat up straight as his mind began

352

to function in a different timbre. "Will you help me, Beñat?"

"Will I help you? Does asparagus make your piss stink?"

"They have French Internal Security forces all over this part of the country with orders to put me away if I attempt to leave the area."

"Bof! The only charm of the Security Force is its epic incompetence."

"Still, they will be a nuisance. And they might get lucky. We'll have to neutralize them. Do you remember Maurice de Lhandes?"

"The man they call the Gnome? Yes, of course."

"I have to get in touch with him. I'll need his help to get safely into Britain. We'll go through the mountains tonight, into Spain to San Sebastian. I need a fishing boat to take me along the coast to St. Jean de Luz. Would you arrange that?"

"Would a cow lick Lot's wife?"

"Day after tomorrow, I'll be flying out from Biarritz to London. They'll be watching the airports. But they're spread thin, and that's to our advantage. Starting about noon that day, I want reports leaked to the authorities that I have appeared in Oloron, Pau, Bayonne, Bilbao, Mauléon, St. Jean Pied de Port, Bordeaux, Ste. Engrace, and Dax—all at the same time. I want their cross-communications confused, so that the report from Biarritz will be just one drop in a torrent of information. Can that be arranged?"

"Can it be arranged? Do . . . I can't think of an old saying for it just now. Yes, it can be arranged. This is like the old days, eh?"

"I'm afraid so."

"You're taking me with you, of course."

"No. It's not your kind of thing."

"Hola! Don't let the gray in my beard fool you. A boy lives inside this body! A very mean boy!"

"It's not that. If this were breaking into a prison or blowing away a guardpost, there is no one I'd rather have with me. But this won't be a matter of courage. It must be done by craft."

As was his custom when in the open air, Le Cagot had turned aside and unbuttoned his trousers to relieve himself as he talked. "You don't think I am capable of craft? I am subtlety itself! Like the chameleon, I blend with all backgrounds!"

Hel could not help smiling. This self-created folk myth standing before him, resplendent in rumpled *fin-de-siècle* evening clothes, the rhinestone buttons of his brocade waistcoat sparkling in the sun, his beret tugged low over his sunglasses, his rust-and-steel beard covering a silk cravat, the battered old *makila* under his arm as he held his penis in one hand and sprayed urine back and forth like a schoolboy—this man was laying claim to being subtle and inconspicuous.

"No, I don't want you to come with me, Beñat. You can help most by making the arrangements I asked for."

"And after that? What do I do while you are off amusing yourself? Pray and twiddle my thumbs?"

"I'll tell you what. While I'm gone, you can press on with preparations for the exploration of your cave. Get the rest of the gear we need down into the hole. Wet suits. Air tanks. When I get back, we'll take a shot at exploring it from light to light. How's that?"

"It's better than nothing. But not much."

A serving girl came from the house to tell Hel that he was wanted in the château.

He found Hana standing with the telephone in the butler's pantry, blocking the mouthpiece with her palm. "It is Mr. Diamond returning your call to the United States."

Hel looked at the phone, then glanced down to the floor. "Tell him I'll get back to him soon."

They had finished supper in the *tatami*'d room, and now they were watching the evening permutations of shifting shadow through the garden. He had told her that he would be away for about a week.

"Does this have to do with Hannah?"

"Yes." He saw no reason to tell her the girl was dead.

After a silence, she said, "When you get back, it will be close to the end of my stay with you."

"I know. By then you'll have to decide if you're interested in continuing our life together."

354

"I know." She lowered her eyes and, for the first time he could remember, her cheeks colored with the hint of a blush. "Nikko? Would it be too silly for us to consider becoming married?"

"Married?"

"Never mind. Just a silly thought that wandered through my mind. I don't believe I would want it anyway." She had touched on the idea gingerly and had fled instantly from his first reaction.

For several minutes, he was deep in thought. "No, it's not all that silly. If you decide to give me years of your life, then of course we should do something to assure your economic future. Let's talk about it when I return."

"I could never mention it again."

"I realize that, Hana. But I could."

PART FOUR

Uttegae

St. Jean de Luz/Biarritz

The open fishing boat plowed the ripple path of the setting moon, quicksilver on the sea, like an effect from the brush of a kitsch watercolorist. The diesel motor chugged bronchially and gasped as it was turned off. The bow skewed when the boat crunched up on the pebble beach. Hel slipped over the side and stood knee-deep in the surging tide, his duffel bag on his shoulder. A wave of his hand was answered by a blurred motion from the boat, and he waded toward the deserted shore, his canvas pants heavy with water, his rope-soled espadrilles digging into the sand. The motor coughed and began its rhythmic thunking, as the boat made its way out to sea, along the matte-black shore toward Spain.

From the brow of a dune, he could see the lights of cafés and bars around the small harbor of St. Jean de Luz, where fishing boats heaved sleepily on the oily water of the docking slips. He shifted the weight of the duffel and made for the Café of the Whale, to confirm a telegraph order he had made for dinner. The owner of the café had been a master chef in Paris, before retiring back to his home village. He enjoyed displaying his prowess occasionally, particularly when M. Hel granted him carte blanche as regards menu and expense. The dinner was to be prepared and served in the home of Monsieur de Lhandes, the "fine little gentleman" who lived in an old mansion down the shore, and who was never to be seen in the streets of St. Jean de Luz because his physiognomy would cause comment, and perhaps ridicule, from ill-brought-up children. M. de Lhandes was a midget, little more than a meter tall, though he was over sixty years old.

Hel's tap at the back door brought Mademoiselle Pinard to peer cautiously through the curtain, then a broad smile cracked her face, and she opened the door wide. "Ah, Monsieur Hel! Welcome. It has been too long since last we saw you! Come in, come in! Ah, you are wet! Monsieur de Lhandes is so looking forward to your dinner."

"I don't want to drip on your floor, Mademoiselle Pinard. May I take off my pants?"

Mademoiselle Pinard blushed and slapped at his shoulder with delight. "Oh, Monsieur Hel! Is this any way to speak? Oh, men!" In obedience to their established routine of chaste flirtation, she was both flustered and delighted. Mademoiselle Pinard was somewhat older than fifty—she had always been somewhat older than fifty. Tall and sere, with dry nervous hands and an unlubricated walk, she had a face too long for her tiny eyes and thin mouth, so rather a lot of it was devoted to forehead and chin. If there had been more character in her face, she would have been ugly; as it was, she was only plain. Mademoiselle Pinard was the mold from which virgins are made, and her redoubtable virtue was in no way lessened by the fact that she had been Bernard de Lhandes's companion, nurse, and mistress for thirty years. She was the kind of woman who said *"Zut!"* or *"Ma foi!"* when exasperated beyond the control of good taste.

As she showed him to the room that was always his when he visited, she said in a low voice, "Monsieur de Lhandes is not well, you know. I am delighted that he will have your company this evening, but you must be very careful. He is close to God. Weeks, months only, the doctor tells me."

"I'll be careful, darling. Here we are. Do you want to come in while I change my clothes?"

"Oh, Monsieur!"

Hel shrugged. "Ah well. But one day, your barriers will fall, Mademoiselle Pinard. And then . . . Ah, then . . ."

"Monster! And Monsieur de Lhandes your good friend! Men!"

"We are victims of our appetites, Mademoiselle. Helpless victims. Tell me, is dinner ready?"

"The chef and his assistants have been cluttering up the kitchen all day. Everything is in readiness."

"Then I'll see you at dinner, and we'll satisfy our appetites together."

"Oh, Monsieur!"

They took dinner in the largest room of the house, one lined with shelves on which books were stacked and piled in a disarray that was evidence of de Lhandes's passion for learning. Since he considered it outrageous to read and eat at the same time—diluting one of his passions with the other—de Lhandes had struck on the idea of combining library and dining room, the long refectory table serving both functions. They sat at one end of this table, Bernard de Lhandes at the head, Hel to his right, Mademoiselle Pinard to his left. Like most of the furniture, the table and chairs had been cut down and were somewhat too big for de Lhandes and somewhat too small for his rare guests. Such, de Lhandes had once told Hel, was the nature of compromise: a condition that satisfied no one, but left each with the comforting feeling that others had been done in too.

Dinner was nearly over, and they were resting and chatting between courses. There had been Neva caviar with blinis, still hot on their napkins, St. Germain Royal (de Lhandes found a hint too much mint), suprême de sole au Château Yquem, quail under the ashes (de Lhandes mentioned that walnut would have been a better wood for the log fire, but he could accept the flavor imparted by oak cinders), rack of baby lamb Edward VII (de Lhandes regretted that it was not cold enough, but he realized that Hel's arrangements were spur of the moment), riz à la grècque (the bit too much red pepper de Lhandes attributed to the chef's place of birth), morels (the bit too little lemon juice de Lhandes attributed to the chef's personality), Florentine artichoke bottoms (the gross imbalance between gruyère and parmesan in the mornay sauce de Lhandes attributed to the chef's perversity, for the error had been mentioned before), and Danicheff salad (which de Lhandes found perfect, to his slight annoyance).

From each of these dishes, de Lhandes took the smallest morsel that would still allow him to have all the flavors in his mouth at once. His heart, liver, and

361

digestive system were such a ruin that his doctor restricted him to the blandest of foods. Hel, from dietary habit, ate very little. Mademoiselle Pinard's appetite was good, though her concept of exquisite table manners involved taking minute bites and chewing them protractedly with circular, leporine motions confined to the very front of her mouth, where her napkin often and daintily went to brush thin lips. One of the reasons the chef of the Café of the Whale enjoyed doing these occasional suppers for Hel was the great feast his family and friends always enjoyed later that same night.

"It's appalling how little we eat, Nicholai," de Lhandes said in his surprisingly deep voice. "You with your monk's attitude toward food, and I with my ravished constitution! Picking about like this, I feel like a rich ten-year-old in a luxurious bordello!"

Mademoiselle Pinard went behind her napkin for a moment.

"And these thimblesful of wine!" de Lhandes complained. "Ah, that I have descended to this! A man who, through knowledge and money, converted gluttony into a major art! Fate is either ironic or just, I don't know which. But look at me! Eating as though I were a bloodless nun doing penance for her daydreams about the young curé!"

The napkin concealed Mademoiselle Pinard's blush.

"How sick are you, old friend?" Hel asked. Honesty was common currency between them.

"I am finally sick. This heart of mine is more a sponge than a pump. I have been in retirement for—what? Five years now? And for four of them I have been of no use to dear Mademoiselle Pinard—save as an observer, of course."

The napkin.

The meal ended with a bombe, fruit, *glacés variées* —no brandies or *digestifs*—and Mademoiselle Pinard retired to allow the men to chat.

De Lhandes slid down from his chair and made his way to the fireside, stopping for breath twice, where he occupied a low chair that nevertheless left his feet straight out before him.

"All chairs are *chaises longues* for me, my friend." He laughed. "All right, what can I do for you?"

362

"I need help."

"Of course. Good comrades though we are, you would not come by boat in the dead of night for the sole purpose of disgracing a supper by picking at it. You know that I have been out of the information business for several years, but I have orts and bits left from the old days, and I shall help you if I can."

"I should tell you that they have got my money. I won't be able to pay you immediately."

De Lhandes waved a dismissing hand. "I'll send you a bill from hell. You'll recognize it by the singed edges. Is it a person, or a government?"

"Government. I have to get into England. They'll be waiting for me. The affair is very heavy, so my leverage will have to be strong."

De Lhandes sighed. "Ah, my. If only it were America. I have something on America that would make the Statue of Liberty lie back and spread her knees. But England? No one thing. Fragments and scraps. Some nasty enough, to be sure, but no one big thing."

"What sort of things have you?"

"Oh, the usual. Homosexuality in the foreign office . . ."

"That's not news."

"At this level, it's interesting. And I have photographs. There are few things so ludicrous as the postures a man assumes while making love. Particularly if he is no longer young. And what else have I? Ah . . . a bit of rambunctiousness in the royal family? The usual political peccadillos and payoffs? A blocked inquiry into that flying accident that cost the life of . . . you remember." De Lhandes looked to the ceiling to recall what was in his files. "Oh, there's evidence that the embrace between the Arab oil interests and the City is more intimate than is generally known. And there's a lot of individual stuff on government people—fiscal and sexual irregularities mostly. You're absolutely sure you don't want something on the United States? I have a real bell ringer there. It's an unsalable item. Too big for almost any use. It would be like opening an egg with a sledge hammer."

"No, it has to be English. I haven't time to set up indirect pressure from Washington to London."

"Hm-m-m. Tell you what. Why don't you take the whole lot? Arrange to have it published, one shot right after the other. Scandal after scandal eroding the edifice of confidence—you know the sort of thing. No single arrow strong enough alone, but in fascine . . . who knows? It's the best I can offer."

"Then it will have to do. Set it up the usual way? I bring photocopies with me? We arrange a 'button-down' trigger system with the German magazines as primary receivers?"

"It's not failed yet. You're sure you don't want the Statue of Liberty's brazen hymen?"

"Can't think of what I'd do with it."

"Ah well, painful image at best. Well . . . can you spend the night with us?"

"If I may. I fly out of Biarritz tomorrow at noon, and I have to lie low. The locals have a bounty on me."

"Pity. They ought to protect you as the last surviving member of your species. You know, I've been thinking about you lately, Nicholai Alexandrovitch. Not often, to be sure, but with some intensity. Not often, because when you get to the bang or whimper moment of life, you don't spend much time contemplating the minor characters of your personal farce. And one of the difficult things for egocentric Man to face is that he is a minor character in every biography but his own. I am a bit player in your life; you in mine. We have known one another for more than twenty years but, discounting business (and one must always discount business), we have shared perhaps a total of twelve hours of intimate conversation, of honest inquiry into one another's minds and emotions. I have known you, Nicholai, for half a day. Actually, that's not bad. Most good friends and married couples (those are seldom the same thing) could not boast twelve hours of honest interest after a lifetime of shared space and irritations, of territorial assertions and squabbles. So . . . I've known you for half a day, my friend, and I have come to love you. I think very highly of myself for having accomplished that, as you are not an easy man to love. Admire? Yes, of course. Respect? If fear is a part of respect, then of course. But love? Ah, that's a different business. Because there is in love an urge to forgive, and you're a hard man to forgive. Half saintly ascetic, half Vandal marauder, you don't make yourself available for forgiveness. In one persona, you are above forgiveness; in another, beneath it. And always resentful of it. One has the feeling that you would never forgive a man for forgiving you. (That probably doesn't mean much, but it rolls well off the tongue, and a song must have music as well as words.) And after my twelve hours of knowing you, I would capsulize you—reduce you to a definition—by calling you a medieval antihero."

Hel smiled. "Medieval antihero? What on earth does that mean?"

"Who has the floor now, you or I? Let's have a little silent respect for the dying. It's part of your being Japanese—culturally Japanese, that is. Only in Japan was the classical moment simultaneous with the medieval. In the West, philosophy, art, political and social ideal, all are identified with periods before or after the medieval moment, the single exception being that glorious stone bridge to God, the cathedral. Only in Japan was the feudal moment also the philosophic moment. We of the West are comfortable with the image of the warrior priest, or the warrior scientist, even the warrior industrialist. But the warrior philosopher? No, that concept irritates our sense of propriety. We speak of 'death and violence' as though they were two manifestations of the same impulse. In fact, death is the very opposite of violence, which is always concerned with the struggle for life. Our philosophy is focused on managing life; yours on managing death. We seek comprehension; you seek dignity. We learn how to grasp; you learn how to let go. Even the label 'philosopher' is misleading, as our philosophers have always been animated by the urge to share (indeed, inflict) their insights; while your lot are content (perhaps selfishly) to make your separate and private peace. To the Westerner, there is something disturbingly feminine (in the sense of yang-ish, if that coinage doesn't offend your ear) in your view of manhood. Fresh from the battlefield, you don soft robes and stroll through your gardens with admiring compassion for the falling cherry petal; and you view both the gentleness and the courage

365

as manifestations of manhood. To us, that seems capricious at least, if not two-faced. By the way, how *does* your garden grow?"

"It's becoming."

"Meaning?"

"Each year it is simpler."

"There! You see? That goddamned Japanese penchant for paradoxes that turn out to be syllogisms! Look at yourself. A warrior gardener! You are indeed a medieval Japanese, as I said. And you are also an antihero—not in the sense in which critics and scholars lusting for letters to dangle after their names use (misuse) the term. What they call antiheroes are really unlikely heroes, or attractive villains—the fat cop or Richard III. The true antihero is a version of the hero —not a clown with a principal role, not an audience member permitted to work out his violent fantasies. Like the classic hero, the antihero leads the mass toward salvation. There was a time in the comedy of human development when salvation seemed to lie in the direction of order and organization, and all the great Western heroes organized and directed their followers against the enemy: chaos. Now we are learning that the final enemy is not chaos, but organization; not divergence, but similarity; not primativism, but progress. And the new hero—the antihero—is one who makes a virtue of attacking the organization, of destroying the systems. We realize now that salvation of the race lies in that nihilist direction, but we still don't know how far." De Lhandes paused to catch his breath, then seemed to be ready to continue. But his glance suddenly crossed Hel's, and he laughed. "Oh, well. Let that be enough. I wasn't really speaking to you anyway."

"I've been aware of that for some time."

"It is a convention in Western tragedy that a man is permitted one long speech before he dies. Once he has stepped on the inevitable machinery of fate that will carry him to his bathetic denouement, nothing he can say or do will alter his lot. But he is permitted to make his case, to bitch at length against the gods— even in iambic pentameter."

"Even if doing so interrupts the flow of the narrative?"

"To hell with it! For two hours of narcosis against reality, of safe, vicarious participation in the world of action and death, one should be willing to pay the price of a couple minutes worth of insight. Structurally sound or not. But have it your way. All right. Tell me, do the governments still remember 'the Gnome'? And do they still scratch the earth trying to find his lair, and gnash their teeth in frustrated fury?"

"They do indeed, Maurice. Just the other day there was an *Amérlo* scab at home asking about you. He would have given his genitals to know how you came by your information."

"Would he indeed? Being an *Amérlo,* he probably wasn't risking much. And what did you tell him?"

"I told him everything I knew."

"Meaning nothing at all. Good. Candor is a virtue. You know, I really don't have any very subtle or complicated sources of information. In fact, the Mother Company and I are nourished by the same data. I have access to Fat Boy through the purchased services of one of their senior computer slaves, a man named Llewellyn. My skill lies in being able to put two and two together better than they can. Or, to be more precise, I am able to add one and a half plus one and two thirds in such a way as to make ten. I am not better informed than they; I am simply smarter."

Hel laughed. "They would give almost anything to locate and silence you. You've been bamboo under their fingernails for a long time."

"Ha, that knowledge brightens my last days, Nicholai. Being a nuisance to the government lackeys has made my life worth living. And a precarious living it has been. When you trade in information, you carry stock that has very short shelf life. Unlike brandy, information cheapens with age. Nothing is duller than yesterday's sins. And sometimes I used to acquire expensive pieces, only to have them ruined by leakage. I remember buying a very hot item from the United States: what in time became known as the Watergate Cover-up. And while I was holding the merchandise on my shelf, waiting for you or some other international to purchase it as leverage against the American government, a pair of ambitious reporters sniffed the story out and saw in it a chance to make their fortunes—and *voilà!* The material was overnight useless to me. In time, each of the criminals wrote a book or did a television program describing his part in the rape of American civil rights, and each was paid lavishly by the stupid American public, which seems to have a peculiar impulse toward having their noses rubbed in their own shit. Doesn't it seem unjust to you that I should end up losing several hundred thousand worth of spoiled stock on my shelves, while even the master villain himself makes a fortune doing television shows with that British leech who has shown that he would sniff up to anybody for money, even Idi Amin? It's a peculiar one, this trade I'm in."

"Have you been an information broker all your life, Maurice?"

"Except for a short stint as a professional basketball player."

"Old fool!"

"Listen, let us be serious for a moment. You described this thing you're doing as hard. I wouldn't presume to advise you, but have you considered the fact that you've been in retirement for a time? Is your mental conditioning still taut?"

"Reasonably. I do a lot of caving, so fear doesn't clog my mind too much. And, fortunately, I'll be up against the British."

"That's an advantage, to be sure. The MI-5 and -6 boys have a tradition of being so subtle that their fakes go unnoticed. And yet . . . There is something wrong with this affair, Nicholai Alexandrovitch. There's something in your tone that disturbs me. Not quite doubt, but a certain dangerous fatalism. Have you decided that you are going to fail?"

Hel was silent for a time. "You're very perceptive, Maurice."

"C'est mon métier."

"I know. There is something wrong—something untidy—about all this. I recognize that to come back out of retirement I am challenging karma. I think that, ultimately, this business will put me away. Not the task at hand. I imagine that I can relieve these Septembrists of the burden of their lives easily enough. The complications and the dangers will be ones I have dealt with before. But after that, the business gets tacky. There will be an effort to punish me. I may accept the punishment, or I may not. If I do not, then I shall have to go into the field again. I sense a certain—" He shrugged. "—a certain emotional fatigue. Not exactly fatalistic resignation, but a kind of dangerous indifference. It is possible, if the indignities pile up, that I shall see no particular reason to cling to life."

De Lhandes nodded. It was this kind of attitude that he had sensed. "I see. Permit me to suggest something, old friend. You say that the governments do me the honor of still being hungry for my death. They would give a lot to know who and where I am. If you get into a tight spot, you have my permission to bargain with that information."

"Maurice!—"

"No, no! I am not suffering from a bout of quixotic courage. I'm too old to contract such a childhood disease. It would be our final joke on them. You see, you would be giving them an empty bag. By the time they get here, I shall have departed."

"Thank you, but I couldn't do it. Not on your account, but on mine." Hel rose. "Well, I have to get some sleep. The next twenty-four hours will be trying. Mostly mind play, without the refreshment of physical danger. I'll be leaving before first light."

"Very well. For myself, I think I shall sit up for a few more hours and review the delights of an evil life."

"All right. *Au revoir,* old friend."

"Not *au revoir,* Nicholai."

"It is that close?"

De Lhandes nodded.

Hel leaned over and kissed his comrade on both cheeks. *"Adieu,* Maurice."

"Adieu, Nicholai."

Hel was caught at the door by, "Oh, Nicholai, would you do something for me?"

"Anything."

"Estelle has been wonderful to me these last years. Did you know her name was Estelle?"

"No, I didn't."

"Well, I want to do something special for her—a kind of going-away present. Would you drop by her room? Second at the head of the stairs. And afterward, tell her it was a gift from me."

Hel nodded. "It will be my pleasure, Maurice."

De Lhandes was looking into the fading fire. "Hers too, let us hope," he muttered.

Hel timed his arrival at the Biarritz airport to minimize the period he would have to stand out in the open. He had always disliked Biarritz, which is Basque only in geography; the Germans, the English, and the international smart set having perverted it into a kind of Brighton on Biscay.

He was not five minutes in the terminal before his proximity sense intercepted the direct and intense observation he had expected, knowing they would be looking for him at all points of departure. He lounged against the counter of the bar where he was taking a *jus d'ananas* and lightly scanned the crowd. Immediately, he picked up the young French Special Services officer in civilian clothes and sunglasses. Pushing himself off the bar, he walked directly toward the man, feeling as he approached the lad's tension and confusion.

"Edxuse me, sir," Hel said in a French larded with German accent. "I have just arrived, and I cannot discover how to make my connection to Lourdes. Could you assist me?"

The young policeman scanned Hel's face uncertainly. This man filled the general description, save for the eyes, which were dark-brown. (Hel was wearing noncorrective brown contact lenses.) But there was nothing in the description about his being German. And he was supposed to be leaving the country, not entering it. In a few brusque words, the police agent directed Hel to the information office.

As he walked away, Hel felt the agent's gaze fixed on him, but the quality of the concentration was muffled by confusion. He would, of course, report the spotting, but without much certainty. And the central offices would at this moment be receiving reports of Hel's appearance in half a dozen cities at the same time. Le Cagot was seeing to that.

As Hel crossed the waiting room, a towheaded boy

ran into his legs. He caught up the child to keep him from falling.

"Rodney! Oh, I *am* sorry, sir." The good-looking woman in her late twenties was on the scene in an instant, apologizing to Hel and admonishing the child all at the same time. She was British and dressed in a light summer frock designed to reveal not only her suntan, but the places she had not suntanned. In a babble of that brutally mispronounced French resulting from the Britisher's assumption that if foreigners had anything worth saying they would say it in a real language, the young woman managed to mention that the boy was her nephew, that she was returning with him from a short vacation, and that she was taking the next flight for England, that she herself was unmarried, and that her name was Alison Browne, with an *e*.

"My name is Nicholai Helm."

"Delighted to meet you, Mr. Hel."

That was it. She had not heard the *m* because she was prepared not to. She would be a British agent, covering the action of the French.

Hel said he hoped they would be sitting together on the plane, and she smiled seductively and said that she would be willing to speak to the ticket agent about that. He offered to purchase a fruit juice for her and little Rodney, and she accepted, not failing to mention that she did not usually accept such offers from strange men, but this was an exception. They had, after all, quite literally run into one another. (Giggle.)

While she was busy dabbing her handkerchief at Rodney's juice-stained collar, leaning forward and squeezing in her shoulders to advertise her lack of a bra, Hel excused himself for a moment.

At the sundries shop he purchased a cheap memento of Biarritz, a box to contain it, a pair of scissors, and some wrapping paper—a sheet of white tissue and one of an expensive metal foil. He carried these items to the men's room, and worked rapidly wrapping the present, which he brought back to the bar and gave to Rodney, who was by now whining as he dangled and twisted from Miss Browne's hand.

"Just a little nothing to remind him of Biarritz. I hope you don't mind?"

"Well, I shouldn't. But as it's for the boy. They've called twice for our flight. Shouldn't we be boarding?"

Hel explained that these French, with their anal compulsion for order, always called early for the planes; there was no rush. He turned the talk to the possibility of their getting together in London. Dinner, or something?

At the last moment they went to the boarding counter, Hel taking his place in the queue in front of Miss Browne and little Rodney. His small duffel bag passed the X-ray scanner without trouble. As he walked rapidly toward the plane, which was revving up for departure, he could hear the protests of Miss Browne and the angry demands of the security guards behind him. When the plane took off, Hel did not have the pleasure of the seductive Miss Browne and little Rodney.

Heathrow

Passengers passing through customs were directed to enter queues in relation to their status: "British Subjects," "Commonwealth Subjects," "Common Market Citizens," and "Others." Having traveled on his Costa Rican passport, Hel was clearly an "Other," but he never had the opportunity to enter the designated line, for he was immediately approached by two smiling young men, their husky bodies distorting rather extreme Carnaby Street suits, their meaty faces expressionless behind their moustaches and sunglasses. As he always did when he met modern young men, Hel mentally shaved and crewcut them to see whom he was really dealing with.

"You will accompany us, Mr. Hel," one said, as the other took the duffel from his hand. They pressed close to him on either side and escorted him toward a door without a doorknob at the end of the debarcation area.

Two knocks, and the door was opened from the other side by a uniformed officer, who stood aside as they passed through. They walked without a word to the end of a long windowless corridor of institutional green, where they knocked. The door was opened by a young man struck from the same mold as the guards, and from within came a familiar voice.

"Do come in, Nicholai. We've just time for a glass of something and a little chat before you catch your plane back to France. Leave the luggage, there's a good fellow. And you three may wait outside."

Hel took a chair beside the low coffee table and waved away the brandy bottle lifted in offer. "I thought you had finally been cashiered out, Fred."

Sir Wilfred Pyles squirted a splash of soda into his brandy. "I had more or less the same idea about you. But here we are, two of yesterday's bravos, sitting on opposite sides, just like the old days. You're sure you won't have one? No? Well, I imagine the sun's over the yardarm somewhere around the world, so—cheers."

"How's your wife?"

"More pleasant than ever."

"Give her my love when next you see her."

"Let's hope that's not too soon. She died last year."

"Sorry to hear that."

"Don't be. Is that enough of the small talk?"

"I should think so."

"Good. Well, they dragged me out of the mothballs to deal with you, when they got word from our petroleum masters that you might be on your way. I assume they thought I might be better able to handle you, seeing that we've played this game many times, you and I. I was directed to intercept you here, find out what I could about your business in our misty isle, then see you safely back on a plane to the place from whence you came."

"They thought it would be as easy as that, did they?"

Sir Wilfred waved his glass. "Well, you know how these new lads are. All by the book and no complexities."

"And what do you assume, Fred?"

"Oh, I assume it won't be quite that easy. I assume you came with some sort of nasty leverage gained from your friend, the Gnome. Photocopies of it in your luggage, I shouldn't wonder."

"Right on top. You'd better take a look."

"I shall, if you don't mind," Sir Wilfred said, unzipping the bag and taking out a manila folder. "Nothing else in here I should know about, I trust? Drugs? Subversive or pornographic literature?"

Hel smiled.

"No? I feared as much." He opened the folder and began to scan the information, sheet by sheet, his matted white eyebrows working up and down with each uncomfortable bit of information. "By the way," he asked between pages, "what on earth did you do to Miss Browne?"

"Miss Browne? I don't believe I know a—"

"Oh, come now. No coyness between old enemies. We got word that she is this moment sitting in a French detention center while those gentlemen of Froggish

374

inclination comb and recomb her luggage. The report we received was quite thorough, including the amusing detail that the little boy who was her cover promptly soiled himself, and the consulate is out the cost of fresh garments."

Hel couldn't help laughing.

"Come. Between us. What on earth did you do?"

"Well, she came on with all the subtlety of a fart in a bathosphere, so I neutralized her. You don't train them as you did in the old days. The stupid twit accepted a gift."

"What sort of a gift?"

"Oh, just a cheap memento of Biarritz. It was wrapped up in tissue paper. But I had cut out a gun shape from metal foil paper and slipped it between the sheets of tissue."

Sir Wilfred sputtered with laughter. "So, the X-ray scanner picked up a gun each time the package passed through, and the poor officials could find nothing! How delicious: I think I must drink to that." He measured out the other half, then returned to the task of familiarizing himself with the leverage information, occasionally allowing himself such interjections as: "Is that so? Wouldn't have thought it of him." "Ah, we've known this for some time. Still, wouldn't do to broadcast it around." "Oh, my. That *is* a nasty bit. How on earth did he find that out?"

When he finished reading the material, Sir Wilfred carefully tapped the pages together to make the ends even, then replaced them in the folder. "No single thing here sufficient to force us very far."

"I'm aware of that, Fred. But the mass? One piece released to the German press each day?"

"Hm-m. Quite. It would have a disastrous effect on confidence in the government just now, with elections on the horizon. I suppose the information is in 'button-down' mode?"

"Of course."

"Feared as much."

Holding the information in "button-down" mode involved arrangements to have it released to the press immediately, if a certain message was not received by noon of each day. Hel carried with him a list of thirteen addresses to which he was to send cables each morning. Twelve of these were dummies; one was an associate of Maurice de Lhandes who would, upon receipt of the message, telephone to another intermediary, who would telephone de Lhandes. The code between Hel and de Lhandes was a simple one based upon an obscure poem by Barro, but it would take much longer than twenty-four hours for the intelligence boys to locate the one letter in the one word of the message that was the active signal. The term "button-down" came from a kind of human bomb, rigged so that the device would not go off, so long as the man held a button down. But any attempt to struggle with him or to shoot him would result in his releasing the button.

Sir Wilfred considered his position for a moment. "It is true that this information of yours can be quite damaging. But we are under tight orders from the Mother Company to protect these Black September vermin, and we are no more eager to bring down upon our heads the ire of the Company than is any other industrial country. It appears that we shall have to choose between misfortunes."

"So it appears."

Sir Wilfred pushed out his lower lip and squinted at Hel in evaluation. "This is a very wide-open and dangerous thing you're doing, Nicholai—walking right into our arms like this. It must have taken a great deal of money to draw you out of retirement."

"Point of fact, I am not being paid for this."

"Hm-m-m. That, of course, would have been my second guess." He drew a long sigh. "Sentiment is a killer, Nicholai. But of course you know that. All right, tell you what. I shall carry your message to my masters. We'll see what they have to say. Meanwhile, I suppose I shall have to hide you away somewhere. How would you like to spend a day or two in the country? I'll make a telephone call or two to get the government lads thinking, then I'll run you out in my banger."

Middle Bumley

Sir Wilfred's immaculate 1931 Rolls crunched over the gravel of a long private drive and came to a stop under the porte cochère of a rambling house, most of the charm of which derived from the aesthetic disorder of its having grown without plan through many architectural impulses.

Crossing the lawn to greet them were a sinewy woman of uncertain years and two girls in their mid-twenties.

"I think you'll find it amusing here, Nicholai," Sir Wilfred said. "Our host is an ass, but he won't be about. The wife is a bit dotty, but the daughters are uniquely obliging. Indeed, they have gained something of a reputation for that quality. What do you think of the house?"

"Considering your British penchant for braggadocio through meiosis—the kind of thing that makes you call your Rolls a banger—I'm surprised you didn't describe the house as thirty-seven up, sixteen down."

"Ah, Lady Jessica!" Sir Wilfred said to the older woman as she approached wearing a frilly summer frock of a vague color she would have called "ashes of roses." "Here's the guest I telephoned about. Nicholai Hel."

She pressed a damp hand into his. "So pleased to have you. To meet you, that is. This is my daughter, Broderick."

Hel shook hands with an overly slim girl whose eyes were huge in her emaciated face.

"I know it's an uncommon name for a girl," Lady Jessica continued, "but my husband had quite settled on having a boy—I mean he wanted to have a boy in the sense of fathering a son—not in the other sense—my goodness, what must you think of him? But he had Broderick instead—or rather, we did."

"In the sense that you were her parents?" Hel sought to release the skinny girl's hand.

"Broderick is a model," the mother explained.

Hel had guessed as much. There was a vacuousness of expression, a certain limpness of posture and curvature of spine that marked the fashionable model of that moment.

"Nothing much really," Broderick said, trying to blush under her troweled-on makeup. "Just the odd job for the occasional international magazine."

The mother tapped the daughter's arm. "Don't say you do 'odd jobs'! What will Mr. Hel think?"

A clearing of the throat by the second daughter impelled Lady Jessica to say, "Oh, yes. And here is Melpomene. It is conceivable she might act one day."

Melpomene was a substantial girl, thick of bosom, ankle, and forearm, rosy of cheek, and clear of eye. She seemed somehow incomplete without her hockey stick. Her handshake was firm and brisk. "Just call me Pom. Everyone does."

"Ah . . . if we could just freshen up?" Sir Wilfred suggested.

"Oh, of course! I'll have the girls show you everything—I mean, of course, where your rooms are and all. What must you think?"

As Hel was laying out his things from the duffel bag, Sir Wilfred tapped on the door and came in. "Well, what do you think of the place? We should be cozy here for a couple of days, while the masters ponder the inevitable, eh? I've been on the line to them, and they say they'll come up with a decision by morning."

"Tell me, Fred. Have your lads been keeping a watch on the Septembrists?"

"On your targets? Of course."

"Assuming that your government goes along with my proposal, I'll want all the background material you have."

"I expected no less. By the bye, I assured the masters that you could pull this off—should their decision go that way—with no hint of collusion or responsibility on our part. It is that way, isn't it?"

"Not quite. But I can work it so that, whatever their

suspicions, the Mother Company will not be able to *prove* collusion."

"The next best thing, I suppose."

"Fortunately, you picked me up before I went through passport check, so my arrival won't be in your computers and therefore not in theirs."

"Wouldn't rely on that overly much. Mother Company has a million eyes and ears."

"True. You're absolutely sure this is a safe house?"

"Oh, yes! The ladies are not what you would call subtle, but they have another quality quite as good—they're totally ignorant. They haven't the slightest idea of what we're doing here. Don't even know what I do for a living. And the man of the house, if you can call him that, is no trouble at all. We seldom let him into the country, you see."

Sir Wilfred went on to explain that Lord Biffen lived in the Dordogne, the social leader of a gaggle of geriatric tax avoiders who infested that section of France, to the disgust and discomfort of the local peasants. The Biffens were typical of their sort: Irish peerage that every other generation stiffened its sagging finances by introducing a shot of American hog-butcher blood. The gentleman had overstepped himself in his lust to avoid taxes and had got into a shady thing or two in free ports in the Bahamas. That had given the government a hold on him and on his British funds, so he was most cooperative, remaining in France when he was ordered to, where he exercised his version of the shrewd businessman by cheating local women out of antique furniture or automobiles, always being careful to intercept his wife's mail to avoid her discovering his petty villainies. "Silly old fart, really. You know the type. Outlandish ties; walking shorts with street shoes and ankle stockings? But the wife and daughters, together with the establishment here, are of some occasional use to us. What do you think of the old girl?"

"A little obsessed."

"Hm-m. Know what you mean. But if you'd gone twenty-five years getting only what the old fellow had to offer, I fancy you'd be a little sperm mad yourself. Well, shall we join them?"

*   *   *

379

After breakfast the next morning, Sir Wilfred sent the ladies away and sat back with his last cup of coffee. "I was on the line with the masters this morning. They've decided to go along with you—with a couple of provisos, of course."

"They had better be minor."

"First, they want assurance that this information will never be used against them again."

"You should have been able to give them that assurance. You know that the man you call the Gnome always destroys the originals as soon as the deal is made. His reputation rests on that."

"Yes, quite so. And I shall undertake to assure them on that account. Their second proviso is that I report to them, telling them that I have considered your plan carefully and believe it to be airtight and absolutely sure not to involve the government directly."

"Nothing in this business is airtight."

"All right. Airtight-ish, then. So I'm afraid that you will have to take me into your confidence—familiarize me with details of dastardly machinations, and all that."

"Certain details I cannot give you until I have gone over your observation reports on the Septembrists. But I can sketch the bold outlines for you."

Within an hour, they had agreed on Hel's proposal, although Sir Wilfred had some reservations about the loss of the plane, as it was a Concorde, ". . . and we've had trouble enough trying to ram the damned thing down the world's throat as it is."

"It's not my fault that the plane in question is that uneconomical, polluting monster."

"Quite so. Quite so."

"So there it is, Fred. If your people do your part well, the stunt should go off without the Mother Company's having any proof of your complicity. It's the best plan I could work up, considering that I've had only a couple of days to think about it. What do you say?"

"I don't dare give my masters the details. They're political men—the least reliable of all. But I shall report that I consider the plan worth cooperating with."

"Good. When do I get the observation reports on the Septembrists?"

"They'll be here by courier this afternoon. You know,

something occurs to me, Nicholai. Considering the character of your plan, you really don't have to involve yourself at all. We could dispose of the Arabs ourselves, and you could return to France immediately."

Hel looked at Sir Wilfred flatly for fully ten seconds. Then they both laughed at once.

"Ah well," Sir Wilfred said, waving a hand, "you can't blame me for trying. Let's take a little lunch. And perhaps there's time for a nap before the reports come in."

"I hardly dare go to my room."

"Oh? Did they also visit you last night?"

"Oh, yes, and I chucked them out."

"Waste not, want not, I always say."

Sir Wilfred dozed in his chair, warmed by the setting sun beyond the terrace. On the other side of the white metal table, Hel was scanning the observation reports on the PLO actives.

"There it is," he said finally.

"What? Hm-m? There what is?"

"I was looking for something in the list of contacts and acquaintances the Septembrists have made since their arrival."

"And?"

"On two occasions, they spent time with this man you have identified as 'Pilgrim Y'. He works in a food-preparation service for the airlines."

"Is that so? I really don't know the file. I was only dragged into this—unwillingly, I might mention—when you got involved. What's all this about food preparation?"

"Well, obviously the Septembrists are not going to try to smuggle their guns through your detection devices. They don't know that they have the passive cooperation of your government. So I had to know how they were going to get their weapons aboard. They've gone to a well-worn method. The weapons will come aboard with the prepared dinners. The food trucks are never searched more than desultorily. You can run anything through them."

"So now you know where their weapons will be. So what?"

"I know where they will have to come to collect them. And that's where I'll be."

"And what about you? How are you going to get arms aboard for yourself, without leaving trace of our complicity in this?"

"I'll carry my weapons right through the checkpoint."

"Oh, yes. I'd forgotten about that for a moment. Naked/Kill and all that. Stab a man with a drinking straw. What a nuisance that's been to us over the years."

Hel closed the report. "We have two days until the plane departs. How shall we fill our time?"

"Loll about here, I suppose. Keep you out of sight."

"Are you going up to dress for dinner?"

"No, I think I'll not take dinner tonight. I should have followed your example and forsaken my midday lie by. Had to contend with both of them. Probably walk with a limp the rest of my life."

Heathrow

The plane was almost full of passengers, all adults,
most of them the sort who could afford the surcharge
for flying Concorde. Couples chatted; stewards and
stewardesses leaned over seats making the cooing noises
of experienced nannies; businessmen asked one another
what they sold; unacquainted pairs said those inane
things calculated to lead to assignations in Montreal;
the conspicuously busy kept their noses in documents
and reports or fiddled ostentatiously with pocket re-
corders; the frightened babbled about how much they
loved flying, and tried to appear casual as they scanned
the information card designating procedures and exits
in case of emergency.

A muscular young Arab and a well-dressed Arab
woman sat together near the back, a curtain separating
them from the service area, where food and drinks were
stored. Beside the curtain stood a flight attendant who
smiled down at the Arab couple, his bottle-green eyes
vacant.

Two young Arabs, looking like rich students, entered
the plane and sat together about halfway down. Just
before the doors were closed, a fifth Arab, dressed as
a businessman, rushed down the mobile access truck
and aboard the plane, babbling to the receiving steward
something about just making it and being delayed by
business until the last moment. He came to the back
of the plane and took a seat opposite the Arab couple,
to whom he nodded in a friendly way.

With an incredible roar, the engines tugged the plane
from the loading ramp, and soon the bent-nosed pterodactyl was airborne.

When the seat-belt sign flashed off, the pretty Arab
woman undid her belt and rose. "It is this way to the
ladies' room?" she asked the green-eyed attendant,
smiling shyly.

He had one hand behind the curtain. As he smiled back at her, he pressed the button on which his finger rested, and two soft gongs echoed through the passenger area. At this sound, each of the 136 passengers, except the PLO Arabs, lowered his head and stared at the back of the seat before him.

"Any one of these, Madam," Hel said, holding the curtain aside for her to pass through.

At that instant, the Arab businessman addressed a muffled question to Hel, meaning to attract his attention while the girl got the weapons from the food container.

"Certainly, sir," Hel said, seeming not to understand the question. "I'll get you one."

He slipped a comb from his pocket as he turned and followed the girl, snapping shut the curtain behind him.

"But wait!" the Arab businessman said—but Hel was gone.

Three seconds later he returned, a magazine in his hand. "I'm sorry, sir, we don't seem to have a copy of *Paris Match*. Will this do?"

"Stupid fool!" muttered the businessman, staring at the drawn curtain in confusion. Had this grinning idiot not seen the girl? Had she stepped into the rest room upon his approach? Where *was* she?

Fully a minute passed. The four Arabs aboard were so concerned with the girl's failure to emerge through the curtain, an automatic weapon in her hands, they failed to notice that everyone else on the plane was sitting with his head down, staring at the seat back before him.

Unable to control themselves longer, the two Arab students who had sat together in the waist of the plane rose and started back down the aisle. As they approached the smiling, daydreaming steward with the green eyes, they exchanged worried glances with the older businessman and the muscular lad who was the woman's companion. The older man gestured with his head for the two to pass on behind the curtain.

"May I help you?" Hel asked, rolling up the magazine into a tight cylinder.

"Bathroom," one of them muttered, as the other said, "Drink of water."

"I'll bring it to you, sir," Hel said. "Not the bathroom, of course," he joked with the taller one.

They passed him, and he followed them behind the curtain.

Four seconds later, he emerged, a harried expression on his face. "Sir," he said confidentially to the older businessman, "you're not a doctor by any chance?"

"Doctor? No. Why?"

"Oh, it's nothing. Not to worry. The gentleman's had a little accident."

"Accident?"

"Don't worry. I'll get help from a member of the cabin crew. Nothing serious, I'm sure." Hel had in his hand a plastic drinking cup, which he had crushed and creased down the center.

The businessman rose and stepped into the aisle.

"If you would just stay with him, sir, while I fetch someone," Hel said, following the businessman into the service area.

Two seconds later, he was standing again at his station, looking over the passengers with that expression of vague compassion airline stewards affect. When his gaze fell on the worried muscular young man beside him, he winked and said, "It was nothing at all. Dizzy spell, I guess. First time in a supersonic plane, perhaps. The other gentleman is assisting him. I don't speak Arabic, unfortunately."

A minute passed. Another. The muscular young man's tension grew, while this mindless steward standing before him hummed a popular tune and gazed vacantly around, fiddling with the small plastic name tag pinned to his lapel.

Another minute passed.

The muscular lad could not contain himself. He leaped up and snatched the curtain aside. On the floor, in the puppet-limbed sprawl of the dead, were his four companions. He never felt the edge of the card; he was nerve dead before his body reached the floor.

Other than the hissing roar of the plane's motors, there was silence in the plane. All the passengers stared rigidly ahead. The flight crew stood facing the front of the plane, their eyes riveted on the decorated plastic panel before them.

Hel lifted the intercom phone from its cradle. His soft voice sounded metallic through the address system. "Relax. Don't look back. We will land within fifteen minutes." He replaced the phone and dialed the pilot's cabin. "Send the message exactly as you have been instructed to. That done, open the envelope in your pocket and follow the landing instructions given."

Its pterodactyl nose bent down again, the Concorde roared in for a landing at a temporarily evacuated military airfield in northern Scotland. When it stopped and its engines had whined down to silence, the secondary entrance portal opened, and Hel descended on mobile stairs that had been rolled up to the door. He stepped into the vintage 1931 Rolls that had chased the plane across the runway, and they drove away.

Just before turning off to a control building, Hel looked back and saw the passengers descending and lining themselves up in four-deep ranks beside the plane under the direction of a man who had posed as senior steward. Five military buses were already crossing the airstrip to pick them up.

Sir Wilfred sat at the scarred wooden desk of the control office, sipping a whiskey, while Hel was changing from the flight attendant's uniform to his own clothes.

"Did the message sound all right?" Hel asked.

"Most dramatic. Most effective. The pilot radio'd back that the plane was being skyjacked, and right in the middle of the message, he broke off, leaving nothing but dead air and the hiss of static."

"And he was on clear channel, so there will be independent corroborations of your report?"

"He must have been heard by half a dozen radio operators all across the North Atlantic."

"Good. Now, tomorrow your search planes will come back with reports of having found floating wreckage, right?"

"As rain."

"The wreckage will be reported to have been picked up, and the news will be released over BBC World Service that there was evidence of an explosion, and that the current theory is that an explosive device in

386

the possession of Arab skyjackers was detonated accidentally, destroying the plane."

"Just so."

"What are your plans for the plane, Fred? Surely the insurance companies will be curious."

"Leave that to us. If nothing else remains of the Empire, we retain at least that penchant for duplicity that earned us the title Perfidious Albion."

Hel laughed. "All right. It must have been quite a job to gather that many operatives from all over Europe and have them pose as passengers."

"It was indeed. And the pilots and crew were RAF fellows who had really very little check-out time on a Concorde."

"Now you tell me."

"Wouldn't have done to make you edgy, old man."

"I regret your problem of having a hundred-fifty people in on the secret. It was the only way I could do it and still keep your government to the lee of the Mother Company's revenge. And, after all, they are all your own people."

"True enough. But that is no assurance of long-term reliability. But I've arranged to manage the problem."

"Oh? How so?"

"Where do you imagine those buses are going?"

Hel adjusted his tie and zipped up his duffle. "All hundred-fifty of them?"

"No other airtight way, old boy. And within two days, we'll have to attend to the extermination crew as well. But there's a bright side to everything, if you look hard enough. We're having a bit of an unemployment problem in the country just now, and this will produce scads of openings for bright young men and women in the secret service."

Hel shook his head. "You're really a tough old fossil, aren't you, Fred."

"In time, even the soul gets callused. Sure you won't have a little farewell drink?"

PART FIVE

Shicho

Château d'Etchebar

His muscles melting in the scalding water, his body weightless, Hel dozed as his feet enclosed Hana's in slack embrace. It was a cool day for the season, and dense steam billowed, filling the small bathing house.

"You were very tired when you came home last night," Hana said after a sleepy silence.

"Is that a criticism?" he muttered without moving his lips.

She laughed lightly. "On the contrary. Fatigue is an advantage in our games."

"True."

"Was your trip . . . successful?"

He nodded.

She was never inquisitive about his affairs; her training prohibited it, but her training also taught her to create opportunities for him to speak about his work if he wanted to. "Your business? It was the same sort of thing you did in China when we met?"

"Same genre, different phylum."

"And those unpleasant men who visited us, were they involved?"

"They weren't on the ground, but they were the enemy." His tone changed. "Listen, Hana. I want you to take a little vacation. Go to Paris or the Mediteranean for a few weeks."

"Back only ten hours and you are already trying to be rid of me?"

"There may be some trouble from those 'unpleasant men.' And I want you safely out of the way. Anyway"—he smiled,—"you could probably use the spice of a strong young lad or two."

"And what of you?"

"Oh, I'll be out of the enemy's range. I'm going into the mountains and work that cave Beñat and I discovered. They're not likely to find me there."

"When do you want me to leave, Nikko?"

"Today. As soon as you can."

"You don't think I would be safe here with our friends in the mountains protecting me?"

"That chain's broken. Something happened to Miss Stern. Somebody informed."

"I see." She squeezed his foot between hers. "Be careful, Nikko."

The water had cooled enough to make slow movements possible, and Hel flicked his fingers, sending currents of hotter water toward his stomach. "Hana? You told me that you could not bring up the subject of marriage again, but I said that I could and would. I'm doing that now."

She smiled and shook her head. "I've been thinking about that for the past few days, Nikko. No, not marriage. That would be too silly for such as you and I."

"Do you want to go away from here?"

"No."

"What then?"

"Let's not make plans. Let's remain together for a month at a time. Perhaps forever—but only a month at a time. Is that all right with you?"

He smiled and nestled his feet into hers. "I have great affection for you, Hana."

"I have great affection for you, Nicholai."

"By the Skeptical Balls of Thomas! What's going on in here?" Le Cagot had snatched open the door of the bathing room and entered, bringing unwelcomed cool air with him. "Are you two making your own private whiteout? Good to see you back, Niko! You must have been lonely without me." He leaned against the wooden tub, his chin hooked over the rim. "And good to see you too, Hana! You know, this is the first time I've seen all of you. I shall tell you the truth—you are a desirable woman. And that is praise from the world's most desirable man, so wear it in health."

"Get out of here!" Hel growled, not because he was uncomfortable with nudity, but because Le Cagot's tease would go flat if he didn't seem to rise to the bait.

"He shouts to hide his delight at seeing me again, Hana. It's an old trick. Mother in Heaven, you have fine nipples! Are you sure there isn't a bit of Basqu

392

in that genetic stew of yours? Hey, Niko, when do we see if there is light and air at the other end of Le Cagot's Cave? Everything is in readiness. The air tank is down, the wet suit. Everything."

"I'm ready to go up today."

"When today?"

"In a couple of hours. Get out."

"Good. That gives me time to visit your Portuguese maid. All right, I'm off. You two will have to resign yourselves to getting on without my company." He slammed the door behind him, swirling the scant steam that remained in the room.

After they had made love and taken breakfast, Hana began her packing. She had decided to go to Paris because in late August that city would be relatively empty of vacationing bourgeois Parisians.

Hel puttered for a time in his garden, which had roughened somewhat in his absence. It was there Pierre found him.

"Oh, M'sieur, the weather signs are all confused."

"Is that so?"

"It is so. It has rained for two days, and now neither the Eastwind nor the Northwind have dominance, and you know what that means."

"I'm confident you will tell me."

"It will be dangerous in the mountains, M'sieur. This is the season of the whiteout."

"You're sure of that?"

Pierre tapped the tip of his rubicund drunkard's nose with his forefinger, signifying that there were things only the Basque knew for certain, and weather was but one of them.

Hel took some consolation in Pierre's assurance. At least they would not have to contend with a whiteout.

The Volvo rolled into the village square of Larrau, where they would pick up the Basque lads who operated the pedal winch. They parked near the widow's bar, and one of the children playing *pala* against the church wall ran over and did Hel the service of bashing the hood of the car with a stick, as he had seen the man do so often. Hel thanked him, and followed Le Cagot to the bar.

"Why are you bringing your *makila* along, Beñat?" He hadn't noticed before that Le Cagot was carrying his ancient Basque sword/cane under his arm.

"I promised myself that I would carry it until I discover which of my people informed on that poor little girl. Then, by the Baby-Killing Balls of Herod, I shall ventilate his chest with it. Come, let's take a little glass with the widow. I shall give her the pleasure of laying my palm upon her ass."

The Basque lads who had been awaiting them since morning now joined them over a glass, talking eagerly about the chances of M'sieur Hel being able to swim the underground river to the daylight. Once that air-to-air exploration had been made, the cave system would be officially discovered, and they would be free to go down into the hole themselves and, what is more, to talk about it later.

The widow twice pushed Le Cagot's hand away; then, her virtue clearly demonstrated, she allowed it to remain on her ample bottom as she stood beside the table, keeping his glass full.

The door to the W.C. in back opened, and Father Xavier entered the low-ceilinged bar, his eyes bright with fortifying wine and the ecstasy of fanaticism. "So?" he said to the young Basque lads. "Now you sit with this outlander and his lecherous friend? Drinking their wine and listening to their lies?"

"You must have drunk deep of His blood this morning, Father Esteka!" Le Cagot said. "You've swallowed a bit of courage."

Father Xavier snarled something under his breath and slumped down in a chair at the most distant table.

"Holà," Le Cagot pursued. "If your courage is so great, why don't you come up the mountain with us, eh? We are going to descend into a bottomless pit from which there is no exit. It will be a foretaste of hell for you—get you used to it!"

"Let him be," Hel muttered. "Let's go and leave the silly bastard to pickle in his own hate."

"God's eyes are everywhere!" the priest snarled, glaring at Hel. "His wrath is inescapable!"

"Shut your mouth, convent girl," Le Cagot said, "or

I shall put this *makila* where it will inconvenience the Bishop!"

Hel put a restraining hand on Le Cagot's arm; they finished off their wine and left.

Gouffre Porte-de-Larrau

Hel squatted on the flat slab that edged their base camp beside the rubble cone, his helmet light turned off to save the batteries, listening over the field telephone to Le Cagot's stream of babble, invective, and song as he descended on the cable, constantly bullying and amusing the Basque lads operating the pedal winch above. Le Cagot was taking a breather, braced up in the bottom of the corkscrew before allowing himself to be lowered into the void of Le Cagot's Cave, down into the waterfall, where he would have to hang, twisting on the line, while the lads locked up and replaced the cable drum.

After ordering them to be quick about the job and not leave him hanging there, dangling like Christ on the tree, or he would come back up and do them exquisite bodily damage, he said, "All right, Niko, I'm coming down!"

"That's the only way gravity works," Hel commented, as he looked up for the first glimpse of Le Cagot's helmet light emerging through the mist of the waterfall.

A few meters below the opening into the principal cave, the descent stopped, and the Basque boy on the phones announced that they were changing drums.

"Get on with it!" Le Cagot ordered. "This cold shower is abusing my manhood!"

Hel was considering the task of carrying the heavy air tank all the way to the Wine Cellar at the end of the system, glad that he could rely on Le Cagot's bull strength, when a muffled shout came over the earphones. Then a sharp report. His first reaction was that something had snapped. A cable? The tripod? His body instinctively tightened in kinesthetic sympathy for Le Cagot. There were two more crisp reports. Gunfire!

Then silence.

Hel could see Le Cagot's helmet lamp, blurred

396

through the mist of the waterfall, winking on and off as he turned slowly on the end of the cable.

"What in hell is going on?" Le Cagot asked over the phones.

"I don't know."

A voice came over the telephone, thin and distant. "I warned you to stay out of this, Mr. Hel."

"Diamond?" Hel asked, unnecessarily.

"That is correct. The merchant. The one who would not dare meet you face to face."

"You call this face to face?"

"It's close enough."

Le Cagot's voice was tight with the strain on his chest and diaphragm from hanging in the harness. "What is going on?"

"Diamond?" Hel was forcing himself to remain calm. "What happened to the boys at the winch?"

"They're dead."

"I see. Listen. It's me you want, and I'm at the bottom of the shaft. I'm not the one hanging from the cable. It is my friend. I can instruct you how to lower him."

"Why on earth should I do that?"

From the background, Hel heard Darryl Starr's voice. "That's the son of a bitch that took my piece. Let him hang there, turning slowly in the wind, the mammy-jammer!"

There was the sound of a childish giggle—the PLO scab they called Haman.

"What makes you think I involved myself in your business?" Hel asked, his voice conversational, although he was frantically playing for time to think.

"The Mother Company keeps sources close to our friends in England—just to confirm their allegiance. I believe you met our Miss Biffen, the young model?"

"If I get out of here, Diamond . . ."

"Save your breath, Hel. I happen to know that is a 'bottomless pit from which there is no exit.' "

Hel took a slow breath. Those were Le Cagot's words in the widow's bar that afternoon.

"I warned you," Diamond continued, "that we would have to take counteraction of a kind that would satisfy the vicious tastes of our Arab friends. You will be a while dying, and that will please them. And I have arranged a more visible monument to your punishment. That château of yours? It ceased to exist an hour and a half ago."

"Diamond . . ." Hel had nothing to say, but he wanted to keep Diamond on the other end of the line. "Le Cagot is nothing to you. Why let him hang there?"

"It's a detail sure to amuse our Arab friends."

"Listen, Diamond—there are men coming to relieve those lads. They'll find us and get us out."

"That isn't true. In fact, it's a disappointingly pallid lie. But to forestall the possibility of someone stumbling upon this place accidentally, I intend to send men up to bury your Basque friends here, dismantle all this bric-a-brac, and roll boulders into the pit to conceal the entrance. I tell you this as an act of kindness—so you won't waste yourself on fruitless hope."

Hel did not respond.

"Do you remember what my brother looked like, Hel?"

"Vaguely."

"Good. Keep him in mind."

There was a rattling over the headphones, as they were taken off and tossed aside.

"Diamond? Diamond?" Hel squeezed the phone line in his fingers. The only sound over the phone was Le Cagot's labored breathing.

Hel turned on his helmet light and the ten-watt bulb connected to battery, so Le Cagot could see something below him and not feel deserted.

"Well, what about that, old friend?" Le Cagot's half-strangled voice came over the line. "Not exactly the denouement I would have chosen for this colorful character I have created for myself."

For a desperate moment, Hel considered attempting to scale the walls of the cave, maybe get above Le Cagot and let a line down to him.

Impossible. It would take hours of work with drill and expansion bolts to move up that featureless, over-hanging face; and long before that, Le Cagot would be dead, strangled in the harness webbing that was even now crushing the breath out of him.

Could Le Cagot get out of this harness and up the cable to the mouth of the corkscrew? From there it was

398

barely conceivable that he might work his way up to the surface by free climbing.

He suggested this to Beñat over the phone.

Le Cagot's voice was a weak rasp. "Can't . . . ribs . . . weight of . . . water . . ."

"Beñat!"

"What, for the love of God?"

A last slim possibility had occurred to Hel. The telephone line. It wasn't tied off firmly, and the chances that it would take a man's weight were slight; but it was just possible that it had fouled somewhere above, perhaps tangled with the descent cable.

"Beñat? Can you get onto the phone line? Can you cut yourself out of your harness?"

Le Cagot hadn't breath enough left to answer, but from the vibration in the phone line, Hel knew he was trying to follow instructions. A minute passed. Two. The mist-blurred helmet lamp was dancing jerkily up near the roof of the cave. Le Cagot was clinging to the phone line, using his last strength before unconsciousness to hack away at the web straps of his harness with his knife.

He gripped the wet phone line with all his force and sawed through the last strap. His weight jerked onto the phone line . . . snatching it loose.

"Christ!" he cried.

His helmet light rushed down toward Hel. For a fraction of a second, the coiling phone line puddled at Hel's feet. With a fleshy slap, Le Cagot's body hit the tip of the rubble cone, bounced, tumbled in a clatter of rock and debris, then lodged head-downward not ten meters from Hel.

"Beñat!"

Hel rushed to him. He wasn't dead. The chest was crushed; it convulsed in heaving gasps that spewed bloody foam from the mouth. The helmet had taken the initial impact but had come off during the bouncing down the rubble. He was bleeding from his nose and ears. Hanging head down, he was choking on his own blood.

As gently as possible, Hel lifted Le Cagot's torso in his arms and settled it more comfortably. The damage he might do by moving him did not matter; the man was

399

dying. Indeed, Hel resented the powerful Basque constitution that denied his friend immediate release into death.

Le Cagot's breath was rapid and shallow; his open eyes were slowly dilating. He coughed, and the motion brought him racking pain.

Hel caressed the bearded cheek, slick with blood.

"How . . ." Le Cagot choked on the word.

"Rest, Beñat. Don't talk."

"How . . . do I look?"

"You look fine."

"They didn't get my face?"

"Handsome as a god."

"Good." Le Cagot's teeth clenched against a surge of pain. The bottom ones had been broken off in the fall. "The priest . . ."

"Rest, my friend. Don't fight it. Let it take you."

"The priest!" The blood froth at the corner of his mouth was already sticky.

"I know." Diamond had quoted Le Cagot's description of the cave as a bottomless pit. The only person he could have heard it from was the fanatic, Father Xavier. And it must have been the priest who gave away Hannah's place of refuge as well. The confessional was his source of information, his Fat Boy.

For an endless three minutes, Le Cagot's gurgling rasps were the only sound. The blood pulsing from his ears began to thicken.

"Niko?"

"Rest. Sleep."

"How do I look?"

"Magnificent, Beñat."

Suddenly Le Cagot's body stiffened and a thin whine came from the back of his throat. "Christ!"

"Pain?" Hel asked stupidly, not knowing what to say.

The crisis of agony passed, and Le Cagot's body seemed to slump into itself. He swallowed blood and asked, "What did you say?"

"Pain?" Hel repeated.

"No . . . thanks . . . I have all I need."

"Fool," Hel said softly.

"Not a bad exit line, though."

"No, not bad."

400

"I bet that you won't make so fine a one when you go."

Hel closed his eyes tightly, squeezing the tears out, as he caressed his friend's cheek.

Le Cagot's breath snagged and stopped. His legs began to jerk in spasms. The breath came back, rapid gasps rattling in the back of his throat. His broken body contorted in final agony and he cried, "Argh! By the Four Balls of Jesus, Mary, and Joseph . . ."

Pink lung blood gushed from his mouth, and he was dead.

Hel grunted with relief from pain as he slipped off the straps of the air cylinder and wedged it into an angle between two slabs of raw rock that had fallen in from the roof of the Climbing Cave. He sat heavily, his chin hanging to his chest, as he sucked in great gulps of air with quivering inhalations, and exhalations that scoured his lungs and made him cough. Sweat ran from his hair, despite the damp cold of the cave. He crossed his arms over his chest and gingerly fingered the raw bands on his shoulders where the air tank straps had rubbed away the skin, even through three sweaters under his parachutist's overalls. An air tank is an awkward pack through rough squeezes and hard climbs. If drawn up tight, it constricts movement and numbs the arms and fingers; if slackened, it chafes the skin and swings, dangerously threatening balance.

When his breathing calmed, he took a long drink of water-wine from his *xahako,* then lay back on a slab of rock, not even bothering to take off his helmet. He was carrying as little as possible: the tank, all the rope he could handle, minimal hardware, two flares, his *xahako,* the diving mask in a rubberized pouch which also contained a watertight flashlight, and a pocketful of glucose cubes for rapid energy. Even stripped down to necessities, it was too much for his body weight. He was used to moving through caves freely, leading and carrying minimal weight, while the powerful Le Cagot bore the brunt of their gear. He missed his friend's strength; he missed the emotional support of his constant flow of wit and invective and song.

But he was alone now. His reserves of strength were

401

sapped; his hands were torn and stiff. The thought of sleep was delicious, seductive . . . deadly. He knew that if he slept, the cold would seep in, the attractive, narcotic cold. Mustn't sleep. Sleep is death. Rest, but don't close your eyes. Close your eyes, but don't sleep. No. Mustn't close your eyes! His eyebrows arched with the effort to keep the lids open over the upward-rolling eyes. Mustn't sleep. Just rest for a moment. Not sleep. Just close your eyes for a moment. Just close . . . eyes . . .

He had left Le Cagot on the side of the rubble heap where he died. There was no way to bury him; the cave itself would be a vast mausoleum, now that they had rolled stones in over the opening. Le Cagot would lie forever in the heart of his Basque mountains.

When at last the blood had stopped oozing, Hel had gently wiped the face clean before covering the body with a sleeping bag.

After covering the body, Hel had squatted beside it, seeking middle-density meditation to clear his mind and tame his emotions. He had achieved only fleeting wisps of peace, but when he tugged his mind back to the present, he was able to consider his situation. Decision was simple; all alternatives were closed off. His chance of making it, alone and overloaded, all the way down that long shaft and around Hel's Knob, through the gargantuan chaos of the Climbing Cave, through the waterfall into the Crystal Cavern, then down that foul marl chute to the Wine Cellar sump—his chances of negotiating all these obstacles without belaying and help from Le Cagot were slim. But it was a kind of Pascal's Bet. Slim or not, his only hope lay in making the effort. He would not think about the task of swimming out through the pipe at the bottom of the Wine Cellar, that pipe through which water rushed with such volume that it pulled the surface of the pool tight and bowed. He would face one problem at a time.

Negotiating Hel's Knob had come close to ending his problems. He had tied a line to the air tank and balanced it on the narrow ledge beside the stream rushing through that wedge-shaped cut, then he undertook the knob with a strenuous heel-and-shoulder scramble, lying back at almost full length, his knees quivering with the strain and the extra weight of rope cross-coiled bandolier style over his chest. Once past the obstacle, he faced the task of getting the tank around. There was no Le Cagot to feed the line out to him. There was nothing for it but to tug the tank into the water and take up slack rapidly as it bounced along the bottom of the stream. He was not able to take line in quickly enough; the tank passed his stance underwater and continued on, the line jerking and bobbing. He had no point of belay; when the slack snapped out, he was pulled from his thin ledge. He couldn't let go. To lose the tank was to lose everything. He straddled the narrow shaft, one boot on the ledge, the cleats of the other flat against the smooth opposite wall where there was no purchase. All the strength of his legs pressed into the stance, the cords of his crotch stood out, stretched and vulnerable. The line ran rapidly through his hands. He clenched his jaw and squeezed his fists closed over the rope. The pain seared as his palms took the friction of the wet line that cut into them. Water ran behind his fists, blood before. To handle the pain, he roared, his scream echoing unheard through the narrow diaclose.

The tank was stopped.

He hauled it back against the current, hand over hand, the rope molten iron in his raw palms, the cords of his crotch knotting and throbbing. When his hand touched the web strap of the tank, he pulled it up and hooked it behind his neck. With that weight dangling at his chest, the move back to the ledge was dicy. Twice he pushed off the smooth wall, and twice he tottered and fell back, catching himself again with the flat of his sole, his crotch feeling like it would tear with the stretch. On the third try he made it over and stood panting against the wall, only his heels on the ledge, his toes over the roaring stream.

He moved the last short distance to the scree wall that blocked the way to the Climbing Cave, and he slumped down in the book corner, exhausted, the tank against his chest, his palms pulsing with pain.

He couldn't stay there long. His hands would stiffen up and become useless.

He rerigged the tank to his back and checked the fittings and faceplate of the mask. If they were damaged, that was it. The mask had somehow survived banging against the tank. Now he began the slow climb up the corner between the side of the shaft and the boulder wall under which the river had disappeared. As before, there were many foot- and handholds, but it was all friable rottenrock, chunks of which came off in his hands, and grains of stone worked their way into his skinless palms. His heart thumped convulsively in his chest, squirting throbs of blood into his temples. When at last he made the flat ledge between two counterbalanced boulders that was the keyhole to the Climbing Cave, he lay out flat on his stomach and rested, his cheek against the rock and saliva dripping from the corner of his mouth.

He cursed himself for resting there too long. His palms were growing sticky with scab fluid, and they hinged awkwardly, like lobster claws. He got to his feet and stood there, opening and closing his hands, breaking through the crusts of pain, until they articulated smoothly again.

For an unmeasurable time, he stumbled forward through the Climbing Cave, feeling his way around the house-sized boulders that dwarfed him, squeezing between counterbalanced slabs of recent infall from the scarred roof far above the throw of his helmet light, edging his way along precariously perched rocks that would long ago have surrendered to gravity, had they been subjected to the weather erosion of the outside. The river was no guide, lost far below the jumble of infall, ravelled into thousands of threads as it found its way along the schist floor of the cavern. Three times, in his fatigue and stress, he lost his way, and the terror of it was that he was wasting precious energy stumbling around blindly. Each time, he forced himself to stop and calm himself, until his proximity sense suggested the path toward open space.

At last, there was sound to guide him. As he approached the end of the Climbing Cave, the threads of water far below wove themselves together, and slowly he became aware of the roar and tympani of the great waterfall that led down to the Crystal Cave. Ahead, the roof of the cave sloped down and was joined by a block-ing wall of jagged, fresh infall. Making it up that wall, through the insane network of cracks and chimneys, then down the other side through the roaring waterfall without the safety of a belay from Le Cagot would be the most dangerous and difficult part of the cave. He would have to rest before that.

It was then that Hel had slipped off the straps of his air tank and sat down heavily on a rock, his chin hang-ing to his chest as he gasped for air and sweat ran from his hair into his eyes.

He had taken a long drink from his *xahako,* then had lain back on the slab of rock, not bothering to take off his helmet.

His body whimpered for rest. But he mustn't sleep. Sleep is death. Just rest for a moment. Not sleep. Just close your eyes for a moment. Just close . . . eyes . . .

"Ahgh!" He started awake, driven from his shallow, tormented sleep by the image of Le Cagot's helmet light rushing down toward him from the roof of the cave! He sat up, shivering and sweating. The thin sleep had not rested him; fatigue wastes in his body were thick-ening up; his hands were a pair of stiff paddles; his shoulders were knotted; the nausea of repeated adren-aline shock was clogging his throat.

He sat there, slumped over, not caring if he went on or not. Then, for the first time, the staggering impli-cations of what Diamond had said over the phones burst upon his consciousness. His château no longer existed? What had they done? Had Hana escaped?

Concern for her, and the need to avenge Le Cagot, did for his body what food and rest might have done. He clawed his remaining glucose cubes from the pouch and chewed them, washing them down with the last of his water-wine. It would take the sugar several min-utes to work its way into his bloodstream. Meanwhile, he set his jaw and began the task of limbering up his hands, breaking up the fresh scabbing, accepting the gritty sting of movement.

When he could handle it, he slung the air tank on and began the hard climb up the jumble of infall that blocked off the mouth of the Crystal Cave. He recalled Le Cagot telling him to try a bit to the left, because he was sitting in the line of fall and was too comfortable to move.

Twice, he had to struggle out of the tank harness while clinging to scant points of purchase because the crack he had to wriggle through was too tight for a man and tank at once without risking damage to the mask slung from his chest. Each time, he took care to tie the tank securely, because a fall might knock off its fitting, exploding the cylinder and leaving him with no air to make the final cave swim and making all this work and torture futile.

When he achieved the thin ledge directly above the roaring waterfall, he directed his lamp down the long drop, up which mist rose and billowed in the windless air. He paused only long enough to catch his breath and slow his heartbeat. There could be no long rests from now on, no chances for his body and hands to stiffen up, or for his imagination to cripple his determination.

The deafening roar of the falls and the roiling 40° mist insulated his mind from any thoughts of wider scope than the immediate task. He edged along the slimy, worn ledge that had once been the lip of the waterfall until he found the outcrop of rock from which Le Cagot had belayed him during his first descent along the glistening sheet of falling water. There would be no protecting belay this time. As he inched down, he came upon the first of the pitons he had driven in before, snapped a carabiner into the first and tied off a doubled line, threading and snapping in another at each piton, to shorten his fall, should he come off the face. Again, as before, it was not long before the combined friction of the line passing through these snap links made pulling it through difficult and dangerous, as the effort tended to lift him from the scant boot jams and fingerholds the face provided.

The water and the rope tortured his palms, and he clutched at his holds ever harder and harder, as though to punish the pain with excess. When he reached the point at which he would have to break through the sheet of water and pass behind the falls, he discovered that he could no longer drag down slack. The weight of water on the line, the number of carabiners through which it was strung, and his growing weakness combined to make this impossible. He would have to abandon the rope and climb free from here on. As before, he reached through the silver-and-black surface of the falls, which split in a heavy, throbbing bracelet around his wrist. He felt for and located the sharp little crack, invisible behind the face of the falls, into which he had wedged his fingers before. Ducking through the falls would be harder this time. The tank presented additional surface to the falls; his fingers were raw and numb; and his reserves of strength were gone. One smooth move. Just swing through it. There is a good ledge behind the cascade, and a book corner piled with rubble that made an easy climb down. He took three deep breaths and swung under the face of the falls.

Recent rains had made the falls twice as thick as before and more than twice as heavy. Its weight battered his helmet and shoulders and tried to tear the tank from his back. His numbed fingers were pried from the sharp crack; and he fell.

The first thing he became aware of was the relative quiet. The second thing was the water. He was behind the falls, at the base of the scree pile, sitting hip-deep in water. He may have been unconscious for a time, but he had no sense of it. The events were strung together in his mind: the battering of the water on his back and tank; the pain as his skinless fingers were wrenched from their hold; clatter, noise, pain, shock as he fell to the rubble pile and tumbled down it—then this relative silence, and waist-deep water where, before, there had been wet rock. The silence was no problem; he was not stunned. He had noticed last time how the falls seemed to muffle the roar once he was behind it. But the water? Did that mean recent rains had seeped down, making a lake of the floor of the Crystal Cavern?

Was he injured? He moved his legs; they were all right. So were his arms. His right shoulder was hurt. He could lift it, but there was gritty pain at the top of its arc. A bone bruise, maybe. Painful, but not debilitating. He had decided that he had come through the fall miraculously unhurt, when he became aware of a peculiar sensation. The set of his teeth wasn't right. They were touching cusp to cusp. The smallest attempt to open his mouth shocked him with such agony that he felt himself slipping toward unconsciousness. His jaw was broken.

The face mask. Had it taken the fall? He tugged it from its pouch and examined it in the light of his lamp, which was yellowing because the batteries were fading. The faceplate was cracked.

It was a hairline crack. It might hold, so long as there was no wrench or torque on the rubber fittings. And what was the chance of that, down in the ripping current at the bottom of the Wine Cellar? Not much.

When he stood, the water came only to midshin. He waded out through the largely dissipated waterfall into the Crystal Cavern, and the water got deeper as the mist of frigid water thinned behind him.

One of the two magnesium flares had broken in his fall; its greasy powder had coated the other flare, which had to be wiped off carefully before it could be lighted, lest the flame rush down the sides, burning his hand. He struck off the flare on its cap; it sputtered and blossomed into brilliant white light, illuminating the distant walls, encrusted with glittering crystals, and picking out the beauty of calcite drapery and slender stalactites. But these last did not point down to stumpy stalagmites, as they had done before. The floor of the cave was a shallow lake that covered the low speleothems. His first fears were supported: recent rains had filled this nether end of the cave system; the whole long marl chute at the far end of the cave was underwater.

Hel's impulse was to give in, to wade out to the edge of the cave and find a shelf to sit on where he could rest and lose himself in meditation. It seemed too hard now; the mathematics of probability too steep. At the outset, he had thought that this last, improbable task, the swim through the Wine Cellar toward light and air, would be the easiest from a psychological point of view. Denied alternatives, the weight and expanse of the entire cave system behind him, the final swim would have the strength of desperation. Indeed, he had thought his chances of making it through might be greater than they would have been if he had Le Cagot to belay him, for in that case he would have worked to only half the limit of his endurance, needing the rest to return, should the way be blocked, or too long. As it was, he had hoped his chances would be almost doubled, as there was no coming back through that force of water.

But now . . . the Crystal Cave had flooded, and his swim was doubled in length. The advantage of despair was gone.

Wouldn't it be better to sit out death in dignity, rather than struggle against fate like a panicked animal? What chance did he have? The slightest movement of his jaw shocked him with agony; his shoulder was stiff and it ground painfully in its socket; his palms were flayed; even the goddamned faceplate of his mask was unlikely to withstand the currents of that underground pipe. This thing wasn't even a gamble. It was like flipping coins against Fate, with Fate having both heads and tails. Hel won only if the coin landed on edge.

He waded heavily toward the side wall of the cavern, where flowstone oozed down like frozen taffy. He would sit there and wait it out.

His flare sputtered out, and the eternal spelaean darkness closed in on his mind with a crushing weight. Spots of light like minute crystal organisms under a microscope sketched across the darkness with each movement of his eyes. They faded, and the dark was total.

Nothing in the world would be easier than to accept death with dignity, with *shibumi*.

And Hana? And that insane Third World priest who had contributed to the death of Le Cagot and Hannah Stern? And Diamond?

All right. All right, damn it! He wedged the rubberized flashlight between two outcroppings of aragonite, and in its beam attached the mask to the air tank, grunting with pain as he tightened the connections with his flayed fingers. After carefully threading the straps over his bruised shoulder, he opened the inflow valve, then dipped up a little spit water to clear the faceplate of breath mist. The pressure of the mask against his broken jaw was painful, but he could manage it.

His legs were still unhurt; he would swim with legs only, holding the flashlight in his good hand. As soon as it was deep enough, he laid out on the water and swam—swimming was easier than wading.

In the pellucid water of the cave, unclouded by organisms, the flashlight picked up underwater features as though through air. It was not until he had entered the marl chute that he felt the influence of the current —more a suction downward than a push from behind.

The pressure of the water plugged his ears, making his breathing loud in the cavities of his head.

The suction increased as he neared the bottom of the marl chute, and the force of the water torqued his body toward the sunken sump of the Wine Cellar. From here on, he would not swim; the current would carry him, would drag him through; all his effort must be bent to slowing his speed and to controlling his direction. The pull of the current was an invisible force; there was no air in the water, no particles, no evidence of the tons of force that gripped him.

It was not until he attempted to grasp a ledge, to stop for a moment and collect himself before entering the sump, that he knew the power of the current. The ledge was ripped from his hold, and he was turned over on his back and drawn down into the sump. He struggled to reverse himself, tucking up and rolling, because he must enter the outflow pipe below feet first if he was to have any chance at all. If he were carried head first into an obstruction, that would be it.

Inexplicably, the suction seemed to lessen once he was in the sump, and he settled slowly toward the bottom, his feet toward the triangular pipe below. He took a deep breath and braced his nerves, remembering how that current had snatched away the dye packets so quickly that the eye could not follow them.

Almost leisurely, his body floated toward the bottom of the sump pit. That was his last clear image.

The current gripped him, and he shot into the pipe. His foot hit something; the leg crumpled, the knee striking his chest; he was spinning; the flashlight was gone; he took a blow on the spine, another on the hip.

And suddenly he was lodged behind a choke stone, and the water was roaring past him, tearing at him. The mask twisted, and the faceplate blew out, the broken pieces cutting his leg as they flashed past. He had been holding his breath from fear for several seconds, and the need for air was pounding in his temples. Water rushed over his face and eddied up his nostrils. It was the goddamned tank! He was wedged in there because the space was too narrow for both his body and the tank! He gripped his knife with all the force of his body focused on his right hand, as the water sought to twist the knife from his grasp. Had to cut away the tank! The weight of the current against the cylinder pressed the straps against his shoulders. No way to slip the knife under. He must saw through the webbing directly against his chest.

White pain.

His pulse throbbed, expanding in his head. His throat convulsed for air. Cut harder! Cut, damn it!

The tank went, smashing his foot as it rushed out under him. He was moving again, twisting. The knife was gone. With a terrible crunching sound, something hit the back of his head. His diaphragm heaved within him, sucking for breath. His heartbeat hammered in his head as he tumbled and twisted in the chaos of foam and bubbles.

Bubbles . . . Foam! He could see! Swim up! Swim!

PART SIX

Tsuru no Sugomori

Etchebar

Hel parked the Volvo in the deserted square of Etchebar and got out heavily, forgetting to close the door behind him, neglecting to give the car its ritual bash. He drew a long breath and pushed it out slowly, then he walked up the curving road toward his château.

From behind half-closed shutters women of the village watched him and admonished their children not to play in the square until M. Hel was gone. It had been eight days since M. Hel had gone into the mountains with Le Cagot, and those terrible men in uniform had descended on the village and done dreadful things to the château. No one had seen M. Hel since then; it had been rumored that he was dead. Now he was returning to his demolished home, but no one dared to greet him. In this ancient high mountain village, primitive instincts prevailed; everyone knew it was unwise to associate with the unfortunate, lest the misfortune be contagious. After all, was it not God's will that this terrible thing happen? Was not the outlander being punished for living with an Oriental woman, possibly without the sanction of marriage. And who could know what other things God was punishing him for? Oh yes, one could feel pity—one was required by the church to feel pity—but it would be unwise to consort with those whom God punishes. One must be compassionate, but not to the extent of personal risk.

As he walked up the long allée, Hel could not see what they had done to his home; the sweeping pines screened it from view. But from the bottom of the terrace, the extent of the damage was clear. The central block and the east wing were gone, the walls blown away and rubble thrown in all directions, blocks of granite and marble lying partially buried in the scarred lawn as much as fifty meters away; a low jagged wall rimmed the gaping cellars, deep in shadow and dank with seep water from underground springs. Most of the west wing still stood, the rooms open to the weather where the connecting walls had been ripped away. It had been burned out; floors had caved in, and charred beams dangled, broken, into the spaces below. The glass had been blown from every window and *porte-fenêtre*, and above them were wide daggers of soot where flames had roared out. The smell of burned oak was carried on a soft wind that fluttered shreds of drapery.

There was no sound other than the sibilance of the wind through the pines as he picked his way through the rubble to investigate the standing walls of the west wing. At three places he found holes drilled into the granite blocks. The charges they had placed had failed to go off; and they had contented themselves with the destruction of the fire.

It was the Japanese garden that pained him most. Obviously, the raiders had been instructed to take special pains with the garden. They had used flame throwers. The sounding stream wound through charred stubble and, even after a week, its surface carried an oily residue. The bathing house and its surrounding bamboo grove were gone, but already a few shoots of bamboo, that most tenacious grass, were pushing through the blackened ground.

The *tatami*'d dependency and its attached gun room had been spared, save that the rice-paper doors were blown in by the concussion. These fragile structures had bent before the storm and had survived.

As he walked across the ravished garden, his shoes kicked up puffs of fine black ash. He sat heavily on the sill of the *tatami*'d room, his legs dangling over the edge. It was odd and somehow touching that tea utensils were still set out on the low lacquered table.

He was sitting, his head bent in deep fatigue, when he felt the approach of Pierre.

The old man's voice was moist with regret. "Oh, M'sieur! Oh! M'sieur! See what they have done to us! Poor Madame. You have seen her? She is well?"

For the past four days, Hel had been at the hospital in Oloron, leaving Hana's side only when ordered to by the doctors.

Pierre's rheumy eyes drooped with compassion as he realized his patron's physical state. "But look at you,

M'sieur!" A bandage was wrapped under Hel's chin and over his head, to hold the jaw in place while it mended; bruises on his face were still plum colored; inside his shirt, his upper arm was wrapped tightly to his chest to prevent movement of the shoulder, and both his hands were bandaged from the wrists to the second knuckle.

"You don't look so good yourself, Pierre," he said, his voice muffled and dental.

Pierre shrugged. "Oh, I shall be all right. But see, our hands are the same!" He lifted his hands, revealing wraps of gauze covering the gel on his burned palms. He had a bruise over one eyebrow.

Hel noticed a dark stain down the front of Pierre's unbuttoned shirt. Obviously, a glass of wine had slipped from between the awkward paddles at the ends of his wrists. "How did you hurt your head?"

"It was the bandits, M'sieur. One of them struck me with a rifle butt when I was trying to stop them."

"Tell me what happened."

"Oh, M'sieur! It was too terrible!"

"Just tell me about it. Be calm, and tell me."

"Perhaps we could go to the gate house? I shall offer you a little glass, and maybe I will have one myself. Then I shall tell you."

"All right."

As they walked to Pierre's gate house, the old gardener suggested that M. Hel stay with him, for the bandits had spared his little home.

Hel sat in a deep chair with broken springs from which litter had been thrown by Pierre to make a space for his guest. The old man had drunk from the bottle, an easier thing to hold, and was now staring out over the valley from the small window of his second-floor living quarters.

"I was working, M'sieur. Attending to a thousand things. Madame had called down to Tardets for a car to take her to where the airplanes land, and I was waiting for it to arrive. I heard a buzzing from far out over the mountains. The sound grew louder. They came like huge flying insects, skimming over the hills, close to the earth."

"What came?"

"The bandits! In autogiros!"

"In helicopters?"

"Yes. Two of them. With a great noise, they landed in the park, and the ugly machines vomited men out. The men all had guns. They were dressed in mottled green clothes, with orange berets. They shouted to one another as they ran toward the château. I called after them, telling them to go away. The women of the kitchen screamed and fled toward the village. I ran after the bandits, threatening to tell M'sieur Hel on them if they did not go at once. One of them hit me with his gun, and I fell down. Great noise! Explosions! And all the time the two great autogiros sat on the lawn, their wings turning around and around. When I could stand, I ran toward the château. I was willing to fight them, M'sieur. I was willing to fight them!"

"I know."

"Yes, but they were by then running back toward their machines. I was knocked down again! When I got to the château . . . Oh, M'sieur! All gone! Smoke and flame everywhere! Everything! Everything! Then, M'sieur . . . Oh, God in mercy! I saw Madame at the window of the burning part. All around her, flame. I rushed in. Fiery things were falling all about me. When I got to her, she was just standing there. She could not find her way out! The windows had burst in upon her, and the glass . . . Oh, M'sieur, the glass!" Pierre had been struggling to contain his tears. He snatched off his beret and covered his face with it. There was a diagonal line across his forehead separating white skin from his deeply weatherbeaten face. Not for forty years had his beret been off while he was outdoors. He scrubbed his eyes with his beret, snorted loudly, and put it on again. "I took Madame and brought her out. The way was blocked by burning things. I had to pull them away with my hands. But I got out! I got her out! But the glass! . . ." Pierre broke down; he gulped as tears flowed from his nostrils.

Hel rose and took the old man in his arms. "You were brave, Pierre."

"But I am the *patron* when you are not here! And I failed to stop them!"

"You did all a man could do."

"I tried to fight them!"

"I know."

"And Madame? She will be well?"

"She will live."

"And her eyes?"

Hel looked away from Pierre as he drew a slow breath and let it out in a long jet. For a time he did not speak. Then, clearing his throat, he said, "We have work to do, Pierre."

"But, M'sieur. What work? The château is gone!"

"We shall clean up and repair what is left. I'll need your help to hire the men and to guide them in their work."

Pierre shook his head. He had failed to protect the château. He was not to be trusted.

"I want you to find men. Clear the rubble. Seal the west wing from the weather. Repair what must be repaired to get us through the winter. And next spring, we shall start to build again."

"But, M'sieur! It will take forever to rebuild the château!"

"I didn't say we would ever finish, Pierre."

Pierre considered this. "All right," he said, "all right. Oh, you have mail, M'sieur. A letter and a package. They are here somewhere." He rummaged about the chaos of bottomless chairs, empty boxes, and refuse of no description with which he had furnished his home. "Ah! Here they are. Just where I put them for safekeeping."

Both the package and letter were from Maurice de Lhandes. While Pierre fortified himself with another draw at the bottle, Hel read Maurice's note:

My Dear Friend:

I wadded up and threw away my first epistolary effort because it began with a phrase so melodramatic as to bring laughter to me and, I feared, embarrassment to you. And yet, I can find no other way to say what I want to say. So here is that sophomoric first phrase:

When you read this, Nicholai, I shall be dead.

(Pause here for my ghostly laughter and your compassionate embarrassment.)

There are many reasons I might cite for my close feelings for you, but these three will do. First: Like me, you have always given the governments and the companies reason for fear and concern. Second: You were the last person, other than Estelle, to whom I spoke during my life. And third: Not only did you never make a point of my physical peculiarity, you also never overlooked it, or brutalized my sensibilities by talking about it man to man.

I am sending you a gift (which you have probably already opened, greedy pig). It is something that may one day be of benefit to you. Do you remember my telling you that I had something on the United States of America? Something so dramatic that it would make the Statue of Liberty fall back and offer you whatever orifice you choose to use? Well, here it is.

I have sent you only the photocopy; I have destroyed the originals. But the enemy will not know that I have destroyed them, and the enemy does not know that I am dead. (Remarkable how peculiar it is to write that in the present tense!)

They will have no way to know that the originals are not in my possession in the button-down mode; so, with a little histrionic skill on your part, you should be able to manipulate them as you will.

As you know, native intelligence has always saved me from the foolishness of believing in life after death. But there can be nuisance value after death—and that thought pleases me.

Please visit Estelle from time to time, and make her feel desirable. And give my love to your magnificent Oriental.

With all amicable sentiments,

PS. Did I mention the other night during dinner that the morels did not have enough lemon juice? I should have.

Hel broke the string on the package and scanned the contents. Affidavits, photographs, records, all revealing the persons and governmental organizations involved in the assassination of John F. Kennedy and with the cover-up of certain aspects of that assassination. Particularly interesting were statements from a person identified as the Umbrella Man, from another called the Man on the Fire Escape, and a third, the Knoll Commando.

Hel nodded. Very strong leverage indeed.

After a simple meal of sausage, bread, and onion washed down with raw red wine in Pierre's littered room, they took a walk together over the grounds, staying well away from the painful scar of the château. Evening was falling, wisps of salmon and mauve clouds piling up against the mountains.

Hel mentioned that he would be gone for several days, and they could begin the work of repair when he returned.

"You would trust me to do it, M'sieur? After how I have failed you?" Pierre was feeling self-pitying. He had decided that he might have protected the Madame better if he had been totally sober.

Hel changed the subject. "What can we expect for weather tomorrow, Pierre?"

The old man glanced listlessly at the sky, and he shrugged. "I don't know, M'sieur. To tell you the truth, I cannot really read the weather. I only pretend, to make myself seem important."

"But, Pierre, your predictions are unfailing. I rely on them, and they have served me well."

Pierre frowned, trying to remember. "Is this so, M'sieur?"

"I wouldn't dare go into the mountains without your advice."

"Is this so?"

"I am convinced that it is a matter of wisdom, and age, and Basque blood. I may achieve the age in time, even the wisdom. But the Basque blood . . ." Hel sighed and struck at a shrub they were passing.

Pierre was silent for a time as he pondered this. Finally he said, "You know? I think that what you say is true, M'sieur. It is a gift, probably. Even I believe it is the signs in the sky, but in reality it is a gift—a skill
421

that only my people enjoy. For instance, you see how the sheep of the sky have russet fleeces? Now, it is important to know that the moon is in a descending phase, and that birds were swooping low this morning. From this, I can tell with certainty that . . ."

The Church at Alos

Father Xavier's head was bent, his fingers pressed against his temple, his hand partially masking the dim features of the old woman on the other side of the confessional's wicker screen. It was an attitude of compassionate understanding that permitted him to think his own thoughts while the penitent droned on, recalling and admitting every little lapse, hoping to convince God, by the tiresome pettiness of her sins, that she was innocent of any significant wrongdoing. She had reached the point of confessing the sins of others—of asking forgiveness for not having been strong enough to prevent her husband from drinking, for having listened to the damning gossip of Madame Ibar, her neighbor, for permitting her son to miss Mass and join the hunt for boar instead.

Automatically humming an ascending interrogative note at each pause, Father Xavier's mind was dealing with the problem of superstition. At Mass that morning, the itinerate priest had made use of an ancient superstition to gain their attention and to underline his message of faith and revolution. He himself was too well educated to believe in the primitive fears that characterize the faith of the mountain Basque; but as a soldier of Christ, he felt it his duty to grasp each weapon that came to hand and to strike a blow for the Church Militant. He knew the superstition that a clock striking during the *Sagara* (the elevation of the Host) was an infallible sign of imminent death. Setting a clock low beside the altar where he could see it, he had timed the *Sagara* to coincide with its striking of the hour. There had been an audible gasp in the congregation, followed by a profound silence. And taking his theme from the omen of impending death, he had told them it meant the death of repression against the Basque people, and the death of ungodly influences within the revolutionary movement. He had been satisfied with the effect, manifest in part by several invitations to take supper and to pass the night in the homes of local peasants, and in part by an uncommonly large turnout for evening confession—even several men, although only old men, to be sure.

Would this last woman never end her catalogue of trivial omissions? Evening was setting in, deepening the gloom of the ancient church, and he was feeling the pangs of hunger. Just before this self-pitying chatterbox had squeezed her bulk into the confessional, he had peeked out and discovered that she was the last of the penitents. He breathed a sigh and cut into her stream of petty flaws, calling her his daughter and telling her that Christ understood and forgave, and giving her a penance of many prayers, so she would feel important.

When she left the box, he sat back to give her time to leave the church. Undue haste in getting to a free dinner with wine would be unseemly. He was preparing to rise, when the curtain hissed and another penitent slipped into the shadows of the confessional.

Father Xavier sighed with impatience.

A very soft voice said, "You have only seconds to pray, Father."

The priest strained to see through the screen into the shadows of the confessional, then he gasped. It was a figure with a bandage around its head, like the cloth tied under the chins of the dead to keep their mouths from gaping! A ghost?

Father Xavier, too well educated for superstition, pressed back away from the screen and held his crucifix before him. "Begone! *I! Abi!*"

The soft voice said, "Remember Beñat Le Cagot."

"Who are you? What—"

The wicker screen split, and the point of Le Cagot's *makila* plunged between the priest's ribs, piercing his heart and pinning him to the wall of the confessional.

Never again would it be possible to shake the villager's faith in the superstition of the *Sagara,* for it had proved itself. And in the months that followed, a new and colorful thread was woven into the folk myth of Le Cagot—he who had mysteriously vanished into the mountains, but who was rumored to appear suddenly whenever Basque freedom fighters needed him most. With a vengeful will of its own, Le Cagot's *makila* had flown to the village of Alos and punished the perfidious priest who had informed on him.

New York

As he stood in the plush private elevator, mercifully without Musak, Hel moved his jaw gingerly from side to side. In the eight days he had been setting up this meeting, his body had mended well. The jaw was still stiff, but did not require the undignified gauze sling; his hands were tender, but the bandages were gone, as were the last yellowish traces of bruise on his forehead.

The elevator stopped and the door opened directly into an outer office, where a secretary rose and greeted him with an empty smile. "Mr. Hel? The Chairman will be with you soon. The other gentleman is waiting inside. Would you care to join him?" The secretary was a handsome young man with a silk shirt open to the middle of his chest and tight trousers of a soft fabric that revealed the bulge of his penis. He conducted Hel to an inner reception room decorated like the parlor of a comfortable rural home: overstuffed chairs in floral prints, lace curtains, a low tea table, two Lincoln rockers, bric-a-brac in a glass-front étagère, framed photographs of three generations of family on an upright piano.

The gentleman who rose from the plump sofa had Semitic features, but an Oxford accent. "Mr. Hel? I've been looking forward to meeting you. I am Mr. Able, and I represent OPEC interests in such matters as these." There was an extra pressure to his handshake that hinted at his sexual orientation. "Do sit down, Mr. Hel. The Chairman will be with us soon. Something came up at the last moment, and she was called away briefly."

Hel selected the least distasteful chair. "She?"

Mr. Able laughed musically. "Ah, you did not know that the Chairman was a woman?"

"No, I didn't. Why isn't she called the Chairwoman, or one of those ugly locutions with which Americans salve their social consciences at the sacrifice of euphony: chairperson, mailperson, freshperson—that sort of thing?"

"Ah, you will find the Chairman unbound by conventions. Having become one of the most powerful people in the world, she does not have to seek recognition; and achieving equality would, for her, be a great step down." Mr. Able smiled and tilted his head coquettishly. "You know, Mr. Hel, I learned a great deal about you before Ma summoned me to this meeting."

"Ma?"

"Everyone close to the Chairman calls her Ma. Sort of a family joke. Head of the Mother Company, don't you see?"

"I do see, yes."

The door to the outer office opened, and a muscular young man with a magnificent suntan and curly golden hair entered carrying a tray.

"Just set it down here," Mr. Able told him. Then to Hel he said, "Ma will doubtless ask me to pour."

The handsome beachboy left after setting out the tea things, thick, cheap china in a blue-willow pattern.

Mr. Able noticed Hel's glance at the china. "I know what you're thinking. Ma prefers things to be what she calls 'homey.' I learned about your colorful background, Mr. Hel, at a briefing session a while ago. Of course I never expected to meet you—not after Mr. Diamond's report of your death. Please believe that I regret what the Mother Company special police did to your home. I consider it unpardonable barbarism."

"Do you?" Hel was impatient with the delay, and he had no desire to pass the time chatting with this Arab. He rose and crossed to the piano with its row of family photographs.

At this moment, the door to the inner office opened, and the Chairman entered.

Mr. Able rose quickly to his feet. "Mrs. Perkins, may I introduce Nicholai Hel?"

She took Hel's hand and pressed it warmly between her plump, stubby fingers. "Land sakes, Mr. Hel, you just couldn't know how I have looked forward to meeting you." Mrs. Perkins was a chubby woman in her

427

mid-fifties. Clear maternal eyes, neck concealed beneath layers of chin, gray hair done up in a bun, with wisps that had escaped the net chignon, pigeon-breasted, plump forearms with deeply dimpled elbows, wearing a silk dress of purple paisley. "I see that you're looking at my family. My pride and joy, I always call them. That's my grandson there. Rascally little fella. And this is Mr. Perkins. Wonderful man. Cordon-bleu cook and just a magician with flowers." She smiled at her photographs and shook her head with proprietary affection. "Well, maybe we should turn to our business. Do you like tea, Mr. Hel?" She lowered herself into a Lincoln rocker with a puff of sigh. "I don't know what I'd do without my tea."

"Have you looked at the information I forwarded to you, Mrs. Perkins?" He lifted his hand to Mr. Able, indicating that he would forego a cup of tea made from tea bags.

The Chairman leaned forward and placed her hand on Hel's arm. "Why don't you just call me Ma? Everyone does."

"Have you looked at the information, Mrs. Perkins?"

The warm smile disappeared from her face and her voice became almost metallic. "I have."

"You will recall that I made a precondition to our talk your promise that Mr. Diamond be kept ignorant of the fact that I am alive."

"I accepted that precondition." She glanced quickly at Mr. Able. "The contents of Mr. Hel's communication are eyes-only for me. You'll have to follow my lead in this."

"Certainly, Ma."

"And?" Hel asked.

"I won't pretend that you do not have us in a tight spot, Mr. Hel. For a variety of reasons, we would not care to have things upset just now, when our Congress is dismantling that Cracker's energy bill. If I understand the situation correctly, we would be ill-advised to take counteraction against you, as that would precipitate the information into the European press. It is currently in the hands of an individual whom Fat Boy identifies as the Gnome. Is that correct?"

"Yes."

"So it's all a matter of price, Mr. Hel. What *is* your price?"

"Several things. First, you have taken some land in Wyoming from me. I want it back."

The Chairman waved a pudgy hand at so trivial a matter.

"And I shall require that your subsidiaries stop all strip-mining in a radius of three hundred miles from my land."

Mrs. Perkins's jaw worked with controlled anger, her cold eyes fixed on Hel. Then she blinked twice and said, "All right."

"Second, there is money of mine taken from my Swiss account."

"Of course. Of course. Is that all?"

"No. I recognize that you could undo any of these actions at will. So I shall have to leave this leverage information on line for an indefinite period. If you offend me in any way, the button will be released."

"I see. Fat Boy informs me that this Gnome person is in poor health."

"I have heard that rumor."

"You realize that if he should die, your protection is gone?"

"Not exactly, Mrs. Perkins. Not only would he have to die, but your people would have to be sure he was dead. And I happen to know that you have never located him and don't have even an idea of his physical appearance. I suspect that you will intensify your search for the Gnome, but I'm gambling that he is hidden away where you will never find him."

"We shall see. You have no further demands upon us?"

"I have further demands. Your people destroyed my home. It may not be possible to repair it, as there no longer are craftsmen of the quality that built it. But I intend to try."

"How much?"

"Four million."

"No house is worth four million dollars!"

"It's now five million."

"My dear boy, I started my professional career with less than a quarter of that, and if you think—"

429

"Six million."

Mrs. Perkins's mouth snapped shut. There was absolute silence, as Mr. Able nervously directed his glance away from the pair looking at one another across the tea table, one with a cold fixed stare, the other with lids half-lowered over smiling green eyes.

Mrs. Perkins drew a slow, calming breath. "Very well. But that, I suggest, had better be the last of your demands."

"In point of fact, it is not."

"Your price has reached its market maximum. There is a limit to the degree to which what is good for the Mother Company is good for America."

"I believe, Mrs. Perkins, that you'll be pleased by my last demand. If your Mr. Diamond had done his work competently, if he had not allowed personal enmity for me to interfere with his judgment, you would not now be facing this predicament. My last demand is this: I want Diamond. And I want the CIA gunny named Starr, and that PLO goatherd you call Mr. Haman. Don't think of it as additional payment. I am rendering you a service—meting out punishment for incompetence."

"And that is your last demand?"

"That is my last demand."

The Chairman turned to Mr. Able. "How have your people taken the death of the Septembrists in that plane accident?"

"Thus far, they believe it was just that, an accident. We have not informed them that it was an assassination. We were awaiting your instructions, Ma."

"I see. This Mr. Haman . . . he is related to the leader of the PLO movement, I believe."

"That is true, Ma."

"How will his death go down?"

Mr. Able considered this for a moment. "We may have to make concessions again. But I believe it can be handled."

Mrs. Perkins turned again to Hel. She stared at him for several seconds. "Done."

He nodded. "Here is how it will be set up. You will show Diamond the information now in your hands concerning the Kennedy assassination. You will tell him you have a line on the Gnome, and you can trust no one but him to kill the Gnome and secure the originals. He will realize how dangerous it would be to have other eyes than his see this material. You will instruct Diamond to go to the Spanish Basque village of Oñate. He will be contacted by a guide who will take them into the mountains, where they will find the Gnome. I shall take it from there. One other thing . . . and this is most important. I want all three of them to be well armed when they go into the mountains."

"Did you get that?" she asked Mr. Able, her eyes never leaving Hel's face.

"Yes, Ma."

She nodded. Then her stern expression dissolved and she smiled, wagging a finger at Hel. "You're quite a fellow, young man. A real horse trader. You would have gone a long way in the commercial world. You've got the makings of a real fine businessman."

"I'll overlook that insult."

Mrs. Perkins laughed, her wattles jiggling. "I'd love to have a good long gabfest with you, son, but there are folks waiting for me in another office. We've got a problem with some kids demonstrating against one of our atomic-power plants. Young people just aren't what they used to be, but I love them all the same, the little devils." She pushed herself out of the rocker. "Lord, isn't it true what they say: woman's work is never done."

Gouffre Field /
Col. Pierre St. Martin

In addition to being exasperated and physically worn, Diamond was stung with the feeling that he looked foolish, stumbling through this blinding fog, clinging obediently to a length of rope tied to the waist of his guide whose ghostly figure he could only occasionally make out, not ten feet ahead. A rope around Diamond's waist strung back into the brilliant mist, where its knotted end was grasped by Starr; and the Texan in turn was linked to the PLO trainee Haman, who complained each time they rested for a moment, sitting on the damp boulders of the high col. The Arab was not used to hours of heavy exercise; his new climbing boots were chafing his ankles, and the muscles of his forearm were throbbing with the strain of his white-knuckled grip on the line that linked him to the others, terrified of losing contact and being alone and blind in this barren terrain. This was not at all what he had had in mind when he had postured before the mirror of his room in Oñate two days earlier, cutting a romantic figure with his mountain clothes and boots, a heavy Magnum in the holster at his side. He had even practiced drawing the weapon as quickly as he could, admiring the hard-eyed professional in the mirror. He recalled how excited he had been in that mountain meadow a month before, emptying his gun into the jerking body of that Jewess after Starr had killed her.

As annoying as any physical discomfort to Diamond was the wiry old guide's constant humming and singing as he led them slowly along, skirting the rims of countless deep pits filled with dense vapor, the danger of which the guide had made evident through extravagan mime not untouched with gallows humor as he opened his mouth and eyes wide and flailed his arms about in imitation of a man falling to his death, then pressed his palms together in prayer and rolled his impish eyes upward. Not only did the nasal whine of the Basque songs erode Diamond's patience, but the voice seemed to come from everywhere at once, because of the peculiar underwater effect of a whiteout.

Diamond had tried to ask the guide how much longer they would be groping through this soup, how much farther it was to where the Gnome was hiding out. But the only response was a grin and a nod. When they were turned over to the guide in the mountains by a Spanish Basque who had contacted them in the village, Diamond had asked if he could speak English, and the little old man had grinned and said, "A lee-tle bit." When, some time later, Diamond had asked how long it would be before they arrived at their destination, the guide had answered, "A lee-tle bit." That was an odd-enough response to cause Diamond to ask the guide his name. "A lee-tle bit."

Oh, fine! Just wonderful!

Diamond understood why the Chairman had sent him to deal with this matter personally. Trusting him with information so inflammable as this was a mark of special confidence, and particularly welcome after a certain coolness in Ma's communications after those Septembrists had died in that midair explosion. But they had been two days in the mountains now, linked up like children playing blind man's bluff, bungling forward through this blinding whiteout that filled their eyes with stinging light. They had passed a cold and uncomfortable night sleeping on the stony ground after a supper of hard bread, a greasy sausage that burned the mouth, and harsh wine from some kind of squirt bag that Diamond could not manage. How much longer could it be before they got to the Gnome's hiding place? If only this stupid peasant would stop his chanting!

At that moment, he did. Diamond almost bumped into the grinning guide, who had stopped in the middle of a rock-strewn little plateau through which they had been picking their way, avoiding the dangerous *gouffres* on all sides.

When Starr and Haman joined them, the guide

433

mimed that they must stay there, while he went ahead for some purpose or other.

"How long will you be gone?" Diamond asked, accenting each word slowly, as though that would help.

"A lee-tle bit," the guide answered, and he disappeared into the thick cloud. A moment later, the guide's voice seemed to come from all directions at once. "Just make yourselves comfortable, my friends."

"That shithead speaks American after all," Starr said. "What the hell's going on?"

Diamond shook his head, uneasy with the total silence around them.

Minutes passed, and the sense of abandonment and danger was strong enough to hush even the complaining Arab. Starr took out his revolver and cocked it.

Seeming to come from both near and far, Nicholai Hel's voice was characteristically soft. "Have you figured it out yet, Diamond?"

They strained to peer through the dazzling light. Nothing.

"Jesus H. Christ!" Starr whispered.

Haman began to whimper.

Not ten meters from them, Hel stood invisible in the brilliant whiteout. His head was cocked to the side as he concentrated to distinguish the three quite different energy patterns emanating from them. His proximity sense read panic in all three, but of varying qualities. The Arab was falling apart. Starr was on the verge of firing wildly into the blinding vapor. Diamond was struggling for self-control.

"Spread out," Starr whispered. He was the professional.

Hel felt Starr moving around to the left, as the Arab went to his hands and knees and crawled toward the right, feeling before him for the rim of a deep *gouffre* he could not see. Diamond stood riveted.

Hel cocked back the double hammers of each of the shotgun pistols the Dutch industrialist had given him years before. Starr's projecting aura was closing in from the left. Hel gripped the handle as tightly as he could, aimed for the center of the Texan's aura, and squeezed the trigger.

The roar of two shotgun shells firing at once was

deafening. The blast pattern of eighteen ball bearings blew a puffing hole through the mist, and for an instant Hel saw Starr flying backward, his arms wide, his feet off the ground, his chest and face splattered. Immediately, the whiteout closed in and healed the hole in the mist.

Hel let the pistol drop from his stunned hand. The pain of the wrenching kick throbbed to his elbow.

His ears ringing with the blast, the Arab began to whimper. Every fiber of him yearned to flee, but in which direction? He knelt, frozen on his hands and knees as a dark-brown stain grew at the crotch of his khaki trousers. Keeping as low to the ground as he could, he inched forward, straining to see through the dazzling fog. A boulder took form before him, its gray ghost shape becoming solid only a foot before he touched it. He hugged the rock for comfort, sobbing silently.

Hel's voice was soft and close. "Run, goatherd."

The Arab gasped and leaped away. His last scream was a prolonged, fading one, as he stumbled into the mouth of a deep *gouffre* and landed with a liquid crunch far below.

As the echoing rattle of dislodged stones faded away, Hel leaned back against the boulder and drew a slow deep breath, the second shotgun pistol dangling from his hand. He directed his concentration toward Diamond, still crouching motionless out there in the mist, ahead of him and slightly to the left.

After the Arab's sudden scream, silence rang in Diamond's ears. He breathed shallowly through his mouth, so as to make no sound, his eyes darting back and forth over the curtain of blinding cloud, his skin tingling with anticipation of pain.

A ten-second eternity passed, then he heard Hel's prison-hushed voice. "Well? Isn't this what you had in mind, Diamond? You're living out the machismo fantasies of the corporation man. The cowboy face to face with the *yojimbo*. Is it fun?"

Diamond turned his head from side to side, trying desperately to identify the direction from which the voice came. No good! All directions seemed right.

"Let me help you, Diamond. You are now approximately eight meters from me."

Which direction? Which direction?

"You might as well get a shot off, Diamond. You might be lucky."

Mustn't speak! He'll fire at my voice!

Diamond held his heavy Magnum in both fists and fired into the fog. Again to the left, then to the right, then farther to the left. "You son of a bitch!" he cried, still firing. "You son of a bitch!"

Twice the hammer clicked on spent brass.

"Son of a bitch." With effort, Diamond lowered his pistol while his whole upper body shook with emotion and desperation.

Hel touched his earlobe with the tip of his finger. It was sticky and it stung. A chip of rock from a near stray had nicked it. He raised his second shotgun pistol and leveled it at the place in the whiteout from which the rapid pulses of panicked aura emanated.

Then he paused and lowered the gun. Why bother?

This unexpected whiteout had converted the catharsis of revenge he had planned into a mechanical slaughter of stymied beasts. There was no satisfaction in this, no measurement in terms of skill and courage. Knowing they would be three, and well armed, Hel had brought only the two pistols with him, limiting himself to only two shots. He had hoped this might make a contest of it.

But this? And that emotionally shattered merchant out there in the fog? He was too loathsome for even punishment.

Hel started to move away from his boulder noiselessly, leaving Diamond to shudder, alone and frightened in the whiteout, expecting death to roar through him at any instant.

Then Hel stopped. He remembered that Diamond was a servant of the Mother Company, a corporate lackey. Hel thought of offshore oil rigs contaminating the sea, of strip-mining over virgin land, of oil pipelines through tundra, of atomic-energy plants built over the protests of those who would ultimately suffer contamination. He recalled the adage: Who must do the hard things? He who can. With a deep sigh, and with disgust souring the back of his throat, he turned and raised his arm.

Diamond's maniac scream was sandwiched between the gun's roar and its echo. Through a billowing hole in the fog, Hel glimpsed the spattered body twisting in the air as it was blown back into the wall of vapor.

Château d'Etchebar

Hana's posture was maximally submissive; her only weapons in the game were voluptuous sounds and the rippling vaginal contractions at which she was so expert. Hel had the advantage of distraction, his endurance aided by the task of controlling movement very strictly, as their position was complicated and arcane, and a slight error could do them physical hurt. Despite the advantage, it was he who was driven to muttering, "You devil!" between clenched teeth.

Instantly she was sure he had broken, she pressed outward and joined him in climax, her joy expressed aloud and enthusiastically.

After some minutes of grateful nestling, he smiled and shook his head. "It would appear I lose again."

"So it would appear." She laughed impishly.

Hana sat at the doorway of the *tatami*'d room, facing the charred ruin of the garden, her kimono puddled about her hips, bare above the waist to receive the kneading and stroking that had been set as the prize in this game. Hel knelt behind her, dragging his fingertips up her spine and scurrying waves of tingle up the nape of her neck, into the roots of her hair.

His eyes defocused, all muscles of his face relaxed, he permitted his mind to wander in melancholy joy and autumnal peace. He had made a final decision the night before, and he had been rewarded for it.

He had passed hours kneeling alone in the gun room, reviewing the lay of the stones on the board. It was inevitable that, sooner or later, the Mother Company would rupture his gossamer armor. Either their relentless investigations would reveal de Lhandes to be dead, or the facts concerning Kennedy's death would eventually come out. And then they would come after him.

He could struggle, cut off many arms of the faceless

438

corporate hydra, but ultimately they would get him. And probably with something as impersonal as a bomb, or as ironic as a stray slug. Where was the dignity in that? The *shibumi*?

At last, the cranes were confined to their nest. He would live in peace and affection with Hana until they came after him. Then he would withdraw from the game. Voluntarily. By his own hand.

Almost immediately after coming to this understanding of the state of the game and the sole path to dignity, Hel felt years of accumulated disgust and hate melt from him. Once severed from the future, the past becomes an insignificant parade of trivial events, no longer organic, no longer potent or painful.

He had an impulse to account for his life, to examine the fragments he had carried along with him. Late into the night, with the warm Southwind moaning in the eaves, he knelt before the lacquered table on which were two things: the Gō bowls Kishikawa-san had given him, and the yellowed letter of official regret, its creases furry with opening and folding, that he had carried away from Shimbashi Station because it was all that was left of the dignified old man who had died in the night.

Through all the years he had wandered adrift in the West, he had carried with him three spiritual sea anchors: the Gō bowls that symbolized his affection for his foster father, the faded letter that symbolized the Japanese spirit, and his garden—not the garden they had destroyed, but the idea of garden in Hel's mind of which that plot had been an imperfect statement. With these three things, he felt fortunate and very rich.

His newly liberated mind drifted from wisp of idea to wisp of memory, and soon—quite naturally—he found himself in the triangular meadow, one with the yellow sunlight and the grass.

Home . . . after so many years of wandering.

"Nikko?"

"Hm-m-m?"

She snuggled her back against his bare chest. He pressed her to him and kissed her hair. "Nikko, are you sure you didn't let me win?"

"Why would I do that?"

439

"Because you're a very strange person. And rather nice."

"I did not let you win. And to prove it to you, next time we'll wager the maximum penalty."

She laughed softly. "I thought of a pun—a pun in English."

"Oh?"

"I should have said: You're on."

"Oh, that is terrible." He hugged her from behind, cupping her breasts in his hands.

"The one good thing about all of this is your garden, Nikko. I am glad they spared it. After the years of love and work you invested, it would have broken my heart if they had harmed your garden."

"I know."

There was no point in telling her the garden was gone.

It was time now to take the tea he had prepared for them.